BLOOD CREED

BOOK ONE

GENESIS

BY

ERIC STILL

Content Warning

First and foremost, thank you for choosing to read Blood Creed Genesis. Within our endeavors to not forgo our humanity, it is important to recognize the things that aren't conducive to our own wellbeing. As such, below are the relevant themes that will be found within the book that you are to be advised of.

Trauma
Grief
Violence (blood, death, etc.)
Racism
Allusions to sexual abuse

ISBN: Paperback: 978-1-965988-00-8

ISBN: Hardcover: 978-1-965988-01-5

ISBN: eBook: 978-1-965988-02-2

First printing 2024 by **Eric Still**

Book Cover and Chapter Decoration by **Anna-Mariya Georgieva**

Interior illustrations by **Philip Neumeister**

Edited by **Maddi Leatherman**

Proofread by **Salman Azhar**

Author photo by **Dwight Taylor**

To my cat, Grim.

Because I found you, I didn't forgo my humanity.

Table of Contents

Within the ensemble of the soul, there is sin and virtue seeking control.

Within this battle's reticence, all who would live find their

Genesis

PROLOGUE

Blood coursed down Kendra's pale cheek. Strung up and bound by rope, she hung, unconscious, head dangling. The fluid gathered at the tip of her chin before it fell to the musty floor below, casting a subtle echo through the cell she was confined within.

She awoke. A rush of stimuli bombarded her groggy senses. Peeking an eye open, she immediately recoiled from the light that singed it. Harsh white rays beamed through the mesh of wires plastered in the door opposite her, flickering fluorescent lights emitting from outside.

After a few moments of easing her eyes open, the drab scenery seeped into her. Stone walls surrounded her, dirty with scum leftover from Gods know what. She wouldn't deign to venture a guess. The dark corners were taunting her anxious imagination, only faintly visible with the minimal light that bled through the door. To spare her nerves, she ceased staring into the dark.

As she took a deep breath to collect herself, the faint, pungent scent of sulfur invaded her nostrils, causing her to wheeze in shock. *Is that my blood?* Exhaling roughly, she attempted to muster her thoughts, despite her jagged memory.

Abrupt, sharp footsteps emanated from somewhere outside the cell, pulling her further from her stupor. Her nostrils twitched, a familiar, musky scent coursing through the mesh. *Shit.* Wrestling her hands against the coarse strand of rope, she only strained her wrists. Despite the stinging burn plaguing them, she persisted in her struggle with teeth tightly gritted against one another as labored breaths gusted through them, followed by tenuous grunts. After several moments, she stopped thrashing, her arms going limp as she resigned herself to efforts of remembrance.

Voices replayed in her head, broken in a hall of hollow echoes and distortion. In the end, it was all indiscernible noise, with nothing useful to amass. Her head throbbed with raucous applause. Saturated brown hair clung to the back of her head. The wound beneath it was the source of the blood that sprawled down her cheek. The futility of her actions became apparent, and she hung her head in defeat, surrendering the prospect of recollection.

Tears welled in her eyes until they spilled, commencing an unsightly marriage with the blood streaking down her cheek. Emotionally distraught, panic swelled in her chest as the footsteps drew nearer. She didn't know why, but their approach spurred a single memory: loathsome, crimson eyes invaded her mind, their sentiment imposing on her and executing her naivety. She clung to the damning phrase *he* had spoken to her. Of all the things she could recall through the fog that pervaded her mind, she cursed it being those words. Those damned words that spurred her impulsive decision, arguably plunging her into this predicament. However true it was, her desperation compelled her to rebel instead.

The steps drew near, their arrival only seconds away. She hadn't much time before her abductor would confront her. It was a pointless parroting, but the words he had spoken gnawed at her throat, seeking escape. They were all that anchored her at that moment—the only thing permeating her shattered memory. She gathered her breath, and with a raspy voice, she resuscitated the words.

"You're not human anymore. Stop pretending you still are."

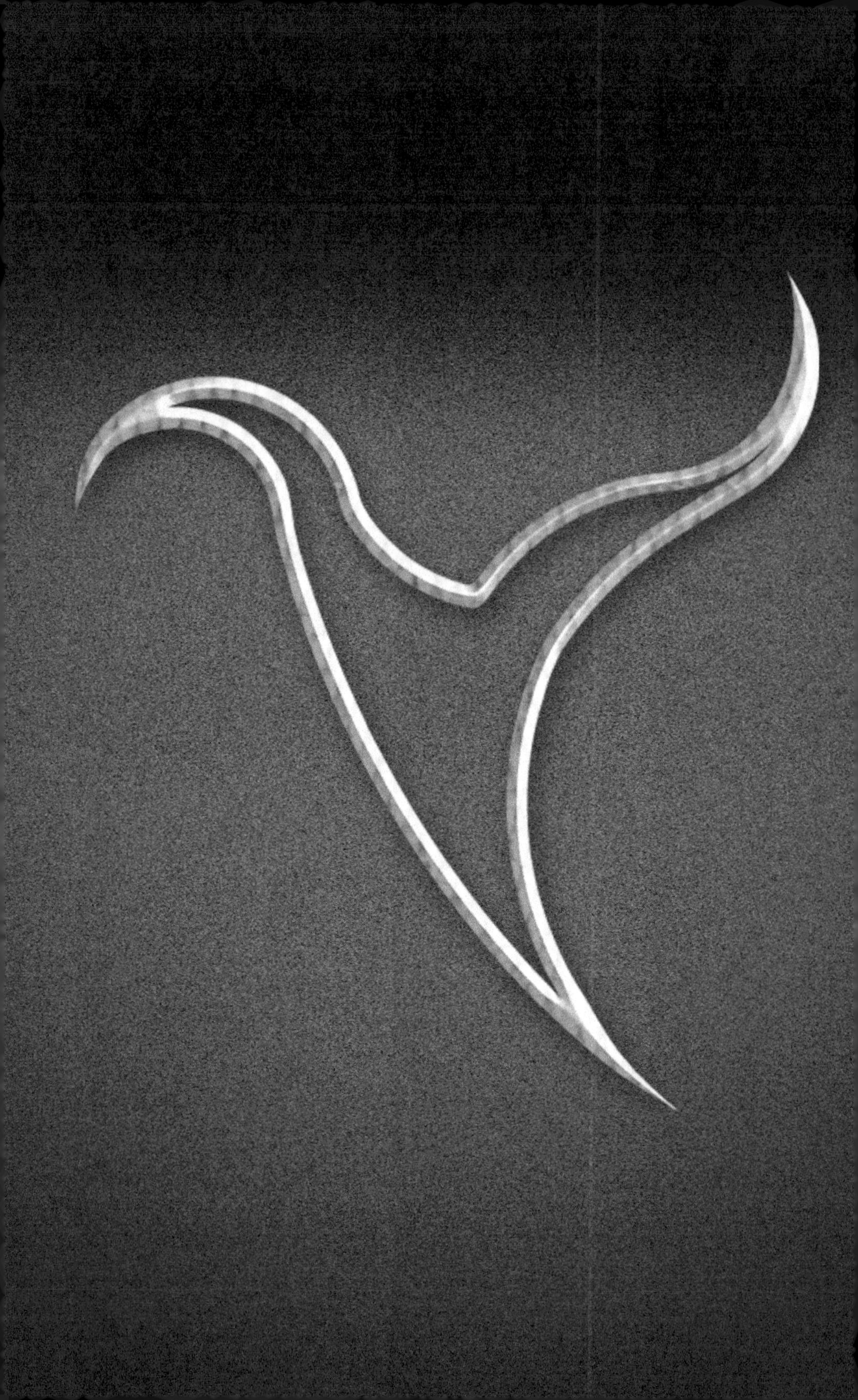

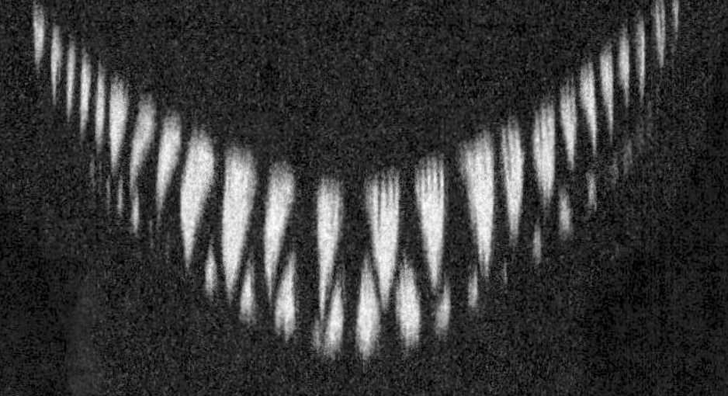

ONE

BURNING EYES

T ucked within the shadow of man lay the foregone tales of malevolent entities—demons. Minds long since primitive dismissed the potential threat, sequestering it to the sands of time, and while empires had prospered and evanesced, humanity still reigned. But regardless of the reality humanity failed to fathom, one truth transcends the arbitrary borders of race or creed: in spite of the darkness that dwells within, never forgo your *humanity*.

Kendra, an eighteen-year-old girl, was oblivious to such a sentiment, unperturbed by any such darkness or the alleged existence of demons. A teenager, as invincible as any other, stumbling her way into adulthood. But as mature as she feigned to be, there was mischief in her yet. At least in the perpetual rivalry between her and her sixteen-year-old sister, Kendall.

With carefully placed steps, Kendra crept down the hallway. The objective was simple: scare Kendall. It wasn't particularly thought out, but Kendall was hardly ever awake on time, whereas Kendra was already showered and dressed. The prank required little prompt. As far as she surmised, there was barely a margin of error, no matter how insufficient the plan was.

Walking along the guardrails of the stairs, Kendra approached Kendall's room. The door was still shut, a sure sign that Kendall was still asleep. She had been made aware on numerous occasions that Kendall always opened her door when she was awake, citing superstitious reasons.

She reached, gripped the knob, and nudged the door open to avoid an untimely creak. Kendra had her this time. The sunlight shrouding the room spilled through the door, and she briefly glimpsed the room and the bed—empty.

Then, there was a pop from two hands that clapped together in front of her, and Kendra yelped, wind gushing in her face. Unbalanced, gravity invited her ceremoniously to the ground, causing her to grunt upon impact. Her glasses had jerked down her face, prompting her to readjust them subconsciously as a groan spilled from her lips.

"Gotcha!" Kendall chirped out in her light, flowery voice as she lowered her hands. She broke into a snicker from the opposite side of the door as she swung it open completely.

Kendra saw her younger sister's black nails with cyan flowers painted on them as she held her hips. With their cutesy, almost thoughtless design—the kind of thing Kendra condemned—they served as a subtle mockery of her witless plan.

"Hey, what happened to that whole *connecting with the world* crap you talked about for waking up?" Kendra huffed, squinting at Kendall through the doorway.

"First of all … that's about me opening the window when I'm awake. And second … do you even know what's coming up?" Kendall took a step back, coming into Kendra's view. She wore high-waisted jeans with a beige anime T-shirt tucked into them, topped by a flowing black cardigan. Wavy brown hair spilled down her shoulders and framed her round face, and thick black-framed glasses accentuated her large hazel eyes, which were fixed on Kendra with a challenging gaze.

Kendra muttered to herself, shuffling to her feet as she racked her brain for an answer. Moments later, it occurred to her. The track race was days away, and whenever an important race approached, Kendall was far more disciplined about good routines.

"The … big track race is this week," Kendra said, her cheeks flushed.

Kendall snapped her fingers, pointing to the ceiling with a shit-eating grin adorned by braces.

"Bingo! Shame on you for forgetting, and even worse ... for doubting me!"

Kendra was sheepishly quiet for a moment but couldn't help breaking out into laughter. Second-hand pride washed over her, overtaking her embarrassment.

Kendall cocked an eyebrow, scoffing.

"What's so funny?" Kendall asked.

Kendra reached out, flicking Kendall's forehead before snagging her in a headlock. Then she ruffled Kendall's hair with her knuckles.

"Ow, ow, ow!" Kendall yelped, tugging to break away.

Kendra released her, nodding with a sheepish smirk.

"Okay, you're not supposed to be this clever—yet. You've made me proud, Kenny."

"Uh, thanks?" Kendall fixed her hair, pouting with annoyance.

Kendra dusted off her jeans, sighing as she calmed down. She twisted her hand and glanced at the midnight-blue smart band on her wrist. A holographic projection of the time read *6:15 a.m.* The glossy black surface projecting the hologram blinked with a green light, and she swiped the hologram to dismiss it before lowering her wrist.

"Anyway, how about breakfast before we head out?" Kendra probed.

Still pouting, Kendall sighed before a smirk snaked across her face.

"Sure. I think I earned my Greek yogurt today!"

Sweat dripped down Kendra's forehead, her feet barraging the ground beneath her as she advanced, her attention—locked on a soccer ball. With a heavy swing of her leg, she kicked the ball and lunged after it. Particles of grass and dirt swarmed before scattering in the wind with each successive step. With indomitable focus, she paid heed to the girls running after her, hugging her tail.

Kendra revised her strategy, reorienting the ball's trajectory before kicking it diagonally across the field. Using her momentum to change the direction, she raced after it. The abrupt motion brought the fervent girls behind her to a momentary pause, and she kicked the ball once more and juked right, following it. With each kick, the ball's momentum increased.

In the near distance, a tanned woman with sun-damaged skin watched through black and blue sunglasses. Coach Springfield. She wore burgundy track pants with a white track jacket framing her slender form. Her messy blond hair was tied up in a bun, blending with the midday sunlight.

The woman patrolled the boundary of the field, spectating her players' performance, albeit the spectacle was dominated by Kendra's. All the girls wore the same practice uniform of plain crimson sports tops and black mesh shorts with twin white stripes down the outer seam. They had run through a few drills already, with Kendra assisting in overseeing the new junior varsity players' sense of the game: tracking the ball, developing pace, and evasive maneuvers. A talented team captain—fastidious of their strengths and flaws even in the fray of their hunt for the ball.

Kendra stopped, pinning the ball with her left foot. A whistle shrieked from their coach. The girls came to a halt before Kendra, their chests rising and falling, skin saturated with sweat. Adorned with fatigue, they stood at attention for the incoming feedback.

Kendra studied them briefly, silently praising herself for how their faces were marred with frustration and exhaustion alike due to her performance.

"I think you're all at a great starting point. I was kept on my toes. Your stamina is gonna need work, but I think what we should work on next is pursuit and recapture. The drills showed you all know how to work around the ball, but I think that will be an important thing to brush up on, regardless." Her tone was firm but avoided unnecessary harshness. Being strident wasn't her forte. Neither would she dare to rob Coach Springfield of that luxury, if she were.

Instead, the two usually played good cop, bad cop: the talented captain with construction and approachability, kindly sharing her knowledge, and the brash coach, who'd keep them in shape and hammer the fundamentals home. Except now, Kendra handled most of this on her own, and she didn't play the coach's role too well.

As if on cue, Coach Springfield made her way over and snatched their attention with a sharp clap.

"You heard her. We'll be running through some more drills for the rest of practice. Kendra won't be here tomorrow. Instead, Vice-Captain Candace will be running drills with you, so don't slack off!" she barked.

The discouraged expressions on the girls' faces reminded Kendra of when she first joined the team. She saw her freshman self, battered and bruised—ego deflated. They had to earn the pride that Kendra had developed in her capabilities, but she had faith in them. It would be odd if she didn't, since she wanted them to make varsity when she was gone. They had to be prepared for when she'd graduate next year. Still, no matter how good they could be, she held that she was a tough act to follow.

Kendra adjusted her sports glasses and brushed the grass from her shorts. She walked toward the bench with a renewed thirst from her tiring display. Her sports bottle sat atop the faded bleachers, which were caked in chipped paint and dirt that had fused to them over the years. But before she could approach it, a warm hand rested on her shoulder. She glanced back at Coach Springfield, her eyes softening.

"Hey, thank you again, Ken. I—"

"Don't apologize. They're my responsibility too," Kendra interjected. "You still need time to process."

Coach Springfield sucked her lower lip in, her glassy eyes becoming distant as she nodded in tepid agreement. Kendra pressed her forehead to the woman's, her hands resting on the back of her head. Springfield reached up, placing her hands on Kendra's wrists, closing her eyes while shaky breaths fled her trembling lips.

"Stay strong, Coach." Kendra pulled away, turning away from the woman before making her way to her sports bottle for a much-needed drink.

She littered her face with cool splashes, washing away the warm sweat from her forehead. Once her face was clean, she took long swigs from the bottle, at last quenching her thirst. A gasp burst from her when she finished, and she gave a long sigh of reprieve. While sweat no longer saturated her face and stung her eyes, she could practically imagine how she smelled. A shower was in order.

Because she had to work two hours from then, she left practice early to prepare. She loved that her boss was flexible with her schedule; abandoning Coach Springfield was unthinkable. The coach's husband had been murdered the summer prior. He was a police officer, just like Kendra's mother. The murder was an abrupt shock to the community at the time, which Kendra could only dread to imagine if it had been her mother instead. He had been found in his patrol vehicle—mutilated. The body cam was stolen from the officer's clothing and the dashcam footage was completely corrupted. No perpetrator was ever found, and there was no tangible evidence left behind, according to her mother. Whoever had done it had gone to great lengths to erase their presence, much to everyone's dismay. The police chief gave regular press conferences over the past few months regarding the matter, but the suspended nerves of the citizens' anxiety persisted.

With a passing glance, Kendra returned her attention to the team, seeing the coach hounding the individual girls who fumbled some of the routines. If she hadn't known better, she'd have guessed her coach was already back to normal. Kendra had seen her have random breakdowns, preventing her from fully committing to her role. But if she were to step down without a replacement, the team would probably dissolve. Because of that, Kendra agreed to take on more responsibilities as captain, ensuring that Coach Springfield could take bereavement days as needed.

Kendra turned on her heel, heading to the locker room to shower and change before leaving.

When she made it to the bike racks in the courtyard, she prepared the NFC module on her smart band to unlock the electronic stall. Her fingers danced across the number pad, entering her passcode on the holographic display. A flash of twinkling red streaked across the corners of her vision. The hairs on her neck stood up, a spark shooting down her spine as she turned to see the not-so-subtle approach of a boy with short, choppy red hair. Her *close friend,* Allen.

He was tall with large shoulders on a sturdily built frame. Fitting, given he was the star quarterback and captain of the football team. A boy one would never guess was from an affluent family of prominence with his regular fashion choices—disparate from the flashy garnishes of his family and others in his social class. He and Kendra had known each other for the better part of a decade—since elementary, in fact.

"You can't be serious, Allen. You thought you were gonna sneak up on me?" Kendra alleged, her pensive gaze challenging him.

Allen stood straight, chuckling as he snapped his fingers.

"Drats! The Fox of Ashwood High has once again thwarted my attempts at stealth!" he quipped theatrically, avoiding her gaze suddenly.

Kendra snorted, rolling her eyes. She scanned her smart band over the lock, causing it to unlatch.

"They should pull you back a few grades with that freshman sense of humor. Also, you're calling me a fox? You're the one with red hair."

"Hey, it's what they call you, I swear!" He approached the bike rack, leaning against an empty slot. "Geez, my ego hurts. Would it kill you to be kinder?" he proposed.

Kendra kicked the stand of her bike up before facing him. Now that he was close, she couldn't help but notice the small bruise on his face. It stuck out quite apparently because she hardly ever saw him with even a blemish. Between that and his sloppier movements, she chalked it up to him taking a tumble at football practice yesterday.

"Nope, I'm afraid I'd combust immediately." She feigned melodrama, placing her hand across her chest as she flashed an insincere grimace.

"You're real cute whenever you're snarky."

"Cute? Last week you called me adorable. So which is it, fox boy?" She stared expectantly.

Allen paused for a moment, resting his chin on his palm.

"Both. It's called nuance, Kendra." Allen smirked.

Kendra's lips parted, but she couldn't find words. She was momentarily speechless in the face of another clever development on the same day.

The same phrase was something she had said to him a month prior during one of their ever-so-fruitful exchanges. *Nuance? That's not even a word he uses!*

Kendra snapped around, pulled the bike from the slot, and sat on it. With a push of her heel, she rolled past him to make a swift escape.

"Keep working on those jokes and maybe one day you'll impress me." She stifled a smile, her royal-blue eyes averting from him as she pulled onto the pavilion leading out the main gate.

"Who said I was joking!" he called after her, but she hadn't remained to hear.

Kendra sat on her bike, waiting for the light to turn green. Patience was never her strong suit, and the anticipation building inside her during her wait reminded her of that. She much preferred riding home at night, when the traffic lights would be green almost all the way home for her. They were set up to orient their hue based on the traffic condition, as opposed to the system from decades ago.

Soon, she arrived at her job, an old storefront with the name plastered on a large sign, *Ohm's Cadence*, and parked her bike in the designated rack out front. The shop found its inception after a big legislative battle several years prior. Whatever kept them busy ensured Kendra would have her part-time job. She enjoyed working there, earning a slight amount over minimum wage, despite only being in high school—a quality she was grateful for within the work environment. The owner, James Ardent, respected her work ethic, and he sought to give her the financial advantage he thought she deserved, knowing she'd attend college soon.

Upon entering, she was greeted by the scent of metal lubricant and cheap, flower-scented air freshener. The white marble floor of the reception area had three pleather couches; a cheap waiting area fashioned by James. *Truly Ohm's Cadence,* she thought.

"Hey, Chelsea," Kendra greeted.

A tall, glossy black-and-white cylinder sat behind the counter, Chelsea's avatar dock. Chelsea was the AI that ran the menial tasks of customer service and operated the store systems. An oblong pod with four propulsors fixed beneath it leaped from the dock, its digital blue eyes manifesting on the screen as it hovered near Kendra.

"Welcome, Kendra. Clocking in?" spoke a robotic female voice. Kendra turned to Chelsea and nodded her head.

"Yes, indeedy." She had gotten that quote from a commercial that played on a podcast her coworker, Jones, listened to.

"I must inform you that Mr. Ardent wishes to speak with you. He is currently at workstation five."

"Did he tell you what he wanted to speak with me about?"

"He didn't say."

Kendra sighed, hoisting her bag up as she walked through the dual counter doors to access the back of the store. She went through the walkway that led into a larger area with numerous workstations, all littered with electronic components and a plethora of tools. It appeared outdated for 2042, but the store was reminiscent of another, simpler time—a driving reason for James's customer base, or so she liked to think.

The other on-duty technicians, Sal, Jones, and Arman, sat at workstations, busy working on a range of technological components. Fluorescent lights dangled above them, along with smaller work lights clipped to the desks, bent at an angle for better clarity.

From the monitor adjacent to Jones's workstation, the news played.

"Here on Fox thirty-two Chicago, another police interceptor was found abandoned off the I-90 east-bound near South Ruble Street, making it the second in a spree of these incidents this week. Here we have Police Chief Archer Bronson to deliver an important update on this matter."

A news transition played, cutting to a podium, and behind it, Archer stared into the camera. He was a stocky man with a shaved head, black skin, and hard brown eyes filled with certainty. Kendra had met the man once before, recalling how sturdy and reliable he appeared to be—exactly what she'd expect of her mother's boss.

"I can assure the citizens of our strong city that we will not bend, break, or yield until whoever is responsible for these abhorrent attacks are dealt with. We are expending any and all resources in our endeavors to not only locate and deal with the perpetrators, but to further protect our officers and community."

Kendra pursed her lips, turned away from the TV, and walked past Jones's workstation.

Jones peered up from his project, his nostrils flaring as he furrowed his brow.

"Crazy stuff, right, Ken? Hope your mom stays safe ... but how's school, kid? I've been waiting for my favorite fetch-monkey to come back," Jones said. His deep voice flowed smoothly while his fingers fiddled with a ribbon cable he was reattaching to a circuit board. Kendra smirked as she walked by him.

"I don't know what you've been waiting for. Sal's already here," she retorted.

Sal peered up from his workstation, grimacing at the two of them.

"Shut it," he warned, causing the others to chuckle.

Sal gave Kendra grouchy-old-man vibes in most interactions, which was how she knew he feigned his agitation in this one.

"Ken, would you mind bringing me a box of 805 capacitors?" Arman requested. Kendra walked over to a shelf by his station, grabbing a radio and earpiece. She couldn't help chuckling at his thick accent and the way he pronounced capacitors as *cuh-pass-it-ores.*

"Sure, as soon as I'm done talking to James," she replied.

Kendra made the short walk to workstation five, where James was absorbed in a motorized gauntlet. James wore special goggles as he fiddled with the device, the zoomed lenses adjusting as he threaded a wire through a slot. The gauntlet confused Kendra, as she had never seen anything akin to it before.

"Uh, you wanted to speak to me, J-man?" Kendra asked.

"One sec." James fiddled with the components, screwing a bracket back into the device before he sighed in satisfaction. He removed the goggles from his eyes, the harness causing his shoulder-length, frayed silver hair to fall free. His gloomy hazel eyes found her as he reoriented his vision with a few blinks, exhaling hard.

"Mornin', Ken," he spoke with his gruff voice. Kendra typically had to pay close attention whenever he spoke due to his southern accent, excessive contractions, and ambiguous inflections. This usually resulted in her having to tread the shop to find him if he needed to tell her something, or his incomprehensible shouting would effectively land on deaf ears.

"Uh, it's early evening."

"Well, it's mornin' somewhere in the world." He cleared his throat. "Anyway, I wanted to make a request. Got a special client comin' by to pick this thing up. Can I trust yah to hand it off to 'im? I gotta step out. My son ain't been too well, and I gotta go see 'im shortly."

"Um, sure. Is there a reason Chelsea can't do it, though?" Usually, many of the orders were delivered by Chelsea or James's wife on the days she was in, but she hadn't been present lately.

"Special. Client," James echoed.

Kendra gave a wry smile, tepidly nodding.

"Right, right. Okay, consider it done." Kendra attached her radio to her belt and snapped the earpiece into her ear. "Anything else?"

"Yeah ... don't let Arman boss yah around too much. He's got legs." He flashed Arman a sour expression.

"Oh, then what are you paying me for?" Kendra questioned with a creeping smirk.

James snorted, returning his attention to the device on the table.

"Never have enough legs aroun'!" he said, cackling as he fiddled with the device.

Kendra rolled her eyes, a smile snaking across her face as she went to the storage room, brushing aside James's faux concern.

Nine O'clock came, and the technicians were settling their projects before the store closed to the public. Kendra clocked out, preparing to head home to beat curfew. The glass door shut behind her, and brisk night air rushed to greet her. LED streetlights radiated miniature moons that stretched endlessly into the urban scape. The orange-tinted, teal sky was all that was left to paint the city, a fall-themed tapestry that cascaded behind the high-rises.

She unlocked her bike and observed the streets, now reduced to a crawl of cars straggling about. There was plenty of foot traffic in the heart of the city, bleeding out to the eastern border where she was. With a soft sigh, she mounted the bike and pedaled to its designated lane on the shoulder, her legs pumping as she accelerated through the streets.

Her braided ponytail whipped through the wind, the cool night air fanning her as she pedaled. In the solace of her commute, she thought ahead to her uncertain future—colleges and vocations. The prospect of becoming a detective like her mother enticed her, but she didn't think herself analytical enough for that. However, forensics interested her plenty, as she discovered watching her favorite TV show: Decker.

In a disparate thought, she remembered having virtually no interest in engineering. *Anything but.* She couldn't fathom getting anywhere near the curriculum that informed her coworkers or father—especially if it meant having to entertain the math. She'd had metaphorical aneurysms simply thinking about the concept of linear algebra.

There was time to decide, however. Kendra's mother, being a Boston University alumna, could potentially play a role in earning Kendra a scholarship to the university. And being an athlete, which she currently leaned toward, was an option, but she feared that, too, could squander her potential.

On autopilot, Kendra reached the border of downtown. Her attention shifted to the transition of the surrounding lights to the less-advanced models of the posts leaching into the neighborhoods. The bright white became a dim yellow with glimmers of—red.

Red lights?

Her eyes caught glimpses of twinkling scarlet sprites radiating with a burning flicker. They rose from the ground and wandered with indiscernible intent. She was alone, and nobody was out. The usually vibrant street of the familiar neighborhood was dead-silent, unusual even when late. No rowdy neighborhood kids, chattering residents, or stray joggers. She initially assumed it was some kind of decorative holographic display—similar to the ones the city used to usher in the New Year.

Burning air singed Kendra's neck. With the sweltering breeze assailing her, it was as if an oven radiated against her back. The streetlights flickered, burning out with a crunchy pop, and she yelped. These variables compelled her to look back, and when she did, something stared back at her, drawing nearer despite the speed she was traveling at. In the dark, burning eyes bore into her, and a putrid scent followed. A quadrupedal creature's paws met the asphalt, audibly carving it with each collision.

Kendra didn't dwell long on the revelation. Snapping her head forward, she slammed her foot down, pedaling faster. Quick, shallow breaths burst from her lips, and snarls filled her ears, each raspy growl growing louder as it gained on her.

Kendra wheezed, whimpering as her body ceaselessly tensed. Whatever it was, her bike wouldn't be fast enough to escape it. She needed a plan before it was too late.

They approached an older home enclosed by a dilapidated wooden fence. The creature gained on Kendra, a loud snarl ripping through the cold air and tickling her ears. *Now!* She banked hard on her bike, slowing at a slant for a few moments, and the thing hurtled above her. With a crash, the creature collided with the fence, breaking through it.

Kendra resumed pedaling as fast as she could, and the gnashes, snarls, and heavy footfalls of the creature finally diminished after several seconds.

The swarming red sprites faded along with the presence of the ghastly beast she had evaded.

But even then, Kendra didn't stop. There would be no contentment until she was home, and she navigated the dark with haste. When she pulled into the driveway of her home, she skidded to a stop and haphazardly tossed her bike onto the lawn. She sprinted to the doorway, her vision pulsing as she fiddled with the doorknob in clumsy desperation. When it was open, she threw herself inside, stumbling to the floor of the foyer. Without pause, she kicked the door shut with a loud thud.

Kendra's father, Aaron, had come home not long ago, explaining why the door wasn't locked. She was thankful for his careless habit in that instance, but that was overshadowed when the tightness in her chest sank to her stomach. Kendra pulled herself to her feet. She slogged to reach the nearest bathroom, gagging as she slumped in front of the toilet, proceeding to puke.

When she raised her head, her father stood in the doorway. A tall man with shoulder-length brown hair and eyes framed in glasses. She met his gaze, her breathing labored as she held a trembling hand up to signal him to wait. Standing on unsteady legs, she used the nearby faucet to gargle until her mouth was cleansed of the lingering taste. Once she had regained herself, she breathed fresh air and gripped the hem of her shirt, gathering her thoughts.

"What happened?" Aaron asked.

"I was chased by something. I don't know how I escaped." She hiccupped. "It was like ... a dog. A *big* dog. And there were red lights all around."

"Woah, woah, Ken. It sounds like you freaked out while being chased by a dog. Was it that scary?"

"Yes!" Kendra drew a deep, unsteady breath, her grip on her shirt tightening as she avoided her father's gaze. Moments later, he pulled her into a firm hug, shushing her before she could sob. The only thought running through her head was the heat, scent, and sinister aura of the beast.

"I'm sorry, Ken. I didn't mean to downplay it. Listen, I'll call animal control about it. They'll look into it, kay-kay?"

Kendra reluctantly nodded while her face was still buried in his shoulder. She broke away from the embrace after a moment, wiping at her eyes and taking another unsteady breath.

"I'm heading to bed ..." she said, stumbling past him and heading upstairs, but the memory assailed her still, and as she was lying in bed, she saw it again when her eyes shut.

It wasn't a damn dog.

"Sounds similar to that coyote that lunged at me the other day when I was out on a call," Kendra's mother, Katherine, said. She was a middle-aged woman who shared Kendra's appearance, bearing the same facial features and royal-blue eyes; albeit, her eyes were currently sunken from restlessness and her gaze suggested she was more aloof than Kendra. She stood at the sink in the kitchen, washing the dishes. It was the night after Kendra had been chased, and the family had finished dinner for the evening. Across from the island, separating the kitchen from the dining room, Aaron, Kendra, and Kendall sat at the table.

"I'm telling you, it wasn't a coyote, Mom!" Kendra protested with ferocity, gripping the edge of the table.

While they spoke, Kendall idly texted on the projected keyboard from her cyan smart band, occasionally glancing up and pursing her lips before returning her attention to the holographic screen.

"We all know what coyotes look like, and not to say I believe or don't believe—but I don't understand how she'd have seen red lights or fire coming from it. Anything you can think of that would provide a good explanation, Kat?" Aaron said, unbuttoning the second button from the top of his shirt, further loosening his collar.

Katherine paused for a moment, warm water running over her hands as she thought about a good explanation. As her tired eyes glazed over, the mention of lights stirred a memory, but she shook her head before shrugging.

"Honestly, no idea right now. I've been working overtime on these cases, and between the insomnia problem and our colleagues going missing, I'm pretty soup-brained at the moment," Katherine admitted, looking back at her husband and daughters. "What *do* you think it was, Ken?"

Kendra lowered her head, running her nails along the smooth surface of the table repeatedly as she thought back to the monstrous visage that leered at her from the dark. The scratchy, shuddering breathing and the embers she had witnessed. None of it made sense, but the image had thoroughly embedded into her memory, evoking her fear with every recollection.

"You're chock-full of inhibitions that you need to let out," Kendall said, flicking the holographic screen away as she abruptly joined the conversation.

"Inhibitions … That's what you're going with?" Kendra spoke dryly, both she and their mother giving Kendall *that* look.

"You'd be surprised what the mind is capable of conjuring when you're scared—like when you can swear you saw something move in the dark. You know … tricks of the mind. That sort of stuff," Kendall mentioned, nodding satisfactorily as she waited in the ensuing silence.

"… Kenny, show me your search history," Kendra demanded, earning a pout from Kendall.

"I'm trying to help you! Stop trying to change the subject!" Kendall protested and frowned as she looked at her mother, who conveniently turned her head away at the last second—hiding an obvious smile of amusement. "*Mom …*" Kendall whined.

Katherine broke out chuckling, placing a plate in the drying rack before she grabbed her stomach. For several seconds, she was paralyzed by the humor she found in the situation, and even Kendra cracked a reluctant smile, averting her gaze to her father. Kendra was astounded by how much of a poker face he held—not even a hint of smiling.

"Unironically, I think Kenny's onto something," Aaron began, spreading his arms out and placing them around both daughters. "You do that yoga stuff or something, right? Why don't you do that taro thing for Ken?"

Kendall scowled at her father, baffled by what he had said.

"It's *Wicca*, Dad. And it's *tarot*, not *taro*."

"Isn't tarot that boba flavor I get you?" Aaron cocked an eyebrow.

With a dull thud, Kendra planted her forehead onto the table. In unison, both she and Kendall sighed.

"... I've been saying it wrong this entire time, haven't I?" Aaron asked.

"You're such a dork!" Katherine declared, bursting out laughing harder than she had before.

Aaron furrowed his brow and leaned back, placing his hands behind his head as he shut his eyes.

"You're the one who married me. I must be doing *something* right."

"Julian's gonna love this one. He always said you were too smart for your own good—but now, you've refuted him."

Aaron sat up straight and stood from his seat, waltzing over to Katherine before wrapping his arms around her. He proceeded to lean on her as he nestled his face into the crook of her neck.

"If I'm a dork, and you're soup-brained—what does that make our daughters?" he asked.

Katherine hummed lightly, nuzzling into him as she pondered the question.

"Tweedle Dee and Tweedle Dum," she answered, sticking her tongue out playfully at her daughters.

Kendra sat up, scoffing at the insinuation before glancing at Kendall, who smirked at her with a knowing glint of confidence. Long ago, they had come up with their signature sister name, which, *unfortunately*, had never stuck.

"Kendra and Kendall—a ferocious duo with no equal," Kendall began, turning her attention to their mother and father.

Kendra rolled her eyes, folding her arms as she averted her gaze.

"With fire and fury—we're ..." she spoke unenthusiastically, but stifled a smirk.

"*The Kamikaze Sisters*," the sisters spoke in unison.

Their parents exchanged glances for a few moments, and Katherine gave a sly smirk as she eyed them.

"So ... you guys both crash and burn, or ..."

"I *told* you that was cringey, even back when you came up with it," Kendra complained, turning her attention back to Kendall and huffing.

Kendall rolled her eyes, folding her arms with a pout.

"Well, I thought it was pretty cool," Aaron alleged, earning a nod of approval from Kendall.

"You"—Kendall pointed at her father—"are redeemed."

"You are your daughter's father," Katherine said to Aaron. She squirmed in his grip before he swung her around, poking her nose playfully while twisting a strand of her brown hair around his finger.

"Kenny, why don't you go do a *tarot* reading for Kendra? Clear up her inhibitions."

"At once, sir!" Kendall said, giving a dramatic salute as she stood from the table.

Kendra shook her head as she reluctantly stood, glancing at her parents and grimacing.

"If it means not witnessing this ... fine."

The sisters exfiltrated from the kitchen—Kendall, eager to do a tarot reading, and Kendra, desperate to not watch their parents *fall in love again*.

Kendra entered Kendall's room, shoving her hands into the pockets of her joggers as Kendall approached her dresser. She grabbed a glass jar half-full of tangerine-colored candle wax and approached the rug beside her bed before gesturing for Kendra to sit.

Shrugging, Kendra briefly scrutinized the rug, embroidered with golden threads that illustrated a triple moon, and in the center—a pentagram. Kendra sat cross-legged on the rim of the rug, positioned atop the crescent. Serendipitously, Kendall grabbed the candle and gave an approving nod to Kendra.

"Totally my idea," Kendall alleged, causing Kendra to snort and roll her eyes.

As Kendall paced, her eyes brightened for a moment, and she looked at Kendra.

"Oh, I just remembered. I'll be doing a reading for your classmate, Eden, after my race. He has these ... really intense green eyes. I'm curious about what'll come up for him."

"Oh ... yeah, Eden Blackwell. Funny you should mention him. He came by the shop the other day. Apparently, he's a special client of James? I don't know much about him, honestly. But he probably enjoys anime, just like you. He was wearing red contacts."

Kendall giggled and shrugged, taking her seat across from Kendra. Both girls now occupied the space atop the two crescents.

"Badass name, by the way. I guess our mutual appreciation of anime explains the good vibe I got from him. I'll have to ask him what his favorite one is," Kendall said, clearing her throat as she took a deep breath. "Alright ... now for the reading." She placed the candle outside of the moon in the center. Pulling a lighter from within the jar, she lit the candle carefully and set the lighter down beside it. She pulled up a projection from her smart band, dragging her finger down, which caused the light above them to dim.

With the small flame subtly pulsing atop the wick, Kendra eyed it curiously. After a few moments of it burning, she inhaled the scent and snorted.

"Pumpkin? For the ritual?"

"It's not a ritual," Kendall scolded, rolling her eyes. "It's for the vibes. I love pumpkin." Kendall shuffled her tarot deck, humming a tune to herself, which, as Kendra recalled, came from an anime featuring a character who looked like a witch that sang about pumpkins. "Alright, cut the deck," Kendall instructed.

Kendra tentatively reached out, her nail gliding down the side of the deck until she caught a groove. With a shaky exhale, she split the upper portion of the deck, setting it beside the lower half.

"Ok ... what would you like to know?" Kendall asked.

With careful consideration, Kendra thought back to the burning eyes that had haunted her—the uncertainty that had prevailed within her left a yearning for answers. She wanted to know her future.

"What is my future?"

One by one, Kendall drew three cards, placing them face down before Kendra. Then she revealed the first.

The Tower.

"Oh?" Kendall chirped, tapping her chin as she pondered the card, studying it intently for several seconds.

"What does it mean?" Kendra asked.

Kendall shifted her gaze up to Kendra, her eyes obscured in the glint cast by the flickering candle.

"Well ... something dire is approaching. You'll be forced to contend with something challenging, and you'll have to let go of beliefs and ideas that'll keep you from facing it."

Kendall carefully reached out, flipping the second card over.

Six of Swords.

"This one is ... transitory. A journey away from darkness and toward something more hopeful. Typically, this means you will seek healing from something that has harmed you—or another."

Kendra bit her bottom lip, her eyes lowering as she fixated on the cards—especially the last one.

Kendall glided her fingers over to the final card, flipping it over slowly.

Death.

Kendra didn't need Kendall to explain what this card was. The visage of the Grim Reaper leered at her, its shadowy appearance obscured even in the soft light of the dancing flame and the dim ceiling light that loomed above them.

"I'm going to die ..." Kendra muttered breathlessly, earning a series of snaps from Kendall. This garnered Kendra's attention, and Kendall frowned at her, shaking her head.

"That's not what *death* means, Tweedle Dee. It can mean a lot of things, but in this context ..." Kendall paused. "It stands for the end of something and subsequently, the genesis of another. You will relinquish something, and in turn, something new—something better—will take its place." Kendall offered a soft smile, clasping her hands together as she nodded enthusiastically.

"Altogether, you have a tribulation, a journey, and a new beginning."

Kendra's eyes narrowed, her breath quickening as the vision of the infernal eyes burned into her. Darkness encroached on her vision, stretching with inky tendrils that latched to her eyes and pried them open. *Closer and closer.*

"So that's how my story ends?" Kendra croaked silently, the phantom question escaping her without conscious thought.

An impact jostled Kendra from her thoughts, causing the creeping despair to abscond momentarily. Across from her, her younger sister held her shoulders, staring with an unyielding hazel gaze that served as a spear to challenge the treachery Kendra had deigned to utter. Accompanying her stare, was an impervious grin that could shield against any excuse she could conjure.

"It's never too late to change your story!"

Kendra was speechless for several seconds, her breath still jagged.

Kendall placed the lid over the top of the candle, starving it of oxygen and putting it out.

"Those damned inhibitions are getting to you, so do exactly as I say, K?"

Kendra remained silent, nodding her head tepidly.

"Shut your eyes."

Kendra did as she was told.

"Inhale ..." Kendall instructed, and the anxious older sister took a deep breath.

Several seconds passed, and Kendra's lungs remained swollen, her abdomen tensing as her mind became foggy. It quickly became excruciating, but she obediently awaited Kendall's next instruction.

Kendra's face turned red, and she felt she would explode at any moment.

"Release!"

With that, Kendra unleashed a long breath, causing the tarot cards beneath her to shift slightly. She relaxed her shoulders as she went limp. Much to her surprise, she no longer saw the burning eyes pervading her mind.

Then a gust of wind and a clap caused her to jump, her eyes shooting open as she fell back—again. Quickly realizing that Kendra had gotten her with the same trick as before, she glared up at her cheeky younger sister.

Kendall snorted as she separated her hands and gathered her tarot cards, placing the three cards back on top before standing up.

"Stop doubting me." Kendall approached her dresser, tucking the deck inside before shutting it promptly. "These events are subject to change, depending on a bunch of things. If this one bugged you this much, I'll do another reading for you—after my race, of course."

It was the next morning. Following Kendall's reading, Kendra had been convinced that she had been delirious when she saw the creature; every memory of the event in her head made no logical sense, and her parents agreed, too. At least now, when she closed her eyes, she wasn't constantly haunted by the memory. Kendall was to thank for that.

Maybe she's surpassed me after all.

Kendra was lying in bed. Her blanket was half-strewn across her body, and her head throbbed as light spilled in through her curtains, scorning her blurry vision. A groan escaped her as she kicked the blanket from her form. She couldn't afford to stay in bed that morning, less Kendall be up and ready first—again. Despite the satirical thought she had entertained, she still intended to remain the superior Mallory.

The notification light on her smart band blinked. She placed her glasses on and grabbed it, tapping the surface to bring up the holographic display of a text from Allen.

Hey Ken, just wanted to say that whatever's been on your mind the past couple of days, you can talk to me about it.

Kendra had avoided many people the past few days—Allen included. It was nothing she held against him, but she didn't want to drive him away with her crappy mood. She sighed and flicked the hologram, dismissing it. She had to get ready.

The day proceeded quickly, and she found herself in her final class period, French. For this reason, she had worn her hair in a French braid to be cheeky. Her teacher, Ms. Boulier, found it to be endearing, at least, often discussing French fashion trends with Kendra as a result. The distinct qualities interested both of them, but Ms. Boulier insisted they speak in French more often than not as a part of the curriculum—something Kendra enjoyed about the class, along with the students not being too pretentious.

When class commenced, one such student was paired up with her for their assignment. They were to present a French fairytale—in French, to no one's surprise. The student in question was a friend of hers, Natalie Lewis. She had strawberry-blond hair and aquamarine eyes that contrasted cutely with her freckles and peach-colored skin. Natalie was dressed in blue jeans and a red flannel shirt, finished with brown leather boots that had engraved designs along the sides. Kendra found the outfit characteristic of her, given she came from the South for school; an aspiring country girl stuck in the big city, as many saw it. Natalie, on the other hand, only found a mild interest in all the outdoors and farm activities and was enthralled with life in the city. From the infrastructure to the technological support systems, she grew giddy at the opportunity of living with her uncle while she studied.

"Ken-Ken, hey!" she chirped.

Kendra nodded her head, a smile drawn out of her.

"Hey, Nat. So. Any ideas on where to start?" she asked. The chatter of their classmates ensued around them, but the girls maintained their focus on each other.

"Well, let's ask good ole Google!" She pulled a tablet from her bag, one that had to be at least a decade old at this point. A proprietary piece of technology that didn't rely on the cloud to function.

"Geez, Nat, how old is that thing?" Kendra asked in awe.

"Still working, something Mama gifted me. Besides, it works when out of range of yer fancy clouds!" Natalie giggled and navigated the website on the tablet. After a few minutes, she snapped her fingers. Natalie proposed one idea she had found, a weird French fairy tale about an ogre raising a princess. But having spoken the words aloud and watching Kendra's expression sour, Natalie became reluctant.

Kendra sighed, shaking her head in refusal.

"Nope, not even gonna entertain that. Especially with the implied incest."

"Aw, come on. Can't we embellish details like the movies do?"

"We can find another one, okay?"

"Fine," Natalie whined. She continued tapping along the screen of her tablet while Kendra waited. Minutes later, Natalie jumped in excitement.

"I didn't even know Little Red Riding Hood was originally French. Let's do this one!" Natalie's eyes glimmered with excitement. Kendra stared at an exuberant Natalie with hesitation but relented.

"Fine, let's hear it. What's the bloody tale? I'm imagining something like the Grimm brothers' books."

Natalie nodded her head in confirmation, a sheepish grin growing on her face. Natalie explained how Red Riding Hood was depicted as a fair young woman who was tricked by the wolf into telling where her grandmother was. The wolf ate the grandmother, tricked Riding Hood into bed, and ate her too. That was where the story ended. Then, there was the moral plastered at the end:

Children, especially attractive, well-bred young ladies, should never talk to strangers, for if they should do so, they may well provide dinner for a wolf. I say "wolf," but there are various kinds of wolves. There are also those who are charming, quiet, polite, unassuming, complacent, and sweet, who pursue young women at home and in the streets. And unfortunately, it is these gentle wolves who are the most dangerous ones of all.

Kendra's eyes were fixed on the text, unsure what to make of it. In her current state of mind, it was jarring. With a blank stare, she turned the tablet around and nodded her head in approval.

"Let's do it."

The class finished with them working on the translations, and the rest was spared for their next meeting where they would present the story. Class had ended, and Kendra prepared to head home for the day. Pausing beneath the covered pathway, she briefly wondered what happened in Kendall's race, but imagined Kendall would volunteer the information when they'd leave school together. Blocking the harsh sunlight from her eyes, she left from beneath the overhang, making her way to the courtyard.

The fall sky glowed with a scarlet hue. Eastern redbud leaves frolicked and nonchalantly descended to litter the courtyard, which the students dispersed through with crunchy steps—a tempo for the whistling wind. The ensemble attributed its song to the passing, unwitting musicians, their banter serving as indiscernible lyrics.

Briefly enthralled, Kendra couldn't stifle the gentle smile on her face. She loved fall for this reason: agreeable weather, beautiful scenery, and the impending encroachment of winter—the precursors of renewal and all it invited. At least that was the way Kendall explained the season, and it was one of the few things she agreed with her on.

Exiting her pause, she walked to the front of the school to the bike racks. Approaching her bike, she felt eyes on her again, a twinkle of scarlet red bordering her vision. She spun around to meet the stern gaze from stark gray irises. Allen. *I forgot to text him back. Right.* Kendra offered a bashful smile as he approached her.

"You always wait by a girl's bike?" she said meekly.

Allen pulled her into a warm hug. His embrace was gentle and caring—a welcomed feeling. Still, she hesitated for a moment before returning the hug, her eyes downcast as she blushed.

"You know me better than that, Ken. I shouldn't be finding out stuff from Kenny. Don't be afraid to share this stuff with me. I'm here for you." Kendra was silent for a few moments as she wrestled the frog in her throat.

"You're right … I'm sorry, Al. I'll make it up to you. How about we talk about it over dinner? No better way to flush out traumas than over food, right?"

Allen separated from the hug.

"So … a date? You're asking *me* out?" Allen cocked an eyebrow.

Kendra snorted, rolling her eyes.

"However you want to picture it is fine. I'm just being selfish. That's all," she laughed.

"I won't argue it, but you know that we both know the optics of this, miss norm-breaker."

Kendra unlocked her bike, seeing Kendall peering from behind a tree. The younger sister smiled wryly at the two and approached.

"That's my cue. I'll see you … Saturday? We'll discuss more over text."

Allen nodded in approval, averting his gaze and falling silent for several moments.

"Hey, hey, lovebirds. I miss anything?" Kendall asked, offering a tepid smile to the two.

"Chivalry isn't dead, for Kendra has resurrected and usurped it," Allen said, stirred from his momentary silence.

"Chivalry?" Kendall skeptically stared at Kendra.

"Oh, shut it. Let's go, Kenny!" Kendra ushered Kendall to her cyan bike.

Allen smirked and waved as he walked backward.

"See you soon, Ken …" He then walked off.

The sisters left in tow, pedaling their bikes out of the school. Side by side, they rode together. Kendra was surprised Kendall didn't immediately bombard her with questions, seeing as she always enjoyed teasing Kendra about Allen. She was about to bring up why Kendall told Allen about what happened, but when she looked over, she saw her pouting. *The race.* Kendra cleared her head and sighed.

"So—"

"Second place! I can't believe I bombed to second place! I got caught in that Woodrow girl's slipstream!"

"The hell's a slipstream?" Kendra waited for an answer, but Kendall was too busy fuming to explain.

Kendall ranted as they pedaled, a mixture of disappointment and anger plaguing her. Kendra listened diligently, avoiding offering input for now since it was clear Kendall wanted to vent.

They were riding on the outskirts of Lincoln Park, their preferred path home. Kendall's long brown hair whipped in the wind, her cardigan rippling. She came to a stop at one of the park path entrances, a hiking route of sorts that the two were familiar with from weekend trips.

"Kendall?" Kendra questioned, coming to a stop behind Kendall.

Kendall huffed, kicking the ground beneath her as her hazel glare met Kendra.

"Let's go on a ride through the park. I still have some steam to blow off."

"Are you nuts? It'll be dark before we finish!" The sky was now orange with hints of midnight blue creeping from the horizon, signaling the approaching night.

Kendall knew this, of course, but she didn't mind some darkness for a few minutes, especially since she carried her charm on her person. However, Kendra had residual trauma from the incident the other night.

"Please, oh, please, my brave big sister. A ride through the park with you would get my mind off my failure." Kendall pleaded with puppy-dog eyes. Kendra debated herself, finding it hard to resist Kendall's begging. She remembered making Kendall cry when she didn't tag along on her adventures when they were growing up. The thought of seeing Kendall moping around, or worse, getting lost by herself—in the dark—was hardly a palatable alternative.

"Fine, but only for a while. I really wanna get home." A pit grew in Kendra's stomach.

"Yay!"

With the debate settled, the sisters pedaled onto the path leading through the park. The deeper they went, the darker it became. Kendra was thankful the trail lit up from the numerous posts lining the path. It wasn't as dark anymore, but the white lights created speckled shadows through the tightly packed leaves.

Kendra let her mind drift. She was mostly focused on getting through the ride, as opposed to engaging in conversation. The two reached the mile mark, and Kendall interrupted the silence.

"Honk, honk. Watcha thinkin' 'bout?"

Kendra popped her head up to see that Kendall was riding close to her side. She shook her head with a flushed face.

"Memories. Graduation is next year and all. I don't stress about it nearly as much as the rest of my class. You should have seen Natalie. She was having a nervous meltdown at one point because of a college admission practice essay. She's about as good with English as she is with French," she spoke, playfully mocking Natalie in her absence.

"So mean! Natalie is amazing and smart in ways you don't even know. Not to mention cute ... but that's beside the point. Kendra, you won't ever get asked to prom with those nasty habits of yours," Kendall jabbed.

"Like I care. I don't expect to get asked," she muttered.

"I don't believe that for a sec—" Kendall's wheel hit a rock, causing it to lose traction and tip over. She yelped. The bike's pedal dug into her calf and ripped across, creating a nasty gash as she slid along the path.

Kendra skidded to a stop alongside Kendall, panic sewn on her face.

"Holy crap, Kenny, you okay?"

Kendall groaned, stirring on the ground while she pushed her bike from atop her form.

"Fuck. That hurt ... ah!" She inhaled sharply, blood seeping from the gash on her leg.

"Shit—you need to be more careful!" Kendra kicked her bike stand, rushing over to Kendall and assessing the wound. Without hesitating, Kendra removed her shirt, revealing the black tank top she wore underneath. She carried little packs of disinfectant wipes in her bag when she worked, a handy resource in this situation. Kendra reached into her bag, fished one out, and ripped the packet open. She tossed the trash into her bag and hovered the wipe above the wound.

"This is going to sting. Brace yourself," she warned.

Kendall bit her bottom lip, giving a quick nod as she shut her eyes. Kendra pushed the wipe to her wound, causing the girl to stifle a gasp of pain and convulse. Kendra had to pin her leg down, ensuring she stayed still while the disinfectant did its job. She traced it up and down until it was saturated with Kendall's blood. She folded the shirt and wrapped it around Kendall's leg to serve as a bandage.

Kendall breathed heavily, dizzy from the process.

"Attagirl. Come on. Let's get you up." Kendra stood, grabbed Kendall's hands, and attempted to pull her up. Kendall aborted and yanked away from Kendra's hand, shaking her head in refusal.

"I can't put pressure on it. How the hell am I gonna get my bike home?" she seethed.

Kendra shrugged.

"Look, we're going to have to leave it and hope it's still here tomorrow. I'll let Mom know." Kendra opened the hologram of her smart band and navigated the menu. However, when she reached the call menu, there was no service as she tried to call. *Strange.* Usually, there was reliable service throughout the trail, but she didn't dwell on why there wasn't this time. "Alright, change of plan. I take you on the back of my bike until we reach civilization again. I don't have reception here." Kendall raised her eyebrow skeptically. She checked her own smart band, coming to the same conclusion.

"Fine," she groaned, conceding.

Kendra hoisted Kendall's bike and wheeled it over to one of the light posts. After she grabbed Kendall's bike lock from the frame, she pried the code from Kendall, who gave a brief fuss over Kendra knowing it. She unclasped it before wrapping it around the frame of the bike a few times, clasping it together once again with the bike firmly attached to the pole. It was good enough by her standards.

"Alright, think you can stand?"

"Maybe." Kendall pulled herself to her feet, wincing in pain. Shockwaves coursed through her calf, but she managed to stay upright. Kendra walked over to her, carefully escorting Kendall to her bike. Kendra mounted the bike, and moments later, Kendall hopped on the back and carefully hoisted her legs up, sitting on the back of Kendra's seat. It was barely big enough for the two of them. Luckily, Kendall was petite enough for it to work.

"Alright, I'll hang on to you. Go slow," Kendall commanded.

"You don't have to tell me that part," Kendra muttered.

She pedaled, careful at first to ensure Kendall had balance. It managed to work, albeit they crawled, but Kendra cared about getting both of them home, regardless of the pace.

Kendra was unsure if her eyes were playing tricks on her or not, but thin streaks of smoke appeared to be seeping from the bushes and shrubs around them. She squinted, the skeptic she was, to see if it was indeed true; the longer she stared, the thicker the smoke became. *Is there a fire?* Kendra glanced back, seeing Kendall completely spaced out.

"Kenny, you seeing this?"

Kendall perked up.

"Seeing what?" She searched.

"The smoke." Kendall squinted her eyes, searching for a few moments before sighing.

"I'm the one who fell off the bike. Are you okay?"

The light flickered. The light from the posts waned with a momentous buzzing. Moments later, they went out—reminiscent of the night that Kendra had been fearful of.

Kendra's heart stopped. The blaze of the evening sky became the only source of light and the wavering shadows from the dancing leaves coordinated with the wind. It was once again dark. And Kendra's fear was reborn. Her breathing oscillated wildly. This time, Kendall didn't doubt her; even she manically glanced around with a worried expression, breathing harder.

Kendra's visceral recollection of that scornful night replayed in her head, and she snapped her head around to scan the cascading darkness.

She saw it. With her heart drumming, she pedaled as fast as her legs would allow. The darkness surrounding them became claustrophobic, and a pungent scent assailed their nostrils. There. In the creeping shadows, shrouded in smoke, they stared at her.

Burning eyes.

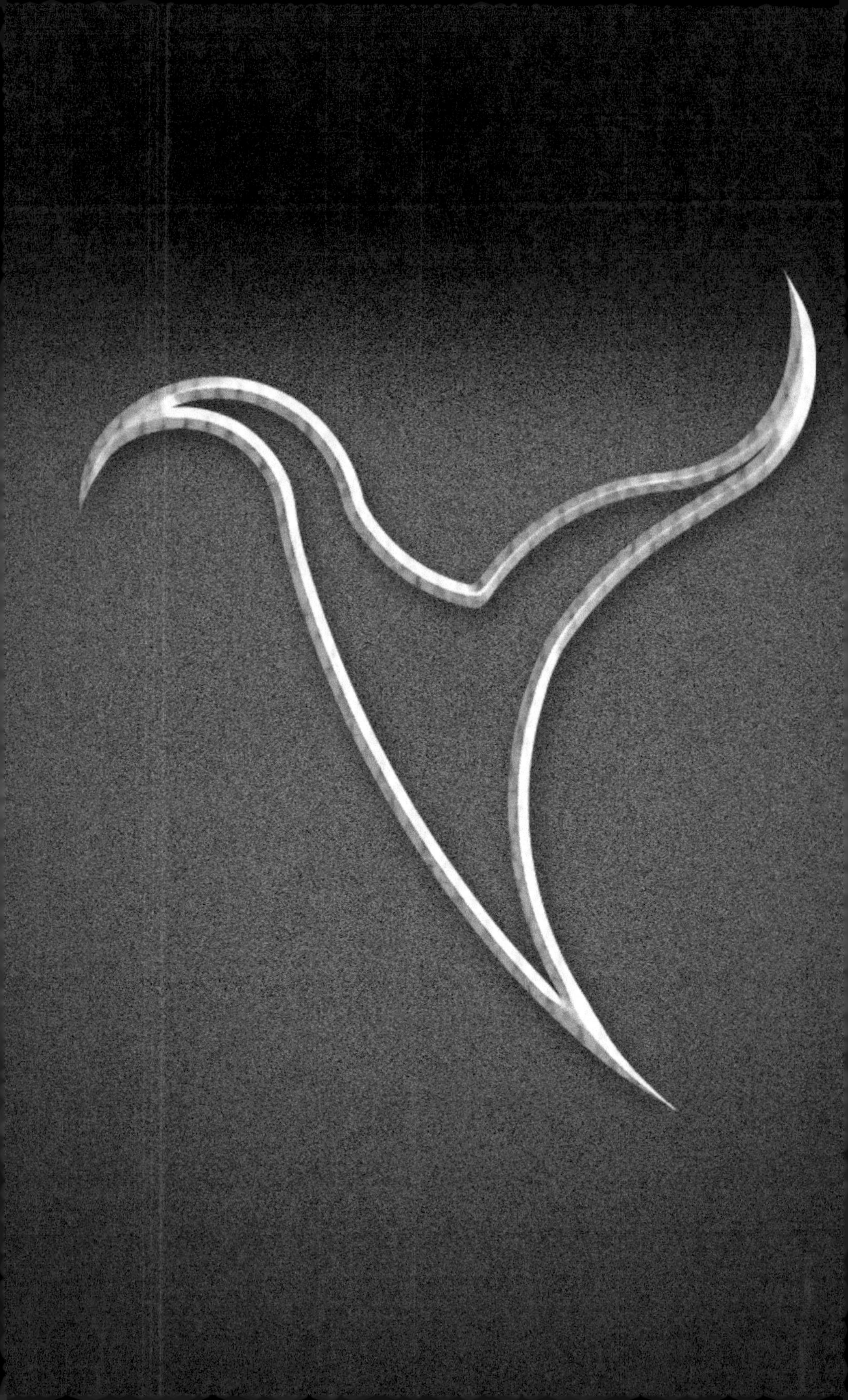

TWO

LEERING SHADOWS

I chor was the source of all life, and all that lived and breathed through her veins. Betrothed to the world, dazzling sprites—the omens—permeated the farthest reaches of Ichor's embrace. Floating about innocuously, their presence was mostly routine for those privy to their existence, but a phantom energy disrupted their journey, a force scarcely detectable by most. Underneath the harmonious thrumming of these sprites, there was a clamorous hiss—one which sought to rhyme with the sprites in order to usurp them.

An envious, near-perfect mimicry.

For less than a month, the Hunters had established their operations in Chicago. Within the anomalies they investigated, humans found themselves preyed upon—as was usually the case in matters of demons. That day, Eden Blackwell, a seventeen-year-old hunter, was sent to the Chicago Police Department's HQ to assist in the investigation surrounding the potential demonic conspiracy.

Eden stared up at the modern building. The glass panes were framed by steel and aluminum, and a foundation of bricks climbed to the top with large, metallic letters reading *Chicago Police Department*. At one time, it had served as an indictment of the city's historic crime rate and any future crimes that would seek to test it. However, Eden and the Hunters suspected its promise was being tested by demons.

Eden entered and approached the lobby's counter. A short line of people waited to speak with an available receptionist. However, Eden was spotted by a female officer behind the desk who avoided interacting with any of the citizens, having anticipated his arrival.

The officer waved Eden over, and he approached the desk with urgency in his stride. He raised his wrist, revealing a device strapped to it, his hunter bracer. He tapped a button, and it displayed a holographic ID to the woman. She scanned it, and moments later, a beep sounded from behind the desk before she resumed typing on her keyboard.

"Mr. Blackwell, Chief Bronson will be here shortly," she spoke in a meek voice. She shifted visibly, wariness filling her gaze as she looked up at Eden. His grim gaze, possessing a focus filled with an aimless disdain, caused her to stir in discomfort.

Eden's absorption in his thoughts consumed his attention, disregarding all other irrelevant details around him. All that mattered was his current objective: investigate the evidence he was sent there to examine. There was an innocence within his obliviousness—a genuine disassociation from his imposing demeanor. Daunting and aloof, the medley of his presence challenged the nerves of most.

A short distance away, the one Eden would meet with first approached. Police Chief Archer Bronson, a man whose own stature aspired to the effortless astonishment of Eden's. Striding beside him was another officer, whose more ordinary appearance and stature self-effaced his own title: Deputy Police Chief Darrel Carver. A smaller man with neatly combed black hair that matched his obsidian eyes, and further contrasted with pale, nearly unblemished skin that posed a question of his strife as an officer. The two spoke with a hint of contention, slowly coming into earshot of Eden.

"Archer, you're already stressed up to your shoulders with reports and requests for interviews on this persisting issue. Let me take the lead so you can prepare for the press conference tomorrow," Darrel said, but Archer was not quick to relent to the salience of his subordinate's insistence.

"Darrel, you undersell my capabilities. For five years, I've been chief, and in the last twenty, I was an officer of various ranks. The pressures I experienced with our predecessors make this multitasking seem like ... a blink for me. Have faith. Besides, if I stress out enough, I may retire early, and you'll take my place. I'm sure that's a positive for you, isn't it?" Archer spoke, his deep voice booming with unbridled positivity, alleviating the surrounding tensions.

Darrel gave a wry smile, snorting as he shook his head at the suggestion.

"You're a terrible salesman, Archy. Keep reminding me you chose the right career."

The two officers came to a stop before Eden, and Archer nodded at him.

"Eden Blackwell, correct? Big man from an elusive organization ... that some kind of code-name?" Archer alleged, holding his hand out to the young man before him. Behind him, Darrel briefly watched, his reticent, dark gaze scanning Eden warily.

"It's my name," Eden said flatly, briefly glancing at Archer's hand before shaking his head.

Archer stared hard into Eden's green eyes, his own brown ones seeking to gauge him and understand the rejection of a handshake.

In their stare off, Eden had gleaned what most would assume to be irrelevant information. Despite Archer's dark complexion, Eden's attention drew to the dark circles beneath his eyes. However, the firm countenance in his eyes contradicted the fatigue. Within their conflicting gazes, he could tell how ignorant he truly was. *A blink* was all it would take for things to go awry, and Eden sought to ensure that brief stretch of darkness, which he knew all too well, would never arise.

After a moment, Archer frowned. He had almost expected Eden would change his mind if he had held firm. This wasn't the case, however, and after several awkward seconds, he lowered his hand and cleared his throat, glancing at Darrel.

Without another word, Darrel turned from the two, walking away to leave them to their meeting.

"Let's not waste any time, then," Archer muttered.

He guided Eden to the upper level of the building—the Criminal Intelligence sector. During their travel, Archer ran through an overview of the case they had investigated. All he had spoken of was information Eden was already privy to. As they traveled through the open floor, Eden detected the gloominess. Tired faces pervaded the floor and solemn voices croaked dull chatter. Sunken faces were tucked into cubicles, and employees slogged through their work on borrowed time.

Eden and Archer came to a stop at a door, the plaque on it reading *Det. Stroth*. Archer knocked, opening the door when a man's voice invited them in.

Entering, Eden stood in front of the desk and gave the detective a once-over. Julian Stroth. He wore a black suit with a white collared shirt. Shoulder-length black hair framed his face, and hard black eyes pierced the lenses of his glasses. And similar to Archer and the other officers, dark circles hung beneath his eyes.

Julian gestured Eden to a seat opposite him while Archer closed the door behind them and planted himself on the frame.

Eden took his seat.

"Detective," Eden said. His somber greeting prompted Julian to nod.

"I'm not sure exactly how much I can tell you. It's not like we have a promising trail ourselves ... but I'll share what I have."

"Even obscure details you'd sooner forget, I want to hear all of it." He was told Julian was meticulous in his work. Whether this was the case, Eden cared little for—so far as if it would benefit him and the Hunters.

Julian captured the brief silence, fixating on the gravity Eden's tone carried. He reached up to a shelf next to his head and removed a worn-out leather folder.

Julian laid out several photos and their corresponding reports, all printed on crisp paper—an antiquity still utilized for less vulnerable record keeping. His focus on the pages obscured; the absurdity of the situation was far too prevalent for him not to ponder this scene. Eden, a *kid*, looking over the case he had worked day and night to solve with his colleagues.

After his initial scan, Eden picked the most pronounced of the photos, one containing a police vehicle etched with smoldering claw marks. He grabbed and inspected it, his eyes shifting from detail to detail. A familiarity to the scenes caused him to frown, and he eyed the marks carefully.

Stirring memories long since buried, he was intimately acquainted with what caused them. With each mark etched into the ground or vehicles, he could practically hear the heavy growls and the sound of flesh being torn from bone. The recollection caused him to exhale unsteadily.

"These marks. The report mentioned that the scenes where they were present had a distinct scent. Did you take these photos and write this report?" Eden asked.

"Didn't personally take the photos, but I can attest to all the information in the report. They're mine."

"Great—then I'll jog your memory. The distinct scent ... did it remotely resemble sulfur?"

Stroth's shoulders perked. He was quiet for a few moments, his gaze falling to the desk as he rubbed the bristles of his shaved chin. *Was it?* he thought. He could scarcely remember, but the rousing memory of pungency was far too familiar.

"I can say that it's possible ... could have been. It was sort of pungent, but it was faint, if any."

Eden nodded. When he reviewed the other reports and images, a pattern formed. A plethora of marks carved the vehicle or some area near it.

"Would you say that a significant portion of these other scenes also had a faint scent of sulfur?" Eden persisted.

"Some more than others. At the scenes where no damage was sustained to the vehicles, there was no scent I can recall." Stroth stared, suspicious of what Eden was surmising.

Eden's eyes flicked from photo to photo, a cursory glance for good measure. He had what he needed, and he straightened his posture before standing.

"I would like a copy of photos nine A through F, seven C through G, and four B through D. I'll also need their corresponding reports. Send them to my RFID tag," he demanded promptly, not wanting to linger longer than he had to.

Julian glanced at Archer. Stern eyes stared back at him and gave a nod of approval. He then looked back to Eden and shrugged.

"I'll send them."

When Eden received the copies on his hunter bracer, he turned on his heel and approached the door—still impeded by Archer. After a brief clash of their respective gazes, Archer opened the door and led Eden through the sector once more.

They walked in silence for several moments before Archer cleared his throat, snatching Eden's attention.

"I hope that whatever organization you're with can solve this quicker than we will. Too many good men and women are dead or missing. My obligation to cooperate with your organization is the only reason I'm giving you access to these documents. You better not misuse them, young man," he huffed, his deep voice thumping against Eden's ear.

Eden focused ahead, reflecting briefly before sighing.

"The only worry you should have is strengthening your current protocols." Venom lingered in the sentiment of his statement.

Archer frowned, shaking his head.

"You guys may not be beholden to our procedures, but the law still applies either way. Due process stands, even if whoever is behind this *is* scum ..." he warned. He stopped at the stairwell and leaned against the banister, expecting a quip from Eden.

Eden held his tongue, raising his hand in a departing gesture before he descended the stairs. Whereas the ignorant chief thought due process was applicable, Eden saw differently. That was *too good* for the perpetrators, and no such mercy would come from him if he were to meet them. Demons would sooner kill themselves than accept it, either. He wouldn't expect a human to understand such sentiments—he certainly couldn't, either.

The engine's soft whirr faded as Eden pulled his motorcycle into the driveway. It was a quiet electric vehicle—a surreal experience he came to enjoy the more he drove it. He had studied all last summer for the tests he took to get a license to drive one. Frugal, he scarcely spent the money he earned, and he saved up enough for a decade-old motorcycle, a Wattz Night Ripper model T. As a casual enthusiast, he studied the mechanisms and systems for several days before purchasing it.

The garage opened when he hit the clicker, and he parked his bike inside next to a black car caked in dust. He removed the helmet from his head, snapped it securely to the bike, and stretched before making his way inside.

Eden's eyes carefully scanned the dark hall as his boots drummed against the lacquered floorboards. Soft, glowing protection runes decorated random sections of the walls. Akin to a long shield in shape, the runes pulsed with a soft blue light. Toward the top of the runes, there was a singular eye with two pupils on either side that shimmered with a white energy. His shoulders dropped as he took in the tranquil silence around him, breathing in the brief respite before he removed his suit jacket and set it on a hook by the door.

He raised his wrist, moving the hunter bracer toward his face as its interface flickered to life. After navigating to the channel he wanted, he fished an earpiece from his pocket, fastened it to his ear, and sat on one of the several couches in the living room. Moments later, the hologram displayed the notification of the broadcast being established.

"Took you long enough. Ready to talk now?" a stern feminine voice prompted. The voice of General Jessica Blackwell.

"I drove home. Better for privacy," Eden justified. "I have their reports and the evidence, along with my own notes. Open an encryption tunnel, and I'll send the documents to you—General."

There were several seconds of silence.

"Go ahead and send them. The tunnel is active for fifteen seconds," she flatly informed him.

Eden's fingers tapped along the interface, navigating to the documents Julian had sent him. He then dragged the folder to the adjacent one labeled *tunnel*, which had a decreasing timer hovering above it.

"Done. Open it, and I'll walk you through the reports along with the pertinent details of the meeting."

"Ready when you are."

"Review files four and nine, along with their corresponding photos. My current hypothesis is hellhounds, based on the picture evidence of burned claw marks. The detective, Stroth, recanted to me that there was a faint pungency—potentially sulfur. All telltale signs of hellhound activity."

"Would seem so. Astute a guess as any," Jessica sighed.

Hellhounds were not native to the realm of Mortale, the realm humans and most other life resided in, and were almost always summoned by demons of a higher order. Given their voracious appetite, for both the physical and spiritual essence of a being, they hardly ever thrived in ecosystems they were not native to—let alone a city where their predation on humanity would be met with swift retribution.

Eden hesitated to speak again yet, recollecting the hiss that he detected within the station. He could only hypothesize it was of greater significance than he currently fathomed. Somnium were exceptionally rare demons born from a collection of malice within Ichor that thrived upon fear—especially nightmares. However, they were not especially capable of remaining in the corporeal realm for long. How the somnium tied together with hellhounds, he could only think of umbra demons—the most prominent of sapient demons not restricted by pesky limitations. Some of the prominent families that the Hunters kept track of, had a history of plotting nefarious schemes at the expense of various life forms.

"The waves encumbered the station. Signs of the somnium," Eden said.

"Wait, you detected them? The hissing and all?"

"Yes."

"The Covenant of Augury may be involved after all ..." Jessica mumbled.

"Not only that. Many members of the police department had dark circles beneath their eyes. Lots of restlessness. It's like—"

"They're being targeted."

Eden shut his eyes, his mind drifting briefly to the energies that were present at the station. He imagined that if he were to try, he could make out more details if he conducted a thorough investigation. The waves were hard to detect, and the hunter devices couldn't reliably tune in on them to triangulate their source. It was a job that required intimate vigilance, and that was a dangerous ask—for most.

"Likely," Eden affirmed.

"I had a hunch, and this just grants me more leverage to send additional help there, considering how few can detect it."

Eden perked, and Jessica continued, "Yet, even we can't reliably track their source. Private Ardent was ambushed during his recon of the department only three days into his assignment. And now that I think about it, based on the marks he has on his leg, hellhounds are an obvious answer in relevance to our earlier guess. I'll make sure to probe him when he wakes from his coma."

Eden hadn't been aware of Joseph Ardent being assigned to investigate the department prior to him. However, he knew it would be difficult to juggle a longer investigation and his homework simultaneously. With the suggested direness mounting, he wished graduation would come sooner.

"Thank you for your work ... I know you're busy with school as well, but I'm sure you understand the difficult situation we're in. Captain Larson was pulled to assist with another matter today, so this was a good experience opportunity for you."

"I want to patrol there tonight. Stealthy recon would—"

"No," Jessica objected. "Focus on homework. I get that you're eager to resolve this dilemma, but you can worry more about hunter duties when you graduate."

"But I can detect them. If I can keep these *things* from harming anybody else, I should! I won't fall behind on my schoolwork."

"I don't authorize it, Eden."

Jessica's verdict solidified.

Eden fell silent. His white-knuckled fists vibrated with constriction. Of all opportunities and times for him to intervene and commit to his *purpose,* Jessica denied him, and a familiar ire echoed repeatedly in his head.

"Aside from that, how was your day? You never tell me about how school goes ... make any friends? Your grades are great. Instead of hunting, have you ever considered becoming a—"

"I'm going to go do my homework." Before Jessica could respond, he disconnected their comm channel and lowered his wrist. The interface disappeared, and he stood up.

Ridiculous. Eden walked upstairs. As it stood now, his mind throbbed in discontent and would remain that way should he abide Jessica's official orders. He stared in the mirror, meeting his crimson eyes, his true eye color, and he sought the conviction that drove him the most. His gaze deigned to descend. On his neck, he leered at the faint markings: bite shaped scars. A reminder. His face contorted in disgust, condemning the associated memories. But he refused to grant those memories further audience.

Eden dragged his gaze left, eyeing a translucent orange bottle. Without a second thought, he snatched it, popped it open, tumbled a pill out, and swiftly swallowed it. After several moments, he straightened, sealed the bottle, and set it back down.

Eden kicked his shoes off, grabbing and stacking them on his closet shelf before stripping from his suit. He spun around and clutched the red crystal dangling from the black cord around his neck. The gem gleamed in his grip, his reflection in it blending with his similarly hued eyes. A verdict was decided.

The crystal twinkled before bursting with white light that swallowed Eden. Shimmering particles dispersed in the air, the rush of wind causing his bangs to flick, and he shut his eyes. Black attire materialized, weaving around him: pants with the ends tucked into shin-high combat boots and steel plate tips. His torso was shrouded in the confines of a trench coat, the front clasping together but parting below his hips.

Eden rolled his shoulders and bounced to adjust to the additional weight the layered jacket provided; as designed, a layer of graphene-coated armor embedded into the coat. He clenched his fists, now covered by tactical gloves. Muscles primed, he ceased his movements and stared down at his chest.

An ethereal essence tugged within Eden—a visceral, intimate force complimentary to his vindictive spirit. He relaxed his right hand, his fingers unfurling slightly. *Avenger,* he called from within. A flash of red light took shape in the palm of his hand, extending and forming a long obsidian-black blade, an odachi. Unlike his apparel, the blade, despite its corporeal, formidable presence, bore no weight in his grasp.

Engraved upon the base of Avenger's blade were runes. On one side, a curvy symbol with forks: two outwardly curved ones at the tops and two thick, straight ones at the bottom. The symbol signified vengeance. On the opposite side of the blade, there were two vertically imposed circular symbols with three curved wings. The rune signified blood—the most sacred, encompassing rune.

With a brief entrancement to Avenger's dark luster, he shifted the hilt in his palm and slid it into the sheath on his hip.

"*Homework,*" Eden mocked.

Eden treaded through the hallway of the school building. The school day, as insufferable as it was to the enigmatic young hunter, proved to go by quick enough. He was eager to continue immersing himself in the troubling circumstances brewing—against the foreknowledge and wishes of his superiors.

Eden had plenty of time to ponder and get lost in his thoughts with no one bothering him—as was typical. He didn't make it easy to be approached; he was at least aware of that much. The few times he conversed with his classmates, pertained to school work, usually group projects or being called on by his teachers.

There were straggling students left in the halls, it being a few hours after class had let out. He would have been gone sooner if not for an art project he had to spend time to complete and turn in. Mrs. Pernell, his art teacher, had generously granted him the extension—on the condition he turned it in that day. She wasn't usually magnanimous, but because of his dedicated participation in class, she had made an exception this time. Of all the subjects Eden endured, he enjoyed art. If he wasn't training, he was either drawing or brooding—sometimes both at once.

He descended the stairwell to the first floor and continued down the hall, approaching the exit of the building. Faint chatter near the lockers caught his attention the closer he got to the door, but he paid it little mind.

"So … like, what does it mean when you draw the magician card? I don't imagine it means you'll start casting fireballs or something," Allen said.

"No, no," Kendall said with a hint of amusement. "It doesn't mean one static thing, let alone a literal thing. The cards are a representation of something. That one is a major arcana, and it can mean a few things, depending on what position it comes up in, or even when you draw it. I wanna practice more, but Ken isn't willing—yet."

As Eden passed by the two, he glanced in their direction, meeting Kendall's hazel gaze, framed by her glasses. For a brief moment, she stared at him, her lips parting as her attention shifted.

"Hey!" she called out, waving to Eden.

Eden stopped, giving a puzzled expression since he wasn't overly familiar with the girl who called to him. When he looked Kendall's way, he saw her and Allen leaning on the lockers, next to a classroom he was vaguely aware of for hosting a club.

"You're Eden, right? You're in my sister's year. Mind if I get a closer look at your eyes?" Kendall continued.

Eden froze, his mind stirred by her exuberance. For as tenaciously as he trained his body, spirit, and his vigilance, it was ironic that Kendall had staggered his poise effortlessly.

As elusive as he was, he was far more prone to being the one to exhibit awkward mannerisms when confronted with socialization—especially by a brazen extrovert. With a frozen silence, Eden shifted uncomfortably for a moment, pondering what to do.

Allen stood straight, pensively eyeing Eden, then Kendall again. He frowned, shrugging after a few moments.

"I'm gonna go wait for Ken. Catch you later, Kenny." Briskly walking past Eden, Allen left the building.

Eden broke from the shackles of his hesitation finally, sighing as he approached Kendall.

Clasping her hands together, Kendall stepped closer to Eden, looking up at him with a brimming curiosity in her gaze. He shifted before her, perturbed by the silent scrutiny. After a few moments, Kendall smiled.

"Your eyes are very captivating. A deep shade of green with a verdant luster befitting your name—a sacred garden embroiled in tragedy."

Eden's cheeks flushed, and he briefly met her gaze once more before nodding.

"Thanks," he spoke, pursing his lips. Perhaps too shrewd an analysis, Eden suddenly became interested if she was more perceptive than she let on. However, that thought quickly refuted itself, given the color his eyes appeared to her.

"I'm curious what lies in store for you. I was just talking with Allen about tarot, and I've been wanting to practice more. If you'd care to glimpse your destiny, I'll happily do a reading for you."

No.

That was what Eden wanted to say. He saw those large hazel eyes twinkling with a curiosity and enthusiasm toward him—conjuring a familiar, troubled memory.

"Sure," he resolved tepidly.

Kendall jumped, causing her black cardigan to bob as she landed. Without consideration of his boundaries, Kendall snatched Eden's hand.

"Let's go then!" As she tugged, Kendall met a resistance she couldn't overcome, causing her to relent as she met his gaze again.

"Oh, uh ... I can't today. I have some errands to run, and I'm behind on homework," Eden said sheepishly, averting his gaze.

Kendall frowned, groaning for a moment before releasing Eden's hand.

"Oh, what a shame. I won't be free until next week. How's Monday sound?"

Eden thought for a moment, shifting as he drew his hand back.

"That can work."

Kendall nodded, shifting her hair from her face and readjusting her glasses.

"It's a date, then!" She paused for a moment, gasping before she shook her head. "Figuratively! Sorry, I kind of have my eyes set on this cute girl my sister knows, and you're really handsome and all ... but y'know? I would totally try to set you up with Ken if she were available, but she and Allen are kind of a thing but don't know it yet." She scrunched her face. "You know how these things go. Anyway, we can meet after school on Monday right here. Sound good?"

Eden couldn't help but snort, shifting, averting his gaze as he offered a tepid nod.

"I'll see you Monday, then," Eden said simply. With the details confirmed, Kendall waved goodbye. Turning on his heel, Eden left.

As he traveled through the courtyard to reach the parking garage, Eden thought back to the serene gaze Kendall had shown him. The memory it had unearthed from him played faintly, and succinctly, he buried it with haste. Still, the lingering warmth from Kendall's soft hand reminded him of fonder times. A time free from the tethers of his self-imposed obligation. A time when he had known what it was to be human. A time before caution was such a prevalent habit in his life. He failed to stifle a small smile, his mind briefly liberated from the tribulations he had been fixated on.

The amicable interaction, while leaving a hint of sweetness for Eden to dwell on, hadn't lasted long. Soon, his mind had returned to the infernal plot he sought to uncover and crush. When he had secretly scouted the night prior, he was stumped to be met with mediocrity and silence. The moment he scrutinized anything, the repugnant hissing permeating Ichor would cease. While he planned to scout again that night, he had to pick up a piece of his gear from a repair shop.

For that purpose, Eden had made his way to the city when he had gotten the message that it was ready. His maneuver bracers had suffered a bad malfunction during one of his hunts. Luckily, the line hadn't snapped mid-grapple, which would have caused him to plunge from a high height. Regardless, it was beyond his means to service on his own, and instead, he had brought it to Ohm's Cadence a week prior.

Parking at a meter, Eden dismounted his bike, tucked his helmet underneath his arm, and made his way into the shop. Joseph's father, James Ardent, was a former hunter whom the organization still subcontracted work to. It wasn't frequent, but James specialized in legacy systems most others didn't, and he offered valuable schematics for the engineers in the organization to further develop the technology. Given the highly proprietary nature, it wasn't something that could be contracted to an average company. Eden had known it would be a while before he'd get his maneuver bracer back, which annoyed him since he had to expend far more energy jumping to higher vantage points during his scouting.

He entered, and Chelsea, the AI clerk, floated from its dock to the reception desk.

"Welcome, Mr. Blackwell. Your order is ready for pickup."

"I know. Where's James?"

"James is out for the afternoon, but we have your order ready. Please wait briefly."

With a sigh, Eden shrugged before he leaned against the counter, waiting patiently for whoever would deliver his maneuver bracer. Drilling, clicking, and knocking droned on in the background. It was typical of the store, but it kept Eden's mind from wandering. While the reception was clean, he could only imagine the mess the technicians made in the back; engineers and technicians were scarcely organized back at base, let alone at a meager shop.

"Hello, I have your order right here ... Eden?" a female voice called. Eden perked up, a familiar human woman's voice rousing his curiosity. Kendra appeared from the doorway leading to the back. The two shared physics and art class together, and while they hadn't interacted much, they had worked together on a few projects. She was one of the few who was comfortable interacting with him. Not that Eden minded his effective ostracization. He wasn't eager to get cozy with others, anyway.

Neither of them had expected to come across each other there. Eden expected James but figured that he must have visited Joseph out of concern about the attack he had recently suffered.

"Kendra ... hey. Didn't know you work here," he spoke quietly, averting his eyes.

Kendra nodded her head slowly, slightly perplexed for a reason undisclosed. She held a box in her hand, which presumably housed his mobility gauntlet.

"So, my order ..." he spoke tepidly.

Kendra perked up, nodding her head.

"Right. Right. Sorry, I was focused on your contacts. You doing some kind of cosplay?"

Eden froze. He had been reaching to take the box, but her statement prompted hesitation.

"Contacts ... what?"

"The red eyes, I mean. They're contact lenses, right? Like out of some anime or whatever. My sister, Kendall, would probably know it, too."

Eden frowned, but then his eyes widened at the implication of her inquiry. If Kendra saw his red eyes, it begged whether she was connected. Faintly, his memory stirred with the eccentric younger sister she had mentioned. He had awkwardly agreed to let Kendall do a tarot reading on him, but as intrigued as she was with the supernatural, he could tell she wasn't connected when they spoke. With the startling possibility presented, Eden sought to explain away the oddity Kendra interrogated him over.

"Just ... trying them out. Forgot I had them in," he lied. However, his deviating inflection challenged the legitimacy of his claim.

Kendra snorted, holding the box out to him until he took it. Knowing Eden to be an aloof boy of few words, she thought little of his odd speech pattern.

"Chelsea already confirmed your identity, and no signature is required, so you're good to go. I'd love to talk more, but I'm pretty swamped today with James out," Kendra turned, holding her hand up. "Later, Eden," she chimed before entering the back of the store.

"Later ..." Eden said, staring skeptically for several moments before he took the box and left the shop. He was suddenly tense, wondering if Kendra had truly become connected to Ichor. *But why and how?* Eden racked his brain, walking back to his bike. Adding to his recent streak of impulsivity, he opted to watch over Kendra that evening; he needed to be certain.

The Hunters' purview was almost exclusive to demons and anything related to their dealings. With the rigid structure of the organization, there would be far too many roadblocks in effectively investigating the matter with the urgency he knew it needed. Killing rogue or feral demons was one thing—protecting someone suspected of being a target of demons on nothing more than suspicion, no matter how warranted, was another matter. If it turned out to be nothing, it wouldn't matter, anyway.

With disregard for the optics, he committed to his own investigation. He parked his bike elsewhere and made his way across the street from the shop. Ducking into an alleyway, he searched his mind for the incantation of imperceptibility. Latin was difficult for him to remember, so he took a few minutes iterating several terms until he recalled it.

"Insenseilis," he whispered. His body briefly quivered, a subtle blue hue cloaking his form. He had successfully increased his connection to Ichor and entered the veil, the boundary that separated all of those within it from those residing outside of it. He was now imperceptible to anybody who would otherwise see him if the basic spell hadn't bent the laws of physics. However, he'd still need to remain plainly hidden from Kendra—should the strength of her connection be strong enough to bypass the spell. Magic wasn't Eden's forte, making that a presumable possibility, and with that, he waited.

A few hours later, he saw the door to the shop swing open, and out stepped Kendra. Cloaked in darkness, he was unseen by her. When he focused on her, the prominence of her aura was more notable than was typical of humans, confirming his suspicions.

When Kendra took off on her bike, he took off after her. The darkness surrounding them would keep him hidden if he was careful, and he ensured he maintained a safe distance from his vantage point.

A surge of malevolent energy spiked in the air, distortion encompassing the nearby space as a heavy breath would. The streetlamps shorted, and he witnessed something leap down from a building behind Kendra. He couldn't see it clearly, but it was a quadrupedal demon with burning eyes and ember-kissed bristles along its coat. *A hellhound.*

It charged after Kendra, a ferocious motivation driving its dastardly pursuit.

Shit, Eden thought. Picking up his pace, he rushed after them. He held his hand out and summoned Avenger, tightly gripping the hilt in his hand.

Upon being alerted to the hellhound, Kendra pedaled with an urgency to escape it, which more than confirmed the extent of her connection. The demon was fast—faster than her bike, but it didn't matter. The hound made a lunge at her and missed. It tumbled into a fence.

Eden bolted forward, channeling a burst of energy into his legs, and closed in on the hound. It had rebounded, scurrying after Kendra again, but it didn't get far. Eden leaped and took out the hind legs with a clean swipe of his blade. The hound tumbled, yelping as its own momentum drove it into the asphalt. Eden didn't let its suffering continue for long. Clutching Avenger, he jumped at the creature and swiftly plunged it through the hound's chest. He pierced the heart, decisive and clean. Silence.

Eden withdrew Avenger, flung the blood from its length, then sheathed it. Now that it wasn't a blur in the night, he examined the dead hound. Burning bristles in its thick fur, fiery eyes that ignited with fury, and a mangled maw with gnarly fangs protruding. The pungency of sulfur permeated the air, originating from its breath that it, much to Kendra's benefit, neglected to use. The outcome could have been grave if it had spat fire instead of lunging.

With the creature being a hellhound, he couldn't help but draw a connection to the police attacks. His eyes scanned the street behind him, seeing burned claw marks carved into the ground from where the demon had been. The scorched marks on the asphalt denoted the same as those he saw in the crime scene photos, comporting with his hypothesis.

"Someone summoned it."

Eden's impromptu mission had been off-the-record—unauthorized. A swift rebuke from his superiors recanted that fact upon him making a report. *It's integral we seek authorization for all actions and operations expressly outside of core duties. You saved the girl, but we will have someone else investigate this matter—something you should not have been doing.* Eden hated bureaucracy. No matter; he knew he was best suited to watch over her. He doubted the covenant had such barriers to their schemes.

Eden passed by Kendra the following morning and saw her in their classes. Her connection to Ichor had faded over the past few days. His doubts lurked, but he passively reminded himself to find her throughout the days. He doubted it had been an opportunistic hunt the hound engaged in, given how they had only been used to target police and those connected to the police up to that point. Feral demons usually couldn't enter their realm without some kind of rift or being summoned. No such naturally occurring rifts were apparent, which insinuated its presence was a deliberate targeting by whoever had summoned it. *But why Kendra?* he wondered.

He surmised the hit was deliberate, and as a result, he feared that she would be connected once again and lured to an untimely demise should he relent. *Someone* had connected her to Ichor. Whoever it was, he couldn't detect them. They had to be remarkably talented at hiding their energy signature—that much he knew—and few demons naturally possessed such a talent.

The end of the school day arrived. A Friday. The reveling students praised the day vocally. A school event was coming up: a dance. Eden had no interest in it, only knowing about it from all the conversations he overheard.

Eden stared up at the gates of the school's main entrance. Through it, Eden saw a concrete block with a bronze statue of an Ashwood tree planted in the center of the courtyard. It wasn't an entirely familiar sight to him, as he hadn't been at the school long, only about a year, but he memorized the layout in a short time. He was never comfortable not knowing his environment; he needed the familiarity.

He paced back and forth in front of the school, waiting for Kendra to make an appearance. He needed to confirm his concerns. If Kendra was back to normal, he'd go home. A short time later, Kendra came coasting by on her bike, accompanied by Kendall.

Unlike earlier that day, Kendra had a faint, thrumming aura permeating her form. His crimson eyes widened. She had been connected—again. Eden jogged across the sidewalk after them. As he uttered the concealment spell, a blue hue shimmered around his form. He usually never used it in public spaces, but there was no real harm. Many perceived him as disappearing into the crowd of students exiting the school. He snatched the red crystal on his neck; light dispersed as his clothes dissipated, quickly being replaced by his hunter attire.

He must have followed them for half an hour, only stopping once they had entered the depths of Lincoln Park. It was an optimal terrain for tailing her, but before he could enter, he grew suspicious. Carried through the wind, a hiss emerged, and accompanying it, a field of distortion from a demonic entity.

Eden placed an idle hand on Avenger's hilt. The wind became furious and heavy, carrying an ominous aura. Then, a surge of red omens coalesced around him.

"Come out!" Eden called out. A few bystanders were near, but they strolled along blissfully unaware of his presence or the stalker he turned his attention to. Manifesting from a shadow several feet from Eden, a humanoid form emerged. Several feet taller than him, it had long, outstretched limbs with pointed digits. The surface of its skin resembled waves of rippling smoke. Large, curved white eye sockets glowed with sinister intent, staring directly at Eden. It smiled with an impossible grin, long white fangs that served an obvious purpose. *A somnium.*

Eden's eyes narrowed, and he drew his blade carefully, taking an attack position.

This roused it to snicker and widen one eye, as if raising a brow.

"Hunter, you take such curiosity in that girl. You should be focusing on your own well-being ..." it said, its voice sounding as if it echoed around Eden from an indeterminable source. Somnium were known to use illusions and incite psychosis, but this was his first time witnessing one directly. It had a raspy whisper of a voice, unpleasantly tickling Eden's ears, but he paid it little heed and remained stoic.

"Tell me, who's after her? What are the somnium up to?" Eden asked, but it stood there grinning, its eyes narrowing as it refrained from responding.

"Answer me, *now*," he demanded.

The somnium turned its wrist, palm facing outward as it curled its fingers slightly. Its chitinous digits extended with the sharp tips pointed at Eden.

With no more patience, Eden understood the challenge, lunging forward with rapid steps that barraged the ground. His approach was brief, and he swung Avenger down when he came into range. The somnium parried, catching it with its armored fingers.

The somnium took a quick step backward and darted forward with its arm shooting out, attempting to impale Eden, but Eden reacted too quickly, catching its wrist while sidestepping. His muscles tightened as he overpowered the demon. He yanked it into a lower position and kicked its chest, causing it to skid backward with a thunderous clap from the impact.

Eden didn't relent, charging forward and parading a combination of slashes and kicks. He whittled away at the demon's defenses, keeping it on guard to block or dodge his attacks. The demon attempted to impale him again, but he ducked. His skin rippled with red energy, and he became cloaked in heat as he swung Avenger up, dismembering the somnium's arm.

A burst of white luminescent sludge spilled from the stump left behind as the demon stumbled back. With its incorporeal *blood,* cold air flashed over the area. It hissed in what Eden assumed was pain, grasping the stump of its arm with wide eyes. He knew that would hardly be enough to finish it off, and he suspected it would regenerate the limb shortly. If Eden intended to slay it, he would have gone for its head, where he could inflict an injury that it couldn't regenerate from with its limited energy supply.

After a few moments, a bipolar cackle erupted from the demon. Eden held his blade out, threatening another attack, but refrained from finishing it there. He needed the thing to divulge its plans in order to discern the Covenant of Augury's plot.

"Speak!"

The somnium's stump ceased to bleed, sealing over as haze oozed from the stump. Tiny, inky tendrils formed along it, slowly reforming into the shape of its severed hand. It puffed its chest out, appearing to inhale deeply, but it was not breathing. With a loud, breathy screech, it expelled a thick, tar-like smoke coursing with ripples of glowing red streaks that resembled torn fiber. Somnium miasma. It violently expanded toward Eden.

Evasively, Eden jumped back and poised Avenger, channeling power into its blade. With an upward swipe, the wind dispersed the miasma into the sky. He dreaded to imagine breathing it in, having read the reports of the miasma causing hallucinogenic exhaustion among its lighter symptoms.

But the somnium didn't expect to inflict him with it. As a clever creature, it harnessed the diversion to flee. It hadn't gotten far, but its intentions were further enacted.

Eden growled and dashed after it. The *thing* couldn't be allowed to escape; he needed answers. When he closed the distance, now within yards of the somnium despite its stride being easily twice his own, he held his wrist up, aiming his maneuver bracer. With a pop, a projectile with a line attached to it shot through the air, piercing the somnium in the chest. With the somnium now anchored to him, he yanked it to the ground with a draw of his arm.

Eden skidded to a stop and released the tension in his knuckles, and the line retracted with a zip; the creature clawed at the pavement, its fingers raking the concrete. When it looked back, it saw the bottom of Eden's boot as it stomped into its back, pinning it. He hovered the tip of Avenger above the somnium's neck.

"I won't ask again." As Eden's ire-filled gaze scorned the somnium beneath him, he thought of killing it then and there, but he was more tactical than his exhibited might and brutality suggested. It would have been easy to take its life, and the cracks beneath his boots suggested as much.

A breathless cackle left the somnium.

"You're forgetting someone. Someone ... in danger," it declared with a vindicated gaze, its mission complete.

Eden's projectile released, zipping back into the socket as he cursed under his breath. *The girls!* The demon was a distraction, not an assassin. As he turned his attention to where Kendra and Kendall were, a ripple in the air brushed over him. It was a greater pocket of distortion, deep into the path they had taken.

Eden sheathed Avenger, breaking into a sprint back toward Lincoln Park.

Satisfied with its results, the creature returned to the amorphous black shadows it had emerged from.

"Good job, hunter," it mocked, the shadows lashing from the ground and swallowing it.

Eden caught Kendra's energy signature from afar—fading. His body flickered red as he bolted through the thick of trees and foliage. In a short time, he reached Kendra's location. Now covered in nature's debris, he emerged in the opening where Kendra and her sister were.

Blood and chunks of torn flesh painted the ground. A mangled bike, scorched beyond recognition, was strewn to the side of the only living person present. Barely recognizable, a corpse was still being gnawed on by hungry hellhounds. The demons had feasted for some time already, their monstrous maws dripping with viscera and blood-saturated fabric.

A short distance away, hounds pinned Kendra. Her brown hair was sprawled in a pool of blood, and her limbs were being nipped at by the hounds that skipped the feeding frenzy, their razor teeth gouging her flesh. All it would take was a single precise bite to end her if they weren't interrupted soon.

Before a fatal bite came, Eden lunged, kicking the two hounds that were atop Kendra. They went flying, one colliding into a tree and the other into the shrubbery. He took a deep breath, his eyes narrowed with crimson vitriol.

The hounds, licking their muzzles clean of their meal, were aroused by Eden's arrival. His scent and aura alike alerted their keen instincts, captivating their voracious hunger. One of the hound's eyes glimmered with a blue twinkle. It had devoured a soul—Kendall's soul. Its objective imperative above all else, it snarled at the pack and turned, dashing off deeper into the park.

Kendra moaned, blood spilling from her gashes and punctures. She needed immediate medical attention should she hope to survive. The agony in her breaths indicated an indeterminable pain permeating her veins and boiling her overwhelmed psyche; there was hardly any time to waste. Her energy faded, and her body was feverish.

In a coordinated formation, the hounds dashed in an attempt to blitz Eden, but he drew Avenger in a clean arch, swinging it to cleave through the hounds that jumped at him. Seeing this, the others hesitated in their lunge.

Eden stomped, causing the ground to splinter and destabilize the pack. Momentarily crippled, he kicked one with ferocious strength coursing through his leg. The hound howled as it slammed into a tree with a crack, falling limp from the damage. Eden exhaled with a menacing glare, his eyes becoming streaks of red in his unrelenting assault. He cleaved, crushed, and launched the low-level demons with attack after attack. His vision throbbed, a sting coursing through his brain due to his exertion—hardly a deterrent in his adrenaline. He didn't stop until the red omens had faded and the demons were eradicated.

Eden flicked the blood off Avenger and sheathed it, turning on his heel to rush to Kendra. She was still alive—barely. Her breath was sporadic, bones crushed, muscles torn, and skin seared. So much blood had pooled beneath her. There'd have been more if not for the flame-melded flesh that closed some of the grievous lacerations.

"This is my fault ..." he muttered, his throbbing focus blurring with memories of the viscera he had seen in his life. Gore of a similar visage paraded in his mind—an incessant, grim reminder of his truths about demons. *Not again,* he promised himself. *They would never take again.*

Eden grasped her body carefully, lifting her into his arms. Kendra screamed in protest, but undoubtedly, she had lost consciousness by that point and only reacted on instinct. He reached into a pouch on his thigh, removing a light-blue crystal—a teleportation crystal that would greatly hasten their departure to receive aid. It was good for only one use, something for emergencies, and with the distortion that accompanied the hellhounds, it could be used without hinderance. The hellhound that had consumed Kendall's soul had fled. While going after it could lead him to answers about his investigation, there was still a chance to save Kendra, something far more important.

Eden glanced one last time at the scene, at the various corpses of the demons he eliminated.

"Sanguine," Eden spoke, the returnal incantation resonating with Ichor and the dead demons he had targeted with the words.

The demons' dead bodies dissipated into white light, and their lingering energy recycled into Ichor. The crystal in Eden's palm glowed brightly, his focus and power channeling into it as he crushed it. When it shattered, a light swallowed the two, carrying them away from the tarnished park trail.

The carnage of that evening entailed a much grander scheme—one unknown by Eden or his organization. Nefarious entities tugged strings yet seen, puppeteering the events they sought to materialize. The blood spilled that day was but a small tribute to those who lurked in darkness. Nightmares unrealized, manifestations of fear culminated within the eyes of those born from the collective fear of man. Kendall was dead—just one of the many who served as kindling for insidious ambitions. But Kendra had lived, a breach in the timeline that originally saw darkness consume light.

Infernal divergence.

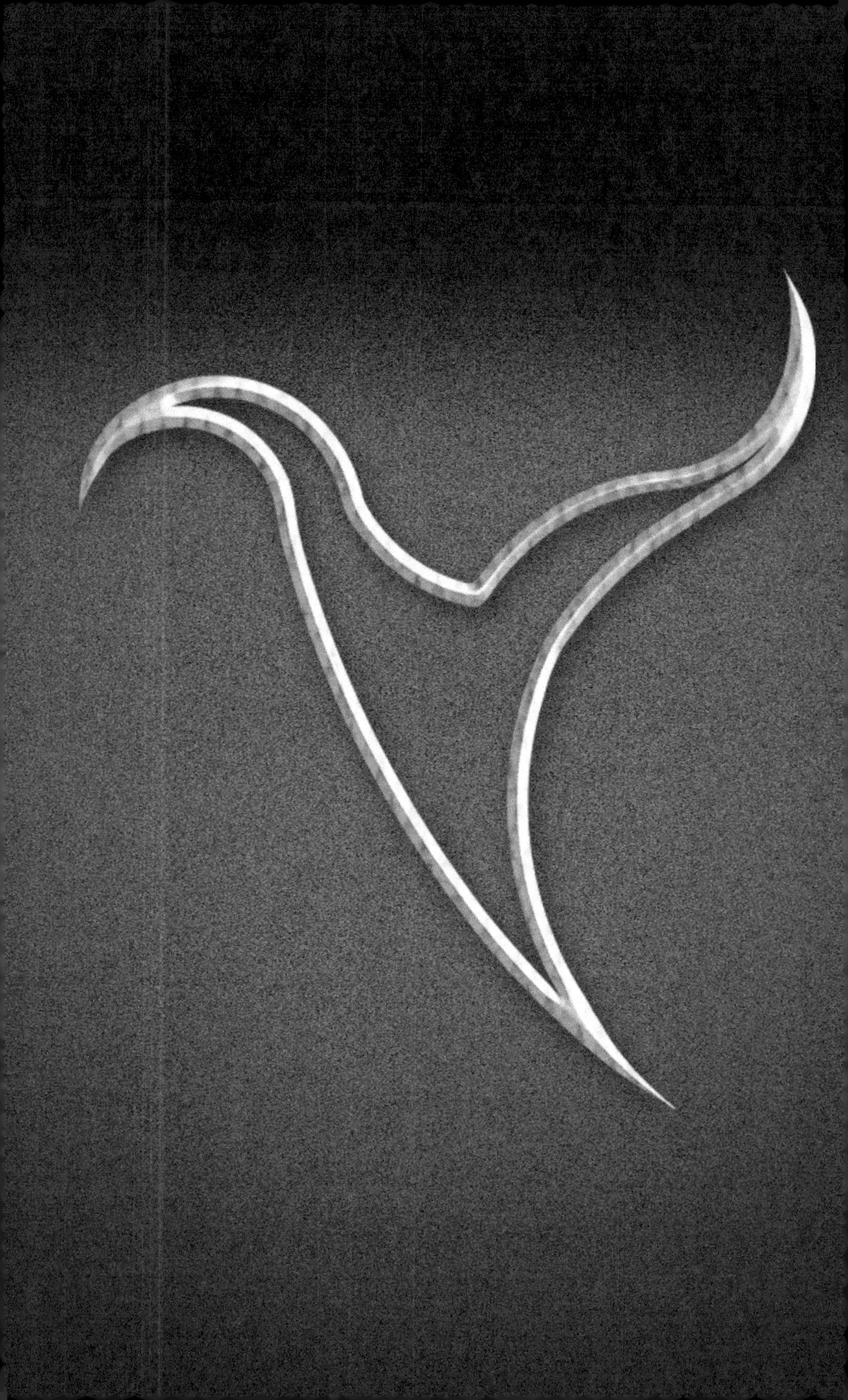

THREE

OATH OF BLOOD

Heat sweltered in the depths of Kendra's chest, seeping through her lips in a fiery bellow. As if she had been encased in flames, everything burned. She had yet to grasp reality; it tore right through her unsteady fingers, and she fought to flee the permeating darkness, her eyes fastened and heavy. Metallic clamps pinned her limbs to the tables beside the cot she was stuck on. A faint red hue invaded the darkness that consumed her vision—fluorescent lights blaring through her eyelids.

Aches and stinging throbs barraged her form, causing her to flinch and writhe with each sizzling second. Her left breast, neck, calve, and shins burned with a ferocity she had never known. Her memory was ash, but it gradually coalesced into a burned effigy. Sporadic images of gnarly teeth gnashing and gnawing flashed through her mind. They tugged and resonated with burning eyes that danced and gouged her—the hounds tearing away at her supple flesh with ease and reducing it to pulp and blood. They had consumed her. Maimed her. She was left with a single thought: *I shouldn't be alive.*

No matter the impossibility of her survival, she clung to what mattered most. *Kendall.* Her fingers curled tightly, clenching into a vise. Her nails dug into her palm. It hurt. Too much, in fact. Claws protruding from her fingertips sank into her skin, drawing blood.

She whimpered, heat surging through her once again, with a feverish pitch overtaking her skin. The pain throughout her body intensified. Ears ringing, senses on overdrive. She could smell the surrounding humans. *Smell them?* She could taste them in the air. *Taste them?* The pain in her chest swelled and came to a boil, and she let out a deafening roar of pain.

With the ambience perturbed, panic ensued around Kendra. Doctors and nurses alike rushed to stabilize her, and she convulsed and bucked in an attempt to ease her suffering. For several minutes, the doctors and nurses injected her neck with an unknown concoction and tried to calm her down. Then a wave of coolness washed over her. A machine above her whirred to life with an aquamarine light shimmering around her form. Sprites of light shrouded her, easing her pain bit by bit.

Kendra was grateful in that moment, her body temperature crawling down from the furnace it had been. She breathed a sigh of relief when it had done its job, and her eyes fluttered open to see a shimmering green crystal hovering above her. Her emaciated senses slowly reinvigorated, acclimating to the alien environment. Despite her confusion, one thought perturbed her mind, breaching the cloud of uncertainty.

"Kendall ... where?" Kendra's raspy voice strained, and a female nurse hushed her through the mask she wore. Someone's approach garnered Kendra's attention, each footstep causing her ears to twitch from how loud they seemed to her, but they didn't answer.

"Is she stable?" Eden's voice called through the noise.

"It's looking promising," a doctor replied.

When Kendra's blurred vision slowly came into focus, Eden's crimson eyes met her gaze.

"Where's Kendall?" she asked, focusing on him.

Eden was silent. His eyes shied away from her own.

"I didn't make it in time ... I'm sorry."

Kendra's heart sank, her eyes going wide with the sweltering heat reviving in the depths of her chest. *Liar,* she thought. He had to be lying. She couldn't imagine any other reality where his insinuations stood. *No.* She needed it to be a lie. Before words could form, flames spilled from her lips, brushing the air around her as she wailed. It didn't hurt. Instead, it alleviated some of the heat in her chest, but not nearly enough to quell her unbridled rage and sorrow.

"Kenny!" Kendra cried, her voice shattering.

Eden flinched, watching in disbelief as her fingers extended with flaming bristles protruding from her follicles. The air burned, and he gestured for the nurses and doctors to step back. He lunged forward, quickly pressing his arm to her chest, halting her flaming breath by force as he leaned over her, clasping his hand over her mouth.

"You need to calm down!" he spoke, mortified by the grim outcome she was subject to. "She's gone ..." he whispered. Kendra stared with pulsing pupils, the whites of her eyes swallowed in a fathomless darkness. Her once royal-blue eyes were now slit and a sinister red.

Faltering whimpers marked her arising grief as tears spilled from her fiendish eyes, and a new sensation arose with Eden being as close as he was. The scent of his hand permeated her nostrils. It was a deeply intoxicating scent, one that was entirely too palatable. Delectable even. She couldn't resist the instincts screaming at her, and she chomped down on his hand. Her large canine teeth extended into fangs, piercing Eden's hand.

Eden yelped, freezing as she clamped down.

The doctors and nurses panicked, and then one activated their radio.

"Code nine. I repeat, code nine!" a doctor called out.

Eden raised his free hand to halt them.

"No! You will *not* put her down!" He stared back at Kendra, her eyes quivering with an intense focus as she suckled with a tight hold on his hand. It hurt Eden, of course, but he had endured much worse. The skin around his hand glowed red, a basic energy barrier he channeled that provided a tough resistance that she contended with in her blood frenzy. She jerked her head and growled, vying for the blood her body begged for.

As Kendra's fangs stung Eden, her growls and tugs caused pain to shoot through his hand. His eyes narrowed as uninvited memories were unearthed by the flames that burned within the abysses that were Kendra's eyes. The familiar sting of fangs piercing his flesh caused his head to pulse, and he wrestled with a dark urge to kill her, an instinct that *demons* provoked within him. It, too, was a measure of darkness he passively neglected, but as he stared down at Kendra, his heart calmed. The burning eyes staring back showed not a surrendered conviction to her new urges. They were entrenched in a deep fear buried within their inky depths as tears welled beneath them, spilling upon their eyes meeting. He resolved that they were not eyes that sought to *take,* as demons would.

"Don't give in ..." Eden pleaded.

Hungry. So hungry, Kendra thought. *Why do I crave it?* She contended with herself to discover these answers, but it was a losing battle. Everything around her was mute except for the distinct rushing of Eden's blood through his veins. It was a sound that lured her when she focused on it, the more she surrendered to its call. The enthralling depths of the siren's song grew deeper with each beat of Eden's heart.

Eden's words echoed within those depths, reaching out to her. She didn't grasp them. They grasped her. Those words tore her from those depths, reinstating her stolen agency. Tears spilled heavily from those abysses, her voice croaking as her bloodied lips retracted from Eden's hand.

Eden snatched his hand back, holding it with deep breaths, showing his reservations. As the pain assailed his hand, he clenched his hand tightly as the blood dripped from the puncture wounds. His conflicted gaze showed a measure of trepidation as core memories challenged a resolution of his regard toward Kendra. With her humanity debased and submerged in an abyss, he knew not what to truly consider her anymore.

Kendra's eyes snapped shut, and she sobbed, overwhelmed by her grief and the changes she was still processing. It was too much for her. The hunger, albeit briefly overpowered, still pulsed and gnawed at her dwindling sanity. Her eyes peeked open, granting an apology to him, but despite their remorse, Eden perceived a hunger within the depths of her burning eyes.

Eden turned his attention to the fearful medical staff.

"She needs syn-blood. Hurry," he commanded. He was in no real position of authority, but they quickly abided when they faced his glare. Soon, nurses in white came barging through the door with a bag and a tube attached to it, a mouthpiece at the end that would serve to deliver the substance. They oriented the bag like an IV drip, and Eden carefully placed the tube in her mouth since the nurses were too afraid to get near the daunting, fanged orifice. After being given instructions, Kendra reluctantly drank in accordance with her instincts.

Sighing in relief, Eden watched the staff with careful eyes, seeing them stare at him in disbelief. They were all too scared to try correcting him on the protocol. By all means, Kendra should have been dead. If not by succumbing to her mutation, they would have put her down as a ravenous threat to humans. Even so, it was because of the breach of protocol prior to and during her treatment that she had a chance. He was silent. He didn't owe any of the medical staff an explanation, and they didn't seem interested in asking for one either. Walking to the exit of the room, he stopped as he gripped the door handle, glancing back at the medical staff.

"I will not hear a single code nine again. Steer clear until we have reviewed this matter," he reminded them eerily, having no regard for how he came across. He would see no further harm come to Kendra. Having issued his command, he left with haste.

Heading southwest from the medical building, Eden sat patiently in the back of a car. In the near distance was the tower that comprised the intelligence center of the Hunters' base, a large megalithic building framed in black granite with flecks of gray. Despite its sleek, modern suggestion, it was the most structurally sound building present on base.

Upon arriving, Eden left the car, shut the door behind him, and approached the main entrance. Distending from the building was the doorway with mechanically operated, steel sliding doors. Surrounding the perimeter were multiple security personnel dressed in gray and black tactical suits, the standard hunter uniform. Vigilant and imposing, they all carried high-caliber firearms slung across their bodies, ready to be used should protocol permit it.

Eden came to a pause before the doors with two hunters on either side of him, both of whom remained watchful but not overly concerned by his presence. Now standing on a black pad in the middle of the pavement, he lifted his arms to be patted down by one hunter. No weaponry was allowed inside, so he had stored Avenger, knowing he could call upon it at will if necessary. The hunter cleared him and his bracer beeped. Subsequently, the horizontally mounted cylindrical enclosure above the door shone. A laser darted out, scanned Eden's form, and retreated upon confirming his credentials. The doors whirred and opened, sliding behind the granite. The lobby was revealed, and he entered.

The layout was large, with a reception between Eden and the numerous halls that made up the first floor of the intelligence center. He walked along the rust-red carpet, approaching a desk. A man behind it acknowledged him with a nod, hitting a button before gesturing to the elevators, which he entered promptly.

It was a quick ride to the upper level. Stepping out of the elevator, large, heavy doors waited at the end of the hall to his left—one of the meeting rooms where he had been ordered to deliver his report and assessment.

Eden pushed the doors open and entered the room; he was greeted by the image of a long table with numerous men wearing formal gray military uniforms or suits. High-ranking officers and the general herself were designated to determine Kendra's fate, depending on the specifics of his report, along with her status. His leer cast silent judgment upon the weathered men's taut faces.

At the end of the table, General Jessica Blackwell sat. Her imposing aura loomed over the room, suggesting the gravity of her authority and capabilities alike, something inhuman entirely. She wore a variation of the hunter uniform—one with a waist cloth attached that parted at the front. Her wide-brimmed hat was tilted to shade the upper half of her face as she kept her head down, but the flash of her jade-green eyes occasionally surfaced to scrutinize the room. This was especially the case upon Eden's arrival. A woman of mystery to those who saw her, but Eden was far too familiar with her for such aloofness to sway his conduct toward her.

With Eden having arrived, a man with bronze-colored skin and hazel eyes behind glasses gestured to an empty seat aside him, the Director of Operations, Ethan Ardon.

The gravity of Eden's report dawned on him as all eyes fell on him. Despite the hastiness of the report that he had conjured in the lobby of the medical center, it was at least accurate in his account.

Ethan stood and spoke, rehashing the details of the events as Eden had written them, and upon finishing, he studied Eden expectantly.

Eden cleared his throat.

"Everything is accurate, sir," he said.

"And to my understanding, there was an ... incident during your visitation with her in the medical facility. Word traveled quickly about the code nine ..." he said.

Eden frowned. *Of course they know already,* he thought.

"That is correct as well. I was bitten by a freshly mutated human due to my carelessness with proximity. She regained her senses after a moment and responded positively to the syn—"

"Relevance, Private. He did not ask for the details of the code nine, merely that it was called," a high-ranking hunter with a scraggly brown beard interjected, Commander Evans. He was the hunter charged with facilitating their operations in Chicago. "I believe a single code nine, no matter the excuse, is enough to warrant a procedural termination of the subject in question."

Eden's eyes widened, his hands clenching into white-knuckled fists.

"Under standard protocol, yes, that would be advised. However, there is more to this girl, yes?" Ethan spoke, temporarily assuaging Eden's swelling temper.

"Yes, Kendra appeared to have been targeted specifically in relation to the somnium incidents we have been investigating. One showed up with the express purpose of distracting me from protecting her."

"An assignment you too undertook without prior authorization or proper escalation within our procedures," Commander Evans interjected once more.

"One I undertook within the developing circumstances being too urgent to wait for prior authorization. She was connected not once, but twice. This wasn't a coincidence, but a deliberate targeting that her continued existence will provide us insight into," Eden said, staring daggers at Commander Evans.

"I would suggest, still, that she be granted the proper ... mercy. She is now a danger to the world around her. Should she lose control, pointless lives would be thrown away for nothing. Homuntiums, far and few between, are rarely ever worth preserving," spoke another commander. A consensus was emerging among those at the table before the chatter was adjourned by Jessica.

"Narrowly escaping death for faceless entities to deliberate on her fate ... how heartless. Have you no reservations about executing a confused, freshly turned girl? Need I remind you that I, myself, am a homuntium?" She glared at the commander. "Should you need a reason other than moral considerations, my own preservation has proven auspicious for the Hunt, yes? If there are insights to be garnered through her in our investigation of the covenant, we should pursue them while also preserving her continued existence. Private Blackwell is showing more foresight than the lot of you at this potentially critical juncture," she rebuked, earning a wary glance from Commander Evans when she praised Eden's judgment.

For once in a long while, Eden found himself in agreement with Jessica.

The men at the table argued. Most suggested that Kendra should be put down, while others suggested she should be held for further research. These suggestions were unfavorable to Eden. In his guilt, his insufficient efforts, he assumed a responsibility for Kendra's life, but he wasn't sure he could ever truly ameliorate it.

Turmoil brewed within his spirit, and he recalled the debates he had heard and been subjected to his entire life. In their fear, speculation of one's abnormal existence—the danger it imposed—was all too common among hunters. He knew such danger, for he had no choice, but rather than resigning himself to its grim verdict, he undertook an oath to himself to persist, that the demons may take no more.

Eden held the edge of the table. His grip became an iron vice, his energy suddenly surging as the table between his fingers cracked and splintered. The room became silent as his fierce red eyes scathed them all.

"How could you suggest that she doesn't deserve to live! I'm the one who breached her boundaries while she was in this sensitive state. I take full responsibility for what happened to her and will continue to take responsibility for her going forward. She's confused and contending with things she hasn't even had a chance to understand yet. I know she will with time and our support. I'll remind you all that these soulless deliberations have led to nothing but tragedies in the wake of idleness. Fate is never so kind. Don't keep ignoring its mercy!"

The room was still until Ethan let out a long sigh.

"I've heard enough. Kendra may still indeed show cognition and humanity. We will determine that as soon as possible. Provided she passes our tests, we will accommodate her in returning to her life ... but she will be under the watch of Sergeant Vicente Almazan, Private Blackwell. A probation of sorts to ensure she can re-assimilate."

An uproar started at the table, but Ethan held his fist up, silencing it.

"Under my executive decision, I decree this," Ethan snapped. The table fell silent, surrendering to Ethan's resolution.

Eden stood from his seat promptly, shaking his head at the absurdity of him not being selected to watch over Kendra. He believed himself to be in the best position to do so, both from a practical stance and in terms of his capabilities. Despite this, he was pleased Kendra would be spared, at least.

"Also, Private Blackwell, the damage to the table will be docked from your pay," Ethan remarked.

Eden shook his head, glancing back as he pushed the doors open.

"I don't give a shit," he declared before marching down the hall.

As the doors closed behind Eden, the eyes in the room shifted to Jessica, whose disinterest following the resolution prevailed as she lowered her head, shrugging her shoulders in response to the stares.

"If any of you desire to sanction him further, I implore you to deliver it to him yourselves ..." Jessica mused. There was a tense silence, garnering a smirk from the enigmatic general. "Thought so."

The white fluorescent lights of the medical room beamed down harshly on Kendra, her royal-blue eyes glazed over in disassociation. Days had passed, and her sense of time bled the same as she had when Eden found her. Numerous tests, questions, needles, and scans—she endured them all. Despite this, she struggled to accept the truth of this nightmare.

She wasn't the same, that much she knew. As abnormal as she was, the place she was held was enamored with its own bewildering details; it put her on edge. The clack and scribbles of pens on clipboards, the whispers of conversation that were far too loud, and the insufferable scent she picked up from everybody. She could make out what they were saying, even from within the sound-dampening walls of the room she was confined to. Her ears were now hyperactive and picking up far too much. Every minute detail was noticed, much to her displeasure. Even with all she overheard, she received no answers to her burning questions—no revelations of what would become of her. They even denied her contacting her parents, who had to have been plagued by her sudden disappearance.

She so badly desired to be free from the subjugation of the Hunters, their caution and procedures meaning little in the face of her growing irritability, grief, and trauma. The call to the void had echoed more than a few times; the burning guilt around the memories associated with the assault she had survived ate away at her with each passing day. Even when her eyes were closed, she still heard the haunting screams and the ghastly sounds of her and Kendall's assault, and she desperately wished she could have gone back to act differently, as futile as the desire was.

Kendra's wrists had since gone raw from the bindings she was kept within. She had learned quickly that compliance was mandatory to keep them off for any significant stretch of time—if only to use the bathroom under threat of gunfire if she was daunting enough to refuse going back into them. At the very least, the pain from her initial awakening had subsided quickly, but her new *hunger* gnawed away at her between each dose of syn-blood they gave her.

Soon, the door opened, and remorseless steps echoed in the room. Unfamiliar scents assailed Kendra, and a few hunters had followed Ethan inside. She dared to look up, and their eyes met in a scathing union; her very being was on trial in his hazel gaze. As perturbing as their presence was, she instinctively sat up, and the thick bindings on her wrists pulled taut as her fingers dug into the mattress defensively. The hunters scrutinized her warily, and she could practically smell their fear and loose trigger fingers.

"Ms. Mallory, how are you feeling today?" Ethan asked, his tone far too cordial to resemble genuine sincerity.

"I've been locked up for days, subjected to however many stupid tests, and forced to drink some weird fake-blood shit. How do *you* think I am?"

"About as I expected. But how of reason are you, really? Are you craving blood? Violence? Anything concerning, I mean."

"Wha—no. I just … want to go home." Kendra's voice cracked, a heavy breath leaving her lips. She curled her lip and took an unsteady breath that evoked a deep sadness from within her suppressed thoughts. For days she had cried herself to sleep and begged for answers—for freedom from the twisted joke they were subjecting her to.

"Right then. I only wanted to confirm. You have been deemed of sound mind and rational autonomy, so far as your instincts are quelled. Do understand, we will grant you your freedom, but—"

"What do you mean *but?* My human rights have been entirely violated! My captivity is against the law!"

"No, no, no, Ms. Mallory. Human rights would imply you are still human. I can assure you, and you must know this too, that you are something different now. You are now a mutation, with a DNA sequence matching that of a hellhound—a demon. You're not entirely human, nor entirely demon. We call beings like you homuntiums," Ethan said.

"What the fuck are you even talking about? Hellhounds? I don't even know what the hell any of this means!"

Ethan adjusted his glasses, his expression sour as he took a step toward her bedside.

"You were attacked by demons. Those hounds that nearly killed you were demons called hellhounds. You were saved by a hunter. That is the briefest explanation I can give. You aren't human anymore and could present a danger to humans should you go unchecked. You are showing no such signs of hostility to human life—for now—but that is contingent on you receiving the syn-blood formula. From now on, you will need to take at least one a day, lest you become a threat to be put down." His eyes narrowed on her, a hollow, chilling gaze piercing through Kendra. "And believe me ... we will do what we have to."

Kendra's eyes widened at the insinuation. Her mind rumbled, memories of the past few days flashing through her head as Ethan's words repeated. She had bitten Eden and even indulged in his blood. As faint a memory as that was, it was not lost on her—the phantom urges that surfaced in that instance. She buried her head between her legs to stifle her shallow breaths and gasps.

Queasiness overwhelmed her as it was explained that the torment had not simply relegated itself to that small pocket of tragedy but would remain with her for the rest of her life. The idea was horrifying—craving blood like some fictional fiend on a knife's edge from succumbing to an invasive, primitive desire forced upon her. This burden she carried was because of beings she never knew existed until they had almost claimed her life. And with the continued agony that came with these revelations, she wished they had. Even then, she heard her own blood roiling in her veins, and her heart throbbed with an unsettling cadence that she knew was wrong.

A war drum that was submerged in a lake of despair, her heart trudged through a marsh with each thump that reminded her of the truths Ethan had spoken. The coming verdict of her continued tribulations mattered less and less the more her senses overwhelmed her. The familiar, sweltering despair that Kendall had once jostled her from was born anew—freezing her limbs as if the void of space had manifested around them. Paradoxically, as her body burned anew with the demonic energy that had infested her flesh and soul, frigidness consumed her body as she released a breath that she had held in for too long.

"You will be accompanied for a period by a hunter of ours. You won't need to interact with them. They will keep a watchful eye on you from a distance. Should you show hostility or skip your regiment of syn-blood ... need I say more?" Ethan questioned, his tone falling flat.

This was when Kendra's consciousness was anchored back to reality, and she broke into a spree of uneven sobs, unable to hold the legion of sorrow back anymore. Everything paraded in her overwhelmed head. A monster had been born, and what was left of her was caged within that visage. A creature to be put down should she misbehave.

"You're—heartless. All of you," she spoke damningly, her voice cracked and barely discernible.

Ethan watched curiously for a moment, waving the hunters away as he turned on his heel to leave with them. Stopping in his tracks at the doorway, he glanced back at her, his gaze softening ever so slightly.

"I always am."

The SUV droned with a continuous hum that annoyed Kendra. In the hours that passed, she had at least learned to tune out frequencies that particularly bugged her. She remained tucked firmly in the middle seat of the SUV, trying to avoid the two hunters on either side of her.

Eventually, the vehicle came to a stop at a police station, and she was ushered out of it by a hunter. The familiar stench of Chicago invaded her nostrils. However, it was significantly more pungent than she remembered, but it was one step closer to home. Police officers and their vehicles lined the lot in front of the station.

More importantly, Kendra saw familiar royal-blue eyes fixed on her, glazed with tears and fondness. Her mother. As she would have imagined, her mother's visage was plagued with dark, puffy eyes and was twisted in distress. Kendra sniffled, rushing past the hunters into her mother's arms.

"Mom!" Kendra cried, and her mother shushed her, firmly embracing her and tangling her fingers in Kendra's hair as if she would fade away if she didn't. Her scent filled Kendra's mind, and for once, it was a familiar scent to put her at ease after days of anxiety and foreign stressors. She was alive. She was home.

A hunter spoke with the police supervisor, giving a rehearsed confidentiality statement regarding the matter of Kendra's return. It was a mystery that she had disappeared and now was suddenly being brought back by mysterious people. The pretenses escaped Katherine, however.

Holding her daughter close, Katherine carefully shuffled over to the hunters. In her indomitable maternal instinct, she decided she would interrogate them herself, those of whom she had only known up to that point as Organization X.

"Katherine Mallory, detective with CPD. Why is my daughter being returned by you guys? Where has she been? Where is my other daughter, Kendall Mallory?"

"Confidentiality of Organization X is in effect. We are not allowed to disclose any details. Your chief will remind you of this as well," a hunter said. Upon delivering that statement, the group of them turned from the officers and Katherine and returned to their SUV.

Katherine scoffed in annoyance, marching after them.

"Wait!" Katherine called, to no avail. She would have protested further, but the police supervisor grabbed her shoulder, pulling her back.

"Let it go, Mallory. It's beyond us."

Hesitantly, Katherine relented and spun around, marching back over to Kendra and tucking her against herself. She had no idea what had happened to Kendra, and despite the burning questions eating away at her, she had to attend to Kendra. With confusion still parading through her mind, she watched helplessly as the SUV disappeared into the busy Chicago traffic.

"I can explain," Kendra stuttered to her mother between hiccups, to which she shushed her again. Kendra slowly separated from her mother and noticed her sunken, dark eye sockets. She surmised her mother hadn't been sleeping, which hardly surprised her.

"Explain when we get home," Katherine said.

Kendra swallowed hard and nodded, understanding that the news wouldn't serve as a relief. It was an impossible task she wasn't sure she could do.

It was a long, tense car ride. Katherine was mostly focused on the road, addled by obvious thoughts and concerns. The silence was too loud, and tensions fermented into an unsavory taste in her mouth. Unpleasant memories, or hallucinations as far as she was aware, surfaced, and she glanced at her daughter with apprehensive eyes.

"The night you went missing ... I heard a knock at the door. You and Kendall were asking to come in ... but no one was there when I opened it," Katherine said. Her face went pale, her mouth agape with dazed eyes, as if she were barely anchored to the present.

Kendra chalked this story up to her mother's lack of sleep. Hallucinations, perhaps. It was impossible that she heard either one of them at that door.

"Where's Dad?" Kendra asked, her mind stirring as she tried to imagine how things transpired in her absence. Her father, while not divorced from emotions, always tried to maintain a level head in scary situations. With how much time had passed, she imagined he'd have forced himself back into his work to cope.

Katherine stifled her worries, swallowing the tension that crept up her throat as she quelled her boiling thoughts. She didn't feel particularly strong, but she forced herself to be—for her daughter.

"He's at work. He knows I have you, and he'll talk with you when he gets home later."

Kendra nodded firmly, tucking herself away as she traced the texture of the car panel, desperate to focus on anything but herself as her head throbbed. What she'd give to hug her father, to have him assure her everything would be okay. As much as she had feigned her annoyance with his lackadaisical attitude and terrible jokes, they were a much-desired reprieve from the hell she had gone through.

Kendra drifted off briefly in the passenger seat of the car, waking up when they pulled into the driveway. *Home at last,* she thought. She rubbed the sleep from her eyes and dragged herself into the house, her mother in tow. They sat down on the couch in the dark living room, soon illuminated by warm light from a lamp. Kendra took in the relaxing scent of lemon grass from the oil diffuser. Now in a familiar and welcoming environment, tension fled from her, and she primed the words she was dreading to conjure.

"They never found Kenny. I ... I have very little memory of what happened. We were biking through the park. Then there were these—these things. And now I'm not ... Kenny is ..." Kendra's voice gave, and she broke into sobs. Her mother's concerned expression contorted into shared grief, her lips curling and convulsing before she sobbed with Kendra.

The questions came, but Kendra was unable to answer, and despite the insatiable concern, her mother knew it was unfair of her to ask, but she had tried anyway. The grief consumed both of them, but despite the obvious undertones, Kendra couldn't deliver the grim verdict of what actually happened. She knew that was too cruel. And even if she did, her mother wouldn't be able to understand it or its supernatural nature; Ethan made that much clear before discharging her.

Their session didn't last much longer, and Katherine hugged and kissed Kendra, inspecting the marks on her neck and noting how twisted it was that someone—something—would dare hurt her.

"Go lay down. Rest. We can talk more later and as much as you need me to. Your father will be here soon, too. For now, you need rest," Katherine said.

Kendra was quiet for a few moments, wiping the tears from her eyes. It had occurred to her she was wearing the scrubs the Hunters had provided her, given her initial outfit had been scorched, shredded, and soaked in blood. She made a mental note to throw the scrubs out once she changed into something comfortable.

"I think we both need sleep, Mom."

Katherine nodded in agreement before she stood and made her way to her room.

Kendra slowly ascended the stairs. She was careful with her gaze, less she would be snared by the family portraits lining the home. She dared not pause in the hallway as she glanced at Kendall's room, a quake erupting within her mind and chest as she forwent that spiral again. With great effort, she forced herself to her room, praying that the familiar environment would grant her a semblance of retreat from her ruptured mind. She shakily scanned her fingerprint on her room's door and entered. She stripped from the scrubs and cobbled together a tank top and pajama pants, which were substantially more comfortable, before stumbling over to her bed and falling into it.

Kendra could only stare at the dark ceiling. The sunlight that bled through the gaps of her curtains dimmed as time slipped. Dissociative shadows crept in as the day faded, and the crevices of her mind were haunted once more. Scars that burned fresh into her memory and body, carving her with the twisted truth she was forced to adhere to.

The harrowing pit that developed in Kendra's chest grew, and she reached toward the ceiling with a trembling hand. Her nails extended into obsidian-black claws, causing her to retract and hide her hand beneath the blanket. Her canines grew within her mouth, accompanied by a sick crackling sound. With a flare of embers fluttering in her gaze, tears welled in her burning eyes as the darkness crept in once more. She desperately vied to hold herself together—not wishing for her father to see her this way when he would return, but the effort was in vain.

That pit in her chest burst, and she silently sobbed to herself once more. No longer a human. A being of vagrancy granted mercy.

A demon.

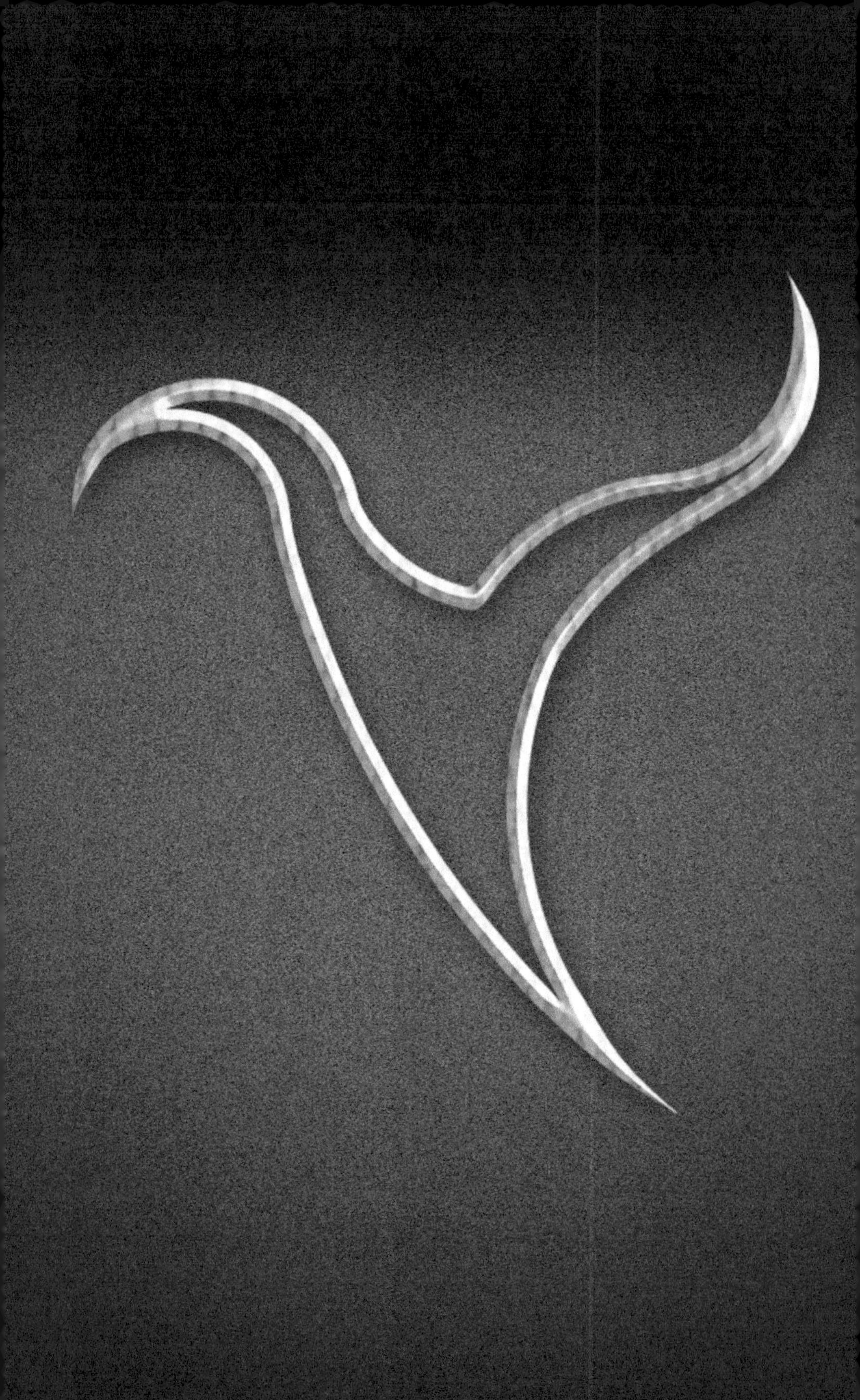

FOUR

OMINOUS SPECULATIONS

Zane enjoyed being an emissary. He had navigated the tumultuous field of demon politics for the entirety of his twenty-six years of life, and he intended to continue to do so. In the roles given to him by the Hunters, nothing was more pertinent than the relationships he fostered with the noble umbra demon houses across the globe. Among all, he found the Siegharts were the most outwardly amenable of the families—jovial and exuberant with a flair for life he scarcely saw among demons. As descendants of Leviathan, the Cardinal Sin Ordinance of Envy, it seemed paradoxical. With an affinity for umbra kinesis—shadow magic—their boisterous displays and vibrant culture hardly matched such a propensity for that arcane attunement.

Their hospitality couldn't be matched, either, and no such envy was apparent in any of Zane's prior interactions with their branches. Still, pretenses loomed above all else, and that hospitality could easily be revoked at the drop of a pin. One wrong statement or development, and the illusion crumbled. Zane liked to think he was a master at maintaining that illusion.

Quirky one-liners coursed through his mind to open the upcoming meeting with the head of the Sieghart family, who primarily resided in Chicago. He had never dealt with the family's patriarch, typically meeting the lesser branches elsewhere throughout the country, so he knew he'd need to tread more carefully than usual. With that in mind, he concluded he'd play confident and cordial, snapping his fingers as he cast his gaze out the window of the car.

The blacked-out SUV Zane, Vicente, and Donovan were in crawled through the busy streets of Chicago. The traffic wasn't as intense on the north side of town as they reached Gold Coast, a high-status area north of downtown Chicago. Zane admired the neighborhood, namely, the proximity to Lake Michigan. While he gazed at the coastline, Donovan ensured to drive carefully when they turned onto narrower roads, making for a claustrophobic drive.

"Finally decided?" Vicente asked, yawning as he cracked his neck and brushed his mustache down. Wearing his hunter uniform, it was easy to see his brawny build, which earned his attendance at the meeting, at least to stay in the car in case something went wrong.

Zane perked his head, sitting straight. His auburn eyes softened as he glanced at Vicente, flashing him a cheeky smirk that pronounced the small scar running down the left side of his lip.

"Yeup," Zane said.

"You know ... you could try to be a little less serious. It's not like you're meeting with a bunch of dangerous demons."

"I don't know about you, but I'm feeling pretty good about this. I doubt we'll need your muscle."

Vicente glanced down at his gloved hand, clenching it before tapping Zane's arm.

"Glad you recognize *I'm* the muscle, captain."

"That's *Captain Larson*, Sergeant Almazan," Zane teased, never taking the formalities of their rank seriously.

Donovan, with his darker complexion and wrinkled face, glanced back at his comrades, sighing.

"Just hit your panic button if anything goes wrong," he spoke, prompting Zane to chuckle.

"I don't think we'll have to worry. This is me we're talkin' 'bout," Zane said.

The certainty in his tone eased Donovan's nerves a bit, but Vicente pouted.

"Been a while since I've seen some action. Haven't seen one of these covenant punks yet."

"Less is more, they say. Careful what you wish for," Donovan said and let out another long sigh, turning the vehicle onto a street with rows of homes and mansions that bordered on flashy. Soon, they arrived at two black gates that blocked a long driveway leading to a mansion. Donovan lowered the window, leaning out slightly to speak into the intercom attached to a post.

"Organization X." Moments later, the automated gates rose vertically, allowing the vehicle to enter. They drove into the driveway of the property, passing under trimmed trees until they reached the driveway roundabout. Topiary and pink azaleas adorned the center, encircled in a short wall of brick. Donovan looped around it before parking in front of the mansion.

Zane's eyes traveled across the property, noting the two-story home, its entrances, its exits, and other fine details—just in case. It was a beautiful home, sporting a modern design with a well-tended, spacious garden surrounding it.

Zane yawned, adjusting his black tie as rows of servants came from the house to greet them at the curb. All were in black formal attire that reminded Zane of the uniforms he'd see in the restaurants he had worked on details at, but he supposed it wasn't too strange given the family's prestige. The Siegharts were flush with funds from their real estate empire. He doubted the upkeep and needs of a demon family warranted such an abundance of workers, at least not in their home.

"See yah in a few," Zane said to Donovan and Vicente. He opened the door, stretching his legs as he straightened the wrinkles from his suit one last time. Easily, his least favorite thing about the role was having to dress up. Despite the years he had grown accustomed to formal attire, it still irritated him over his more comfortable clothing choices. On a positive consideration, he didn't have to wear the overbearing uniforms other hunters wore, much to Vicente's feigned envy.

An older maid with stringy blond hair and firm blue eyes greeted him upon his emergence from the SUV. He shut the door behind him, and she instructed him to raise his arms for the inspection, which he obliged without complaint. Two butlers stepped forward, patted him down, and ran a wand over his body. It was their procedure to sniff out any unauthorized technology. Once he was cleared, the blond-haired maid ushered him to follow her.

The maid tucked her hands behind her back as she escorted Zane through the archway leading to the entrance. They ascended the porch, and the other servants closed in behind them. It would have been intimidating if Zane couldn't tell most of them were human. He was aware that the maid was not. He displayed no trepidation despite this, and the maid opened the door, leading him inside.

The entryway was clad in a decorative carpet, cozily padding their steps as they walked through it. Between the antique decorations and the high-profile art along the shelves and walls, he could have sworn he was getting ready to negotiate a business deal worth millions of dollars. He found that prospect amusing. As he inspected the hall, he caught a familiar sight. A painting hung on the wall depicting a large home encrusted in exotic flowers: calatheas, calla lilies, anthurium, and a variety of other comparable flowers adorned the ancient manor with a vermilion sunset imbued in the background. It was a painting Zane was more than familiar with.

"Ah! The *Chateau De Fleur* is a classic. Mr. Sieghart has excellent taste," he said, attempting conversation with the demonic maid. He would be more impressed if not for the fact it was only a copy, whereas the real one was present with the Alastair family. The demon families appeared to have a symmetry of tastes in their arts—at least among the western demon families. He had yet to meet any of the demon families in the Middle East and Asia, primarily due to the circumstances of his assignments and the language barrier. His fluency in the demon language was still crude.

"Mr. Larson, I am afraid I am not as versed in such art as you or Master Sieghart. I propound you to, instead, share your commentary with him. I plead your understanding," the demonic maid said.

Zane blinked, snickering with amusement.

"What a polite way of telling me to shut up."

The demonic maid was unfazed by his bluntness and remained silent for the rest of the escort.

When they entered the living room, a soft yellow hue radiated, bathing the room in warm light. Sitting on a rust-brown armchair was a large man with shoulder-length, wavy red hair and large gray eyes, with a full beard that accentuated his imposing frame. Oliver Sieghart, a name Zane found peculiar. He resembled a lumberjack, if not for the crimson suit he wore. Zane was ushered to sit on the loveseat opposite him before the demonic maid left the room. A one-on-one conversation as per the agreement.

Zane took his seat, meeting Oliver's intense gaze. Oliver held a pipe in his mouth, their eyes locked in attrition as the crackling fire pervaded their respective silence. Under such rigid scrutiny, Zane took the initiative to break the initial tensions.

"No way you're a billionaire real estate mogul with your build. You sure you're not a boxer?" Zane joked.

Snorting, Oliver drew the pipe from his mouth, blowing a light-pink haze into the air.

"Flattery will get you many places, Mr. Larson." He set his pipe down and continued, "Oliver Sieghart. I understand you have met others in my family, yes?"

"Zane Larson. But you already knew that. I have met the lesser branches of your family before, yes. I find them to be quite agreeable. Stylish homes and quite the resume to boot. Classy, if not a tad more charming to the sensibilities of the common man."

"I presume that we're not as ... bourgeois as the Alastairs, yes?"

Zane snorted, realizing that Oliver, too, had done his homework, researching his background.

"In your own ways. It's still quite the display you boast."

"Such modesty. Even I know of the Alastair's prominence with frills and flourishes."

"Your euphemisms aren't lost on me. Trust me when I say there is extravagant and then there's gaudy."

"And Eridianne? How is she these days? Her interest in socializing has been quite diminutive lately."

"I primarily worked under her brother, Arionne ... but in my few interactions with the mistress of the clan, her vanity is only matched by her ire. She has plenty to dish out where applicable, especially after her husband's death. Still, you can catch her deviating from those characteristics on a good day, and while I won't confirm or deny personally ... those days are pretty good for whoever she fancies."

Oliver chuckled abruptly, smoke spilling from his lips as Zane spared information that he, as the head of the Siegharts, found both amusing and noteworthy.

"Her preferences are as enigmatic as she is."

Zane sighed, clasping his hands together as he straightened his position, clearing his throat.

"But enough about that. Besides the niceties of our respective backgrounds, I need to impose a few concerns you may be able to help the Hunters with." Zane's expression sharpened.

Oliver straightened his position, gesturing toward Zane with a nod.

"Oh, by all means, don't let my blithering distract us further. How can I assist a ... cinder?"

Zane winced and cleared his throat, electing to ignore what was considered by some to be a slur to Zane's kind.

"For the past few months, it has become increasingly more common that police officers are mysteriously going missing in this county. And further evidence is suggesting that they are being methodically taken out in demon attacks, specifically by hellhounds." Zane furrowed his brows, his mind surfacing the memory from the week prior when he stopped a hellhound from attacking a policewoman—a detective who was investigating the very case that he spoke of. "Any information to offer us regarding this phenomenon?"

Oliver furrowed his brow, increasingly showing an inquisitive expression as Zane went on. It became apparent to him—the implication of Zane's questioning.

"By every means available to us, no. We have no information pertaining to this phenomenon you speak of." Oliver adjusted the knot of his tie, shaking his head.

Zane furrowed his brow, his scrutiny intensifying as his expression narrowed.

"Ah, is that so? We have no reason to believe you wouldn't notice *something* pertaining to this. Especially with your reach in this area," Zane said. Moments of silence passed.

"It is certainly strange indeed. We have no such direct information about the police casualties—but we do have information about the rifts that may be responsible."

Zane perked up at his posit.

"A strange energy has been floating about, and more frequent rifts accompany it. My family has worked to close some of these rifts, but the frequency is proving burdensome," Oliver said, his nostrils flaring as he heftily exhaled.

Zane nodded along, his eyes softening.

"I'm aware. You've been following the Kohen Treaty to a T. That's appreciated. However, there is the pressing concern that there are more than a handful of civilian casualties ... meaning this appears targeted rather than just random demon attacks. There's an organization behind this. And while I don't intend to implicate you, your network is more reliable than ours. We've only recently established our own in Chicago." Zane flashed a smirk, leaning into his seat as he waited for Oliver's rebuttal.

The Kohen Treaty, which was signed decades prior by the heads of the noble umbra demon houses, was one of the first efforts demon and man concocted in a reconciliation of their coexistence. Demons were monitored closely to ensure they would not attempt to rebel, usurp, or otherwise undermine the broader considerations of humanity, but they were also ensured that humanity would allow them to live peacefully among them. Various statutes within the treaty ensured this, but the most prominent of note were stipulations of their lack of political power or influence. A mandatory cooperation with the appropriate government organizations regarding supernatural phenomena wherever applicable.

As it stood, as far as Zane could tell, the Siegharts had not done anything to violate the treaty and even abided by the additional ethics clauses that weren't strictly mandatory. It was almost too good to be true, or so Zane suspected.

Oliver countered Zane's insinuations with a smile, crossing his legs as he shook his head.

"Ah, forgive my mistaken grievance. I can understand why this investigation is necessary, for both of our sakes. Unfortunately, we have drawn no conclusions from these attacks. Should we garner further intel into the matters, we'll reach out to the appropriate contact in your organization. I look forward to our continued cooperation, Mr. Larson."

Zane's smirk had turned into an amicable smile, one that begged reservations he may have exhibited. He was satisfied with the conversation—despite how inconclusive it seemed. His demeanor even appeared to put Oliver at ease.

Oliver was more than aware of what violating the Cohen Treaty could entail. Any demon family caught brazenly colluding against the interest of humanity, or at its expense, would be deemed threats to be eliminated.

"I'm glad to hear it then. We'll crack the case soon enough with your help. Until then, I'm relying on your diligence," Zane said, grinning as he stood from his seat. He stretched his legs, internally cursing how cramped he was in the low chair. He was particularly irked by the overpriced sofa, and it was uncomfortable to add to its travesty. *Bourgeois alright,* he thought.

"I look forward to it, Mr. Larson. In the meantime, I apologize for our ignorance."

"Don't go beating yourself up over it. We'll figure it out, remember?" Zane gave a cheeky laugh.

This made Oliver shift uncomfortably, granting a wry smile in response.

"Ah, before you go, can I offer you a drink?" Oliver asked.

Zane shook his head.

"Pft, I can't drink on the job, otherwise I'd take you up. You're awfully kind to consider, however."

"Aw, well, more for me then," Oliver spoke, and the two of them laughed.

The demonic maid returned to the room. Her weary blue eyes found Oliver, who nodded in confirmation toward her. Then she returned her attention to Zane. She beckoned to him, ushering him now that the conversation was over.

"Right on cue, huh? No worries, we're all done," Zane said, yawning. "Remember, Mr. Sieghart, we're allies only if you'll allow us to be. We share common interests. Let's maintain them." Zane glanced at the demonic maid, offering her a sardonic smirk. "Ah, and before I forget, I appreciate the *Chateau De Fleur* in the foyer. It's a well-made copy," Zane said, holding his hand out.

Oliver's hard eyes locked onto Zane's hand, freezing in silent contemplation for a moment. The same apprehension was found in the demonic maid's expression, both warily staring at Zane's hand. Breaching the silence, Oliver reached out, firmly gripping Zane's hand and giving it a hefty shake.

"A man of the arts? I respect that. Guess I should expect no less from you."

The demonic maid, who presented a sterner disposition toward him than before, escorted Zane back through the house. He could practically feel the daggers she would embed into him if given the opportunity. It irked him that she fit the stereotype of a demon, not that he was naïve enough to believe she was a fair representative of most others, including himself.

On the way out, another maid stood beside the door in the foyer. She was a younger, fair-skinned human woman with dark eyes and silky black hair pinned up in a bun. She held her apron, her gaze showing apprehension.

As Zane walked toward her, their eyes met, and he flashed her a smile with a wink. This broke her stance, causing her to avert her gaze meekly and shuffle to hide her flushed face.

"Have a nice day," Zane said. The demonic maid simply bowed, her hands stiffly clutching the front of her apron.

Once Zane was tucked away in the vehicle, he scanned the Sieghart's servants one last time.

On Zane's signal, Donovan drove them off the property. When they rejoined the main street traffic, Zane sighed heavily, relaxing in his seat.

"Talk about suspicious. Can't believe they didn't come up with a better set of excuses before we got there," Zane said, leaning on his elbow.

"Think they're behind this?" Donovan asked, and Vicente folded his arms, watching Zane expectantly.

Zane snorted.

"A lot of demons are guilty of one thing or another, but to what degree? I can't say. They're definitely hiding how much they know about the situation at the very least, but I got nothing concrete. A hunch is a hunch, but they've covered their trail—as any competent umbra demon house would." They fell silent after his comment, and Zane turned to focus on the city once again, his eyes narrowing with suspicion.

"They probably are. From what I read, it wouldn't surprise me if the ones bearing that weird eye ability were cooperating with the covenant somehow," Vicente alleged.

"I wouldn't put it past them. Be it all of them or just a select few at the top of the family, they're on our radar. I'll add my suspicions to my report."

Zane's eyes flickered a bit, noticing a shift in the surrounding energies. The omens became distorted with a rush of red streaking through. Underneath—a hiss. The insinuation hardly perturbed him, however, and he feigned ignorance of the revelation.

"Hey, Don, mind letting me out at the intersection? I'm going to go ahead and grab some tacos before heading back. The Chicago base is only a few miles from here. I'll walk."

Donovan was silent for a few moments, glancing back at Zane in the mirror before pursing his lips. Albeit wary of the reasoning, he nodded, sighing apprehensively.

"Sure, but I won't be coming to pick you up if your legs get tired. I ain't your personal taxi."

Zane snickered.

"Eh, I gotta get my daily steps, anyway."

Vicente perked up, frowning at Zane and Donovan, the undertones dawning on him. With his own senses not as attuned as Zane's, he would have been none the wiser.

"You detected something—didn't you?"

"No idea what you're talking about, man," Zane lied.

Donovan pulled over into a loading zone, and both Zane and Vicente unbuckled their seatbelts, prompting Donovan to glance back at them.

"Think I'll get some tacos too. The more, the merrier, right?" Vicente said.

Donovan reached back, grabbing Vicente's shoulder, staring at him with stern eyes. Without a word, he conveyed what he needed to.

Pursing his lips, Vicente sighed and shook his head.

"Bring me back a couple of chicken tacos, captain." He gave Zane a knowing stare, his nostrils flaring.

Flashing a smile, Zane winked at Vicente.

"No promises."

Zane wanted to spare any coming danger to his less-equipped comrades. He doubted they would be attacked in broad daylight on the road, but being followed was a possibility. Though he somehow doubted that as well. This was something else.

Stepping from the car, a whistle from Donovan prompted Zane to glance back at his older comrade.

"Be careful, kid. I'll see you soon."

Zane shook his head and snickered.

"I heard Chicago's tacos were killer, but you're really hyping me up now, Don."

Shutting the door, Zane stepped out onto the sidewalk, watching as the two drove off, eventually disappearing into the rows of traffic. Looking around apprehensively for a moment, he looked down at his stomach, which rumbled slightly, his mind set on the idea he had conjured.

"Man, really could go for those tacos too ... ah, well. No rest for the wicked," he muttered. Zane pressed through the crowd of pedestrians, eventually finding an alleyway, which he swiftly tucked himself into. Giving a once-over of his environment, he confirmed the coast was clear.

"Insenseilis." The air around Zane warped, and a blue hue flashed over his form. He snapped his fingers as a rush of flames surrounded him, consuming his suit and replacing it. When the flames died, he was clothed in jeans tucked into his black boots, a slim black T-shirt, and a brown parka with fur lining the hood. He let out a sigh of relief, much more comfortable than he had been prior.

"Alright, let's do this." Zane crouched before jumping high into the air and landing atop the building. He stood straight and held out his wrist, the holographic projection illuminating from his bracer. He navigated the menu and dialed into a channel, causing the speaker on the device to ring out. Suddenly remembering he hadn't put his earpiece in, he scrambled to remove it from his coat before command could answer.

"Mr. Larson, are you ready to deliver your report?" a female voice said.

"Barely. Things are gonna get fun here soon, but I'll give the synopsis for now."

"Okay, hit me."

"Oliver is a pretty sneaky man, from what I gathered. Nothing incriminating on the surface—he's covered some tracks for sure. Everything you'd expect from him. But get this, guy pleaded ignorant to what's going on, right? And that's an issue with how connected and in tune the Siegharts are here. No way he isn't aware of how suspicious this all seems. They're probably in cahoots with those covenant guys." Zane paced while speaking, his eyes glancing around. Shortly into his explanation, rifts opened around him. Tears in reality glimmering violet and seeping with darkness—a minor portal to Inferos, the realm of demons that was akin to what humans called hell. Through rifts, lesser demons could invade Mortale.

Zane had never been to the realm, personally, but he had witnessed its rifts and even more intimate bridges on several occasions. The malevolent energy was always a rush to bask in, albeit he still wasn't a fan of it. It spurred a phantom essence within him that he wasn't fond of—a compelling force that urged the darkness at the core of his being. The strength of said force, perhaps, had more to do with his lack of acclimation, as opposed to the primal nature of the sin-spurring realm that Lucifer had created eons ago.

"And now ... looks like I'm getting some company, so how about I formalize this info later? Just wanted to get the synopsis out to command before things picked up."

"We can send back up. I advise retreating until—"

"Nah, don't bother. I've got this," Zane said, appearing disinterested in the immediacy of the situation. "Call you back in a bit with an update."

Zane lowered his wrist and reached behind his back. From beneath his coat, he flicked his wrist out, holding an object that unfolded in conjunction. A blade with a single edge emerged, and a mechanism that resembled a revolver cylinder was built into it. A gunblade he had designed with the help of the engineers back at the Hunters' HQ. His finger hovered over the trigger as he aimed at the creature emerging from one of the rifts.

There it was, the first of the few hellhounds that lunged at him. With a pull of the trigger, he fired. The bullet met its skull, causing it to tumble onto the gravel of the rooftop. From the wound oozed gnarly maroon blood that sizzled with smoke, and the creature went limp.

"How convenient, a bunch of puppies," Zane called out. He found himself surrounded by several hounds that emerged from the rifts. Given the combustible nature of the hellhounds, he knew his only remaining means of attack were his bullets and blade. Snarls and howls ensued as the demons rushed him. He jumped back and aimed. He fired several times, and bangs echoed as a spree of bullets paraded the hounds, hitting all but one who had the foresight to dodge. The two that were hit dropped, twitching.

The other hound circled Zane before rushing at him. It leaped, and Zane took the liberty of poising his blade back before jabbing it forward. The tip pierced the hound's mouth, and he fired. With a point-blank shot, the hound whimpered and slid down the blade, twitching on the ground.

"If your hide and skull weren't so thick, that bullet would've gone straight through you," Zane muttered.

Swiping his blade clean of blood, Zane hit a switch on the side that folded the weapon back into its compact state. He sheathed it in the holster behind his back and wiped his hands together a few times. It had been an easy enough encounter—*too easy*. Given that the hellhounds were summoned and left to him with no further backup, he deduced it had secretly been some sort of trial. With that realization, the last detail to settle to his attention was the droning hiss.

"Now ... there's only you," Zane called out.

As if on cue, a surge of red tore through the air like ripped fabric, and a dark figure emerged onto the rooftop. Standing over the hellhound corpses was a tall somnium demon—taller than the demon compendium listed, at least. Its inky black carapace-like skin shimmered and rippled as it came into view. And unlike other somnium, this one wasn't bare. It sported a top hat and a shadowy black cape that dissipated into mist at the end. A tattered black suit with a red vest lined with golden buttons and a white-collared shirt beneath loosely clung to its emaciated stature. The attire reminded Zane of a magician.

"That's one dapper demon," he muttered.

A dark chuckle echoed through the air, causing Zane's ears to vibrate a bit. Same as the other somnium demons, it spoke as if directly whispering into his ears. He shuddered, holding his hand out to signal the somnium to stop.

"Hold up, before we talk ... cut that shit out. Talk like a normal ... thing."

The somnium's sinister face contorted in perplexity, so far as it could express with its indistinct visage.

"You ... aren't afraid? Good, this'll be much easier." It chuckled again. This time, the voice came directly from it.

"Okay, much better. So ... somnium demon, huh? First time seeing one in person. Kind of ... creepy? Reports don't say you wear clothes ... but I like the hat, really completes the imposing stature. Reminds me of that thing I saw when I took too much Benadryl."

The somnium narrowed its gaze in response, clearly unamused.

"Alright, I presume you wanted to talk to me about something? I imagine that's the case, given you're not trying to kill me ... yet," Zane said. The strange energy it exuded prickled Zane. That signature hiss others had described permeated, but there was a greater depth to it. It was strong, perhaps stronger than he could handle if it decided to attack. Despite this, Zane maintained his composure.

"Hunter ... yet a demonium, yes? Half human, half demon. Peculiar—you side with the humans?"

"Is something wrong with that? Nothing more fun than paying taxes and playing by the rules—don't you think?"

"You surely jest with comedy? Enlighten me. You would choose to remain a slave? Bound by the arbitrary concepts of equality and harmony?" The somnium demon folded its arms, resulting in an awkward overlap over its slender frame.

"At least the rules I'm playing by don't demand mafia-like loyalty and an ethics system that'd make a dictator blush. Been there, done that."

"So, you once tasted freedom and chose chains? A shame, truly." Its grin turned into what appeared as a scowl, but it showed no open hostility—yet. "Irrespective of your foolish decision ... I extend an invitation. I recognize your talent, and offer you pedigree within our dominion," it spoke.

"Dominion? Come on ... you can at least try to negotiate with a better start. Hi, my name is Zane. And you are?" He raised a brow expectantly.

The somnium grunted in irritation.

"I go by no name. I offer you—"

"Nada, no deal. You're obviously some kind of chief or boss. Gotta call you something flashy ... oh! How about Valstrix, or Xeta? Wait, actually ... you remind me more of a color. Scarlet, or Indigo."

In the blink of Zane's eyes, the somnium vanished, emerging from the shadows behind him.

"Intico? I like the sound." Its grin widened beyond its face. "Intico!" it shouted, the air shuddering as it leered down at Zane.

Zane jumped. He hadn't detected movement, but he blamed his distracted pontificating more than Intico's speed. He chuckled lightly, spinning to face the demon. Staring up at it, he was amused by the comical height difference, but he had faced bigger demons before. What fazed him more was how much creepier it was up close.

"Don't wear it out …" Zane suggested. The demon had misheard him, but he didn't think to correct it at that moment. He found it funnier that way, at least.

With a swish of its cape, the shadowy fabric danced in the wind it conjured. A dark chuckle emitted from the somnium's mouth as Zane took a few steps back.

"Call me … Intico. Now. Zane. I offer you dominion. A safe vestige in exchange for cooperation with the Covenant of Augury. You will be granted power and the true depths of its terrors. We somnium have proven resourceful in that department thus far."

"It's always power." Zane rolled his eyes. "Okay. Shoot. What kind of power would I be granted? Nightmare mist? The ability to make people yawn with a snap of my fingers?"

"Among others, yes, actually. We possess a miasma more potent than anesthesia, yet not permanent as death would be. This power and much more could be yours, come Harvest. All you've to do is make a pact as an umbra demon would."

Zane perked up. *Umbra demons?* His suspicion was close to being confirmed. He suspected Oliver and the Siegharts were involved with the covenant, but this was comically convenient for him.

"Alright. And what exactly is this *Harvest* that you mentioned?"

"You may be granted knowledge of this once you have struck the deal."

"So, you wouldn't be able to enlighten me about the true breadth of your grand ambitions right now?" Zane asked.

Intico stared blankly, its eyes wavering with hazy darkness; a gaze that bored into Zane. A gaze that consumed him.

Until then, Zane had maintained his nerve, but now, he realized its unsettling scope. Intico could strike right then and there, but what unsettled him was what hid behind that gaze. He understood why something would seek to recruit him. He wasn't remiss about what he could offer. No. Intico's eyes betrayed it. As fathomless as they were, and with what little emotion he could garner from them, none invoked a sense of trust within him. Aside from his instinct, he had run through the genie scenario in his head far too often to take any transcendent entity promising things at their word.

"Got it," he started. "I'd be inclined to accept your offer if not for the fact that this entire time, you've been looking at me as something to be *used,* not a potential ally. Pretty rude, by the way—should work on your pitch. I give you a five out of ten at best." Zane grimaced.

The rejection showed on Intico's face, albeit not in the way Zane expected. A wicked grin consumed its expression as audacious laughter erupted from it. Intico stepped back, shadows dancing across its form and swallowing it slowly.

"Shame ... but it matters not. You will help us one way or another."

"Hm, we'll see then, I guess. It's been ... unpleasant. Yeah. I'd rather we not meet again, but you don't seem the type to let rejection stop you." Zane scowled. "Go bitch about it on social media or something."

Intico whimsically disappeared into the darkness, its cackles echoing in the wind. Only the bodies of the hellhounds remained present on the rooftop.

"Sanguine," Zane spoke. He swiped his fingers in the direction of the bodies, watching as they dissipated, leaving behind nothing as Ichor reclaimed them.

"Intico ..." Zane said aloud, running a hand through his shaggy brown hair. He paced back and forth, mostly dreading the extra paperwork regarding the encounter with Intico. He looked up to the sky, his expression dead serious now that the confrontation was over. A lot of problems lay ahead of him and the Hunters—he knew that much. Still, he never expected the Chicago assignment to be this convoluted.

"Another ambitious entity of pure evil—great."

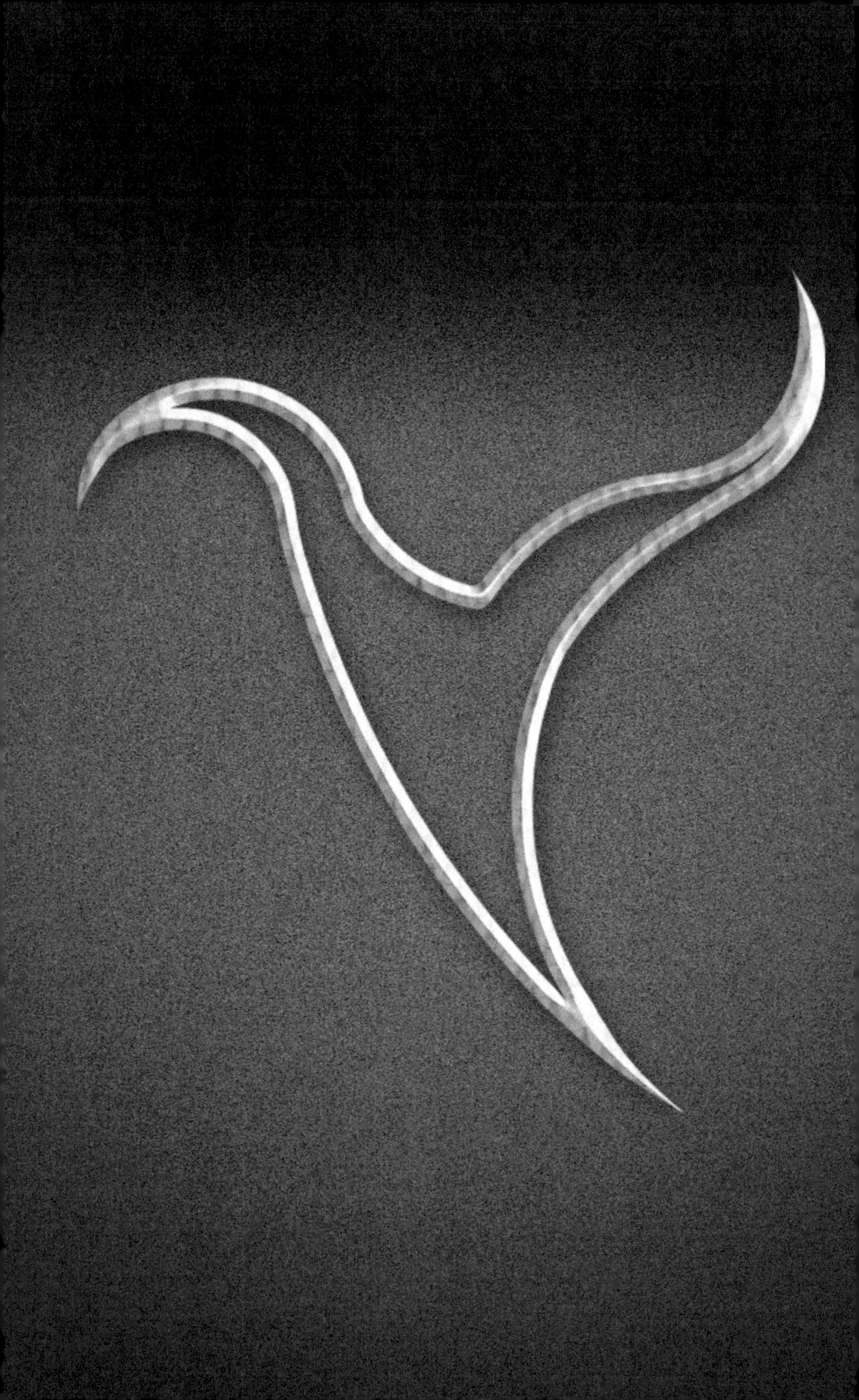

Five

Disparate Harbinger

Why is everything fucked? Kendra thought. Confined within her new body, she remembered everything on repeat: the accursed evening, the Hunters' facility, and the soul-wrenching grief displayed by her mother upon her return. Even her father's stoicism had buckled when they spoke.

Katherine had taken a leave of absence from the department, unable to contend with her grief. Almost every day, after hours of searching, she waited in the living room by the door, as if, miraculously, Kendall would appear behind the door or be returned, like Kendra had been. But the truth remained: Kendall was gone.

Kendra choked up, her breath hitching as she pushed that brutal memory from her head. She couldn't afford to think of it now. She couldn't stand being held up in her home any longer, either. The wallowing turned her room into a den of misery; she sought other stimulation than trying to occupy herself with several videos on prescriptions of the supernatural, several of which were greatly misrepresented. It seemed that was the case when parsed against the slivers of information she had picked up from the Hunters. She hardly understood it herself, even after what happened, but she could at least dismiss the usual suspects of spiritual prescription. With difficulty, she decided to return to school against both her parents' and the Hunters' recommendations.

She was cautioned by the Hunters that she would need to be hyperaware of her status and to ensure she excused herself if any of her demonic symptoms flared up. It was her new reality, similar to managing blood sugar with diabetes—but even more consequential. She loathed it but complied with their orders. The only other choice was death, and remembering the firearms she saw her *handler* carry, she'd deign to guess how that would occur. How it would be covered up, however, she dared not entertain.

Kendra reached across to her nightstand and grabbed a large tablet from an already torn packet, a syn-blood tablet. She dropped it in a glass of water next to the packet and watched it fizz and congeal into a thick liquid. It wasn't red, contrary to what was expected, but a light yellow. She didn't understand it, of course, but she knew it suppressed the symptoms for almost a full day.

Kendra turned her nose to the odd scent, a metallic taste awaiting as she prepared to down the drink. Three. Two. One. Down the hatch. She tried not to savor it. A full eight ounces disappearing with several gulps. She sighed in disgust upon finishing it, but her eyes softened, and she relaxed. The concoction worked efficiently, suppressing her *hunger* and quelling the fire in her chest whenever she went without it for stretches of time.

When Kendra made it to school that morning, she took care to avoid everyone, and most took the hint and avoided her as well. Some offered cheap consolations: the usual, *we can talk if you ever need to*, from those who knew her. But most of all, she avoided Allen. She couldn't bring herself to even look her *closest friend* in the eye. The idea of even broaching the subject was ludicrous to her. And if she lost control ... that was when the Hunters would step in, of course.

She had seen Allen sulking by the bleachers a few times, but she didn't know why. Couldn't be because of her, she figured. She had quit the soccer team. Coach Springfield understood, albeit with remorse. To lose her varsity captain was upsetting, but her sympathy starkly remained on Kendra and what she had gone through, the truth of which almost nobody else would ever know. Everyone knew that Kendall was still missing after they were both *kidnapped*, or at least that was the narrative.

Interactions were short and sweet, the minimum requirement for her classes. All of it was a distraction and nothing more. The semblance of freedom from the Hunters' scrutiny she had at school remained, at least. There was allegedly one hunter that watched over her at school, who she had assumed was Eden, but she dared not inquire. In fact, she avoided him even more than she avoided Allen. And for the most part, that had remained the case until she came face-to-face with him.

Kendra had been tucking her books into her locker, dissociated as she prepared to head to the front of the school to wait for her mother. When she shut the locker, Eden was there; his loathing crimson gaze scrutinized her. She was silent at first, her wariness palpable as she searched for his intentions within those eyes.

"I feel fine, nor do I feel like tearing someone's face off. I swear ..." Kendra spoke meekly and averted her eyes.

"That's not why I'm here, Kendra," Eden said. He folded his arms as he shifted his gaze to the small scar trailing up the left side of her neck.

"Then what is it?" She held her arms, shifting uncomfortably.

"It's hardly my place to speak, and I can't imagine you care to hear what I have to say, but you need to understand that what happened to you wasn't random."

"I don't understand," Kendra said, pursing her lips as she glanced around, seeing the halls gradually empty around them.

Eden cautiously glanced around before stepping closer to her, causing Kendra to retreat against the locker, her eyes wide all of a sudden.

"You were targeted deliberately."

"Those things," Kendra spoke shallowly, her fingers tensing as her nails dug into her palms. Tepidly, she shifted her head up, meeting his remorseful eyes.

"Demons," Eden said, his tone dark and dripping with a contempt that puzzled Kendra.

Kendra recalled the words Ethan had spoken to describe her. Not quite human—not quite demon. *A homuntium.*

"I'm not ... like them. I can't be," Kendra whispered, swallowing the tension building in her throat as she glanced at the exit to the building. A shaky breath left her throat, and she slowly pried herself from the locker, gripping the bag slung over her shoulder. The desire to flee built up inside her, but seeing their respective statures and knowing what he had done to the hellhounds, she knew he'd easily catch her. Forced to contend with his words, the implications of the danger he alleged settled into her stomach as wet concrete would; it roiled inside her in an unsavory message that refused to register among the grief she neglected.

"... I know," Eden said hesitantly, holding his wrist up as he navigated his smart band to reveal his contact screen. "I won't pretend to know the full implications, and I'm not even allowed contact with you, technically ... but still, you should take my number—just in case."

The moment prior, Kendra had considered running past him to get away, convinced he was lulling her into false security so he could eliminate her, but his statement and gesture had placated that worry. She carefully raised her wrist and navigated to her contacts application.

With a flick, Eden's contact showed up, and with shaky fingers, she accepted the exchange request, seeking to get the interaction over with. As unsettling as the ire she gleaned in his gaze was, she assumed that if he had sought to kill her, he'd have done it already. If not him, the other one, maybe.

"If you feel like you're in danger, I'm here," Eden assured, lowering his wrist as the projection from his smart band disappeared. He then turned from her and walked off without another word.

Kendra was frozen in pensive silence for several seconds following their interaction, and she gripped her chest, barely registering her thundering heart as she struggled to catch her breath. As dangerous as the *demons* were, an irrevocable sense of danger assailed her when around the Hunters. An especially damning oppression weighed on her when she saw the inhuman hues of Eden's crimson eyes, which she now knew were not contact lenses.

Tearing herself from her petrification, she made her way out to the front of the school, desperate to go home. When Kendra's mother picked her up, the car rides were quiet. They didn't talk much, but there was at least comfort in their respective presence. She used to prefer biking to school herself, since that usually helped clear her head, but her bike was horribly mangled and scorched, last she saw. Riding it wouldn't have appealed either, given the several dreadful memories surrounding it now.

As her mother drove into the neighborhood, the hunter, Vicente, was waiting for their arrival. He had dark skin, brown eyes, and short brown hair that subtly flared in the front. A large, sheathed knife rested on his hip. Above the knife, a pistol.

Despite him wearing the gray and black hunter uniform she had grown accustomed to seeing, he was hidden in plain sight. She was aware there was a magic that hid them from eyes unattuned to the supernatural—the veil, as the Hunters called it.

Contrasting with his burly imposition, Vicente was kind. Compared to Eden, he was far more inviting, nor did he ever impose himself on her frail boundaries to speak to her. He assured Kendra that she'd be fine whenever he could get a word in with her. She refrained from responding when he did, however. He was present most afternoons, lounging outside her home—her supernatural stalker, as she thought of him. Despite her reluctance to engage with him, a deep curiosity pervaded her mind since the abrupt conversation with Eden about the idea that she had been targeted. She understood little about the supernatural still, and within their custody at the medical facility, she was never given any solid answers or information to enlighten her. Regardless of her lingering fear of the Hunters, Vicente had given her plenty of reasons to believe he would hear her out without condemnation.

Kendra paused by the porch, her gaze flicking to her mother, who ascended it while fumbling with her keys.

"Mom, I'm going for a walk in the neighborhood. I want to stretch my legs a bit," she said.

Katherine thought little of Kendra's alleged walk, and although she worried, she offered no argument.

"Of course ... I won't keep you. Be home for dinner in two hours, tops. Call me if you need to be picked up."

"I won't take that long. Promise." Kendra turned, eyes locking with Vicente, who stood across the street. She approached, his stance shifting as she did. He displayed no defensive body language, but his brow furrowed in surprise.

"Vicente," Kendra called.

"What can I help you with?" he replied in his rough voice.

"I ... I don't think I'll lose control again. You're here in case I go ..."

"Feral? Yeah. I doubt you will, too."

Kendra swallowed hard, eyeing his gun warily before she folded her arms over her chest.

"And what about those ... demons that attacked? Was that just a coincidence? What if"— she froze, her eyes quivering—"they come back?"

Vicente stared quietly for a moment, then ushered her to follow him. She complied, and they walked together.

"Sometimes, these things happen. I can't speak to the reason, but if they come back, we're here to deal with them. That's what we do. Make sense? Hunters hunt," Vicente explained.

Kendra kept her head down, trembling and processing what Vicente said.

"Including me."

"I certainly don't want to."

"How will you know if you *need* to?"

Vicente gave a wry smile.

"We'll know. You'll know. We'll all know. So let's not have it come to that, deal?"

Kendra saw Vicente's hand extending out to her—a gesture of goodwill, and in another way, a vote of his confidence in her.

Kendra was reluctant, reading between the lines that weren't there, parsing out her demise in every nook of the alphabet. Illogical fear coursed through her veins, turning her blood to ice. She couldn't help but imagine that Vicente would sooner turn his gun on her if she so much as flashed a fang, which happened when her emotions became intense—something that occurred a lot recently. But she swallowed her trepidation when she met Vicente's kind eyes, finding no malice hidden within their depths, unlike Eden's.

"Deal, Vicente," she said and took his hand.

Vicente smiled.

"Call me Vic."

They continued on their walk, chatting about various things and exchanging questions. To Vicente, it was a reminiscent conversation that reminded him of his past and how he had become a hunter. As a young man, he was attacked by demons, thrusting him into an unfamiliar world. The Hunters gave him two options: join or be forced to forget. But unlike Kendra, he had retained his humanity—another reminder of how isolating her predicament was.

For Kendra, the conversation was a way of facing her fears—her fear of the Hunters and the demons they hunted. She doubted they would tail her forever, perhaps downgrading her to a less encroaching probation. Her vigilance was essential to prevent a tragic fate, and her newfound hunger was a perpetual battle she would have to fight. Perhaps then she'd be able to focus on living her life again. Hopefully, one devoid of more demons. It was wishful thinking.

As they spoke, the neighborhood became more vivid to Kendra with her newfound senses. Her ears picked up a squabble between squirrels, her eyes tracing the area to see the two small mammals wrestling each other. It was peculiar, but she had been noticing those kinds of things more and more. It wasn't all bad. Paying attention in class was harder for her, sure, but she could gather a lot more information easily. *Is this what it's like to be a dog?* she thought.

The two bantered casually throughout the rest of their walk, and Kendra held her tongue on further questions, opting to save those for another day. Kendra's confidence in Vicente had elevated, a sense of trust brewing with him and what he had said to her. They shook on it, and he hardly suggested himself as a man who would do so cavalierly.

As they returned to her home, Vicente waved Kendra off.

"Keep that head up, Kendra. You're a bright young lady," Vicente said.

Kendra smiled kindly at Vicente.

"Call me Ken."

In the following afternoons, Kendra walked with Vicente around the neighborhood, talking and probing. Vicente didn't suggest he minded the proximity to her either, further displaying his confidence in her self-control. As much as she hated the syn-blood formula, it was essential in her maintaining that control.

"It's gross, in case you were wondering. Tastes like metallic syrup. Would *not* pour it on my pancakes."

Vicente snickered.

"I don't envy you having to take it, but on the bright side, it's free. Can't say that about every essential medication in America. We'll be keeping you supplied until you can afford it yourself. It's pretty cheap and easy to make, believe it or not."

Kendra rose an eyebrow, whipping her head toward him, curiosity overtaking her.

"How *is* it made?"

"Oh, you know—vitamins and minerals packed with Ichor. Stuff is everywhere and manufacturing it isn't too hard anymore."

Kendra pursed her lips and nodded. It was interesting to think that Ichor, the surrounding energy, could be stored in crystals.

"This Ichor stuff ... I need to somehow consume it to maintain my sense of reason and survive. Can't I just ... learn to absorb it through the air?"

Vicente showed an inquisitive expression and shook his head.

"I'm no expert on the subject, but you'd need to consume it in a form your body accepts. This tablet fools you into thinking you're consuming something living, like hellhounds do. That's the case for many demons, actually. Our blood contains the energy naturally, and I guess that's the stuff your body needs more of than it currently produces. It's different for all homuntiums, and it definitely depends on how you became one."

Kendra nodded, letting out a sigh as she stared down at her hand, briefly thinking back to the night she had first seen the hellhound. Demons were fast and dangerous, and came in many forms beyond the feral sorts, from what Vicente had recanted to her.

"The reason nobody knows they're here is because of *the veil.* It's ... a cloak or curtain of sorts that the supernaturally attuned can put up, or refrain from taking down. The reason nobody sees me is the incantation I recite to enter the veil. Insenseilis. Pretty sure it's Latin."

"I take it that's what kept people from hearing me that night that hellhound chased me? I was like ... thrust into the veil?"

"Likely. It's one way they can move around without drawing too much attention to themselves. Once you pierce the veil, you're practically invisible to common people. Otherwise, we'd be on their cases a lot sooner," Vicente spoke assuredly, cracking his knuckles as he strode beside Kendra.

Pensive for a moment, she couldn't help but recall how powerful even the lesser, feral demon—the hellhound—was compared to a human. If her scorned memories weren't embellished, if it was as fast as she remembered, they outclassed humans entirely—even with guns in the equation.

"How do you guys keep up with them? If they're faster, stronger, and have crazy abilities, guns or not, wouldn't they be hard as hell to kill?" Kendra asked, folding her arms as she glanced back at Vicente expectantly.

"We utilize Ichor to augment ourselves. For example, I can bench five hundred pounds on a good day, but with the help of this suit and my training with utilizing Ichor, I can lift roughly triple that."

"I'm sorry. 1500 pounds!" Kendra questioned, her mouth agape. The casual mention, more than anything, astonished her.

"*Roughly,*" Vicente reiterated, stifling a chuckle while patting his left biceps.

Kendra tapped her chin, staring pensively at the street. Vicente was already hulking to her, and the idea of him being more formidable than he already appeared boggled her further.

"Okay, strength is one thing, but unless that combat suit you're wearing is super fortified, wouldn't they still be able to hurt you? I mean ... those hounds' teeth were *really* fucking sharp." Kendra deigned to recall the deadliness that the hounds boasted, and she could only imagine what other abominable types of demons existed.

Vicente snapped his fingers, pausing in the middle of the sidewalk before holding his hand out.

"Right you are. We're still pretty squishy, all things considered. I'd like to think I can take on whatever they throw at us, but if it isn't the physical stuff, it'd definitely be the magic."

"Magic?" Kendra furrowed a brow, stopping and turning to face him, her eyes lowering to his hand.

"Yeah. Some use spells, usually destructive things: fire, electricity, or even pure energy. The suits offer some protection, and we may be strong and fast, but ain't no amount of eating your Wheaties or working out that's gonna protect you from a burning ball of energy hurled at you. So ... we create barriers," Vicente spoke, glancing down at his hand before falling silent for several moments. Faintly, his hand pulsed with a white energy, causing subtle ripples in the nearby air. It was almost invisible if Kendra hadn't focused on it.

"That's a barrier? Doesn't look like it'd do much in the way of defense," Kendra challenged, looking back up at Vicente with doubt written on her face.

"Go ahead and give my arm a punch. You'll see," Vicente said, holding his arm up as he smirked.

Hesitating for a moment, Kendra eyed his arm and the subtle energy that cloaked his skin. She glanced around to see if there were any prying eyes before she raised her arm. Obliging his boast, she jabbed his arm. But rather than meeting the appendage directly, light flickered upon the impact and her fist hovered an inch above the actual arm, repelled by Vicente's energy. Her lips parted, and she lowered her hand, glancing down at her warm knuckles in awe.

"Woah ..." Kendra began watching as Vicente placed his hands on his hips, flashing her a grin. "You've gotta teach me that sometime. That seems super useful."

"I'd be a terrible teacher, honestly. Barriers aren't my forte, and I'm barely passable at utilizing them. Still, I can share some pointers, at least. Some other time, though. When we aren't standing in broad daylight."

Kendra nodded enthusiastically, imagining all the cool things she could do if she learned. Her immediate thoughts drifted to one of the anime Kendall used to watch, and her smile became rueful. She wondered what Kendall would have to say about all of this if she were there.

The two continued on their walk, and Kendra retreated into her thoughts. The days had melded into a blur for her, and going back to school hardly proved sufficient in clearing her head of her fermenting thoughts. There were too many reminders in both environments and not enough distractions. With her bike gone, she also had less exercise than she used to, and she became more sluggish as the days went by, reminding her of another thing she had wanted to ask Vicente.

"I wanted to ask," she said, ducking beneath an approaching branch. A few cars zipped by them as they walked, and it occurred to her that it must look strange, her talking to someone that others couldn't see. She imagined they'd chalk it up to her being on the phone with someone.

"Shoot," Vicente said, ducking under the branch behind her.

"I wanted to go on a small hike. I'd take the Pace bus to the 606 trail. Please, Vic, I need—"

"I'll wait for you at the trail entrance, then. You want some alone time out—I get it. Take an extra dose of your syn-blood formula before heading out on the trail. Just to be safe, k?"

Kendra smiled, her gaze redirecting to the street.

"It means a lot to me, Vic, really. I'll be going tomorrow. I know you'll be on duty."

"Memorizing my schedule now? How sweet. My birthday's next month, if you wanna plan a surprise party or something."

Kendra laughed softly.

"Just ... stalking my *stalker*." She made air quotes, which drew a hearty laugh from Vicente.

Kendra tucked her bangs beneath her hoodie, lowering her head to shield herself from the bright lights on the bus. Sitting across from her was Vicente, who was occupied with scanning through something on his smart band, acting disinterested in the bus ride. Vicente had even kept his hunter uniform hidden to take the bus as a normal person would, apparently not wanting to be bothered with using the concealment spell. Given the uniform was a form-fitting suit, it was indiscernible under his civilian apparel of jeans and a jacket. She couldn't imagine what people would think if they knew he was carrying a gun. Apparently, that wasn't atypical in Chicago in the distant past, from what her mother told her. Kendra wasn't a big fan of guns.

The rickety bus creaked with each groove and dip it ran across in the road. The sounds were significantly worse to Kendra, whose sensitive ears magnified the unpleasant creaking. Luckily for her, this was one of the newer buses, making the ride quieter than it could have been. Even so, she had noticed Vicente shifting uncomfortably throughout the duration of the trip.

Kendra thought about the last time she was out on a hike. It was right before the end of summer. She and Natalie were on the 606 trail. Natalie had never been hiking on a trail not entrenched in nature or on a mountain, and she regaled Kendra with several stories about much better trails that she had been on near home. The 606 trail was at least accessible and well-lit at night; otherwise, Kendra would have preferred one of the nature trails in the daytime. Convincing Vicente to make that commute with her would have proven significantly more difficult, she imagined.

Kendra recalled various trails known for their nature and beauty in Oklahoma when she and her family had taken a vacation to see her grandparents. Her father hadn't been too happy being out in nature; his place was inside with his computers and schematics, unlike her and Kendall.

"Now arriving at—Lawndale Drive."

Vicente slapped the button next to him, eager to get off the bus.

"Stop requested."

Soon, the bus came to a halt at their stop. Kendra stood shakily, holding the grab rail while the bus's wheels squeaked as it stopped. Both she and Vicente made a hasty exit, ducking through the door. When they got off, they had a small distance to walk to reach the 606 trail.

Gray clouds sprawled across the darkening sky, but there wouldn't be any rain that evening. Kendra wasn't a fan of the rain on any day; the thought of cool water droplets on her skin repulsed her even before her change. Instead, brisk fall winds greeted them. However, faintly, there was an even colder bite seeping through the air. Kendra instinctively gripped the inner pockets of her hoodie, wrenching its warmth while praising her decision to wear it.

Kendra and Vicente hadn't spoken much on the way to the trail. Vicente knew that she wanted to be alone with her thoughts, so he was only accompanying her to the trail entrance to wait, as per their agreement.

The rumination crept in, and nearly everything felt lifeless to Kendra. The more her mind drifted, the more her body acclimated to the surrounding stimuli, tuning out things that were previously bothersome. *What's the point?* she thought. She had no Kendall, depreciating motivation, and was constantly wrestling with her own instincts.

Kendra hadn't been horribly disfigured from her attack, but she was left with scars. Each time she saw them, she remembered the stinging, burning, and throbbing that accompanied them, causing her to relive those unpleasant memories again; it was unavoidable to see the way they marred her body. She sought to minimize ruminating on it as much as possible.

When they reached the trail, Kendra made her way to the staircase. Before she could reach it, Vicente whistled to garner her attention. *Right... syn-blood.* Kendra reached into her back and removed her secondary sports bottle. She unscrewed it, dropped the syn-blood tablet in, and waited for it to dissolve before downing it quickly.

Vicente gave a thumbs up before ushering her off with a wave of his hand. He scouted the area for a bench, shambling his way over to it and plopping down. He intended to keep himself occupied until Kendra was done with her hike.

Kendra used her primary sports bottle to rinse her mouth of the metallic taste. She found the aftertaste to be equally unpleasant, reminiscent of a sports drink with a slimy texture. How she'd deal with taking the stuff for the rest of her life escaped her, but at least she could hike in peace now. She jogged up the staircase, making her way onto the paved pathway. It wasn't a loop, so she planned to stop at California Avenue and turn around to head back. She usually would go much further, but she figured she'd have plenty of time to clear her head—and she didn't want to keep Vicente waiting.

Shrubbery and bushes decorated either side of the paved trail, along with the occasional fork into gravel pathways for the bikers to have less foot traffic in their way. Most never used it, however. The trail, being elevated above the streets, carried the same smog scent as the rest of the city, but there was also the scent of nature artificially fused with it. The city's scent was less pleasant to Kendra than before, because of the changes, but she learned to tune it out a bit.

The ambience relaxed Kendra, her tensions melting more with each step. She enjoyed it for all it offered; the breeze that nipped and kissed her skin, the ambience of crickets chirping, the cars passing underneath, and the exercise was humanizing to her. There weren't many other hikers out that evening for reasons unapparent to her. The sun was low, and the trail lights came on. Kendra thanked whatever gods existed for this, praying that they wouldn't short out this time. However, there weren't any red omens gathering to suggest demons would be present. She hadn't been privy to the existence of omens prior to her change. Ever since she woke up in the Hunters' care, she found herself unable to ignore them—their presence always in the corner of her vision if she wasn't focusing on them.

Though the lights granted plenty of luminance to the trail, something else stirred in Kendra's periphery. The blue omens in the area swarmed abnormally, coalescing around one spot in particular: *a man*. He stood a few yards from her, unprovoked by the omens as they danced around him. She couldn't tell at first, but something about him suggested he wasn't human. The omens were too prominent in her vision, and the more she focused on the man, the more she discarded her focus on the omens. They gradually diminished, leaving her with a clear view of the *man* she saw. He wore a black asymmetrical trench coat and black pants tucked into knee-high boots with silver owl crests embedded on top. A strange outfit by human standards, but Kendra was too enamored to pay it much mind.

His silver hair twinkled under the trail light, but more importantly, a similar light shone around him. He shimmered with white particles of energy dissimilar from the omens. His skin was pale as snow, and a winter's chill accompanied his icy visage, and she drew to him and his alluring chill the same as the omens did.

The man slowly turned his head, taking notice of his sole audience. His icy blue gaze pierced any darkness there was and almost literally froze her in place. The man had an aura about him that made Kendra wonder if she was in danger—a strange pressure that he exerted. Transcendent of an earthly presence, he was something beyond what she thought she was *allowed* to see.

"You're not human," he said, his soft voice as chilling as his aura.

Kendra removed her hands from her pockets, her fingers clenched tightly and her mouth agape. She was stuck wondering if she should answer or run. But nothing begged her to run within her body, much to her confusion. Sure, the cold was uncomfortable, but so was the thought of him pursuing her. Something beckoned her curiosity and informed her that running would be both fruitless and unnecessary.

"E-excuse me?" she asked.

"Ah, I mean you no harm. It's just, I can tell. The fact you can see me—react to me. It means you aren't ordinary. And judging by your aura and temperature, you aren't human either."

Kendra swallowed hard. The fact he could peg her status casually confirmed he wasn't normal. No, he was far more peculiar than anything human.

"You're a d-demon ..." Panic swelled in Kendra's chest. The prospect of meeting a demon again terrified her, albeit he was not nearly as imposing as she imagined most demons to be. Logic told her to run, but her instincts refuted it. His claims did little to assuage her trepidation, but he had spoken to something more primal in her, tempering her fear.

"Yes, I am. Allow me to introduce myself," he began, crossing his arms with his palms pressed against his shoulders as he bowed his head. "I am Azazel. Son of Azazel." He noticed Kendra's increasingly confused expression. "Hm ... you aren't familiar with demon customs, are you?" He stared for a moment, examining her carefully. Now that he scrutinized her more thoroughly, it was intrinsically clear to him that she was something in between. "Not quite demon. Not quite human, either. Your fate beckoned a tragedy ... a shame, but you live. No doubt ... under supervision. Am I correct?" Azazel glanced around, his frosty eyes searching for her guardian. However, he found none.

Kendra, petrified, stared in an odd mix of fear and awe. Against her instincts, she determined she needed to flee. Her eyes were wide with fear, but before she could even put thought into action, calmness washed over her, paradoxical to its encroachment into her otherwise reasonable mind. A soft purple energy flashed in her eyes, and her muscles relaxed against her will.

Do not fret. You are safe.

Those were not Kendra's thoughts. They were his, and she somehow knew that—she felt it. Azazel's thoughts and intentions pervaded her own, and a phantom serenity enshrined it. Sincere and true, she determined she was safe.

Azazel frowned at her, his own leer shimmering an indigo color in correspondence with the energy she found herself relaxed by.

"Forgive my intrusive magic, but a surge of energy came from you that suggested panic. Do remain calm, for both our sakes."

Despite how bizarre the situation was to Kendra, he spoke in a calm, soft voice still. She shook her head, biting her lower lip as she choked back her initial worries, primarily because of the spell he had used. Her fingers retracted from her palms, and she breathed a soft sigh.

"Look ... I don't even understand most of this yet, but you're someone important, right? Among the demons? You can make them go away from here, right?" Kendra asked, her voice cracking as she spoke.

Azazel couldn't help but form an amused smile at her question. It was absurd from his perspective, borderline satire, really. He softly chuckled, shaking his head and waving his hands in front of him.

"I'm afraid there's a whole host of reasons why I cannot *make them go away*. Without good reason, I will not indiscriminately infringe upon demons. They are not mine to command, for I am no king, nor do I hold dominion over them. I can, however, stop them with force if I deem it to be pertinent to my wellbeing or the integrity of my missions. Otherwise ... I am but a rime—an ice demon." Azazel sighed, granting a rueful smile. "You are afraid of them, yes? Perhaps the feral bunch, if I were to surmise how you came into your current state."

Kendra shifted on her feet, exhaling a shaky breath. She was baffled at how perceptive Azazel was, or of how transparent she was. It was possible it was both, and both her ignorance and naivety perturbed her frayed nerves.

"Why the hell would a demon like you be here, then?"

Azazel paused, his gaze softening as he offered a paradoxically warm smile.

"Ah, that's simple. There are strange happenings, and I am investigating on behalf of my king and kingdom."

Kendra raised a brow, finding what was coming out of his mouth ridiculous. She wasn't afraid anymore, thanks to the spell he had used on her, but now she was perplexed by this rush of disjointed information, which, in fairness, she had requested. Still, the answers begged more questions.

"Strange happenings?" she echoed.

Azazel stared for a moment, trying to determine what he should reveal to her, or if he should even continue speaking at all.

"Strange energies plague this city, and its denizens go missing or turn up dead. I have a hunch that these things are connected—something pertinent to the kingdom of demons' dominion."

Kendra averted her gaze to the ground. She surmised that the information was relevant to her own plight. The officers going missing, the Hunters' presence, the demons that attacked her and Kendall. It was all connected. The revelation dawning on her inspired a headache to build, and her shaky hand clutched her head as trepidation dripped from her pores.

"It's just a hunch at the moment, however. So don't pay me too much heed." Azazel shifted his gaze elsewhere, his brow furrowing. "Ah, I'm afraid I've spent too much time speaking. A situation begs my attention. Be safe," Azazel said.

Kendra perked up.

"Wait!" she called, but it was too late. Azazel was swallowed by the dazzling energy and carried away in the wind. The omens resumed their normal routines once again in his absence, and the accompanying chill had fled with him. She debated with herself about telling Vicente about this encounter. He'd believe her, surely. *But what good would it do?* she thought. Nothing happened. There was also the off chance that it could lead to a further restriction of her permitted freedoms. She couldn't take that chance, so she kept the encounter with Azazel secret when she headed back to Vicente.

Azazel had perturbed Kendra's returning tranquility, having granted her a revelation that wouldn't settle. *A demon on a mission from a kingdom? Demons have a kingdom?* she thought. Her ignorance only grew the more she learned about the strange, supernatural world she had unknowingly lived in for her entire life. As mysterious as Azazel had been, there was a strange captivation that she couldn't unravel. Powerful and unprovoked by the supernatural world that she had grown to fear, yet possessing a voice that was nothing short of hypnotic and princely—as was his shimmering gaze that froze her mind. Staring into those icy hues of his, she had become oblivious to time. Realizing how long she'd spent thinking about him, she shook her head and banished thoughts of Azazel from her mind.

Kendra was sprawled on her bed, wearing dark gray joggers with a black tank top tucked into the band. Her hair was tied into a neat braid, strewn over her shoulder and curled above her chest. Initially, she hesitated to wear something as revealing due to the visible scarring left from the attack. Atop her right breast were deep marks that showed she had been carved by claws. On her neck and left shoulder, there were several puncture marks from where the demons had torn into her.

Kendra loathed seeing such marks on her once-clear skin. She couldn't help but wonder why they hadn't regenerated. Perhaps due to exactly when she had ceased to be human in her mutation. Even if it had fixed *just* her eyes, it would have been less condemnable.

Kendra's smart band rang, stirring her from her rumination. Accompanying it, a pressure built in the air. Her breathing became labored for reasons she couldn't discern, and her limbs became heavier with the growing intensity in the air. The band continued ringing, and she flicked the projection to see it was coming from Vicente. Vicente never called her that late, immediately warranting her concern. She answered.

"Vic?"

"Ken, leave your house immediately. Something's approaching," Vicente said.

"Huh? What's going—"

"Come out *now*. I have to get you out of here."

Red omens danced into Kendra's vision, pulsing and bobbing. She knew what they meant: demons were near. Kendra scrambled from her bed, fumbling to put on her running shoes she lazily kicked off earlier. She paused for a moment. Both her parents were home. She hesitated to leave them if demons were near.

She resolved herself quickly.

"Mom! Dad!" Kendra called out, but her words were hindered by the building pressure in the air. As if she were speaking into a fan, her voice rippled and caused the omens to jitter. She jogged down the stairs and burst through the front door, not bothering to punch in the disarm code since she assumed her parents would come running out after her. She also assumed the alarm ringing would do them some good.

Upon stepping out the door, the air distorted with contorting energy, as if made of fabric, tearing apart to reveal red thread beneath. The air grew dense, suffocating, even. It was as if weights bore down on her body, making even simple movements more difficult. Albeit dark, the area was faintly illuminated by red omens.

Vicente was across the street, gun drawn and aimed in various directions that beckoned his caution. Upon seeing Kendra, he ushered her to him with a wave. Panic marred his features, and his eyes repeatedly darted from left to right. The increasing gravity pulled on them, but he held steady, refraining from firing until he could confirm an actual target.

"Hurry!" Vicente called.

Kendra dashed forward, but a streak of purple energy shot through the air and crashed into Vicente's chest. A puff of smoke exploded from where the energy impacted, and he went tumbling down. Kendra's eyes widened, and without thinking, she rushed forward and dropped to her knees before Vicente. A sizzling hole was burned into his chest, having seared and contorted layers of his flesh and muscle beyond recognition through his deformed armor. Yet, somehow, he breathed. Whatever minuscule protection his uniform provided had kept him alive—barely. Kendra choked back a gasp, coughing as the smoke infiltrated her nostrils along with tears that encroached on her vision.

A robed figure emerged from the dark. Heavy boots crushed the bushes from which the assailant stepped from. As if materializing from the tears in reality, glowing irises cut through the dark. The being leered at her from within the darkness, their menacing gaze evoking Kendra's fear.

Kendra noticed that the streetlights were off—blown out similar to the night she had been chased. Within the darkness of Kendra's surroundings, the air distorted, shimmering within the scarlet-red omens that shivered within its recesses. And despite how *wrong* it all felt, she turned her attention back down to Vicente, seeing him writhe beneath her. Hearing the difficulties of Vicente's breathing, she held his torso up. Vicente coughed and wheezed, blood pooling in the burned cavity as he gasped for air. There was no way he would survive.

Even so, in Vicente's fleeting moments of life, his one concern prevailed above all else. Backup would be there soon, but Kendra had to last long enough for it to count.

"Run ... Ken," Vicente wheezed out. With his last, raspy breath, he went limp in Kendra's arms.

Kendra sobbed quietly, traumatized by having seen Vicente, the man she had come to know and trust, ruthlessly wrenched into death's grasp. Morbid and grim, she watched helplessly as the life left his eyes. The scent of the violent assault impaled itself in her mind. Burned flesh, armor, and blood alike were amalgamated into a visceral image. Blood pooled beneath Vicente, and she became lost in the glimmer from the omens reflected within it as the light left his body.

Shaking from her petrification, Kendra jumped to her feet, slowly turning to see the assailant that emerged from the bush. The robed entity inched toward her. As she saw their glowing eyes leering at her, she glimpsed several more irises manifest from the shadows surrounding her. Four robed figures, and they all closed in on her. With the faint light, a shared detail among the robed figures assailed her: their varied black horns that protruded from their heads.

Demons.

Kendra didn't know what to do in this moment. Running was a good option, but they surrounded her. She could pick up Vicente's gun and put her minuscule gun training to use. While eyeing the gun warily for a moment, the image of Vicente getting a hole blasted in his chest surfaced—the outcome she assumed awaited her if she pulled such a stunt.

"What do you want?" Kendra shouted, glancing at the door of her house, waiting to see if her parents would come to her aid. The alarm would ring in under a minute if left untouched. She assumed if she made enough noise, someone would notice, but this was to no avail. She was unaware of the precautions taken by the cloaked assailants. They had already cast them all into the imperceptible space of the veil, and those outside of its scope of perception would be none the wiser. No one would perceive them. No one would hear her.

"You will be coming with us," one of the robed demons spoke.

"No. The. *Fuck.* I will not," Kendra said, clenching her hands. "Stay back!"

A demon's gloved hand glowed a soft pink as they conjured magic within it. The aura she detected from it was akin to that of the energy Azazel exuded when he had calmed her down. She presumed it was meant to lull her into a sense of calm, but it was nowhere near as potent as Azazel's magic had been. Still, its influence intruded into her mind, whispering for her to slumber—defying every other instinct present. Unlike the gentle coaxing of Azazel's magic, this magic was anathema to her will—seeking to override rather than persuade, but she resisted. Realizing this, they moved closer. With the subtle pulses of the energy making her queasy, she knew she couldn't let them touch her. Equally perturbing, the lack of a response to her yelling evoked a greater elusiveness to the situation she was confronted with.

An inhuman aura permeated their dark forms, resonating with the surrounding red omens. She had come to learn over the weeks that demons were not only, in fact, real, but that they had discernible qualities to them. One of which was their malevolent auras, at least as told to her by the Hunters. Any other nuances were lost to her.

Paralyzed in fear, she scoured her mind for a plan of action. A buzz came from her smart band, stirring her from her hesitation. She was receiving a call from ... Eden. She answered hastily.

"Kendra, I'm on my way. I got Vicente's distress signal."

Kendra recognized the voice.

"Eden? Shit, shit, *shit*—Vic is *dead*. These demons in weird robes showed up and killed him, and I-I ..." She glanced at the glowering assailants inching closer to her. "I think they want me now," she said, her voice riddled with panic.

The demons approaching her froze at the mention of Eden's name. This had stirred their own hesitation, and they searched around them, unaware of whether Eden was really present or not.

"I've already got a lock on your energy signature. Run as fast as you can from them. I'll be there shortly."

Kendra's lips trembled, and she swallowed hard, her gaze bouncing from demon to demon as they invaded her personal space, now only a few yards from her.

"Please hurry," Kendra whined, and the call ended. She wasn't sure if Eden could make it in time. But she shook the thought from her head. She needed to focus on whether she could even run from her would-be abductors. Her legs tensed as she glanced between the demons surrounding her. As improbable as it was, she saw a slight opening she could take, a spot between two of the demons, neither of which harbored the sinister glowing hand that would put an end to her resistance.

The security alarm of her house blared, briefly distracting the demons, and Kendra dashed toward one, sliding past them when they tried to grab her. Once clear of their immediate reach, she broke into a full sprint, and the demons gave chase to her. With their inhuman speed, it was immediately apparent there was no way a human could outrun them, but Kendra was not human anymore.

Kendra's legs surged with energy, and she sprinted faster than she had ever been capable of doing before. She tore through the wind's resistance, her instincts kicking in as her claws and fangs emerged. The demons called after her, as if that would somehow persuade her. She was quicker than them, that much was evident, but she was not quick enough to shake them off.

Despite the darkness, Kendra's eyes adjusted to it beyond what seemed normal. Nothing was too obscure within its umbrage, something she had noticed ever since her change. She could now see more clearly in the dark, not that she sought to go poking around in it because she could. Because of demons like the ones chasing her, the darkness offered no asylum.

A rush of heat brushed her cheek, and a crackle of purple crashed into the pole in front of her. Streaks of energy left her pursuers' palms, aiming to disable her. They needed her alive, but perhaps aware of what she now was, they were less concerned about inflicting a mortal injury with such magic. Despite how much it caused her heart to swell with fear, she weaved out of their path several times, able to hear the familiar crackles and screeches prior to the magic being launched. Those distinct sounds allowed her to anticipate and dodge them. She avoided all obstacles in her path, reminding her of her time on the soccer team. Much like a game of soccer, she juked imaginary opponents, racing toward her goal. Only, this time, the goal was to not get captured.

They eventually reached the outskirts of the city, and the darkness fled with the well-illuminated block coming into view. She squinted a bit, her eyes taking a moment to adjust as another searing energy blast whizzed past her and hit the wall she had reached. The energy blasted the stone apart with ferocity, and shards of brick projected from the explosion. Shrapnel collided with Kendra's eye, blinding her and causing her to tumble to the ground. Her cracked glasses fell from her face and her left eye bled from the fragment that had lodged in it.

Kendra wheezed and cried as smoke left the wound. She reflexively cupped her eyes, blood spilling between her fingers along with a shooting pain in her head. She turned over and shuffled backward, hyperventilating. The demons closed in on her, and one jumped at her, arm outstretched to grab ahold of her and sedate her. With the excruciating pain that incapacitated her, she scarce had any ability to continue resisting. Shutting her eyes tightly, she whimpered in defeat.

In that moment, the air exploded with the collision of Eden's fist into the encroaching demon's face. They flew back, tumbling across the ground until they crashed into a fire hydrant. With a sick crack, their body contorted in a way it shouldn't have, and the demon went limp. Eden landed in front of Kendra, placing himself between her and the demons.

Kendra panted, her heart catching up to the rest of her as she watched Eden's timely arrival. The demon he had hit stopped moving altogether. Dead. She could even see its faint aura fade, leaving its body entirely. The remaining demons hesitated before Eden, carefully taking their positions in a somewhat triangle-shaped formation.

Cloaked by their hoods, Eden couldn't see their faces. They weren't especially dangerous to him, their energy signatures not at a level he was concerned with. Still, he would eliminate them all, except for one. He had determined he needed one alive. Gripping Avenger's hilt, he took a step toward them, causing them to tense with anticipation of his coming move.

They whispered among themselves, devising a strategy of attack. Kendra wondered why they hesitated to attack with their magic. She blinked in confusion, noticing the pain in her right eye had subsided, smoke sizzling from the wound. The debris had been pushed from it, and when she blinked, her sight was restored, an actual benefit of her change.

"Eden, we should get out of here. There's too many of them," Kendra called to him, but Eden never stirred. Kendra's ears perked, able to hear the demons from where she sat.

"Those eyes ... there's no denying it's him. We need to leave. *Now,*" one whispered.

"Are you dumb? If we return empty-handed, we'll be worse than dead!" another said.

"Shut it and stick to formation. We'll kill him and take the girl."

Eden watched them stir, unable to overhear what they whispered, rousing his ire.

"You guys must be from the Covenant of Augury. This won't end well for you," Eden claimed.

The demons, ignoring his allegation, spread out into the street. Two stood a short distance apart from each other, and the other took a far position beneath a billboard. The formation left Eden and Kendra cornered, but this hardly concerned Eden. Stoic and silent in the face of danger, he didn't waver.

Eden glanced at Kendra, nodding at her assuredly before scowling at the demons. He waited for them to make their move before he'd respond. It was clear from the unperturbed focus in his eyes, however, that he was not afraid.

The demons in front outstretched their arms, fingers opening toward Kendra and Eden. Energy crackled in their palms, and they poised blasts of energy. As they erupted, Kendra flinched, preparing for pain.

Eden drew Avenger, swinging the blade. It shone with his red energy, consuming the magic upon colliding. The blast shrieked, creating a puff of smoke that obscured him for several moments. Before it cleared, he shot forward, emerging from the smoke.

In two blinks, Eden emerged behind the assailants, Avenger coated in their blood with two huge gashes visible atop their cloaks. Blood spilled from their wounds, and they stumbled before falling to the ground in shock.

One more, Eden thought before he darted toward the last demon, who recognized the situation and tried to flee. The demon jumped into the air, seeking an aerial advantage, but Eden aimed his left wrist. The maneuver bracer's projectile fired and streaked through the air before it pierced their shoulder. He jumped into the air after the demon, pulling them toward him with the maneuver bracer's line. Once in range, he sent the demon plummeting to the ground with a kick, resulting in a hard impact.

Eden sheathed Avenger and landed atop the demon, his knee pressing into their chest. He reached down, removing the hood of the demon to reveal the face of a young man with ashen skin, red hair, and green eyes. Such a visage was faintly familiar to him, but he couldn't place it. But what was clear is that they were an umbra demon.

"I suggest you speak before I lose my patience," Eden warned. His harsh gaze bore into the demon, who gawked at him—frozen in fear.

Lying dead around the demon were his comrades. Alive seconds ago, they were all dead by Eden's hand. Before his eyes, he saw only death waiting for him. His fate was sealed no matter if he spoke or not. Its silence was guaranteed.

Kendra's ears twitched, and she shuddered. There was a bite in the air, a raucous pitch that tickled her ears. *A hiss.* The energy shifted in the air once again. It was a pressure dissimilar to the one before, but something much more frightful. A pit grew in her stomach upon the arrival of the appalling energy.

Clapping echoed through the area, and near Eden, Intico coalesced from the shadows.

"Lady and gentleman, it is a pleasure to make your acquaintance," Intico spoke, giving a performative bow as it eyed them with its wide grin and mysterious scrutiny.

Eden was confused at first, staring up at it. Intico was dressed, unlike the other somnium demon he had encountered weeks prior. It leered down at him with its large, ghostly eyes. Eden stood, easing off the demon beneath him, but not before stomping his head to knock him out. Even if he were to have a concussion and broken nose, he didn't want the demon interfering with his stand off against Intico.

"You think you'll have a prisoner? Clever," it said and cackled.

Eden's eyes widened as a foreign energy surged in the air, prompting him to leap back toward Kendra. At that same moment, Eden observed Intico appear above the demon in a flash of shadows and step on his throat with its talon-like feet. The sharp talons pierced the demon's neck fatally, and he gargled blood, choking for a few excruciating moments before falling silent. In the next breath, tendrils of shadows danced around them, latching onto the corpses littered around them and melding them into puddles of darkness.

Eden growled, seeing his best lead murdered by what he presumed was the demon's ally. On top of that, it had cleared the street of their bodies, leaving no tangible evidence the Hunters could perhaps glean pertinent information from.

The sight of Intico petrified Kendra and urged her ensuing silence. Akin to humans in appearance, but not quite; it was the kind of thing that, if viewed from afar down a dark hall, could fool someone. However, its limbs were too long, and its eyes and mouth were hardly contained to its head, permeating a ghastly white color bleeding from its figure. She especially focused her gaze on its gnarly teeth. *Can he kill that thing?* she thought.

"You would kill your own ally?" Eden asked.

"Disposing of a useless vessel, is all," Intico corrected.

"Vessel?" Eden muttered, contemplating the ghastly implications of Intico's phrasing. He gripped Avenger tightly, positioning it defensively.

Intico's left eye expanded, as if raising a brow at the gesture, but it grinned wickedly.

"Eden Blackwell, the infamous demon hunter. This will be a fantastic show, indeed. Now, show me the power of this ... *boogeyman*," Intico implored, shifting its hat.

Eden could tell Intico was stronger than the somnium he had fought weeks prior. In recognition of that reality, he didn't wait for an attack; that could prove fatal, and he needed every advantage he could manifest. He barraged the demon with a flurry of slashes, aiming to wear it down. But the demon was quick to block or dodge any of Eden's attacks. As Eden gained leverage and landed a strike, the demon melded into black smoke around Avenger. Dark mist filled the surrounding area, and his vision became obscured as a thick, pungent miasma covered the surrounding area.

Intico had melded into the asylum of the shadows, becoming a blot of darkness that maneuvered and hid within the miasma. Eden held his breath to avoid breathing it in, more than aware of what it would do if he did. Intico's energy permeated the streets, crawling along his nerves and strumming them deleteriously. It was subtle, serving as an unlikely boon to him, but every disturbance in the air betrayed its position. When he thought it had appeared, it submerged within the shadows once more, employing its umbrage with devious intent. If it had command over taking refuge within the shadows, he surmised he'd have a narrow window of opportunity to counter it.

"Don't tell me such parlor tricks are enough to confound you. I have such high expectations, hunter," Intico's voice taunted, tickling Eden's ears and pricking his nerves.

Time was frozen, but as Eden focused on the faint energy that danced within the veil of miasma and shadows, he waited patiently for the singular moment of its manifestation. In a single instance, it resumed, and Intico emerged from the darkness behind Eden, reaching out to subdue him, but that subtle shift hadn't evaded his unparalleled focus.

Eden twisted. A clean swipe of Avenger severed Intico's arm, the miasma fading quickly. Unrelenting, he continued his assault, slicing off the other arm, then its head. Eden rendered Intico incapacitated entirely, and upon removing its head, Eden held his hand out, palm aimed at the still-standing body.

"Sanguine." As Eden uttered the phrase, Intico's severed parts and body dissipated into white light, scattering into the atmosphere. Eden took a deep breath, the miasma having cleared upon Intico's seeming demise.

Kendra eyed Eden, relieved that he had *killed* it. Her nerve slowly returned, and she stood to her feet shakily, her legs still wobbling.

Eden turned to face Kendra with a stoic expression, if not slightly perturbed from the battle he had emerged from.

"You okay?" Eden inquired.

Kendra nodded, although hesitation was present. She wasn't entirely sure what okay meant in this context. She was fine physically, albeit shaken. Mentally, however, she was more than disturbed.

Eden approached Kendra, observing how disheveled she appeared. Between the chase and the damage she had suffered, he imagined she could be worse for wear.

Eden's ability to single-handedly defeat the several demons left Kendra completely baffled, even more so under the assumption of him being human. It felt too good to be true—the idea that her classmate was a demon hunter. With his inhuman performance, it was no wonder he was the first hunter to arrive. Furthermore, he hadn't shown the hostility she had gleaned in his eyes the day prior as he scrutinized her. She had previously mistaken his aloofness and cold gaze as something to fear, yet there he was, having saved her—again. Still, the thought of Vicente's demise weighed heavily on her conscience. He had died trying to protect her, and the guilt mounted in the brief solace following her assailants' defeat.

Kendra's ears twitched again, her heart throbbing wildly in her chest. However silent things were, however desolate the streets were around her and Eden, something resonated amiss. The omens hadn't lost their sinister scarlet hue, and the air pulsed ominously with the tearing she had witnessed earlier.

Eden stopped in his tracks, and the world itself came to a halt with him. Eden assumed that the disparate omen's malicious aura would have faded already; however, they continued to stir, thrumming with a faint buzz. But beneath this innocuous noise, an ominous clamor persisted among the omens.

A hiss.

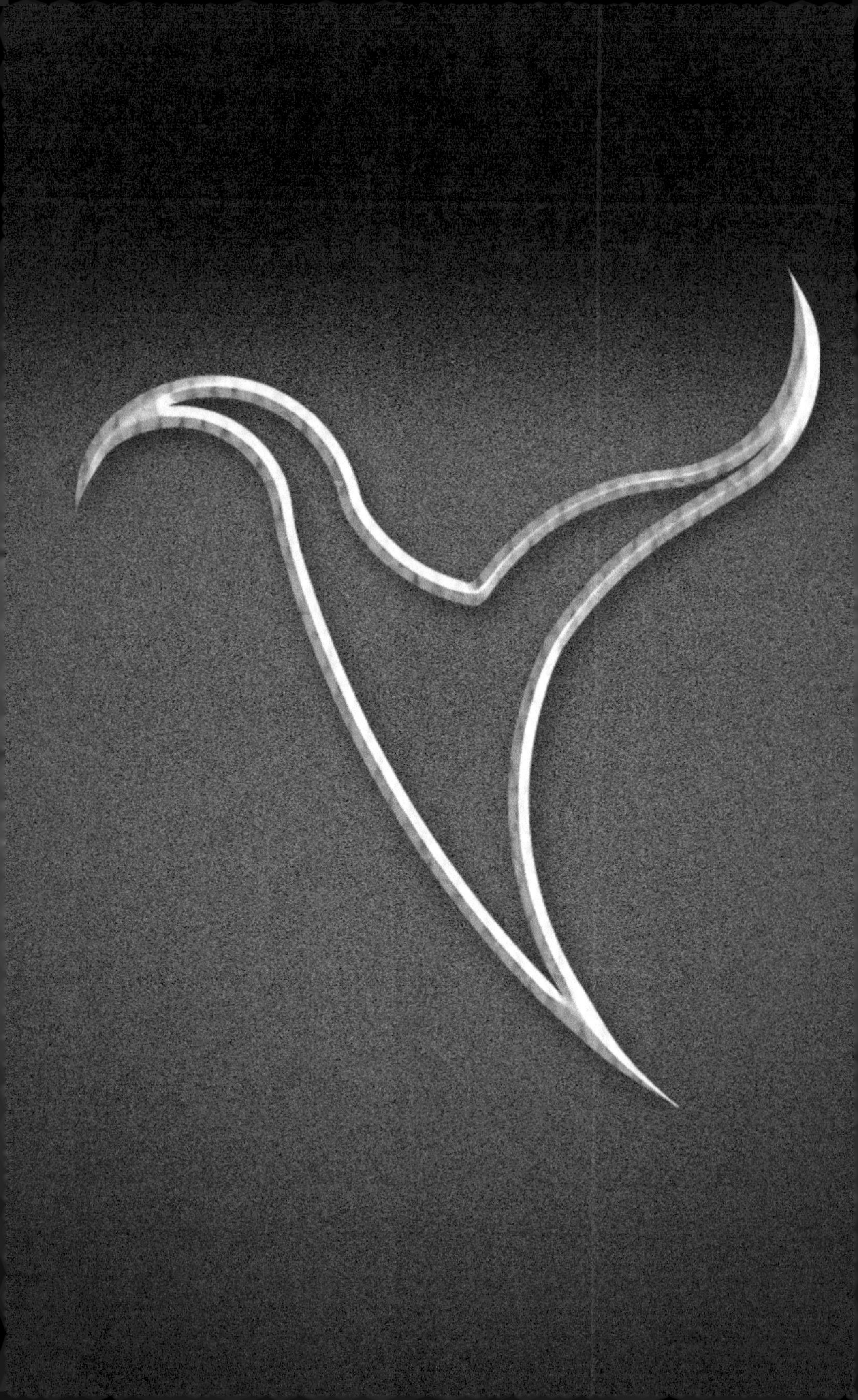

SIX

CRUCIBLE OF NIGHTMARES

Darkness swallowed Kendra and Eden, the miasma swarming around them. While Eden showed a milder reaction, his expression perturbed, Kendra's eyes grew heavy the more she lingered within it. She had seen Eden *kill* Intico. There was no way that its power could still linger, or so she thought.

Eden's heart drummed, the insinuation of Intico's return filling him with concern. The miasma shrouded the streets, trickling from every crevice Eden could discern. There were no visible signs of Intico yet, but despite that, the moments prowled closer, ominously creeping in on him. Hollow breaths left his quivering lips, but his eyes never wavered. He wouldn't relent.

The wind gathered, whipping into a ferocious whirlwind that carried the miasma to a singular spot. The miasma coalesced, manifesting a tall, eerie figure. Intico had returned. Lanky digits extended, gripping the top of its hat and shifting it to an upright position. Chuckling, its voice grew into insidious, audacious laughter.

Eden flinched but drew Avenger from its hilt, finding himself ready to face it once again. But he wasn't sure how he could fight it effectively. Glancing back at Kendra, he gestured with his head to the wall behind her before stepping forward, and she complied, taking several steps back to give him space. He swore he had vanquished Intico, but it evidently sought to install seeds of doubt within their meeting. That false sense of security served as the inception of astounding fear. For a creature of nightmares, a commissioner of fear, there was no greater priority than such a self-ordained prerogative.

"Exemplary. I tip my hat to you, Blackwell. I must say, you show excellent ... potential. But the show is just beginning, and I have so many tricks up my sleeve." Every word that left the being echoed in the air around Eden, suggesting Intico's permeating presence.

Intico held a hand out, beckoning Eden with its long, spindly digits.

"Your move," Intico cooed, its grin widening.

Eden lunged. One slash, two, a kick. Everything failed to connect, a developing pattern in his persistence. Intico whimsically dodged, leaving only a faded silhouette of its cape in Eden's path. His eyes shifted rapidly to track the demon, but Intico danced out of his sight each time he thought he had locked in on its position.

Eden's paranoia mounted, and each of his maneuvers was sloppier than the last. Effortlessly evading Eden's attacks, Intico slowly cracked his resolve. Between the miasma and the fighting, Eden's movements slowed. His eyes grew heavier, vision blurring in and out, as Intico moved out of reach repeatedly. The miasma had worn him down, a mistake he woefully regretted overlooking. Intico had refrained from attacking him back again, tickling his growing concern insidiously.

He slashed, Avenger appearing to cut Intico in two. Its form never bled, however, and it scattered into the wind. *An illusion.* The realization of its sly capabilities—the means by which it had survived the first time—was grossly apparent now.

"Where are you aiming?" Intico cackled, its voice causing Eden to shudder with its oscillating frequency.

Eden quickly turned, facing the tricky somnium once more. Their gazes met, and it held its hat up, performatively spinning the accessory atop its fingers. With a flick, the hat shifted and became a black staff that pulsed and contorted with black particles. Reminiscent of smoke, except it dripped a sludgy substance.

When they lunged at one another again, Intico's staff collided with Avenger, causing sparks and shadowy wisps to scatter into streaks of smoke. If his impairment hadn't presented enough of a challenge, Intico continued to utilize its umbra kinetic affinity throughout their duel. The shadows along the ground lashed at Eden's ankles and served as a retreat for Intico's large form to escape what would otherwise have been a significant blow from him. Eventually, Intico no longer resorted to such tactics and met him head on with their respective weapons, but by then, Eden's vigor had greatly diminished. The crushing pressure behind each collision plagued his muscles, and he was driven back the longer the encounter persisted. An encroaching gravity followed—a heavy contention that would soon be insurmountable in his growing stupor. Vibrations rumbled through his limbs and made his dancing vision skip and jitter.

In a moment of disorientation, Intico took its chance as Eden's arm retreated. Its talon-like feet grasped Eden's sword arm and wrestled it to the ground. As its talons dug into the earth, Intico slammed its staff into Eden's chest, causing him to crash into the ground, landing on his back. This knocked the wind out of Eden, whose energy dissipated from his skin. His barrier was ruptured, leaving him vulnerable.

Eden gasped and clawed at Intico's foot to no avail, unable to gather his power and conjure the strength to free himself. His bones screamed from Intico's strength, but despite how fruitless his resistance proved to be, he tenaciously fought to free himself from its hold on him.

Intico chuckled, amused by Eden's dwindling bravado. As far as it was concerned, he was finally primed for its intentions. Intico's other foot ensnared Eden's chest, talons extending at the webbing to pin him at his shoulders with the middle talon dangerously positioned above his neck, daring him to continue writhing.

Eden deigned to meet Intico's gaze, and it stared down at him with impossibly enormous eyes stretching off its form, consuming the entirety of his focus. Dancing with hazy tendrils of mist, those eyes spelled out an impending fate for him—something other than death. Then it grinned, rows of white sharp teeth glistening, as a dark voice cackled around him. Intico's long fingers closed together, narrowing. Its other hand reached out, clutching his neck in a tight vise, and he gasped for air.

Compelled to watch, Kendra's stomach twisted into knots, her chest constricting as her breathing became labored. With Eden pinned down and vulnerable to a killing blow, the image of Vicente flashed in her mind, gasping as his life fled from him. Eden was next. *Not again,* she thought. She didn't want Eden to die because of her, too.

"You seem winded, Blackwell. Why don't you ... *inhale,*" Intico implored, its other hand drawing closer to Eden's face.

Eden saw lights dancing in his vision from air restriction, but then Intico released his throat, and as Intico instructed, he inhaled reflexively. But it never ended. Intico's hand had contorted into black matter, forcing its way in through Eden's mouth. Intico's arm slowly sank into him through the ceaseless inhale.

Ice coursed through Eden's veins, his face and throat going numb. He had assumed it was a possession ritual of some kind, which neither he nor the Hunters knew somnium to be capable or desiring of such a thing. The somnium consumed the essence of fear, usually through nightmares. They were unlike wraiths, spectral demons that haunted and primed their chosen victim for long durations of time prior to possessing them.

This was no ordinary possession he had ever studied. A visceral and intimate entry, he was invaded as his vision filled with static. Darkness and light danced in an unholy union. Speckles twisted into lines that became a web of numbing darkness before repeating perpetually, crawling toward the center of his vision. Then an image manifested. The black took a bulbous shape, and the white became eyes and teeth. That same inhuman grin mocked him, and those eyes that hungered for a body to inhabit burrowed into him. Soon, he was *there.*

A semblance of light spilled through thick bars opposite him, an unforgiving, cold floor beneath him. When he strained his arms, tension subdued his struggle. He glanced down, seeing his wrist tightly bound in shackles that were bolted to the floor, a faint energy undulating on its etched surface. *Here again,* he thought.

His heart swelled within his chest, shrieking in its own prison. An indiscernible cacophony of treacherous noises reverberated through the insidious halls. He winced, his neck craning as he struggled harder, hyper-ventilating in his futility.

Slowly, the light evacuated, and the darkness crept in on his vision. A whine escaped his trembling lips, and steps approached his cell. His vision was swallowed by obsidian feathers, bathing his cell in darkness. From within its treacherous embrace, an unfeeling, glowing purple eye peered at him, an insatiable greed bleeding from its consuming leer.

Everything faded, leaving Eden to float within a void of pure black. An image suddenly manifested in front of him. As if they were ink on a canvas, several somnium in unison grasped *vessels* that slumbered in the harrows of their own machinations. One by one, they merged into their bodies, becoming something tangible—permanent. No longer were they bound to the constraints of their limited manifestation, no longer dependent on the energy they leeched from humans' fear—liberated from an infernal envy that they were cursed to harbor.

Am I afraid? It was unclear whether it was Eden's thought or Intico's. It was nearly impossible to discern in their melding consciousnesses. Intico was not merely inhabiting Eden's form, pushing him aside to take control. Its thoughts became his, and soon, their respective thoughts coincided. They were becoming one. And it was within the jumbled thoughts he saw it. A darkness marching over the city.

Outside of the insurrection in the depths of his mind, Eden had be-come pale, his eyes consumed by the hazy white that composed Intico's. His skin rippled, contorting with speckles of darkness and light. His fingers twitched, and he stilled, unable to conjure agency over *their* form. And they saw it, a new reach of power capable of containing the mass of Inti-co's being. But as the disparate being behind that power opened its eyes, awakening to Intico's invasion, it blared in a violent rebellion.

Witnessing the horrifying display, Kendra whimpered and dug her claws into her palm, drawing blood as tears welled in her eyes. As if her muscles had atrophied, she couldn't move, and she was forced to watch helplessly. She wanted to run, but her legs disobeyed her desires. Her mind could barely resist the whispers that persuaded her to slumber as is. The miasma, while unintended for her, had been inhaled. But falling asleep was not a permissible option. The image of Intico's uncanny visage crawling in from the corners of her vision was far too haunting to be left with in the seclusion of encroaching dreams.

Intico's entire arm was nearly submerged in Eden, but before the sequence could reach its apex, a bright crimson light shone from Eden's hazy eyes. That light surged through their consciousness, disrupting their unison and ripping them from one another. A loud crack projected from Eden, several crimson arcs of electricity erupting from his mouth.

Intico wrenched back its arm, stumbling away and releasing Eden from its talons. The stump of its arm smoked, and it stared in disbelief as white glowing liquid oozed from it.

The light from within Eden subsided shortly after Intico broke away, and he coughed, hacking up the shadowy essence that had festered within him. He gasped for fresh air and darted to a sitting position. Wide awake, albeit his vision still throbbing and his body waking from its numbness. He trembled, and with a hesitant gaze, he looked up at Intico.

Eden's eyes no longer maintained the crimson glow they had at the beginning of the battle. Now, they were dull, jade-colored irises—wide and quivering. This was the way Kendra had always seen Eden prior to her connection. However, the implications of the crimson hue leaving his eyes spelled something dastardly to her—something she was not yet privy to.

"You couldn't be something divine, could you?" Intico inquired.

Eden's eyes widened, the allegations looming over him with grizzly undertones. Shoving away his fear and trepidation, he returned a dark glare.

"You're no mere mortal. You're something spectacular. A spawn of divinity!" Intico was ecstatic, erupting into discourteous laughter. It widened its stance, its head expanding to encompass a large area of space. The laughter roared as its presence darkened the area. Sapping the light, Intico retained Eden's focus entirely once again. Its laughter shook the air, causing the world to jitter as particles swarmed and the surrounding energy stretched and tore.

"Shut up!" Eden yelled. Ubiquitous in its revelation, Intico had established itself to be his match. But Eden could not afford to be *matched*.

He needed to prevail. There was no other permissible outcome. With his lineage, he should have been more than a match, or so he had thought. *Yet again, too weak.*

Silence ensued. Intico stopped laughing abruptly, and its form shrank to its normal state. It adjusted its hat, white eyes wavering and locked onto Eden with the same inciting expression it persisted in using to antagonize him.

"I am correct, aren't I? Who do you hail from? Twelve deities ... of which only ten are candidates. Your mother is mortal ... so that narrows it to five ostensible candidates, assuming the Primordials hadn't sought to present differently than they are purported to. Who is it? Sere? Verse? Izanagi? Draqul?" Intico pensively tapped its chin, peering hard into Eden's eyes as its grin widened, "Romanus?"

Eden's eyes narrowed, causing Intico to chuckle darkly.

"Ah, of course! The Primordial Deity of Conflict. I gleaned such conflict within the depths of your soul. Rebellious and stubborn—more than I could wish for—and far more than Ichor deemed I deserve," Intico pontificated, shaking its head. Soon, its amusement turned to disdain, and it glared at Eden. "Blackwell, why are you not broken?"

Eden froze. His hand trembled far too much for him to reach for Avenger, and even if he grasped it, his fingers were too weak to hold on to it. He questioned if he was fearful, but he vehemently rejected such a cumbersome feeling. *No, it's the miasma,* he surmised. His adrenaline was the only thing keeping him awake, his vision flickering with darkness as he wrestled his eyelids open.

The merging was a nightmare becoming oneself, and the festering darkness within him had awakened him from it. Despite how uncertain he was in the face of this threat, he knew the answer to Intico's question. He knew why, above all else, he tenaciously fought. Even should he destroy himself in the process, the fearful memory he and Intico had relived was a grim reminder of what was taken from him. What was left of him was a being whose only purpose was to preserve what remained of the world—to deprive demons from satisfying their depravity and quench the undying vengeance that festered in his forlorn heart.

And he would never admit to Intico this sentiment—a near inseparable despair that scorned all that he was.

You can't break what is already broken.

Eden pursed his lips and stumbled back, shifting his position to stand between Intico and Kendra. He raised his trembling hands, willing his body to obey his dwindling imperative. He would protect Kendra above even himself, an extension of a promise he had internalized in the face of the world rejecting such a conviction. *They will not take again,* Eden thought, his sparse breaths no longer catering to his tenacity. For several seconds, he and Intico stared, their gazes locked in a tumultuous duel, for he could offer no other resistance.

Intico's vision flickered, turning its gaze to the side as it detected a shift in the surrounding energy, the surrounding distortion weakening. It snorted, shaking its head. It had run out of time, and hunter reinforcements approached.

"Hm. Seems you are quite fortunate tonight. No matter ... I will have your body soon enough—come Harvest," Intico said.

With its words, an unsettling confusion bore into Eden. He had no conception of what *Harvest* meant. It didn't sound good to him. No matter what, he had to find a way to stop whatever it had planned.

"How do the Alastairs say goodbye?" Intico mused to itself quietly. "Ah, yes—" Intico muttered. "*Au revoir.*" Intico's being melded into a black puddle on the ground, which slowly dissipated into the surrounding shadows. Along with it, the miasma dissipated.

Kendra's head perked, having heard what Intico had said. She understood French enough to know it had said goodbye, and then there was the name she picked up. That name wasn't intended for their ears: *Alastairs.* Kendra knew she'd need to hold on to that information for the Hunters. For reasons she couldn't articulate, she wanted them to know it. Her silence was not an option.

Eden panted heavily, gritting his teeth as he watched Intico dissipate. Intico fleeing hardly made sense until he detected the surge of several energies heading toward him and Kendra. Intico knew it had to flee under those circumstances. He sought to refute its claim of taking his body, but it was correct in one insinuation: there would be a next time, and Eden knew he'd need to be ready for that.

With Intico now gone, the exhaustion hit Eden even harder. His constitution thoroughly battered, and his willpower failing, Eden collapsed to the ground, no longer able to stay conscious. He had reached his limit.

Kendra's trembling legs finally obeyed her with Intico gone, and she rushed to Eden's side. He breathed, albeit shallowly and with strain. He was alive, which was what Kendra cared about most. Despite Eden's slumber, his face contorted in distress, his darkened eye sockets marred with simmering wisps of shadow. She was stumped on what to do next. She didn't have contact with the Hunters directly, only having Eden's number. There were the police, but she hardly could fathom explaining any of this to them.

Kendra heard the distinct revs of large vehicles approaching in the distance. The engines drew nearer until several bulky black SUVs came to a stop next to them. The doors swung open and numerous hunters in uniform rushed out. They brandished their guns, eyes scanning their surroundings while several rested their hands on the sword hilts at their hips. Another black SUV pulled up, and from within it, Jessica burst out of the vehicle, hurrying to Eden's side.

"Eden!" Jessica called. Her fright exploded when she saw him lying on the ground, stirring in distress. She grabbed his wrists, confirming his vitals before turning him over and pressing her ear to his chest. Hearing his heart thumping, albeit slowly, she sighed in relief, her lips curling into a distasteful scowl. She ran her fingers across his jaw before looking up at Kendra. Their eyes met briefly.

"Are you hurt?" Jessica asked.

"No," Kendra said. She had been, but not anymore. Her biology still eluded her, but she was grateful for it at the moment. Between the familiar, maternal fondness, and the similar jade-green eyes and facial features, Kendra easily deduced that Jessica was Eden's mother. She somehow wasn't surprised to know that she, too, was a hunter. Unbeknownst to her, she was detecting energy—Jessica's energy. Its signature and its depth imposed Jessica's status as someone both powerful and prominent. She'd speculate she was even more powerful than Eden. *Guess the apple doesn't fall far,* she thought.

Jessica nodded, carefully and effortlessly scooping Eden into her arms. Despite her smaller stature, she was physically stronger than her size suggested. While her concern and curiosity rampaged inside, a report of what happened could come later. Eden needed medical attention, regardless of what his relatively unmarked form would suggest. The energy invading his mind, along with the darkness around his eyes, reminded her of the affliction that Joseph had incurred. Although asleep, he was not resting soundly. Easing her tense nerves, Jessica carefully carried Eden to the back of one of the SUVs.

"Those covenant worms will pay for this," Jessica muttered.

Kendra heard footsteps approach, urgency and authority in their steps, prompting her to raise her gaze. Ethan. She wasn't too thrilled to see him among all the faces present. Their last interaction was still sour in her memory, which had been particularly devoid of empathy, or even sympathy, for that matter. He incited unease in her with his gaze alone, prompting her to avert her eyes.

"Please enter the vehicle right there. We'll be taking you to our local facility. We have much to discuss," Ethan said.

Kendra didn't know what made her stomach turn worse: his frank tone, or how lacking in empathy his tone suggested. She opened her lips to retort, but then it hit her. A wave of fatigue surged through her, and darkness swallowed her vision. Her eyes sank low, the miasma finally taking effect as her consciousness fled. Her body drained of strength, and she slowly slumped to the ground.

Ethan sighed when Kendra collapsed, annoyance painting his expression.

"Great," he grumbled, carefully lifting Kendra from the ground.

Darkness and cackling. It was all Kendra could see and hear. Intico's echoing voice called and taunted, its white eyes peeking through the dark at chaotic intervals. The shadows flickered and whipped like fireless smoke. Blotches of the smoke swirled and coalesced into various figures with the same white crescent eyes she knew belonged to the somnium. They watched her bumble in the dark. No escape was apparent. Her chest tightened, feeling as if she plunged, albeit nothing contrasted to suggest she was falling. No matter how she flailed, no matter her sense of autonomy, she was as helpless as a floating head.

Distorted voices of those she knew and cared about echoed around her. One after the other, they called her name, crying for her help, followed by snarls and snaps. And the voices drew nearer until they shouted directly into her ear. The voice she heard was the one she dreaded the most: Kendall's voice.

"Ken!"

Kendra shot awake, rising from the bed she had been placed in. Her gaze darted from corner to corner, taking in the surroundings of the unfamiliar room. It was sepia, lit by a single lamp atop the wood-toned nightstand next to the bed. There wasn't a headboard or even any defining furniture in the room other than a faded red single-person couch parallel to the center-positioned bed.

Kendra didn't feel rested at all, prompting her to question if she had slept or had been paralyzed in a hallucination. Her eyes sagged and her exhaustion pervaded her entire body, but she wouldn't dare return to slumber, not after that suffocating nightmare. Kendall's voice had jolted her awake, its insidious undertones weighing heavily on her foggy mind. She was grateful it had awakened her, at least. She could imagine Kendall serving as her guardian angel in whatever afterlife existed; it was certainly something Kendall would have believed in if the situations were reversed. Irrevocably, she missed Kendall, but she shook the thought from her head. More pressing matters were at hand.

With hesitation, she stepped out of bed, realizing her shoes were off, but she found them in front of the nightstand. They were rugged and dirty. Regardless, she put them on; they were intended for heavy use, not fashionable presentation. The unfamiliar floor was not something she sought to creep along in socks, as well. She crept to the door, pressing her hand in front of the glossy black pad next to it, the mechanism releasing and sliding the door open. She faced a long corridor. Several doors lined either side, resembling dormitories from the colleges she had researched.

She calmed her nerves and swallowed her trepidation, tiptoeing her way down the hall, hearing dull chatter through the doors she passed. When she reached the end of the corridor, it opened up into a larger living center with plenty of couches, tables, desks, and other branching hallways. But it was empty, not a soul in sight—initially.

"Yo," a voice called. Kendra's head snapped to her left, taking in the sight of the man who hid in plain sight. It was Zane, who stood a fair bit taller than her, enough to be imposing at first sight.

"Uh ... hey," Kendra said nervously.

With a crisp snap, Zane took a bite of the pear in his hand, his auburn eyes fixed on her. He swallowed, giving a satisfied sigh.

"Awake, huh? You doing okay? Can't imagine you slept well, with the miasma you inhaled and all."

In only a few seconds, Zane's cavalier attitude had managed to dissuade her fear and incite annoyance in its place.

"What the hell are you talking about?" Kendra asked.

"I mean that dark mist stuff, you know ... the stuff that the somnium you guys faced presumably spewed?"

Kendra shook her head, perplexed by the unfamiliar terms he threw at her.

"Never mind," Zane sighed. "In any case, General Blackwell said to take you to her when you woke up. Wants to hear from you what happened."

"General Blackwell? What makes you think I want to talk to some strange woman after waking up? I was getting ready for bed before I ended up here," Kendra said, agitated.

Zane furrowed his brows, glancing down at his half-eaten pear before turning it in his palm.

"General Blackwell is the top general of the Hunters; I highly doubt she'd appreciate being blown off. Besides, she's watching over Eden right now. Didn't he, like ... save your life or something? Least you can do is tell his mom what happened."

Kendra crossed her arms, but his words settled in over the next few moments. She deemed he was partly right. Eden had saved her. And here they were, without any clue as to what fully happened. It was no surprise Eden was still unconscious after the battle against Intico.

"Fine—I'll talk to her."

Zane pretended to wipe his brow and sighed in relief.

"And here I thought I was gonna have to bribe you or something. Alright, let's go."

Kendra rolled her eyes, and Zane ushered her to follow him through the halls.

"I'm Zane, by the way. Kendra, right?"

Kendra nodded her head but refrained from speaking beyond that. She wasn't in the mood for introductions or his jovial demeanor.

Zane choked back a chuckle, shaking his head as he sighed. "Fine, fine. I get it."

They reached an infirmary. It wasn't nearly as big as the other medical facility they had kept her in before, but she assumed it was sufficient for a detached base of operations. It was bright white with a sanitized presentation. Fluorescent lights beamed down, illuminating every corner, much like a normal hospital. Curtains were open, bunched up along the ceiling-mounted railing.

Along the walls were separate, smaller rooms. Zane guided Kendra to the room in the far-left corner and knocked on the door. When Jessica's voice permitted them, they entered. Eden was in the bed, sleeping. Next to him, Jessica sat. Kendra was thankful she'd be delivering her statement to her instead of Ethan, whom she sought to avoid. She had assumed it before, but Zane had confirmed Jessica was, in fact, Eden's mother.

Zane excused himself from the room.

"See yah soon," he said to Kendra, closing the door behind himself.

Kendra met Jessica's gaze. It was still a mystery to her why Eden's eyes had changed colors, distinctly remembering them initially being green—then red—then green again. She approached, glancing down at Eden to see he was still asleep, and his face was contorted in discomfort. He was having a nightmare—just as she did.

"He'll be okay, soon. Just has to tough it out for now," Jessica said. Kendra's eyes softened, taking a seat on the opposite side of Jessica. She wasted no time in explaining the events as she had experienced them: Vicente's call, his death, the chase, Eden's arrival, Intico's arrival, and what it tried to do to Eden.

Jessica's solemn expression held, gradually shifting in perturbance as she carefully absorbed the story. She wasn't entirely sure what to make of it. Kendra was being targeted. That was irrefutable, but the reasoning wasn't apparent. Kendra was a homuntium now, but neither did that suggest any sort of motive the covenant could have to kidnap her. There had to be something more to their actions.

Jessica sighed, reaching out and placing a hand over Eden's chest. Gentle thumps pulsed against her fingers—his heartbeat. Fondness washed through her, easing her tensions slightly. It occurred to her that the reason the Covenant of Augury targeted Kendra coincided with Intico's attempt on Eden, but it was too soon to say.

"I'm glad you're okay. I can't imagine that any of this has been easy on you," Jessica said.

Kendra found Jessica's deep voice to be both melodic and soothing. She reminded her of her own mom, and she imagined her to be just as tough, too.

"I can't say I like any of this ... it's just ... so much. I can't get a chance to breathe," Kendra said, nearly breathless as she contained her emotions. It was difficult. Everything. She hadn't properly grieved, nor was she permitted a normal life following what happened. She thought for a short while with Vicente that she had some sense of normalcy to cling to. But that too was ripped away from her, along with Vicente's life—and nearly Eden's too.

"You should go rest if you can."

Kendra shook her head.

"I've had enough sleep. I'm good," Kendra said. Her head lifted, gasping as a crucial detail emerged in the fog of her mind. *Alastairs.*

"That thing ... the somnium, I think you guys called them. It mentioned a name: Alastair. Then it said goodbye in French. It whispered, so I don't think it knew I could hear it."

"Alastair ..." Jessica muttered, her eyes shifting as she receded into thought. The name, along with the mention of French, all but confirmed a suspicion she had—a lead she would have to chase. Shaking her head, she exhaled raggedly before flashing a smile at Kendra. "I appreciate that information, Ms. Mallory. Thank you."

Kendra stood from her seat, returning the soft smile. Seeing such a stoic bastion of mysticism smile was enough to ease her nerves a bit. It almost suggested things would be okay.

"Before I go, I wanna ask. I'm ... worried about the demons coming again. What happens now?"

"We haven't made that decision yet. Likely, we will be making new arrangements now that it is clear you are being targeted."

"Will ... I be stuck inside again? I don't know if I can mentally handle that, if I'm being honest. I can't allow myself to be alone in seclusion for too long."

Jessica pursed her lips and tilted her hat down as she breathed a soft sigh, shaking her head. There was a sad familiarity Kendra's worries suggested, and she was all too acquainted with their implications.

"Rest assured, we will protect you from them," Jessica began, glancing up with a soft smile, her jade-colored eyes firm and sympathetic. "You won't be suppressed, either."

"But ..." Kendra clenched her hands, gathering the fabric of her joggers in her palms as she exhaled unsteadily. "I'm not human anymore."

"We're one and the same, then," Jessica said, standing from her seat. "I, too, am a homuntium. I'm still here ... and you will be too. You have my word as Mistress of the Hunt."

Kendra's eyes widened, meeting Jessica's as she struggled to find what to say—a protest to conjure. She failed. Her fears remained, but she hadn't a rebuttal to pull from her foggy mind.

Jessica placed a hand on Kendra's shoulder, capturing her eyes as she dauntingly challenged the conflict nestled within Kendra's mind.

"We all have stories, Ms. Mallory. I've heard them all. I've lived them. If you are so perturbed, might I suggest you speak with my hunters? They will gladly share them, and they won't harm you. On the contrary, they would lay down their lives to see your peace undisturbed—like my son has."

Mulling on the idea, Kendra was reminded of the leap of faith she took when speaking with Vicente that afternoon. She'd have never known his story if she had remained sequestered by her fearful caution. The caution, however comforting, fed her ignorance—an ignorance that saw her drowning within uncertainty and rumination. Her thumbs dug into her palm, and she glanced at Eden, seeing his face twisted in a familiar distress, and she could only wonder what *his* story was. After several moments of consideration, she nodded and turned to the door.

"Fine. I'll ... be around."

"As will I, should you have need of me."

Exiting the infirmary, Kendra found her way back to the open area where she had run into Zane. In her absence, the room was now busy. Several hunters walked about with trays of breakfast food. It was morning, as Kendra realized when she checked her smart band. *7:15 a.m.* She fumbled her fingers together, unsure of where to begin, how to approach, or even what to ask exactly. She wasn't sure about interrogating unfamiliar demon killers—as something of a demon herself, no less.

In the background, the television at the far end of the lobby played the local news—another press conference with Police Chief Archer Bronson. Whereas he had once been the affirming, boisterous bastion of the Chicago Police Department, the man who stood behind the podium on TV that morning was hollow and dreary. His sunken eyes and loose, disheveled appearance begged many questions. Even his once stern, booming voice was a croaky whisper of its former nature. Even with the difficult implications, for the duration of his speech, the hunters in the living center watched with skepticism in their gazes.

"I can assure you all—we are sparing no expense in these endeavors. We are not yielding. We draw closer to uncovering these ... evil forces that test us. Hope, love, and your prayers maintain the foundation, the ethos, of our great institution. Continue to bear with us through this trying time ..."

Several times, it had appeared as if Archer would fall asleep mid-sentence, and there was no criticism spared in the following questions from the media. It was genuinely disheartening to watch. With the following chatter in the room, it became the new topic of conversation.

Once again, both exclusion and dejection alike assailed her because of the circumstances that loomed. Repeatedly, she pondered whether that thing, Intico, had been connected to the police disappearances and murders somehow. She felt there was an ominous association with the term it had mentioned: Harvest.

In her persisting uncertainty, she awkwardly sat on a couch, waiting for *something*.

"You know, they aren't that scary. You can talk to them," Zane said, his voice muffled.

But not that something. When Kendra turned her head, she saw Zane with a tray of food, half a bagel hanging from his mouth.

"Hasn't anyone ever taught you not to speak with your mouthful? Plus, that's easy for you to say. Nobody here would try to kill you," Kendra said, scoffing.

Zane took the bagel from his mouth, snickering.

"You don't know that. Besides, we're all friends here. Just go talk to someone. Like ... those two lovely ladies right there." He pointed to Kendra's left.

There were two female hunters by a wall-mounted bar, speaking with one another with an air of familiarity between them. Kendra glanced back at Zane, who was more interested in his food rather than what she'd do following his suggestion. Sighing, she stood up from the couch. *Fuck it,* she thought, approaching them with begrudging conviction.

There was a girl slightly taller than Kendra, who was distinct immediately due to her pale features. She had silky white hair pinned in a braided tail and pinkish-blue-hued eyes. She was an albino woman named Yuki. She was slender, wearing jeans and a red T-shirt that hugged her torso. The other girl was a shorter woman with caramel-colored skin, dark eyes, and neatly combed short black hair. A woman named Emily. She was dressed much less casually, sporting a light gray pantsuit and white cloth gloves.

Their attire hadn't surprised Kendra much, having assumed hunters were hardly present in uniform all the time. With that thought in her head, she thought it fitting that Eden's and Jessica's attired differed from the other hunters.

"Oh, hi," Yuki greeted. Her velvety voice was as delicate as a snowflake.

"Uh, hey. I'm sorry to bother. It's just, I think it's cool that there are even female hunters in this organization," Kendra said.

"Oh? Why does that seem cool to you?" Emily asked, quizzing Kendra with a cocked eyebrow.

Kendra froze in silence for a moment, nervously laughing.

"I'm only teasing." Emily chuckled. "You're that girl we've heard about, right? The one who was attacked by the covenant?"

Kendra sighed in relief, giving a nervous laugh as the women eyed her curiously.

"Sorry, I'm still not used to all of this. Not sure about *the covenant,* but those *demons* came for me ... yeah. I was curious about how things function around here. How you guys came to be hunters ... if you don't mind me asking, that is."

"Well, let's start with names," Yuki said. "I'm Yuki Schaeffer. And this is Emily Grayson."

"Yuki, Emily, I'm Kendra—Kendra Mallory."

"Pleasure to make your acquaintance," Emily said cordially.

Kendra smiled a bit, finding them to be agreeable.

"So, you don't mind me asking questions about all of *this*?" Kendra asked.

"Shoot," Yuki said.

Kendra gathered herself, clearing her throat and taking a seat on the stool beside them.

"Well, it's not like you guys have flyers or anything. How do people join or even come to know about this? Vicente mentioned something about a connection to the military ... but we didn't get far into that conversation before my mom called me back home."

Emily furrowed her brow, snorting as she crossed her arms over her chest.

"Well, sometimes it's a family line thing. Lots of families stay in the field, like mine. Whereas others find themselves joining through exposure to the world of demons, and as Vicente mentioned, some join from the military, should they have the aptitude and a willingness after being briefed. If they refuse, they get their memories wiped and go about normal service. We are technically a *secret* branch of the military, but the specifics are hard coded from public scrutiny."

Kendra nodded along. She was somehow not surprised to learn they could wipe memories. It was the least shocking thing given what she had experienced of the supernatural thus far. She turned her attention to Yuki when Emily stopped speaking, expecting she had an interesting story as well.

"As for me—I was exposed in my late teen years. I was offered a chance to join by Ethan, and I took it," Yuki chimed, keeping her own situation vague and brief.

"So ... you're kind of like me? Except for the joining part, I mean. I was attacked and barely survived. I was saved by a hunter. My classmate—Eden," Kendra said.

"Eden? He's a decent kid. Very strong, almost too much for his own good. I swear that kid doesn't listen to orders for shit sometimes," Emily said.

"Eden is ... nice," Yuki said, prompting Kendra to purse her lips with a skeptical stare.

"I'm not sure ... if that's the adjective I would use to describe him," Kendra said, chuckling nervously as she recalled his blood-hued eyes and how imposing he was.

As Yuki and Emily spoke further about their experiences as hunters, Kendra was amazed by the scope of their work, given how normal they otherwise were.

But before they could explain, Kendra's ears twitched, picking up the sounds of whirring machinery and frequencies neither Yuki nor Emily reacted to. She winced slightly, unable to continue focusing on the conversation. Jolting from her seat, she groaned softly, abruptly excusing herself. She needed to find the source of that noise and shut it up.

Stumbling, her ears led her to a separate section that branched from the lounge. She came to a large doorway that opened into a spacious garage. Various blacked-out vehicles remained stationary inside—the same kind she had seen the night prior.

Several humans tinkered with the vehicles and disassembled machinery and weapons. Some of these devices were foreign to Kendra, which surprised her, especially given her time working in James's shop. The way the people diligently worked on the unfamiliar technology reminded her of the days at Ohm's Cadence with Sal, Jones, and Arman.

She didn't linger to reminisce, however. The pitch shot through her again and she clutched her ears tightly. She whimpered while her body tensed. Eyes fell on her, seeing as she had trespassed into the space.

"Shut—it—off!" Kendra yelled. Cutting through the ambience of the garage, various heads poked out with inquisitive eyes, their expressions contorted with concern. The attention created a contrast, allowing her to pinpoint the direction the pitch came from at last. One head hadn't poked out—a boy with blond hair and muffs over his head, explaining his obliviousness to Kendra's plea. Reacting on instinct now, she marched over with urgent desperation in her steps.

It was a small spherical object with several small holes along its surface. Kendra's hand met the table and clutched the device the pitch came from, her claws scraping across the wood as she crushed it. A growl left her lips, her breathing heavy with puffs of smoke bellowing from the corners of her mouth. She came to her senses shortly, her ears liberated from the torture they had been subjected to. Staring up at her were the largest blue eyes she had ever seen. They showed shock, which hardly surprised her. His glazed eyes beckoned her guilt, causing it to swell inside her as she tore her own eyes away from the boy.

The teenage boy, who wasn't much younger than Kendra, was a junior engineer by the name of Andrew. He swallowed hard, perturbed with both fear and wells of disappointment as he stared up at Kendra's inhuman appearance. Trembling, his gaze warily shifted to the claws that were still deeply embedded in the surface of his desk.

"H-hey, I was working on that," Andrew squeaked.

Kendra's expression softened, and she breathed deeply to ease the tensions in her fingers, causing the claws to retract as she pulled her hand back. Her heart throbbed wildly in her chest, lashing against its constraints despite the relative quietness now. The unpleasant stimulus of the noise had set something primal in her off—something she was both ignorant of and unwilling to delve into.

"I am—so sorry. I-I don't know what came over me. That noise hurt, and I just ... reacted," Kendra said, her voice resigned to shame. "Look, I can pay you back."

"Oh, trust me, you couldn't afford that. It costs, ballpark, around ten thousand a unit," Zane said.

Kendra snapped her head around to see Zane. And more importantly, she saw the other hunters with their guns drawn on her. With the sight of brandished weapons, her fear instantly overshadowed her chagrin. With bated breath, her muscles tensed as she exhaled shakily.

"Now, now, put those things away. She isn't a threat," Zane scolded. Perpetually lackadaisical, he failed to sound concerned even with such dangerous circumstances. Reluctantly, the hunters lowered their weapons, resuming their work.

Kendra breathed a sigh of relief, holding her chest. She thought she had screwed up irreparably there, and she had doubted her excuses would prove sufficient in dissuading them. After a moment, she composed herself, discarding her worries for the moment.

"Are you following me, Zane?" Kendra asked, raising her head to stare him down.

"You went running out of the lounge area all of a sudden and bolt toward the garage while groaning in pain. Excuse my curiosity," Zane protested. "But yeah. I gotta keep an eye on you for now. Nothing personal." Zane yawned, stretching his arms above his head.

Kendra sighed, shook her head, and returned her attention to Andrew, whose large eyes hadn't pulled away from her. She retracted her hand slowly, mumbling another apology to him.

"Wait … did you say *ten thousand?* For *that?* How can you guys even afford all of this?" she asked in exasperation, snapping her attention back to Zane. How a tiny earpiece device cost so much money, she was oblivious to.

"You've seen this country's defense budget, right?" Zane asked, albeit rhetorically.

"Oh, dear God, spare me," Kendra groaned.

"Um … I exist, you know," Andrew interjected.

Despite how imposing Kendra was in Andrew's mind, she was beholden to his mercy, having impulsively and unfairly destroyed his property. There was no way she could afford to replace it. She returned her gaze to him, worry eating away at her. Unintentionally, she gave Andrew puppy-dog eyes while slumping her shoulders.

"S-sorry … I don't know how I'll possibly afford the damage."

Andrew blushed, diverting his eyes to the smashed device and reaching out to fumble with it, peeling away layers of plastic and films.

"Luckily, the casing is the only thing really broken, along with a few pins I can solder back on. Don't worry about it, okay?" Andrew said. Andrew stood, turning to face Kendra with a tense expression. He bit his bottom lip, his posture becoming abnormally stiff. He was shorter than Kendra, prompting him to look up at her timidly.

Kendra furrowed her brows, pursing her lips as she glanced to the side.

"Are, uh, you sure? I feel—"

"Don't worry about it. Changing the subject … you're that guest everybody's been talking about, right? I'm, uh, Andrew. Nice to meet you," Andrew said, his words hurried and his tone shrill.

"Woah, woah, Andrew. One breath at a time, buddy," Zane said, holding in his chuckle. "He's our junior engineer. Kid's one of the best hackers you could ever meet, too," Zane said.

Andrew huffed, folding his arms defiantly.

"I don't need you to introduce me, Zane. I can handle myself just fine." Andrew pouted.

"Oh, my bad. Let me leave you to it, then," Zane replied with an amused smirk before he walked off, waving to one of the other hunters in the room before mingling with them.

Kendra studied Andrew. She found it odd someone as young as him could be a hunter, but then again, so was Eden. Kendra developed a smile, finding his awkward demeanor to be endearingly cute.

"No way. I worked with a bunch of engineers and technicians. How did you even find yourself in this position?"

Andrew's blush darkened. He hadn't expected Kendra to take an interest in an extended conversation. A weight lifted from his chest, his initial hesitation to info-dump assuaged. He shifted his weight on his feet and rubbed the back of his head.

"Total accident, really. So, I used to live in an orphanage for sick kids and really loved technology and computers, so ... I studied all that sort of stuff. Hyperfixation, I think it's called? Anyway, I learned everything I could, and I'm tinkering with this radio device one day, playing with various frequencies. Then, I access this channel where I'm listening to these two *secret agents* discussing some really dark stuff. Demons and the like! I thought it was just some joke until they realized the channel had been compromised and came knocking. It was Zane and another hunter named Yuki. You probably haven't met her, but she's in this base too, so maybe? Anyway, they both started asking me questions.

"One thing led to another, and we end up uncovering this huge conspiracy about demons using children from my orphanage as sacrifices. Almost got sacrificed myself, too. Then next thing you know, I got offered an education, and one of the hunters I met served as my mentor and adopted me. So here I am. Oh, uh ... did I just overload you with all that? I'm sorry ... it all worked out in the end—I swear."

Kendra listened with bated breath, extremely interested in the finer details of the story, and the obvious implications of such a nefarious plot unfolding. *Orphanages and sacrifices to demons? Would make for one hell of a movie,* she pondered, and when Andrew apologized, she shook her head, dismissing it.

"No! Not at all, it's just ... wow. The women I just talked with weren't kidding about the gravity of the stories here. I'm glad that everything worked out for you in the end." Kendra offered a kind smile, leaning down to scan his desk. "We get to meet now, and you get to work on this really expensive tax-funded stuff."

Andrew's eyes sparkled, and he silently celebrated, having kept Kendra's attention. However, he hardly assumed he would retain it, usually finding most weren't interested in his personal projects—like the one Kendra had destroyed.

"So ... I'm currently working on this device. It's a sonic grenade, and I was just testing out the frequencies it could emit. That must have been what you were hearing. Sorry again about that. I didn't know your ears would even pick it up. I'm impressed. The frequency is in a range undetectable by humans, so I'm surprised you can hear it."

Kendra's face sank at the mention, as she was reminded once again of her inhuman traits. Her change in expression had been obvious, and Andrew tugged the webs of his gloves awkwardly, averting his eyes in the extended pause.

"I'm, nothing special, really. Just ... Kendra," she spoke, telling herself this more than him.

"Y-yeah. And I happen to think Kendras are pretty cool," he squeaked, which drew a small laugh from her. Nodding his head with a reassuring grin, he turned back to his desk, grabbing various modules and blueprints he proclaimed he drew up before explaining the inner machinations of his ideas.

Kendra enjoyed hearing him explain more of his technology. She considered his focused rambling to be endearing, albeit with stutters and flustered corrections. Gradually, his words became almost mute to her as a pang shot through her stomach. A dull throb spread throughout the various reaches of her body and pecked at her mind to feed. She was *hungry*. And not in the way that she preferred. With rapid, shallow breaths, she chewed on her lower lip, trying to drown out her instincts and suppress the developing urges.

With a tap on her shoulder, Kendra was pulled back to reality briefly. She turned to see Zane's knowing smile.

"Hey, Andrew, I'm gonna go ahead and steal Kendra. K?" Zane said.

Kendra's pupils dilated, stretching between her inner demon and humanity in a tug-of-war within her mind. With a reluctant nod goodbye, she bit her bottom lip to stifle a groan.

"Talk to you later, Andrew," Kendra said, offering a wry smile before quickly spinning around. "Talk later," Andrew chirped.

With a last glance, Kendra saw his smile, and her own expression softened, warming with the image of such a serene, genuine smile. She followed Zane to the corridor, and he reached into his coat pocket. His hand retreated with a water bottle, already pre-prepared with the familiar amber tint. Kendra clutched the bottle, uncapping it before tepidly sipping from it, causing her face to sour.

"Not bad having me around after all, huh? You gotta be on top of this. Even if it's uncomfortable. Andrew wouldn't have even cared if you said so. Plus, doubt he'd mind if it meant talking your ear off about his projects," Zane said, snickering as he shoved his hands into his coat again.

Reality imposed on her with each dreaded sip she took from the bottle. There was no greater displeasure than her reliance on the syn-blood. As the unsavory serum lingered on her tongue, she wondered if her voracious hunger would forever persist. Perhaps she could abstain more someday. Perhaps she could find solace in some other alternative. Until then, there was a sense of suffocation. A prisoner to her own body, and a rapidly fleeting will in tow.

That was all Kendra could think about. She crushed the bottle in her hand when she finished, clenching it tightly with a trembling fist. Her mind drifted to the festering darkness within her. She hadn't the words or concept to explain it exactly, but there was malice deep within her. She hadn't believed in the soul, no matter how many explanations Kendall had given her. She had thought the fermenting turmoil inside of her to be something bound in flesh—corporeal and observable with science. Regardless of what she understood, despair consumed her mind once again. And even in the glimpse into the paranormal, and how seemingly normal it was among the Hunters, she felt a part of her would never truly be accepted.

Ahead of her, she saw despair and the barrel of a gun. If the trigger was pulled then, she would have been dead before the bullet hit. Something else would die in her place. A creature once called Kendra.

A demon.

Kendra awoke the next morning, her mind temporarily assuaged from rumination. The despair had receded for now. Thoughts of grief forever festering, she buried them to find her will to carry out basic self-care: get up, do her hygiene, and dress. With her own clothing dirty, she was provided with generic, ill-fitting clothes that were likely purchased from the nearest clothing outlet. It was better than wearing the same dirty thing for several days in a row, but she wasn't allowed to go retrieve her belongings at home yet. That would be perilous, a risk they weren't willing to take. She had no guardian with Eden out of commission, and the demons prowling about Chicago, and other unsavory realizations, threatened her wellbeing. There was no hope of her making any sort of argument as things stood.

She had gotten to speak with her parents, at least. The case in which she had left was alarming, to put it both figuratively and literally. When she had remembered to check her smart band, there were several missed calls. Under normal circumstances, as was the case with most teens, she'd be fearful of the consequences of neglecting her phone. In this case, she was remorseful for how worried they must have been again. She worried more about them losing their only remaining daughter than she did her own sanity, in a sense.

It was up in the air what would happen from then on, and the limbo was as oppressive as everything else. Even so, despite the bounty of hunters at their disposal, she hadn't imagined they were eager to throw another into harm's way if it meant she could go home—an idea that would potentially place her parents in peril, too. She dismissed the idea of going home on those grounds alone. She had assured her parents over the phone that she would keep in regular contact in the meantime, a mercy granted by *Organization X.*

Kendra was up earlier than she had been the day prior and with more rest now that the miasma had worked out of her system. It was a wonder what avoiding inhaling nightmare demon miasma could do for the health. With a more rejuvenated mind and her morning intake of syn-blood, she left the room.

Kendra crept through the halls of the corridor, careful not to wake any of the hunters. It was an easy path to the infirmary where she had been the day prior. Although some staff lingered inside, they hadn't paid her much mind, much to her preference, and she stopped at the door to Eden's room. A pin drop could be heard in the silent ward, but in Kendra's case, she could hear every subtle sound: breathing, the siphoning of IVs into patients, and the conversations through the doors. The words were muffled, but she could distinguish what was being said at least. With curiosity, she discreetly propped against the wall next to Eden's door and listened.

"You met Intico? That especially tall somnium wearing a tattered magician's getup, right?" Zane said.

"Yeah. That was it," Eden said. "It wanted me ... my body."

"Checks out. It tried to recruit me a few weeks back. Demon is definitely scheming something big if it wants your body. Called it Harvest, if I remember correctly."

The two were silent for several moments. Eden sat up in his bed. He was groggy after sleeping for so long, but especially prevalent was the memory of Intico's violation. However briefly it had merged with him, it was indescribably traumatizing. He easily considered it to be among the top three worst moments of his life.

"Why did Intico want your body? Don't tell me ..."

Eden shifted in discomfort. He gripped the blanket that covered his lower half tightly. The thought of Intico peering into the fibers of his being, peeling away the veneers and laying him bare before it, encompassing and consuming all he was—almost—was more than terrifying. That *thing* had granted him a fresh reminder of how visceral his reality was. He was unsafe. With an unsteady breath, he nodded, his eyes quivering.

"It knows I'm a demigod."

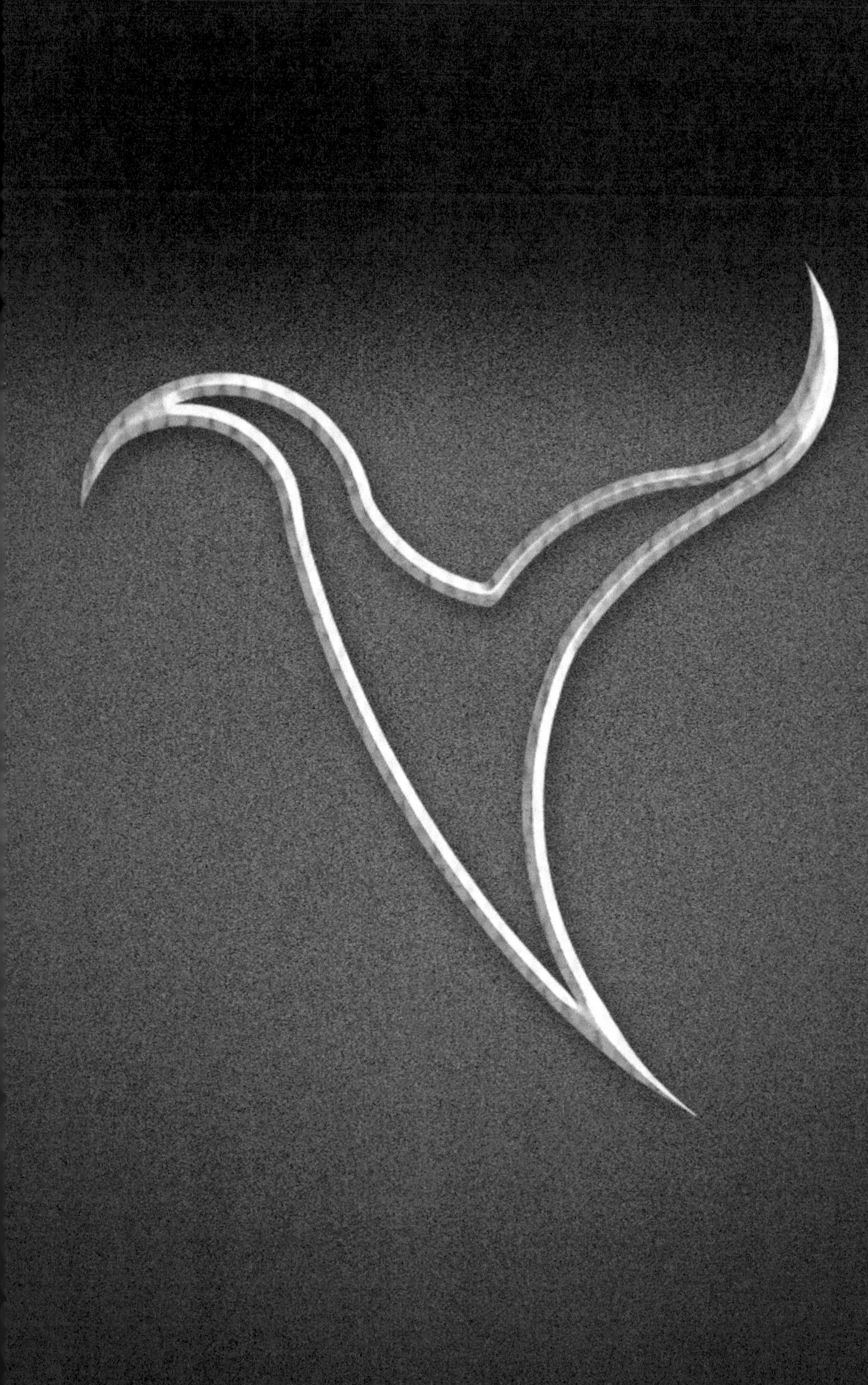

Seven

Remembrance of Repression

As fickle as it seemed of the Hunters, Kendra was still permitted to attend school. Contrary to what she had expected, they did not restrict her freedoms—at least within the bounds of reason. After her attack at home, there was no doubt the Covenant of Augury endeavored to seek her once more. Tribulations aside, she had a new guardian—Eden, much to his vindication. He was appointed to watch over her at school until it was time for her to return to the base. Despite his formidable prowess, danger still presented itself in the ever-looming threat the covenant posed.

With Intico still out on the prowl for Eden, and the pervading faction that sought Kendra, it appeared counterintuitive to pair the two. It begged the question of a greater issue present or a dynamic she was unaware of. Ethan had discussed the arrangements with her and Eden that Sunday. She was to be escorted to and from school, with no unnecessary errands in between. There was a hard curfew before nightfall, something deemed necessary because of the particulars of how most demons operated primarily at night. At night, the collective fear of humankind spurred the pervasive energy to become similar to their home realm. Such fear would cause Ichor's veins to become ripe with sin and malice. Compounding this phenomenon, when human activity was scarce, demons garnered less attention in their predation.

The nature of demons eluded Kendra the more she was informed of it, so far as the human perspective had detailed. She couldn't be bothered to remember it all. Despite her struggle to grasp it, she knew what the Hunters did was necessary—dispatching demons and dealing with the underbelly of the world that eluded greater society.

Ethan had mentioned he would meet with her parents when the agreement would be established, but Kendra knew that wouldn't go well, nor did it. When they had met, her parents protested vehemently. The vague explanations did little to assuage their refusal. Albeit the vagueness was necessary, the parents' ignorance to the supernatural rendered any efforts of rhetorical persuasion ineffective. But there wasn't a negotiation or a compromise; there was an attempt at explanation. And despite Kendra loathing the further loss of her freedom, the terror of potentially involving her parents in the covenant's conspiring was far more pressing.

The conversation became bitter, and her brief time home was drawn to a close. She was instructed to gather her belongings, which she begrudgingly obliged, and she packed a few outfits, hygiene items, and her syn-blood tablets she had left behind. Hearing her parents argue with Ethan downstairs made for a grizzly ambience as she said goodbye to the familiarity of her room.

Kendra rummaged through her drawers, tossing items clumsily into her suitcase. Once she had mostly cleared the drawer, she saw a black feather protruding from beneath one of her bras, and she frowned, remembering what it was. Pulling it from beneath the clothing, she held it up. A small dream catcher Kendall had gifted her years ago. It had been when Kendall first got into Wicca and Spiritualism.

The dream catcher was designed as a triple moon with a pentagram in the center, and dangling beneath it were black and cyan beads along strings decorated with black feathers, making it resemble a bird's tail feathers. Kendall had always been good at crafting things, and Kendra remembered seeing her recording a video when she had made it before gifting it to her.

Setting the dream catcher back in the drawer, Kendra opened the browser on her smart band, typing in the address to the vlog Kendall had made long ago. There was a thumbnail plastered on the front page of Kendall in a dark, flowy shirt with her nails painted the same way they had been when she had died. The videos had been uploaded every morning, titled as daily tarot readings, but there hadn't been one uploaded on the day of the attack. Kendra stifled a sob upon realizing this.

Kendra breathed an agonizing breath, shaking her head before swiping away the holographic projection, closing the drawer, and quickly gathering her suitcase. Making her way downstairs, she came to the foyer where her mother and father spoke with Ethan and a high-ranking hunter she was unfamiliar with.

Kendra's mother turned to face her, wearing a distressed expression that Kendra hated to see. The messy, fraying hairs and sunken features marred her mother's face, and a pang of guilt shot through Kendra as the gravity of the situation dawned on her. It has been more than their safety that was destabilized by the coming arrangements, but the vestiges of their peace as well.

"Please, Kendra," Katherine pleaded, her face glossy with tears.

"It's ... not safe for any of us if I remain here, Mom."

"What's threatening you? What ... really happened that evening, Kendra? I promise I won't be upset—please. I just ... need you to tell me what's happening."

Kendra breathed sharply through her clenched teeth, shaking her head as she cast her gaze to the floor, unable to handle seeing her mother in that state.

"I—can't. I'm sorry. I'll be in contact. I'll continue to call and text every day. I promise. I can't stay, even if I wanted to," Kendra spoke, her voice raspy and quiet as she walked toward her mother, dropping her suitcase and pulling her into a firm hug. Kendra buried her face in the crook of her mother's neck and shoulder, breathing in her scent deeply as she embraced her. Eventually, that eternal embrace came to an end, and she looked up at her father.

Aaron's own expression showed deep sorrow and regret. He approached Kendra, reached out, and pulled her into a firm hug. He placed a palm atop her head and kissed her forehead before exhaling softly.

"I'm sorry I couldn't be here for you more. Don't hesitate to reach out to either of us. We love you more than words could ever describe, and we'll miss you every second you're not here, so don't think we won't expect those calls and texts. Double promise?"

Kendra pursed her lips, shutting her eyes tightly as she gasped and nodded her head against her father's chest.

"Double promise," Kendra spoke, carefully prying away from him, scooping her suitcase up, and marching toward the door, meeting Ethan's divorced gaze, shaking her head before walking past him without another word.

"No harm will come to her in our custody. That is my promise to a mother and a father," Ethan spoke, turning from them as he walked away.

Without further interaction, Katherine and Aaron watched as the hunters and Kendra drove off in a black SUV.

The next morning, Kendra and Eden sat in an SUV on their way to school. It was a Monday, ushering in a long day that followed a long weekend. It was clear to see that Kendra was still exhausted after everything. There was no chance to rejuvenate with everything that occurred, but she imagined she was better off than Eden. Having to take on her safety as a responsibility after what he went through less than two days prior was less than optimal. When she glanced over at him, he suggested himself as stoic as ever. His bold features held with his focused crimson eyes as if he partitioned every contingency, a feature she hardly imagined fostered ease of mind.

"Where do you find time for school? I can't imagine your responsibilities don't get in the way," Kendra inquired.

Eden kept his eyes forward, his focus unwavering.

"I don't get to commit much time to my duties. I'll be a full-time hunter when we graduate," Eden said.

"Yeah, but ... killing demons and homework in senior year? I can hardly imagine they mix."

"I make it work and will continue to do so," Eden sighed, finding the conversation to be fairly pointless. "In case you're worried about that," he added.

"No, I'm not worried about *that*," she replied.

"Then what *are* you worried about?" Eden's gaze turned to Kendra, his inquisitive expression soliciting her to answer.

"... Everything else. I'm confused, okay? That *thing* wanted your body and called you a spawn of divinity? You mean to tell me there are gods too? What else am I missing?"

Eden's eyes narrowed. Curling his fists, he thought back to what Intico said. *Of course she remembered that*, he thought. There was no means by which he could explain away the accusation or her question altogether. The hum of the vehicle's motor whirred in the silence as they were driven.

Kendra wondered why Eden had trouble answering this time. Her own hard blue eyes found his wavering crimson ones, challenging them rather than relenting, but her curiosity was unquenched by the stretch of silence between them. She imagined even the driver noticed the tension.

"They're mysterious, even to me. Don't have much involvement in the day-to-day, nor do they really communicate with humans often, either."

Eden was mostly oblivious to his father, unaware of the details Jessica had withheld from him. He couldn't explain the deities, for he had no means of understanding them entirely himself. They weren't the gods to be revered in religion; their impersonal impression on the universe they ordained required no such devotion, nor granted doctrines. They simply existed as a state of being, governing as the primordial essence of concepts and phenomena.

But there was a notable exception to this impartiality: Ichor. Ichor represented life itself, the animating essence all could bear witness to and through. All the living came from Ichor, and would one day return to Ichor. They all possessed Ichor, just as Ichor possessed them. Some, like Eden, wielded it, manifesting it into might or as a means to manipulate the world around them. Almost nothing could subvert Ichor's eternal dominion.

Eden stirred in his seat. Stoking his tenacity supplanted any lingering trauma—any fear he could suffer. He had failed Kendra once and would not see himself fail her again. That was his vow to her—and to himself. Something deep inside stirred, recalling the misery on her face when he found her torn asunder and caked in blood. It reminded him all too much of his own victimization he sought to bury in the darkness of his convictions.

"Just know, I won't fall to Intico next time. Next time ... it'll be different," Eden said.

Given how little Kendra knew of Eden, she couldn't for certain parse out the inner machinations driving his vow, whether it was for her—or for him. Her faith wavered in the face of her continued predation, and in her alienation. Unsavory and taut, it tugged at her determination, threatening to snap if it were further tested.

Their car ride wasn't much longer, and they were dropped off a short distance from the school to walk the rest of the way—something about safety concerns with patterns being established. Eden escorted Kendra but let her walk ahead. His vigilance never wavered, even though there was hardly a worry in the daytime. He put nothing past the demons and their scheming. It was what he knew them for—what he admonished them for.

They approached the steps leading up to the school, and Kendra dreaded the day ahead for a variety of reasons. Anxiety growing, she desperately sought to keep from ruminating. Eden couldn't assist with that much, especially given how encumbered he seemed by his own brooding tendencies. She pondered how he would watch her, perhaps by monitoring her energy signature through the walls. She was unsure. They shared less than half of their classes, especially on that day's schedule block.

"Remember to take your syn-blood this morning?" Eden asked, staring at her as she ascended the steps.

Kendra scoffed, growling as she nodded.

"Yes," Kendra groaned as she jogged up the staircase and entered the gate, leaving Eden behind. She missed the more personable rhetoric Vicente had employed, finding his more sympathetic approach to be far more accommodating of her stressed nerves. A long week was ahead, and she doubted it would be an easy one.

The week had passed quickly—it was already Friday. Kendra idly solved trigonometry problems that were left for her and the class on the board. The tapping of styluses on old tablets and the ticking of the analog clock set by their trigonometry teacher, Mr. Russo, served as an agitating ambience. Her ears twitched at each incessant noise that disrupted her focus—which was more than usual that day. Before the timer went off, she had finished the problems, and there were a few minutes remaining for her to relax.

While her thoughts drifted, she noticed the omens out of boredom. Seeing them was as easy as focusing until they appeared, like taking her glasses on and off. Mostly blue, they swirled around the students and phased through solid matter in their whimsical bumbling. The occasional sprite of red would mar the spectacle, drifting from the churning minds of the students and blending to create streaks of purple. It was almost comical how much Kendra understood what that entailed. She, too, had hellish thoughts when in math class.

The omens were the resonant frequencies of life, corresponding to the thoughtless endeavors of the living. To those who were aware of them, with enough practice, they could manipulate them—draw energy from them or distribute energy through them. Comparable to the veins Ichor flowed through, they represented the will and sentiments of all who came from Ichor, yet another primordial essence. Kendra still didn't fully understand it, but Eden had insisted they could be thought of as the *vibes* of Ichor's children—all the living who drew breath through her.

The clock chirped loudly, breaching the ambience of the class. Mr. Russo slapped the clock, shutting it off before he clapped his hands.

"Okay, class. Anybody confident in sharing their answers on the board?"

Silence.

Purple omens gathered around Mr. Russo, his lips pursing and twitching as he paid attention to the shy students. Or rather, they were uncertain of their answers to the difficult equations. Some had hoped they'd get the answer and reverse-engineer it with the formula. The tension built, and a heavy sigh left his lips. His crinkly brown face furrowed with a frown, displeased with the class's lack of confidence.

Kendra thought to volunteer, as she was certain of her answers, but she'd be forced to explain it in a presentation—Mr. Russo's expectation of specificity that no one adored. Of course, Mr. Russo didn't take kindly to the class playing coy. He began his tirade, something about the class not having the *cojones* to tackle math problems.

With each second of his complaining, Kendra lost more patience. One deep breath after another, she focused in on her surroundings—a bit too much, in fact. The churnings of blood in the body—hearts pulsing as frustrated breaths paraded. She retreated into her thoughts in an attempt to escape the noise.

The harrowing ache of her heart swelled as she sought the familiar silence she had neglected in her days as a human. The idea of her existence once again invaded her mind, and the rumination ensued once more until the end of class.

Next was her AP English class, where she was only expected to write an essay in class. It was innocent enough—peaceful, even. She wasn't much of a writer, but writing did help focus her thoughts and keep her from delving back into the desolate scape of her mind.

They were required to use pencils and paper in the class—a relatively antiquated idea in later schooling years, but a method, nonetheless. The taps and scribbles bugged Kendra a bit, but she found herself tuning it out as she placed her focus on her own writing. An essay on the migration of birds, and the unseen impacts it spelled out for the environment.

Similar to a bird seeking to flee a stressful ecosystem, she desperately wished she could flee the cage of her own flesh and mind. So did she dream of the days when she was just a girl finding her way—now, the paths ahead were narrow and jagged. Forced to tread this unforgiving terrain, she translated her plight within the details comprising the assignment. That much, she could do.

Then Kendra was off to physics. Eden shared that class with her, and he excelled in it, unlike her, who slid by with a B-minus. She thought he'd make a great engineer with his demonstrated understanding, recalling various times when he loosened his tongue to explain various concepts in their class participation. Aptitude aside, she hadn't assumed he would be a demon hunter, of all things.

They sat together during a group project session. It was a collaborative effort to demonstrate thermodynamics on common household items, while also protecting an egg from a torch. Eden was focused on his tablet, writing down bullet points for them to go over together, while Kendra fidgeted, watching him. She hadn't given it much thought before, but he seemed oddly at peace when he did his schoolwork—a sharp contrast to his usual, high-strung vigilance.

Kendra hadn't thought much of Eden prior to everything that happened, only thinking he came from a troubled home and was studious despite that. However, the more she inspected him, the more she could see how he, too, sought to bury himself in his work. Oddly enough, her scrutiny of him kept her from the turmoil of her own thoughts. She wondered if, despite being a hunter, he sought other aspirations, or even to become an engineer like Andrew—since the Hunters had various vocations, as she had learned.

"My dad—he's an engineer, you know," Kendra said.

Eden grunted in acknowledgment, setting his stylus to the side and grabbing a sheet of aluminum along with a sheet of dry pasta.

"You're good at this. Ever think of becoming one?" Kendra asked.

"No."

Kendra rolled her eyes and looked down at his tablet, spinning it to review his notes, which were hyper specific beyond what they had even reviewed in class.

"Why are you this detailed?"

"Because it's pertinent to my work."

"I guess ... but this is still a bit much for a small project."

Eden shrugged, idly assembling the materials into a shield for their egg.

Kendra pouted, Eden's aloofness taunting her.

"What? No explanation?"

"I didn't get much sleep, so I'm not all that up for conversation ... sorry."

Kendra had become familiar with the tired features of others in recent times, especially her parents. The dark, sunken eyes, the sluggish demeanors, and other relevant signs of restlessness. She figured it had something to do with the somnium—specifically Intico and the thing it had mentioned: Harvest. From everything she had recalled, Eden had always been this way. Reclusive and marred in mystery, with a glint of ire embedded within his distant gaze. His alleged restlessness beckoned her skepticism, as she had always seen him this way. *Maybe he doesn't sleep well in general,* she thought.

"Still thinking about it? That magician-demon?"

"*Not here,*" Eden shushed, glancing around for anyone in earshot. "The veil doesn't disguise words, only what is perceived to be happening."

"Oh ... I see," Kendra sighed, shrugging before she rested her cheek on her palm.

Looking down, Eden scanned his tablet and continued to write on it.

"Anyway, the egg survived thanks to the heat resistance in the starch with added dispersion from the aluminum. That's the summary. The math is irrelevant," Eden said.

Not a moment too soon, their teacher, Ms. Roth, walked by to check on their progress. She was an older woman with silver hair and light green eyes who wore a white lab coat over baggy jeans.

"Eden, Kendra, almost ready to present?" Ms. Roth asked, folding her arms above her chest. She stood at the head of their lab table, staring down at Eden's tablet to glimpse his notes. She gave an approving nod while examining the unsinged egg sitting on the small stand designed for it.

"Just about," Eden said.

She gave a skeptical look between them, earning a wry smile from Kendra.

"Yeah. Almost. Eden is good at physics, so I can't take the credit here," Kendra admitted.

"Aha! I want you to lead the presentation to even it out then. Sound fair?" Ms. Roth suggested.

Kendra internally cursed her modesty. Presenting was hardly preferable, given she wanted to remain inconspicuous. With her bad mood, *fairness* wasn't her consideration at that moment.

"You've got this, don't worry," Eden assured, stifling the smile that tugged at his lips.

When Kendra looked up, she saw his determined eyes and a small smirk plastered on his face—an odd sight coming from him. Despite his alleged faith, it did little to assuage her nerves.

"See? Eden believes in you. Hear from you guys soon," Ms. Roth said before she waltzed off to the next lab table. Kendra reached across the table, playfully punching Eden's arm, causing him to raise a brow in confusion at the gesture.

"Your fault I have to present now," Kendra said with a pout. This earned a small chuckle from Eden, which made her smile.

After Kendra's French class, she was finally free from the tyranny of Natalie's exuberance. She droned on and on about never losing hope in the face of things and how Kendra was a powerful woman. Sure, and fine advice, but she could scarcely resist the urge to curl up and seclude herself by the end of the school day. To stave off her annoyance, she gave simple, flat replies.

Accompanied on the way out by Natalie, she was grateful Natalie switched the subject to her family's crops back home. Because of her interest in politics, Kendra found it to be one of the more interesting topics Natalie rambled about due to the political nature of water allocation.

Natalie stopped by one of the vestigial lockers, which were never uninstalled, kneeling to tie the laces of her boot that had come undone, and Kendra heard footsteps approaching them. In the crowd, she saw Allen, of all people. She hardly wanted to subject him to her foul mood or torture herself by refraining from venting to him about her past few weeks, much like they usually were inclined to do.

Pushing through the crowd, Allen made his way toward Kendra, and she silently cursed to herself. She didn't want to scare him off with the comfort she would seek from him. Eden's statement about being connected to Ichor echoed in her mind, and she imagined Allen being even more confused about the supernatural than she was. While kept at a distance, she didn't want to risk her friendship with him until she had worked through her own demons.

"Ken, hey, I—"

"Allen. I'm sorry … I don't … it's not a good time to talk, yet." Kendra had never been shy toward him before, but her gaze avoided his. She used to be more approachable, the big sister most wished they had. Her new *anxiety disorder* was the excuse that most abided by, granting her leniency with regularly needing to excuse herself to get air. But she couldn't keep conjuring excuses to avoid Allen.

"Ken, please, if I did something, I—"

"She doesn't want to talk, Allen," Natalie spoke sympathetically, stepping between the two and grabbing Allen's shoulders. "She's going through a lot right now. Understand and bear with her."

Kendra lowered her head, squinting. *She chooses now to understand this?* she thought.

Allen stared down at Natalie, his mouth agape. Then he glanced at Kendra, whose gaze was cast to the floor.

Allen was a stubborn boy, tenacious in everything he pursued, but the boundaries were made clear. They had been the closest of friends, but now she was distant. His expression twisted into one exhibiting sorrow, but also his worry.

"I understand ... Ken. If you want to talk, my door is always open," Allen said.

Venturing to look up at him one last time, a deep pit grew in Kendra's stomach. The urge to hug him encumbered her will when she saw his contorted expression. He had shown such an expression at various times in the past, always pertaining to family matters he avoided talking about, and she hated seeing that. She gritted her teeth beneath her clamped lips, turning away from him to snuff her impulsion.

When Allen shambled off through the hall, Natalie sighed in relief, her gaze returning to Kendra with a kind smile. Kendra mouthed a *thank you* before she reached across, gently tugging Natalie into a hug before quickly separating.

"Nat, I'm gonna head home now ... talk to you soon."

"Alright, Ken. Have a good rest of your day, darlin'."

Kendra shifted away from Natalie and dragged herself through the courtyard. The wind was oddly uproarious that afternoon, but the omens were strangely sparse. Their luster was diminished, still present, but less obvious. Cascading leaves were usually accompanied by blue omens that slowly faded when they drifted to the ground. These leaves had fewer omens that faded quickly. She wondered if they had patterns and variations, similar to weather.

Kendra arrived at the front gate of the school, glancing around at the students who made their enthusiastic escape from the campus grounds. Nobody directly paid attention to her, much to her relief. The alienation was renewed in her head following Allen's outreach, and the brewing guilt tore away at her. She kept him at arm's length in fear of being vulnerable. She would rather push him away temporarily than drive him away forever. Kendra once felt she could tell him everything—this was not something she thought she could. For once in her life, she had nobody she could speak with—not her mother, father, sister, or Allen.

Eden waited for Kendra, perching against a telephone pole by the base of the staircase. Splintered, decrepit, and cracked, the old wooden poles contrasted heavily with the newer surrounding infrastructure. Eden was careful not to shift against it in fear of a splinter, but it held steady, still.

"You ready?" Eden asked, his eyes fixed on the sleeve of his shirt, straightening the fold on his wrist. But Kendra didn't answer.

The routine was simple. They would walk to an obscure alleyway, Eden would scan the nearby environment for any threats, and then they would reemerge. There would be a pickup vehicle on the opposite side of this alleyway to take them both back to the Chicago Hunters base. While it was a simple process, to Kendra, who valued her freedom above all else, it was both vexing and demeaning. She had dealt with being followed by a guardian before, but this was something far more oppressive.

Kendra and Eden walked to the pickup spot together. They hadn't spoken during their trek, both occupied with their own thoughts. Eden's silence was far more typical, driven by caution, whereas Kendra tactically held her tongue in fear of snapping, her nerves racked with guilt, fear, and sorrow alike.

Something pulled inside Kendra. The glimmers of normalcy and hope slipped through her fingers, fading into obscurity. The memories flooded her mind. Kendall's demise, her parents' grief—her grief. The alienation and the minnows of humanity she had clung to had been mute for a numbing stretch of time, and it finally exploded.

"I can't," Kendra muttered, pausing in her tracks. They were in the busy sprawl of traveling citizens when she finally succumbed to her rumination. Tears welled in her eyes for the first time all week. It escaped her why her emotions had been held at bay for that long. Obscured for most of the week, it became ubiquitous, overcoming her inhibitions and piloting her.

"You can't?" Eden asked, coming to a stop to glance back at her.

"I-I can't take this, Eden." She quivered uncontrollably. Her fists clenched, and she lowered her head. Her pupils dilated and expanded repeatedly as she wrestled with the *demon* inside of her. It wasn't hunger or bloodlust; rather, it was irrevocable turmoil. *Demons. Hunters. Humans,* her mind repeated incessantly. "I can't deal with this fucking world," she said, barely containing her volume. "I don't want to live like *this*!" she proclaimed. This garnered the attention of those who surrounded them. Most couldn't guess what was going on. None was of positive regard, however.

"Kendra ... hold it together. Take a deep breath."

"I'm. Not. Going. Back!"

Eden's intense gaze prickled her own. He glanced down at her hands. Her claw bored into her palm, yet she never flinched. He saw she was on the verge of a breakdown, and that wasn't good for too many reasons, none fair to her. When he looked up at her face, he saw the festering darkness creep in, consuming her sclera as burning irises carved the center. He was all too familiar with such eyes, and the infernal resemblance beckoned a sentiment he had sought to keep buried. Even though Kendra's eyes were not fueled by an evil voracity, in that moment, Eden failed to distinguish such differences. Sorrow and hate. They were both entrenched in darkness—ready to *take*.

"Kendra"—he released a contemptuous breath—"this is for your own good. You can't go back to the way things were." His voice was hushed, his gaze warily glancing around. However, Kendra's outburst had already garnered unwanted attention. Some passively watched, whereas others showed no concern and kept on with their business, as was typical in Chicago.

"I'm a fucking human, Eden. I. Have. *Rights*." Kendra's fingers spread open, the tips dripping with blood as they tore from her skin, and she backed away from Eden. She wanted to run away. *Somewhere safe.* With her inhuman speed, she assumed she could escape. But then again, Eden wasn't a human either. This question festered as she held his pensive, ire-filled gaze. "You wouldn't understand that, would you? What it's like to be put on a fucking chain and forbidden from just being a person!" she hissed.

When Kendra lurched to run away, Eden caught her wrist. It was an iron grip she couldn't break, no matter how much strength she conjured. And he never flinched, even pulling Kendra in close. Her eyes met his and were indicted upon contact. Her conviction nearly perished under their brutal scrutiny. This gaze was different from any she had seen from him before. It was one of a greater vitriol than her own, reeking of pity and an alien darkness that was foreign to her.

"You're not human anymore. Stop pretending you still are," Eden growled, his eyes burning with a condemnation saturated in cold blood within their crimson depths.

The infraction he had committed against her settled incorrigibly. Her humanity was sundered, battered, challenged, and condemned. She saw no other recourse. Kendra's breath faltered for a moment, her eyes narrowing as she stared deeply into his damning crimson expanses and countered with her burning gaze. She was not human, and she would remind him of his careless words.

Flames erupted from Kendra's wrist, the bristles of her hair standing with ember-kissed tips. Eden's hand was scathed by these flames, forcing him to release her impulsively. The briefest of moments with the most intense of consequences for what was to come. She knew her place was not with the Hunters now, no matter the fragility of her safety.

Kendra dashed away from Eden. She could not confide in Eden or the Hunters, but there was one person she knew she could confide in. And in spite of her impulsivity, a sense of invulnerability whelmed her in that instance. It wasn't a taste of freedom, but of hope she would seek in her desperation.

Holding his singed hand, Eden could tell Kendra hadn't intended to hurt him with that maneuver. The flames were superficial in a way that surprised him more than if they had scathed him. He knew true malice in the crucible of his vendetta against demons, and her actions lacked the lethal forethought he was accustomed to opposing.

Those still around him showed confusion and concern, but none interfered, not having perceived the reality of the situation as he and Kendra had experienced it. Regardless, it was unwise of him to give chase, and he acted accordingly. Informing the Hunters and waiting until nightfall to drag her back seemed a more productive idea.

He had sought to serve as Kendra's guardian, knowing he was most suited to combat any threat seeking to harm her. Yet, it had never crossed his mind that *he* would be one of the things she'd have wanted to flee from. Still, the impulsivity that had festered within her was all too familiar to him, and her rebelliousness—he was hardly one to judge on that front. It left him with uncomfortable ideas to mull over, and he found a seed of sympathy for her, considering the trauma yet addressed.

"Great," Eden grumbled, sighing as he made his way to the alley to rendezvous with the driver and prepare an explanation.

A buzz rumbled on Eden's wrist, snatching his attention. He never wore his hunter bracer while in civilian clothes and instead linked the basic functions to his specialized smart band. The indicator flashed with a hologram ID flickering above the projector. It was Zane, which both annoyed and perplexed him.

The combination of the terrible timing and Eden's personal distaste for Zane added to his irritability. He would have opted to ignore it, but considering the fact that Zane *never* contacted him for anything, ignoring it was probably unwise. Eden walked toward the SUV that was sent to pick him and Kendra up, dreading the explanation he'd have to give. He perched himself against the car, holding up a finger to the driver to request his patience before answering the call.

"Eden, I need you to drop whatever you're doing and come here *now*," Zane's voice rang through the speaker.

"Well, *now* isn't a good time," Eden sighed.

"You don't understand, Eden." Zane sucked air harshly through his teeth. "It's regarding the Covenant of Augury investigation. Chief Bronson is dead."

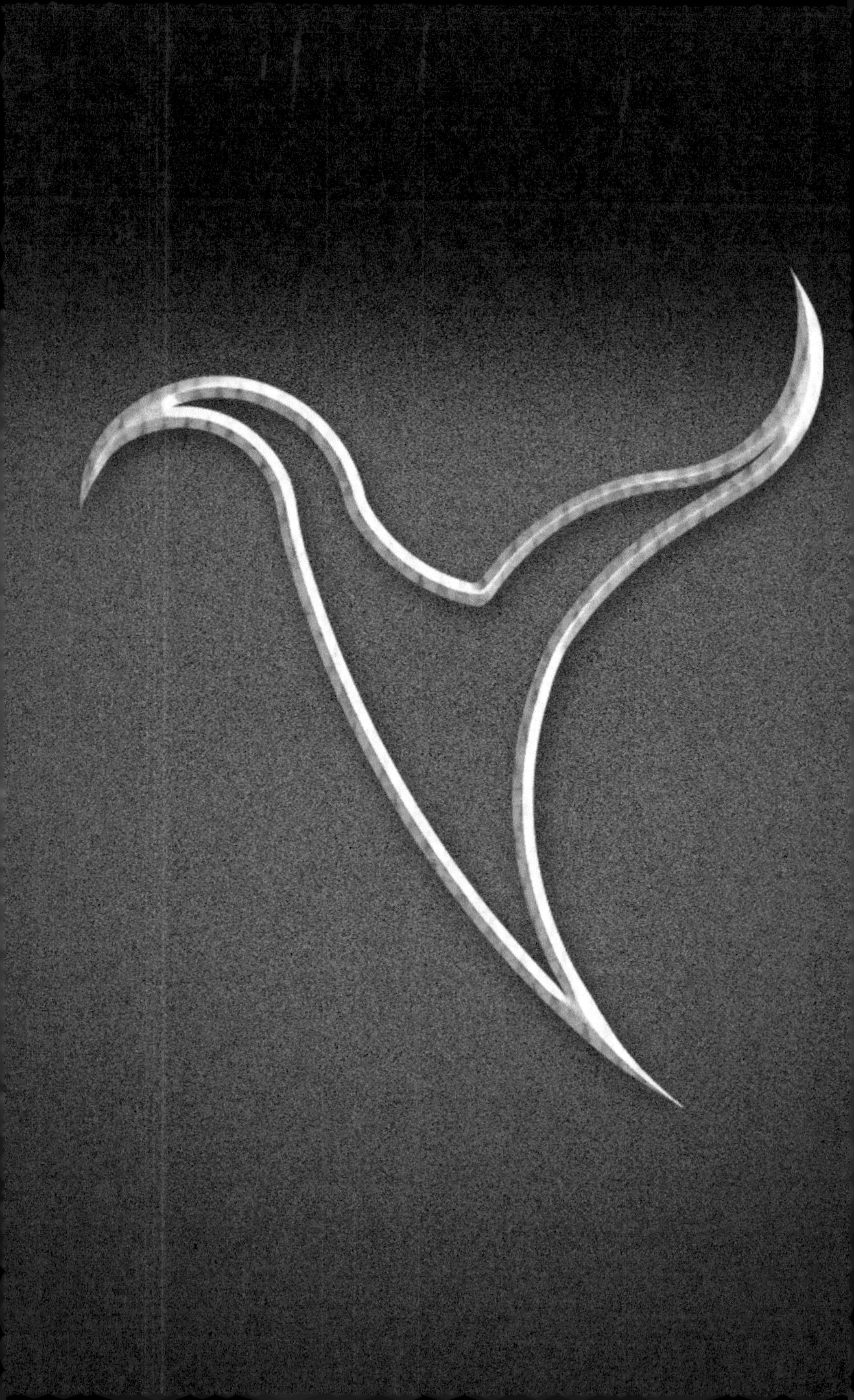

EIGHT

EVERYWHERE SHE'S NOT

Lincoln Park was where Archer had been murdered. How it ended up that way, Zane was oblivious to. He was caught in the middle of the bustling scene that swarmed with police officers securing and examining the crime scene. There, in broad daylight, was the body belonging to the man who he had met some time ago when he had first been stationed at the Hunters' base in the city. The body was too apparent, left perfectly preserved with no significant decomposition, as if it had been frozen that way. *Like it was meant to be found,* Zane thought.

Zane had been attracted to the area by a sudden surge in malicious Ichor, and as indolent as he was, he knew diligence was necessary for the situation. It technically wasn't his duty to examine the scene immediately—that could be left to a hunter whose job was to parse reports with the police, but something didn't settle right with him about the situation. He *needed* to be there. And while he certainly didn't like Eden, he knew that Eden had more familiarity with the police and was as astute as one could be on supernatural phenomena. He had also contacted command about it, and more hunters were on their way already, but Eden would be there first.

It was minutes after the phone call when Eden came bolting up to the scene. Judging by the disheveled faces the officers showed, they immediately prepared to deny entry. But Eden brought up the encrypted ID badge that he was to use with local law enforcement for these matters.

Eden ducked beneath the caution tape sectioning off the cluster of trees, and Zane waved him over to stand in line with the police officers and investigators who processed the scene.

Archer was on his back, his dark skin now pale and his face shriveled and taut. But it wasn't the only body left at the scene. Two other humanoid bodies wearing robes of which Eden immediately recognized, were a short distance away from Archer's corpse, and then there were the bodies of hellhounds strewn close by. The dead demons all had gaping wounds, which appeared to have been caused by a projectile that was no longer present, something that could be removed or dissipate naturally. It wouldn't have been a hunter that killed the demons, as a hunter would have certainly both reported the encounter and would have *cleaned* the scene afterward. Eden knew without a doubt that the dead demons had been associated with the Covenant of Augury.

Bronson was in his police uniform, tattered in various sections which suggested a struggle prior to his death. Other than scrapes and bruises, no apparent wounds marred his form to suggest his death. Both Eden and Zane easily concluded Archer hadn't been the one to afflict the mortal wounds against his assailants. His nine-millimeter rounds wouldn't have been able to damage them significantly, not with their demonic healing abilities and the hounds' thick hides.

Eden glanced to the side, finding a familiar face among the investigators present. Distinguished in a black double-breasted trench coat with a notepad in hand was Julian. *Of course, he'd be the one called to the scene,* Eden thought. They caught each other's gaze, and Julian pushed past his colleagues to approach Eden and Zane.

"You know anything about what happened ... sorry, your name is slipping," Stroth stated.

Eden was quiet for a moment, studying Julian's face to see the dark eye circles beneath. They were more pronounced than when they last met.

"Eden. And no, I'm just as clueless as everybody else here." Eden paused, turning his gaze back to the corpses. "Tell me what you've assessed of the scene so far."

Zane stayed quiet. Despite he and Julian having met briefly weeks ago, he decided to let Eden handle the conversation, since he was caught up in piecing together a hypothesis of what happened exactly. Still, he was vexed by Eden's willingness to speak with a non-hunter, given his reclusive nature and reluctance to speak with anybody in general.

Julian sighed, glancing over at the corpses. His own relationship with Archer aside, it was early and the entire department had already been stressed to no ends—on top of the pervasive insomnia they all reported experiencing.

"Well, our chief is dead. But so are those two other unidentified individuals and some coyotes. Considering this is all at the same scene, there is a lot to disentangle."

Eden nodded along, raising an eyebrow to hear that they perceived the hellhounds as coyotes. It wasn't unusual for them to be perceived that way by humans who were disconnected. However, the mystery of why they were left there was still present.

"You can smell it, right? The sulfur?" Eden asked, and Julian nodded, pinching the bridge of his nose.

"Plenty," Julian replied.

Eden glanced at Zane, who stared intently at the faces of one of the dead demons in robes.

Zane thought it peculiar that both robed demons had red hair—a signature trait of the Siegharts. As suspicious or coincidental as that was, it was only one of his many questions. He turned his gaze back to Archer's corpse, and his unease amplified upon further scrutiny. It was unusual to see someone shriveled up in such a way. He'd be interested to know what a human autopsy would reveal, but he knew the truth: his soul had been ripped out. Likely by one of the hellhounds present, which were known to consume the essence of the soul, leaving only the husk for Ichor to reclaim.

Utilizing hellhounds to collect souls—a hypothesis the Hunters already had—was now all but confirmed. Zane knew that ruses involving a collection of souls usually entailed dark rituals, of which he was viscerally acquainted. He imagined it had something to do with the infamous *Harvest* Intico had mentioned. It reminded him of the unethical practices of the Alastairs. Vehemently haunting his conscience, the ramifications of these kinds of rituals and schemes weighed heavily, the wanton loss of life especially egregious.

"What are you two not telling me? It's obvious this is beyond my usual scope ... and given your mysterious nature, I'd say it's even something ... otherworldly," Julian asked.

Zane furrowed his brow, shrugging.

"Not sure what you're getting at, buddy, but we're not dealing with aliens or anything, if that's what you're thinking," Zane said.

"With all due respect, Mr. Larson, cut the shit. I'm acutely aware that something big is going on, and you guys are investigating it. My colleague you met, a detective of ten-plus years, took a leave of absence after her daughters went missing. And it was right on the precipice of this investigation. The chief wasn't the first, and I have a suspicion he won't be the last. Everybody's exhausted and at their wit's end. What little sleep we *can* get is abysmal and plagued with nightmares. Even I haven't slept well in days, and all this paranormal bullshit is over our heads. You guys know *something*."

Julian pulled his hair back, releasing a long, exhausted sigh. He had always been an exceptionally perceptive person; it was why he became a detective when granted an array of opportunities for his talents. This translated intuitively when faced with matters beyond human comprehension. He worried that if he fell asleep during the most vociferous calls, he'd wake a different person. He was abundantly aware he had no true understanding of these things, and it was becoming more prevalent with each scene involving his dead colleagues.

As Julian focused on the scene, he was reminded of Officers Freeman and Santos. Both were found dead as rubbery, emaciated husks, much like Archer was here. Later, autopsies revealed them to have died from exsanguination—bleeding to death. In this case, drained dry by *something*.

Eden could see it in Julian's abyssal gaze. He was connecting. There was no way to continue hiding the truth from him for long, or at least the supernatural portions of reality best kept obscured. Julian, while naturally sharp, was exuding an aura with a richer depth, one more ingratiated with Ichor herself.

"Take a closer look, Detective Stroth. The answer is becoming clearer to us by the minute. This is the first scene we've been at, whereas you've seen plenty. Perhaps you can help more than you think—provide us insight if you can see this for what it truly is. Look at those other bodies and the *coyotes* again. Don't panic if you notice it," Eden said. He was cryptic in his messaging, providing a hook for Julian to latch onto, provided he could. If he couldn't irrevocably escape the boundaries of his human senses and perceive reality as it truly was, then Eden and Zane would remain enigmatic to him.

Julian stared with impertinence, initially dismissive of the bizarre speech from Eden, a boy half his age. However, reality warped in front of him. The longer he stared at the scene, the less sense it made. Before his eyes, the *coyotes* morphed into large, malformed hounds with black fur and protruding horns, along with impossibly wicked features, ones capable of easily gouging a vehicle's armor.

"Get them out of this crime scene. They have no further jurisdiction to be here!" a voice called from behind the caution tape.

Eden and Zane snapped their attention to the source of the voice: a man dressed in black formalized police attire with various pins and badges attached. The badge pinned atop the left side of his chest read *Chicago Police Deputy Chief.* He had obsidian-black eyes and short, slick black hair that matched. His vanilla skin was fair, albeit on the paler side. He had three small vertical scars beneath his right eye. Deputy Police Chief Darrel Carver.

Darrel gave off a peculiar aura, one that set Zane off for reasons he couldn't discern at a glance, but it also garnered Eden's attention. With both of them on alert, Zane turned to face Darrel.

"No further jurisdiction? Prior to his passing, we've been working closely with your chief. You'd do well to remember that," Zane said.

Darrel's sharp footsteps came to a halt when he planted himself between the pair of hunters and the sight of Bronson's body.

"Julian, you're not to speak or confer with them any longer," Darrel said, and Julian stared with an exhausted expression on his face. He glanced at Eden and Zane once more before nodding.

"Yes, sir," Julian grumbled. He pursed his lips, returned his gaze to the crime scene, and entered the immediate vicinity of it to continue his investigation.

"Got wax clogging your ears? We have jurisdiction, whether you say so or not," Zane said. Eden stared daggers at the deputy chief, unamused by the impertinence. Nothing irritated him more than those who wielded authority dubiously.

"Do you have wax in *your* ears?" Darrel sneered. "I said I want you two out of this crime scene *now*. I don't want to have to arrest you for obstructing an official investigation," Darrel said.

"Official investigation? That's why we're here. We're more official than *you*," Eden spat.

"And our chief is dead. Goes to show what good the most official among us can offer. Now, your continued jurisdiction with the department is under review until further notice," Darrel snapped. He crossed his arms, scrutinizing the two hunters more openly as he committed their faces to his memory. "You won't receive a lick of intel, help, or acknowledgment from any of my officers or detectives. Your superiors have been notified of this as well. Appeal if you'd like. We'll have this case solved before you can so much as get a subpoena. You can wait for updates with the rest of the citizens."

"Being demoted to a citizen?" Zane rolled his eyes.

"I'm second in command and my word is law here. I won't ask again. *Go.*"

If Eden had been staring daggers, his gaze became swords poised to cut Darrel down. This was their first real exposition to what had occurred, and actual demons lay dead at the scene. Numerous confirmations were already made, but now they couldn't collect information to make an in-depth report of their findings. The disobliging Deputy Police Chief was adamant to ensure that.

The coincidental nature of Darrel's approach settled unevenly in Zane, and he had to clarify something.

Eden took a step toward Carver, holding tense eye contact with the smaller man. There was no way any of the officers there could subdue him if they tried, but while the repercussions weren't immediately prevalent to him, they were to Zane.

Zane placed a hand on Eden's chest, stopping his approach. Zane stole Darrel's attention, and he glanced at the name tag on his shirt, gathering his name before offering a small smirk.

"Carver, huh? Alright, we'll be going then. Expect to see us again, though," Zane said. He glanced at Eden, nodding his head.

Eden gave Zane a puzzled look, huffing, before he turned on his heel. He and Zane marched away from the crime scene, and Darrel kept his eyes on the two until they were out of sight. And when they were gone, he resumed barking orders to his subordinates at the scene.

Eden and Zane found their way to a bench some distance away from the scene. When they came to a stop, Eden's harsh crimson gaze fell on Zane, demanding an explanation. He knew Zane enough to know that he had relented far too easily. Zane held a hand up.

"He knows something ... that Carver guy," Zane surmised.

"What makes you say that? He's human," Eden replied.

"A human with authority. You think demon families haven't wormed their way into positions of power in some shape or form? Sure, they can't hold office, but it doesn't mean they don't contribute to campaigns and make good little puppets out of their chosen thralls. Police are hardly any different. The incentive structures are more ... complicated."

"What are you getting at with this?"

"Carver may be a pawn, keeping the Hunters from confirming anything too damning. Something along those lines."

Eden's gaze became pensive, his head running through the scenario that had played out. He saw Carver as an anal cop who wasn't versed in the protocol sufficiently. Still, what Zane said was entirely possible. And above anybody, he trusted Zane when it came to demon politics.

"I'm still confused as to how they pulled this off. The body looks fresh. Did they kill him in broad daylight?"

"Something like that would take coordination from demons who could actively suppress the population ... a Sieghart."

Eden thought about this for a moment. He knew Zane had been working as a liaison between the Hunters and the noble demon families. The fact Zane had floated their name meant he had more than just a suspicion.

"So, they must have some degree of involvement ... one uses the eye of Jugo, the others hunt and kill. Damn ... if we had been able to investigate the scene, we could have confirmed this."

Zane's pensive stare held, and he nodded in confirmation of Eden's assessment.

"Precisely. Carver definitely had something to hide from us."

Eden sighed, shifting uncomfortably as he concluded that he would leave the rest of the situation to Zane. Kendra came back to mind, and he realized that she had been gone long enough. It was time for him to find her.

"Well, since that's settled, you make the report. I have to get back to Kendra. She needed to cool her head."

"You left her unattended? Geez, man, I told you to drop what you were doing, but you could have tucked her into the shuttle first."

"It's ... not that simple," Eden said.

"She ran off, didn't she? Not a good idea to tick ladies off, but you'll learn that eventually." Zane clucked his tongue, shaking his head and waving Eden off with his hand. "Just go find her. I'll take care of the paperwork."

Eden nodded, sighing heavily and turning on his heel. He removed a teleportation crystal from his pocket before crushing it, and in the next moment, he dispersed into light.

Zane slumped his shoulders and made his way back to the base, dreading what was ahead of them. The situation boded poorly, and he had a feeling he'd make liberal use of his flames soon.

Eden re-materialized atop a rooftop overlooking the city. He had focused from a high vantage point near where he last detected Kendra, the city below abuzz with its natural ambience. It'd be easy to get lost in the sea of energies, all similar and ordinary in both frequency and measure, but Kendra's signature was quite distinct, one of which Eden had become acquainted with more thoroughly over the past week.

In a sea of calm, flowing energies, disconnected and free of inhibitions, Eden sought the burning, chaotic energy emblematic of Kendra. A flickering flame flaring with swarming embers. Kendra's energy was distinctly demonic and impossible for him to not notice.

Eden knew she couldn't have gone far. He tried to narrow his focus on a handful of locations he suspected she would seclude herself in. More than anybody else, given his reclusive nature, he could understand hunting for solitude in times of psychological strife, but the circumstances hardly proved logical for such. No matter how or where he searched, he could not locate Kendra.

Within the boundaries of energy detection, limitations were determined by the intensity and distance of an energy signature. Kendra had no training or real conception of controlling her energy, and the suspicion of her hiding it was farfetched. Even with considerable distance, Eden would have been able to detect a hint of her energy with how it contrasted. A light in a dark room, it would pronounce itself, but it never did. Once that had failed, he tried calling her—several times—to no avail.

Time to worry, he thought. There was no good explanation for why her energy was without even a wisp. There was suppression, and then there was death. He had already ruled out the former, and now, the latter was a haunting possibility. But he refused to believe it. There had to be some kind of explanation or some obscure probability he hadn't considered.

Eden took a deep breath and paced atop the gravel of the roof he was on. He looked down to see the streets below him, the streets he had diligently scouted. He remembered seeing her head east.

"Insenseilis."

Eden leaped from building to building, his anxious visage magnifying the longer he searched. He racked his mind for ideas on how to find her, irrespective of her energy signature. He landed hard on one rooftop that stood in the eastern district of the city, his eyes dancing across the various roads and architecture. After several minutes, he concluded that the lack of her energy entirely suggested something sinister.

Briefly, the idea of her having perished festered within him, and he worried he had, once again, failed to protect her. For his entire life, he had known demons to plot in the shadows and take their opportunities to strike. He had seen it countless times. He had experienced it personally. The modicum of safety he had dedicated to maintaining on her behalf appeared to slip away in those trying moments, and his chagrin swallowed his fermenting hatred of demons.

However, he remembered a crucial detail from his studies when he had trained to become a hunter. When energies escaped the body after death, there was usually a *stench* left behind, one that permeated the surrounding area and signified death's essence. No such essence perfumed with an energy akin to Kendra's, and he ruled it out, much to his relief.

That was when an idea surfaced. Kendra had on her smart band, as he distinctly recalled—a midnight-blue Voltia H-12. The model utilized cloud computing for most of its functionality, and as such, it could be located by the right person—a person who understood technology. He recalled Andrew at the Chicago base, primarily because the boy had informed him he couldn't fix his damaged maneuver bracer, prompting him to take it to James for repair.

He mulled this over for several seconds, considering the ostensible benefit of seeking Andrew's help. He could keep Kendra's absence a secret longer than he could otherwise and remedy the situation organically. Should Jessica discover what had happened, he expected more consequences than just his guardianship over Kendra being revoked. Such an outcome caused his chest to tighten, and he wished he would have gone after her immediately, optics aside. Now, he needed to swallow his dwindling pride and take the necessary measures.

"Wait, so … Kendra's missing?" Andrew asked.

"Keep your voice down," Eden said, glancing around before leaning in. "Yes, now, can you help me or not?"

"Do you have her IMEI, by chance? Or the serial number?"

"The wha—no. Do you need it?"

"Not technically, but it would make it a whole lot easier." Andrew shifted his gaze down to his laptop. He flicked his wrist up, causing two holographic interfaces to manifest from his desk. "Listen, I'll need like … a solid hour before I have tangible results. You're gonna have to wait."

"Any way to get those sooner?" Eden spoke, leaning in closer to see what Andrew was doing on the monitors.

Andrew cocked his brow and shook his head.

"This isn't like those corny movies or whatever. I have a lot of digging and technical jargon to comb through. Consider yourself lucky I can even do it at all, seeing as you don't have any of the other information." Andrew scolded but bit his bottom lip when he realized how harsh he had sounded. Not having intended to sound demeaning, he muttered an apology.

Eden sighed, shrugging in defeat as he stood straight and folded his arms. He glanced around the engineering center, briefly distracted by the loud sounds of maintenance taking place on the equipment and vehicles. Eden never enjoyed being in there for too long. It was too convoluted and noisy. He could withstand loud noises, but not a lot of them all at once for extended periods. It was almost ironic, given the nature of his job, but it was different considering the state of mind he was in while hunting.

"I'll call for you when I finish, k?" Andrew continued. Eden nodded and turned on his heel, walking to the connecting corridor that led back to the main lounge.

He turned into the dorm corridors, heading a few doors down until he reached his room. It had been made available to him if he ever desired to stay at the base instead of home, but there was no point in doing so. Still, he used it as additional storage. Propped up on a hook was a hunter uniform, which he had worn once. He much preferred the one personally designed to his liking. The standard hunter suit offered humans the ability to amplify their speed and strength with their energy, providing power to the exoskeletal enhancements built into it. The system was a way of ensuring humans could more competently contend against demonic forces. He had no need for it, given his lineage and biological abilities that surpassed anything the suit would offer him—it, in fact, would hinder him more than anything. He also thought he looked ridiculous in it.

A sigh escaped his lips, his underlying attitude becoming increasingly more agitated as he counted the seconds. It was largely unproductive, but he didn't know what else to do. Anxiety having made a home in his chest, he sat on his bed and idly scrolled through online content on his smart band. Eventually, when that no longer held his attention, he reclined back and stared at the ceiling. With no further distractions, he reflected on what he had said to Kendra. Soon, the seed of regret took root, and it sprouted in the uncomfortable silence.

Then, his band vibrated on his wrist, and an incoming text from Andrew flickered on the indicator projection. He stood and promptly marched to the engineering center once more. When he turned the corner, he froze. Standing next to Andrew was Zane, whose pensive gaze scrutinized the monitor in front of Andrew. The two idly chatted with one another, oblivious to Eden's arrival. *Why is Zane here?* Eden thought. He approached after his initial hesitation, his sharp footsteps alerting the two, causing them to glance back at him. Zane turned on his heel, ushering Eden over with a grim expression on his face.

"What is it?" Eden questioned, worry present in his tone.

"Nothing good ..." Zane said.

Andrew cleared his throat, gesturing to the blinking locator on the map.

Eden recognized the map of Chicago and the primary districts that resided within it. The blinking locator that he assumed to be Kendra's smart band signal was flickering at the center of the map, which was zoomed in on the Gold Coast.

"Address look familiar at all?" Zane asked.

"Cut to the point," Eden snapped, his eyes narrowing with impatience.

Zane crossed his arms, sighing as his expression showed apprehension.

"It's where the damn Sieghart family is. Down to the street. This means that Kendra's in a noble demon family's custody," Zane scolded, understanding the troublesome nature of the development. Zane had suspected the Siegharts were unwitting accomplices at least, but the broader ramifications of this discovery were far more entrenched in their investigation—crucial, in fact. "Those demons ... the one at the scene earlier. They *had* to be a part of the Sieghart family. The red hair, the hellhounds ... we both know that umbra demons utilize feral demons for their schemes. They're with the covenant."

"*Shit*," Eden said, clenching his fists. The Siegharts were suspects as it stood, but there were no concrete ties to pin on them—until now. Kendra ending up at their home couldn't have been a coincidence, especially with her energy signature vanishing. It made sense to him and Zane. The Sieghart family was renowned for some of their members possessing a power within their eye that was capable of doing such a thing: the eye of Jugo, the *eye of connecting*. Colloquially, it was known as *the leer of envy*. The use of that eye allowed the host to connect and disconnect individuals from Ichor as they saw fit, effectively nullifying enemies or amplifying their allies' abilities. Such a thing perfectly explained both Kendra's initial connection prior to her first two attacks and her energy signature disappearing now.

"We have to report this and do something as soon as possible ... we don't have much time," Eden said. Andrew kept quiet, unsure of what to say in this instance other than meekly nodding along in agreement.

Zane shifted uncomfortably, grabbing his chin as he shifted his gaze elsewhere.

"This one's on you. I have somewhere I have to be tonight," Zane said.

"You're seriously going on a date at this time?" Andrew squeaked, and Zane lowered his gaze. Andrew was confused, seeing remorse in Zane's eyes, an emotion not commonly expressed by him.

"I wish it was a date," Zane sighed, shaking his head. "Look, just keep me updated on the developments. We've got a lot of work to do."

Eden had his reservations about what Zane said, but for all his disdain, he didn't distrust him. Zane had a less-than-stellar past, and he knew all too well how the past could come back to haunt.

"Thanks again, Andrew, I owe you one," Eden said before he walked off.

"Uh, yeah ... no problem ..." Andrew muttered, eyeing Zane with a hint of concern. He still had his own work to do, but he suspected the workload would swell soon.

Dismissing himself, Eden left and found seclusion in the base. He was ill-prepared for such a report, seeing little saving grace even with the revelation pertinent to the Hunters' investigation. Enthusiasm didn't manifest from the discovery either. The Siegharts were working with the Covenant of Augury or were a part of it.

There was still the mystery of Kendra's condition looming over Eden. The covenant had sought her for reasons unknown to him, but with the Sieghart family at the core of it, he knew it was potentially grimmer than death. In the period of unraveling mysteries, Eden was at least certain of the promise he made to himself: he would get Kendra back safely.

No demon would stand in the way of that.

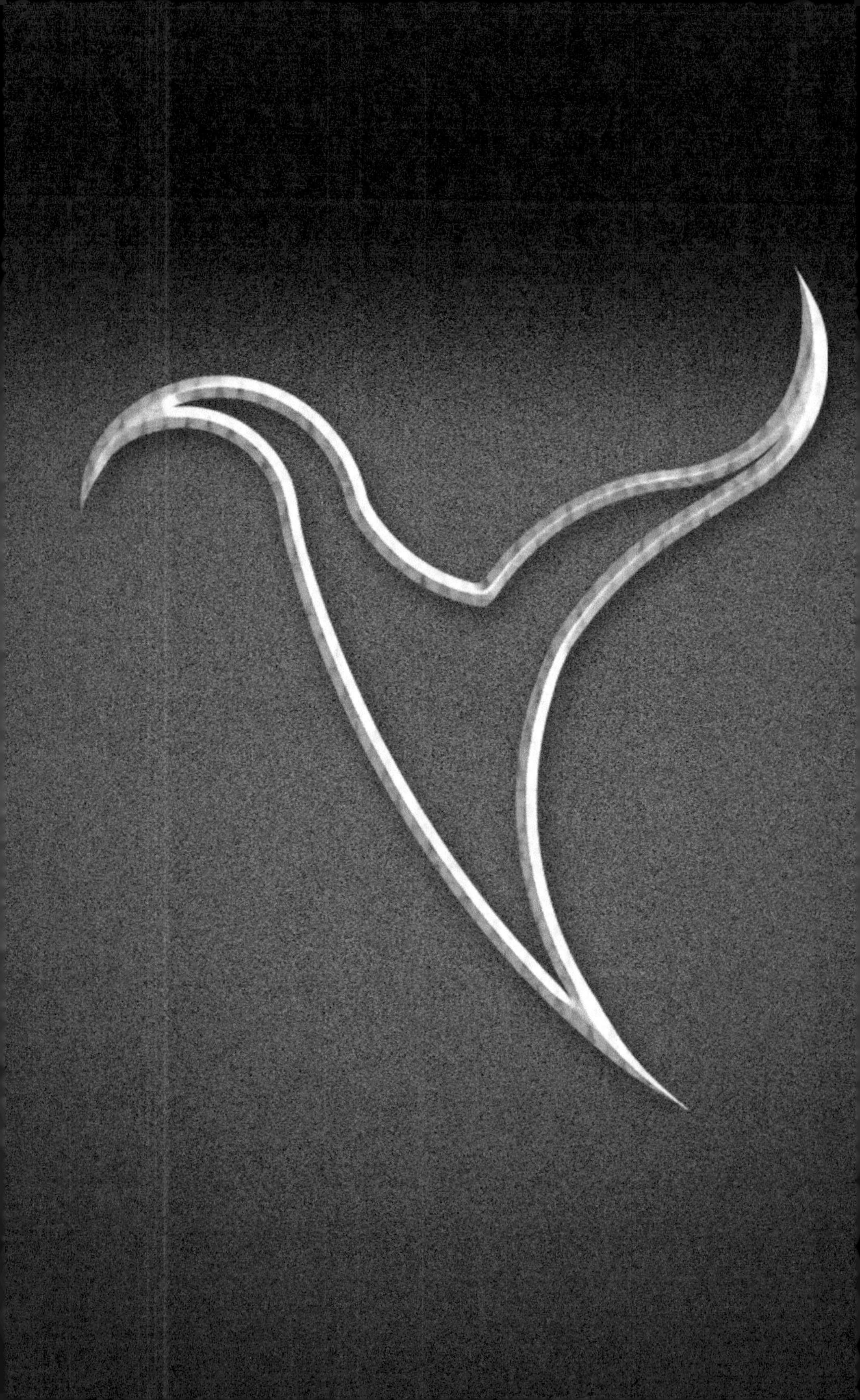

NINE

Eye of the Scorned

Darrel Carver had been the deputy chief of police for almost a year. With his title, he was granted the prestige of overseeing the department alongside Police Chief Archer Bronson, the man he sought to usurp. For Harvest to succeed, he needed absolute authority over the department. To that end, Archer had to die. There was less than a week until Harvest was to commence, and there was far too much he needed to prepare, should the Hunters become a greater impediment than they already were.

"Our subordinates should have killed and seized Bronson's soul for Harvest by now. He's only human. He shouldn't have provided any substantial resistance," Darrel said, his dark eyes scanning his cohorts. At his side was a black-haired woman with equally dark eyes and moonlight-pale skin, his trusted familiar and lover, Alysium. Slouched to fit within the room, Intico and another somnium Intico claimed to be its lieutenant stood in the corner. Splayed on the rust-brown armchair was Oliver Sieghart, whose pensive gray stare equally scrutinized Darrel. Several robed figures stood as silent sentinels on display, ultimately inconsequential to the conversation taking place.

"I'll believe it when I see it, Carver. Neither I nor the somnium will accept failure. Either you seize power, or we take it by force. There have been too many setbacks as is," Oliver said, his deep voice crackling in frustration. As inscrutable as the way of the somnium could be, there was a pact to be respected, and Oliver was more than aware of the consequences of deviating from that pact. He was grimly reminded when he met Intico's hollow gaze.

"Adequate bodies are needed, and I've taken to my own ventures in seeking out proper vessels capable of housing myself and my brethren. It is my understanding you have failed to capture that homuntium girl, yes?" Intico inquired. Aware of Kendra's change, the somnium deemed her a high-quality vessel, one that Intico would have sought itself, if not for being set on claiming Eden.

Oliver's brow knitted with apprehension as he scraped his nails along the arms of his chair. The consequences became far more pertinent, and the stakes were entrenched in the future of the Siegharts, something of great pertinence to him as the head. Should he see them prosper and one day overtake the Alastairs, it was too important for him to maintain the good graces of the somnium—to maintain the Covenant of Augury. Averting his gaze from Intico, he glanced at Darrel briefly, who stringently avoided his gaze.

"I can assure you, in due time, that perfect vessel will be in our possession ... it is not the easiest to procure the girl with a hunter's—"

"Ah, counting chickens before they hatch? Quite the hypocrite, Sieghart ... you'd do well to mind your promises," Intico said, its tone trailing off with a sense of foreboding lingering with each wisp of its words.

"I don't make assurances cavalierly, Lord of the Somnium. It won't be long before you may have the girl as your vessel," Oliver spat, losing his patience.

Intico appeared to scowl.

"The homuntium girl is not for me. Scarlet has insisted on claiming her. The girl's mother is for Lapis. Speaking of which ... you may all refer to me as Intico now. That is my name."

Oliver cocked an eyebrow.

"You're naming the individual somnium?" he asked.

A smirk formed on Intico's face, supplanting its scowl.

"Just a scheme a certain hunter inspired."

"I swear, you're about the most vapid *thing* I've ever had the displeasure of dealing with," Oliver grumbled.

"Gentlemen and entities of unfathomable fear, we can tear each other apart when time isn't scarce," Darrel reminded the two demons, a heavy sigh escaping his lips as he lowered his head. With a frown, he collected his thoughts. It was always difficult to hold covenant meetings with how inhospitable the somnium could be, but it was to be expected; the nature of demons was that of volatility. There was always a tug-of-war in the interactions between demonic parties. And through sheer guile, Darrel navigated the conversations as any skilled rhetorician should.

"And what say you, Carver? I witnessed these goons in action directly. They were less than impressive against the Blackwell descendant. Although ... they did inspire other such interests within me," Intico pontificated.

Alysium stepped forward, turning her onyx gaze onto the pair of somnium demons. Having held her tongue and remained meek until then, she found herself impatient with Intico's insinuated incompetence of Darrel.

"Gauging the strength of our underlings against a vessel worthy of you would be an insult to your power, right, fiend?" Alysium retorted, her voice, albeit sharp and challenging, flowing with tranquility and elegance. The polarity between her dark gaze and Intico's fathomless depths diminished, and Alysium relaxed before the somnium lord.

A wicked grin formed on Intico's face, its eyes narrowing with intrigue.

"Good answer," Intico cooed. "From where I stand, I can see that we are more than adequately supplied to commence Harvest ... what delays impede us?"

Oliver held his chin, his hard eyes glancing between Intico and Darrel again. The disparate variables at play weren't to be easily discounted, as was grossly apparent in his conversation with Zane. He sincerely wished he had prepared better for it, but there was hardly any means of obscuring all the details with how disjointed their respective efforts were between the somnium and his own umbra kin.

"If you want the plan to be susceptible to the impudence of the Hunters, by all means, let's commence immediately. I care to ensure that all the pieces are where they need to be. One of which is Carver installing himself as the chief of police and ensuring their formation is as vulnerable as possible. In the event that the citizens don't all fall asleep, as is likely with our current stockpile of soul power the hounds have reaped, we'll need to launch a supplemental assault. Just because their bullets pose little threat to demons doesn't mean the dithered won't be susceptible during the initial merging process," Oliver explained. He clenched his fists, cracking his large knuckles as he shifted his attention to Darrel.

Pensive and shrewd, Darrel leered at Oliver. He had set in motion for Bronson to be eliminated following his methodical and unassuming plunge into restless turmoil. He had planned to frame it as a disappearance, one that would fit the profile of the officers he had the covenant eliminate over the past few months. Archer Bronson was a restless, diligent man—one fundamentally incapable of resting, even if he was required to. The effects of the miasma released among the department scarcely affected him as it should have. *An outlier of most unfortunate standings.*

He leaped to order the covenant to lure the chief off into the depths of Lincoln Park and disconnect him prior to eliminating him. His soul was to make another addition to the pool that would be used for Harvest. Upon collecting his soul, they were to leave the scene spotless to avoid cluing in the Hunters. As if in a cruel twist, rapid steps perturbed the following silence, alerting the group to the door swinging open.

"Excuse the intrusion, Master Sieghart. We have an urgent report from the party sent to eliminate Chief Bronson," spoke the demonic maid. Her weary blue eyes tiredly examined the room, whose guests scrutinized the space directly behind her. A silent ire was birthed in the room, as if they had been interrupted at the cusp of some inextricable revelation.

"Jacob Sieghart—reporting in," a cloaked male said and stepped from behind the demonic maid, who then quietly excused herself from the room. Cloaked in a dark robe with the embroidery of the covenant stitched around the plackets, he removed his hood, revealing the emblematic red hair and gray eyes many Siegharts possessed. With a reluctant gaze, he sought Oliver, who stared back. But more inescapable was the haunting gaze of the somnium, who appeared, paradoxically, both eager and cynical.

"Yes, yes. Hurry and speak!" Oliver snapped, the room rumbling with his voice. The demon flinched, nodding his head before straightening his posture.

"Chief Bronson has been killed—but we came under assault."

"Assault by whom?" Darrel interjected, leaning forward with his harsh gaze directed at the demon.

"W-we don't know! A rime eliminated my squad entirely. The fact I live ... is not an accident. He spared me." He recalled the haunting image of the icy gaze glowing within the dark, wielding ice magic to skewer his squad and hounds. Even in the face of the somnium, he dreaded the leer of that rime far more.

"The body, boy! Did you dispose of the body?" Oliver inquired with urgency in his tone, his eyes bulging from his head. Tense silence pervaded the room, overstaying its welcome. "Out with it!" Oliver demanded. A rime—demons thought to have been extinct except for a sole surviving member—interfering hardly made sense, and his doubt surfaced.

"I fled when my entire squad was massacred ..." the demon whimpered. His lack of resolve was cemented in the face of the cold terror he had witnessed. It had been with precision that the rime had compromised their objective, with means unknown to any of the parties present.

Oliver had prepared to throw his lesser kin to oblivion with his fist uncurling and crackling with powerful energy, but Darrel snapped his finger, halting him before his rash outrage.

"And what condition was his body left in?" Darrel asked.

"Silent and quick. A soul tear, but the body should still be there," the demon said, his expression showing his resignation to death, understanding firmly what his failure entailed.

Darrel's good grace had since exhausted, and he was left with only unwieldy, fuming rage at the prospects that he had been granted by Oliver's incompetent kin.

"Should? Should isn't good enough," Alysium hissed, snatching the words of condemnation from Darrel. Her magnanimous gaze cast innumerable curses and damnations on the demon, and she was not alone in this sentiment, as both Oliver and the somnium glared.

"Oliver?" Darrel spoke flatly, glowering at the man.

It didn't need to be said, but it was quick. Oliver nodded. Darrel snapped his fingers, and darkness permeated the room. Emerging from the shadows behind the demon, a somnium loomed over its *prey*. Intico's eyes flashed as they made contact with the demon. As if encased in lead, the demon suddenly found himself unable to move but stared in mortification as the somnium loomed over him. Upturning his eyes, he saw ghastly whites consuming his vision from above. The impossible grin of a somnium bore into him, signifying his doom. The terms of the covenant were to be enacted on the recreant demon, as was vowed when he took the oath.

"Care to see how one becomes a dithered?" Intico asked Oliver, chuckling to itself as its eyes cocked with an inquisitive suggestion. Carver's heavy stare bore into Intico now. He was unamused by the transcendent demon's praxis.

"Not in the slightest," Oliver said, deigning to provoke Intico further.

Intico huffed, squinting at its looming kin.

"Fine," Intico sighed. "Elsewhere, Burgundy." Intico shooed the lesser somnium.

With a sneer, Burgundy took hold of the demon and slowly sank through the floor with him. As the two melded into the darkness, the demon's pale face quivered, and he screamed in sheer dread as he and the somnium disappeared.

Brief silence perturbed the ire shared among the demons, and Alysium rolled her eyes, crossing her arms defiantly as she glanced at Darrel.

"It looks like we have a mess to clean ... but before that. I propose we begin Harvest tonight. It won't be long before the Hunters are too entrenched in our operations for it to be an imminent success," Alysium suggested, her tone dry as she eyed the others.

Oliver's fingers rested firmly against the sofa he sat on, incessantly scraping with increasing tempo.

"I have my concerns ... but I reserve judgment of that to you, Carver. After all, you'll be the one gauging how dire the scene is for our plans. Perhaps the body hasn't been discovered yet?" Oliver suggested.

"I'll reserve that decision as a last resort ... it'll be risky if we begin the ritual tonight. Otherwise, I can't guarantee there is enough soul energy for all the somnium to maintain a corporeal form long enough to inhabit a vessel. Now, are there any other matters for us to discuss before I head to clean up after your failures?" Darrel asked Oliver.

Oliver glared for a moment, but he took a deep, shaky breath before composing himself and shaking his head.

The demonic maid stepped toward Oliver, whispering in his ear. He stood up, nodding with a sigh as he snapped at the cloaked demons in the room. "Take your positions. She's arriving soon. Make sure that boy doesn't fail me again."

"Ah, but there is one thing. One piece that may be crucial to our plans. A certain demonium. Should one of a much more fair and familiar affliction, such as the lovely Alysium, interject in my stead ..." Oliver trailed off suggestively as he shot the aloof woman an expectant look. He knew of Zane's prior affiliation with the Alastairs, and was also aware that as their former assassin, he had served alongside Alysium during her own servitude to the Alastairs. He was also aware of Zane's inclinations toward women, as one of his servants had informed him.

Alysium dropped her arms. Her gaze lowered as she ventured into the darkness of her past, the past she had left behind in desperation to escape her dreaded fate and humiliation under the Alastair's oppressive ambitions, especially the current heir.

To her, Zane had always been like a kid brother, one she had protected. He, too, had protected her upon becoming capable of his own prowess. She had no doubts in her mind that Zane would be useful to them. Secretly, when reflecting on the memories of his vicious immolation of several of their foes, she hoped he would defect to their cause, less he serve as a formidable adversary to impede them. He would at least hear her out.

"I will call to meet with him tonight," Alysium said.

"And he will listen to you? Even after my own failed attempt?" Intico asked.

"He will listen to me. And perhaps ... he will join us." Alysium had hoped to manifest these words, to see her old comrade take to her side again in realizing the Covenant of Augury's ambitions—their only hope of seeing the Alastairs, who had wronged them, brought to heel. To see their vengeance exacted.

Shrugging its shoulders, Intico snickered.

"Good luck ..." With a turn, Intico's cape rose in shadowy flaps to cover it and the other somnium demon that had quietly watched. When the cape reached its peak, the two disappeared in a veil of shadows.

Darrel stood up, fixing his uniform before turning to Alysium.

"I'll leave you to it," Darrel remarked, his expression softening for a moment as he met Alysium's despondent gaze. "Be careful, and do what you must in order to come back to me," he demanded, suggesting there was no other option he'd see come to fruition.

Shadows cascaded at Alysium's feet, swallowing her slowly as she met Darrel's concerned expression with a soft, sentimental smile before disappearing.

Darrel had no further words to exchange with Oliver or his subordinates and excused himself from the room. He briskly stormed down the halls to the courtyard out front where his car was. All the while, he pulled up an application through his smart band, which brought up a holographic screen of the recent reports that had come in from dispatch. Typically, none of them had access to these things on their personal devices. However, he hadn't played by the rules for a long time, nor did many other high-ranking officials he had manipulated in his ruse. And with bemusement, he saw it: a report on a dead body found in Lincoln Park an hour ago. He hurriedly scanned the details of the report while walking back to his car.

"A fucking *transient* reported it?" he hissed. Opening the door of his blacked-out interceptor, he threw himself into the driver's seat and hit the button to turn the vehicle on before pulling out of the looped driveway. Having made his way onto the road again, he was left to ponder his thoughts, his nerves rattled by the possibility of his meticulously crafted plan falling apart due to incompetent subordinates, the sole surviving rime, and a homeless man. He had a white-knuckled grip on his steering wheel, the vein on his forehead dancing as he shot a death glare at the car that had merged in front of him. He couldn't afford to let it all fall apart before his eyes.

The plan, Harvest, was carefully built for several months between Darrel, Intico, and Oliver. Failure was far more grave than merely remaining irrelevant among the brutal politics of demons; Darrel cared not for such sentiments. No, for him, it was imperative to reclaiming what was stolen from him in the past by the Alastairs. He was cast from his blood rite, and manifesting his claim as the rightful heir was the one thing driving his existence. Alysium had reinvigorated such a dream within him, and when he and Intico first met, he was granted a hope of achieving it.

With his vision going dark and his left eye flickering with a malevolent energy, Darrel thought back to his and Intico's fateful meeting—an unlikely alliance that would herald the evolution of his ambitions and the depth of their depravity.

It had been the fall of 2041, the year prior, and Darrel had recently been promoted to Deputy Police Chief of the Chicago Police Department after several years of service in law enforcement. Despite his successful navigation and climbing within the department, a void was present in his heart, a demonic void unfilled by his human life. *Revenge.* A motivation as worthy as any for driving a demonium of Darrel's caliber, it festered in his heart, scorned by a cruel lineage that detested his impure blood.

But ambition without an engine to drive it was as pointless as any other fanciful endeavor that could be dreamed up. And to demons, those without power behind their drive were as empty as their desires themselves. What distinguished a demon's desires was the wanton means of manifesting them.

Power, that was what a demon needed to enact their desires. Darrel had a semblance of power now, but no plan, nor a cause that other entities with power would fight for. There was no such way to wage war against the Alastair family with only minuscule influence over the Chicago Police Department. His *family* was sequestered in a mansion in Paris, no doubt counting their abundance of euros from the luxury cars and wine they produced—a fortune he was granted no part of since his expulsion from the family.

He sat in the living room of his condo, having finished his shift for the evening, and relaxed with a glass of wine—Merlot, his favorite. The bitter-sweet liquid flowed past his lips as he tilted the glass back, the rich flavors and notes settling on his tongue. His feet rested atop the footrest of his burgundy sofa, freshly relieved of the boots that had imprisoned them for the past fourteen hours. A series of conferences and meetings in the department had rendered him scarce for the evening, and he wouldn't seek any further activity until he had to prepare for bed.

Alysium had implored him to seek avenues for his revenge. She had urged him to continue gaining power, to continue seeking a rank to garner favors that could be used against the Alastair family. And with time, perhaps that day approached. It was with power that other demons would gravitate to a cause. Of various political and dynamic afflictions, it was in their interest to remain dominant within human society. He also had the benefit of not being known by the Hunters, and with secrecy, he was only known as the human, Darrel Carver. Alysium had insisted on calling him by his birth name, but he had been quick to refuse it. A name from an unscrupulous family that had stripped him of his dignity was unpalatable, unlike their wine.

"Complacency isn't becoming of you, Carver," a whispered voice echoed around him. On cue, the lights failed, and darkness swallowed the room.

Immediately setting his glass down on the rust-accented black coffee table, Darrel lifted his hand. A spiraling orb of purple energy formed in his palm with a flickering pulse, casting vivid waves of light that sparsely illuminated his surroundings, but he saw nothing.

"Reveal yourself, *now*," Darrel spoke in an exigent tone. The cumbersome darkness enveloping his condo settled with menacing undertones of silence. A cold draft carried an insidious energy through the living room. The energy was foreign to Darrel. No amount of examination of it resonates in his memory. *Not a feral ... nor a wraith,* he thought.

"Compose yourself, Carver. I mean no harm. I come with a proposal that could benefit the both of us," the voice called. The deep, raspy voice called. It exuded a haughtiness that suggested a lack of concern for Darrel, as if he was of no threat, and such an insinuation was hardly favorable to him.

"Did I stutter?" Within the perceptually stretched moments, the insidious energy dispersed through the room, amalgamating from the shadows in a surge of red and black. The air shuddered and whipped around the room, causing the furniture to vibrate and the ceiling fan to spin as a smoky substance manifested into a tall, dark figure: the being that would become known as Intico.

Maintaining his stance, Darrel flinched at the initial image, unaware of what stood before him. A tall being that had manifested directly out of nightmares. The being wore tattered magician's clothing. He hated magicians. They had always scared him as a child, and he couldn't help but recall a nightmare he once had about an undead magician chasing him through an unending maze of corridors and hidden crevices.

Shuddering, Darrel held his hand up, the energy still flickering and pulsing in his hand with a newfound resolve plastered on his face.

"What the *fuck* are you?" Darrel demanded. He knew Intico was a demon of some kind, but he couldn't place what kind. He had never seen a demon capable of manifesting nightmares directly, unprovoked at that. It was not an illusion spell. No, the pattern of the energy was not sufficiently perturbed. However, there was an irrefutable quality to the surrounding energy that was intransigent. It *hissed.*

"My kind is long overdue for our debut," it began. "We are the somnium. Beings composed of and driven by fear, born of the omens that create such emotions. Humans call them ... nightmares. We feed on the deepest reaches of fear, be it man"—it gazed deep into Darrel's eyes, its gaze widening with its wicked grin expanding—"or demon."

With the revelation that Intico knew what Darrel truly was, that it had peered into his own sanctuary of repressed fears, the energy in his palm crackled ferociously. His left eye briefly flashed red and purple as he cast his ire on Intico.

"And why should I not blast you into dust, fiend?" Darrel hissed.

"That would be very rude of you. We just met, after all," Intico chuckled. "I'm sure you would be interested to know how I could assist you, an umbra demon capable of forging a pact with others, in reclaiming the rite that was stolen from you."

Darrel, surging with uncertainty and fear alike, considered the vague pitch from Intico. However dubious it sounded, it had piqued his interest, but he was not convinced. Every hair of skepticism he harbored stood on edge under the scrutiny of the ghastly abysses that were Intico's eyes.

"Who would choose to believe a fiend like you? A being of night-mares with every reason to mislead is hardly a trustworthy diplomat, even among the treachery of demons."

Intico chuckled again and held out its hand, long, spindly digits unfurling.

"I offer you my power, the power of the somnium. My brethren awaken for reasons even I have yet to discern, but I presume it is our shared discontent. I have taken the liberty of unifying us." Intico's grin wavered. "Still, there remains an issue even I am incapable of solving. Our corporeal affinity is ... low. We cannot maintain our beings for long outside of dreamscapes embroiled in fear. But we yearn for a solution. A solution that, in turn, would grant you allies capable of assisting in seizing control of the Alastair family. And there is so much more than you could desire in that fiendish heart I glimpsed."

Darrel could discern that Intico spoke the truth about the matter of its ability to remain in a physical form. Even then, he could see its rippling, dark flesh seeping energy, threatening to disperse into nothing if it gratuitously expended itself. Akin to smoke, it bellowed its energy in unstable, hazy discharges. Even so, the entity before him possessed an air of prominence—an irrevocable potential entrenched in its voracious ambitions it sought to manifest with his aid.

"You had my skepticism, but now, you have my attention." The energy in Darrel's hand shrunk, not completely dissipating yet. "Go ahead. What's this odious scheme you think would benefit me and my desires?"

"Excellent decision," Intico said. It kneeled in front of Darrel to meet him more squarely, albeit still towering over him. Only now, as it had more headroom, a top hat manifested, further drawing a distasteful expression from Darrel. "I have already made a pact with the Siegharts, whom you no doubt are aware of within the city. We have forged a new covenant. Now, we require your power and influence to ensure that we can bring about an event that will allow us to seize control of the city. In one night, in one fell swoop, we will claim our vessels, and the Siegharts can further expand their territorial significance. Harvest. Wherein the somnium will meld into the corporeal beings of the city, assuming their form. For this to work, we will need souls to perform the ritual, otherwise my brethren and I cannot maintain our forms or safely meld with these vessels." Intico snickered, its fingers crackling as it curled them into a fist. "We will methodically install ourselves, city after city. And then ..." it trailed off, its eye cocking expectantly.

"We will seize power from the Alastairs when their formidability will be dwarfed by our own," Darrel finished. His indignant gaze shimmered with a hope he had long lacked, a renewal of understanding of the importance his career had served in his grand scheme—their grand schemes.

"Precisely." Intico shifted to stand once more, cackling as its cape whipped ferociously with a rising surge of power coalescing around it.

"But the Sieghart family ... how will they play into this?" Darrel asked. Only then did he lower his hand, the energy that had been poised in his palm dissipating.

"Their alliance grants us corporeal agents capable of acquiring the souls we need for Harvest. They are aware of you and your prowess, and as such, wish to leverage your prestige to streamline such a process." Darrel tensed at the mention of being discovered by the Siegharts. He could only imagine his mother had seen to it that they kept tabs on him.

"And in turn, you will find that your power, your demonic abilities, will significantly grow with our own. I draw from your power, and you will, in turn, draw from mine. That's a fair exchange, yes?" The room distorted, and the air resembled fibers coming undone atop a red canvas. Rippling and waving, Intico's presence consumed the space, filling it with a swarming energy that sought to join with another, to forge a pact as any notable umbra tended to.

But Darrel hesitated. His hands remained clenched at his sides. His revenge could finally be realized, but the currency was steep and tumultuous. Neither his soul nor power was at stake. This was not the pact Intico offered. Instead, there was a price he could not identify, a detail unarticulated. However unwise this pact was, it was a hope he had never been granted before. Even though he would see his comrades in the police force be offered as kindling to the flames of his ambition, he would see the injustice plaguing him remedied.

However meager his own role appeared, Darrel was far from useless, and much to his perturbed awareness, Intico had discovered that spark of power he possessed—the same power he had been prepared to use against it minutes ago. Darrel had been blessed with the abilities of his clan. An Alastair fortunate enough to inherit the ability typically manifested it within their right eye, and he was no exception. However, this challenged a legacy—his impure blood, his humanity they had scorned him for, was impermissible for a prospective heir. With infernal volition, they had extracted the power from his right eye and gifted it to the *rightful* heir to further bolster his powers, for an Alastair of pure lineage with two blessed eyes was more formidable.

But little did the Alastairs know that he later manifested it within his left eye as well, an unforeseen phenomenon even in a pure-blooded Alastair. And with the power still residing within him, he knew that he still had a rightful claim. However crippled his potential was, he could display an overwhelming might the family would be forced to revere. While insufficient by himself, with Intico's power—with the covenant's power—he could discover a new apex of his bloodline.

"Come, Carver—make a deal with the Devil." Intico held its hand out to Darrel again, an outstretched palm with digits that could easily shroud half his arm.

After several seconds, Darrel's pensive dark eyes flickered with purple energy. His arm lurched forward, and his hand grasped Intico's.

"Henceforth, we forge a pact of dark harmony and solidarity!" Darrel declared. With their energies joined together, a dark union commenced between their souls, and the pact was forged.

Intico gave a large, wicked ghost-white grin that curled right off its small face. The air became stagnant, their energies coming to a rousing conclusion with the ritual, and they retracted their hands. Left dangling in Darrel's grasp was a pendant, etched with a screaming face bearing the semblance of a somnium. As it swayed from an obsidian chain, he inspected it. Darrel scowled, finding it to be an ugly, accursed ornament.

"And this is?"

"Henceforth, you are a part of the *Covenant of Augury*. This"—Intico gestured to the pendant dangling in Darrel's grasp—"is a token of our contract, and a means by which you may call upon us. The Siegharts will be in contact, Carver." Intico stood, turning as a rift of darkness opened, ready to swallow it.

"What is your name, fiend?" Darrel asked.

Intico turned its head, eyeing him momentarily before snickering.

"We somnium do not have names. Feel free to continue calling me *fiend*."

As Intico stepped through the dark rift, its presence ceased from within the condo, and the light soon flickered back to life. Chaotic energies had swept through the living room, and the wineglass had shattered, causing the ruby-red liquid to drip from the edge of the table.

Frowning, Darrel sighed, shaking his head as he promptly sought to clean the mess. He tucked the amulet into his pocket, sighing in a shaky exhale. Though he was fatigued from the day, a renewed vigor rushed through him. His first thought was to contact Alysium and inform her of their new alliance, to instill in her the hope she had sought from him long ago. Her unwavering commitment to seeing him triumph in their vendetta against the Alastairs was greatly appreciated by him, and he sought to live up to her expectations, to liberate her from the suffering they had caused the both of them.

"Zaldionne won't stand a chance," Darrel mused to himself as he cleaned. He tentatively raised a shard of glass, still stained in the wine that trailed down its jagged edge. It reminded him of blood dripping from a dagger—*his* blood dripping from the dagger the Alastairs had used to extract the power from his eye. He would conjure such a weapon when the time came, and he contemplated what he would carve from Zaldionne first.

Remembering the tears that streaked from Alysium's face during her plea to him and the visage of Zaldionne wearing the eye that was taken from him, Darrel's lips curled into a malicious grin. He wouldn't simply kill Zaldionne. He wished to have him lament his misdeeds, to see him stripped of his dignity—to see him stripped of the *pillar* of his sins. Whatever torturous fate he'd design for the loathsome man, Darrel would ensure he would never again be able to harm another woman like he had harmed Alysium.

"Legitimate heir."

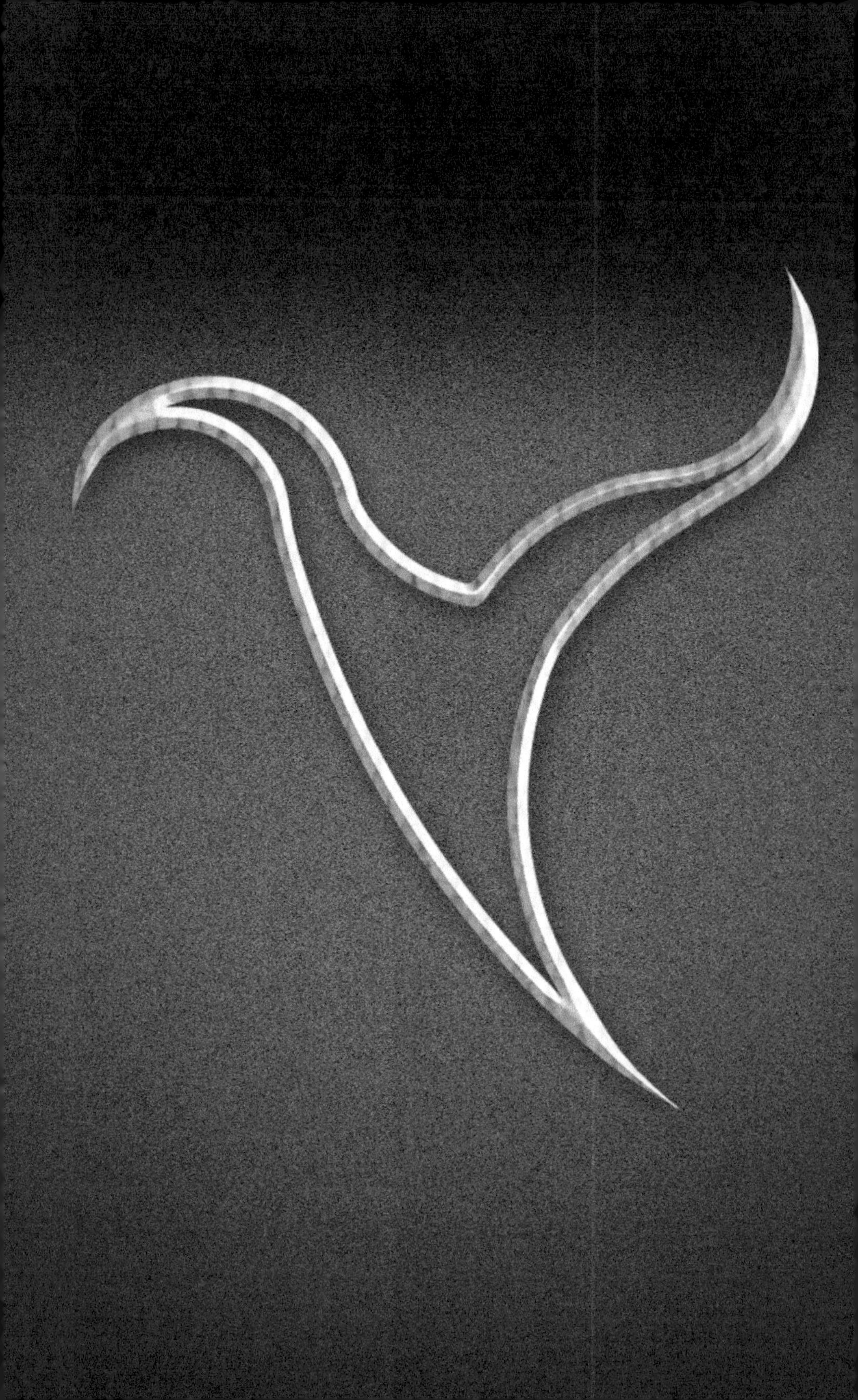

TEN

DIMINUTIVE DESOLATION

S weat dripped from Allen's brow during the drills Coach Meyers ran him and the football team through. They stormed through the obstacles placed before them, cleats scattering the grass and marking the field with their respective dedication. As their captain, Allen had borne the responsibility of leading the team and serving as an inspiration not only to them, but to the school as well.

Ashwood High had always been renowned for their football team especially, a legacy built upon its mantle. He carried the proverbial torch now, and next year, his absence, in the vision he had once sought, would leave a desolate quarry. He had wanted to be the best—but not for himself or the school.

For Kendra.

But even more imperative was the gravity weighing on him—the mantle he was to carry for his family. Kendra had once called them the modern aristocrats, and that was not an inaccurate comparison. With the prestige of their wealth, there was a more infernal prominence he was expected to fulfill one day. With such painful, grating shoes to fill, there was a demand for sacrifice.

Presented to him was a woman with fair skin, the silkiest red hair, and an almost-ethereal radiance. But that was the extent of her appeal—for she dawned such desirability as an ornament that was exceedingly impractical. Beneath the facade, there was a treachery he abhorred. Sooner did he find himself reaching out to Kendra, banishing the idea of his and that woman's union as if he had a choice. Ideally, he would see himself disowned and forced to toil for meager wages if it meant he and Kendra could just remain friends, but that wishful thinking plagued him. Only she had a choice.

Such envy.

That aspiration had faded, and even as he pushed and stressed himself to the brink and back, the hollowness left in his heart ached deeply. If he could get a chance, he doubted there were even words he could conjure that would see the fondness they once shared rekindled.

Once he had cleaned off the mud and grass in the shower, he dressed in a simple outfit of blue jeans, a red shirt with a popular logo on it, black boots, and a white bomber jacket. He always dressed down if he could help it, much to his father's disapproval every morning. He would never go without a reminder.

Then, his green smart band buzzed, and the holographic projection displayed the caller.

Kendra.

He nearly fell from the bench when he realized she was calling him. It had been when school had let out earlier that day that she had declined to speak with him. A reluctance that, in truth, he was paradoxically grateful for. Remembering the stern echoes of his father's voice, he clenched his hand into a tight fist and composed himself.

He answered.

"Ken? Hey!" he spoke, biting his bottom lip.

"Allen ... I want to talk."

"Of course! I wasn't sure if I had done something ... or—yeah, we can talk. When and where?"

"I want privacy ... so, your place. I'm sorry if this is abrupt—"

"Don't apologize. I told you I'd be here for you, right? I'm on my way home now ... did you need a ride?"

"No, no. I'm walking there now. I'll see you soon, k?"

"Right. See you soon."

The call ended, and Allen stood from the bench as he kicked his locker shut. His heart raced, thrashing with paradoxical resolve to see

Kendra—but once again, his father's voice kept reverberating in his head, and he remembered what awaited him. He reached into his pocket, and the cold sting of the amulet within it sank into his skin. With its bite, the reminder of his imperative solidified.

Kendra had a choice. He had none.

As he bolted from the locker room, he reminded himself of this truth repeatedly as he ran home, and there was a deep, festering voice that thrummed alongside his father's—a creed deeper than the imperative his family carried. No matter how much he had pretended, such things unmarred by its stretches would see him never meet redemption.

Kendra found herself at the large, black gates that led into the driveway. She hadn't needed to announce herself over the gate comm, because it was already unlocked. She let herself in, treading down the long stone walkway. Approaching the head of the driveway, she noticed a blacked-out sedan hurriedly speeding to the gate of the driveway. A strange presence tickled her from the vehicle, one that was unfamiliar but dubious.

It wasn't uncommon for Allen's family to have unsavory guests, plenty of whom she had the displeasure of meeting. However, she had always thought it was her *posh radar* going off. She pushed the thought down before approaching the large porch of the mansion.

Before Kendra could even knock, Allen burst through the door, alit with anxiety-addled breaths as if he had been running.

"Ken. It's good to see you."

Kendra froze in her tracks, raising her trembling hand and giving a reluctant wave.

Allen's hair was damp and disheveled, and he had a fresh scent that Kendra picked up on; it was clear he had come from practice. This reminded Kendra of the days when they'd finish their respective drills for their teams and spend the time afterward together. She always found catharsis in his stormy gray eyes and cheap humor. He always smelled of pine tar with his after-practice showers, and she used to love catching his scent, not that she'd have admitted it. Now—it was slightly overwhelming with her change.

Approaching him, Kendra's fingers dug into her shirt for a vestige of security. However, that insecurity melted away when he embraced her in a firm hug, pulling her against his sturdy frame. The doubts ceased, rousing her relief, and her fingers that had been taut and rigid, relaxed, almost going limp as she raised her arms and returned Allen's embrace.

"Let's head to my room," he said, but registered how it sounded upon saying it. "For privacy, and all," he quickly added.

Kendra stifled a chuckle and nodded, finding humor in his gaff. Navigating the gaudily decorated home, they went upstairs to where his room was. Kendra lightly dragged her nails on the wooden banister, which she had done the first and only time she had come over for one of his family's parties. It had been under more challenging pretenses and conceptions of the others present. It hadn't been all family, but the scrutiny she had been subjected to was difficult to disregard. She recalled a younger woman giving her nasty faces. Class division, she supposed.

Kendra *reeked* of her middle-class upbringing, having sported a dress that wouldn't cost an entire paycheck or two. Yet, it still had an iota of quality and style to it. She at least understood that, given her passive interest in fashion. That girl had suggested jealousy in her regard toward her, but Kendra hardly had any mental real estate to entertain such a thing.

Allen waited for Kendra at the top of the staircase. Catching up to him, he continued down the hall and opened the door leading into his room.

Upon entering, there was the queen-size bed, two dressers, a nightstand, and various sports memorabilia from his years of playing. She could only assume he'd be prideful of such accomplishments, but something stuck out to her. Dangling from the drawer was a necklace that was etched with an elongated face and a gaping hole where the mouth was. Reminding her of *The Scream* painting, it harbored an eerie appearance. She always assumed it was another one of the weird things his family had given him—similar to their family crest. The idea of them even having a crest peeved her, but she hardly blamed Allen for that. It wasn't his choice that they had one, after all. He mentioned how much it annoyed him, too. In fact, he had always declared he hated the flashiness of his family.

Kendra was still afraid of what Allen would think—what he'd say about her trauma dumping. But, beyond the measures of the absurdity and what it entailed, she found hope when she gazed into his sympathetic eyes, which were similarly marred with sorrow. Guilt racked her to know she had inspired such anxiety within him, or she assumed that was why he was so tense and eager to speak with her.

In spite of any sympathy he could impose, or if he deigned to *believe* her, she saw her demonic nature to be antithetical to a continued friendship with Allen. She believed he was under no volition or scope in which he could accept her as she was now. A monster. One that could tear him apart if she forgot to take her medicine.

She crept toward his bed and took a seat. She was prepared for him to stand, but in her moments of preparations to speak, he took his seat beside her. Her gaze became more evasive, fixating on her lap. It was the only way she could focus. He was silent—and patient—as he had suggested the last time they saw each other. Eventually, she found her words.

"I ..." she stammered. "I'm not the person you used to know ... and it happened that night that—that Kenny and I were ..." The word got caught in her throat. "Attacked."

Allen nodded along, sucking his bottom lip as he focused, his gaze pensive.

"They were some kind of creatures ... demons that looked like wolves. They attacked us ... and I'm the only one who made it before someone showed up and saved me. But now I'm this ... thing. I'm a mon—"

"You're not a monster. I'd never consider you one," he spoke preemptively, almost as if rehearsed.

"You don't understand, Allen," she snapped, throwing her head side to side. *He still has no idea,* she thought. "I'm not human anymore ... I'm some mix of whatever the fuck they were. I'm some kind of demon now!" she stuttered.

Allen never flinched or wavered. His hard gaze rose to challenge her own gaze of self-loathing.

"You're not a demon, monster, or whatever. You're Kendra, and that's all I care about," he said.

Kendra went quiet, her teeth grinding as they sharpened. Her eyelids blackened, her sclera consuming itself with inky darkness as her irises cast aside their royal-blue hues in favor of a burning crimson and orange. With elongating fingers becoming tense, her nails took on a similar darkness as they extended into sharp claws.

She wasn't consistently of a demonic aspect, and in fact, could hide her features from herself if she focused on keeping calm. However, Eden had told her before about humans being unable to perceive the change, should she lose track. If someone was connected to Ichor, they could easily see what happened to her, but she had no idea what someone who wasn't connected to Ichor would see. As such, she waited to see if he'd react, shutting her eyes tightly as if it would cloak her.

"Do you see? This ... thing I am?" she asked. Allen watched with unwavering determination, reaching out and gently resting his palm on her shoulder. Kendra jumped, reflexively turning her head away from Allen. She waited for anything. And then she felt his warm embrace once more. She gasped, his scent bombarding her demonic senses with a renewed acuteness. It was different.

"You're still my Kendra ..." he spoke in a hushed tone.

The sense of relief lasted but for a moment, if not for her carnal instincts urging her otherwise. As Allen held her, a subtle red hue danced in her vision, and a thousand needles prickled her skin. She was suddenly alert ... Allen's energy was absent now, along with all the other energies she had noticed within the mansion. It was a subconscious process she had been used to washing over her since her change. It was as if she were completely human once again, both in her physical and spiritual perceptions.

As Allen embraced her, her eyes fluttered open to stare down at her hands, now strangely devoid of her demonic qualities. *Human hands.* She couldn't feel the familiar pulsing focus within her eyes, and they, too, had returned to their royal-blue hue. Though her senses were dulled, they were not fully withdrawn, as was evident when she heard faint vibrations from the stairs.

She drew back, her gaze still downcast as she shook herself from the comfort of Allen's arms. Then she looked up at him. Her eyes widened, her heart racing fast as she registered what she saw. His right eye was irrevocably different from his left eye, a green slit pupil with incandescent purple veins trailing to the edges of its black sclera. When she blinked, it was gray once more, but she knew what she had seen.

"You'll always be—"

"What did you *do*?" she strained out, her voice endeavoring not to break.

Allen stared blankly for a moment, his face showing a perturbed sorrow, and then he reached out slowly with a shaky hand.

"Shh ... it's okay, Ken. I know you're on edge. You'll be okay."

"Don't touch me!" She slapped his hand away. Her eyes narrowed as she threw herself from the bed, stumbling back unsteadily. Her eyes locked onto his, afraid to let him leave her sight. She had never seen his eyes like this—filled with sheer despair a thousand miles away. The hall outside creaked with footsteps, and her gaze briefly shot to the door. In that brief moment she took her eyes off Allen, something hampered her. She writhed and tossed herself to break free, glancing down to find tendrils of shadow enveloping her form and constricting her limbs.

The door burst open. Breath halting in her throat, Kendra's pupils dilated in horror as she saw them. Robed figures—the same that had come for her that night Vicente died.

"I'm sorry, Ken ..." Allen called out from behind her.

A robed demon inched closer to her, hand poised and cloaked in an indigo aura that made Kendra woozy in its proximity. They drew nearer, and Kendra's eyes swelled with fear. Hands tightly clenched, she waited, and the hand outstretched to grasp her. Kendra's body lurched back despite her restraints, but she lost her balance and fell back, slamming her head against the edge of the dresser. Her world danced in flashes of moving images, distorting and re-centering in her vision until it settled on a face that loomed over her—Allen's.

She writhed in her constraints, focusing on the swelling chaos within her mind—the rage that consumed her each time her flames had accidentally been conjured from her body. But they never came. As if the spark within her was deprived of oxygen, those flames never kindled. Her efforts proved fruitless after several excruciating seconds, and then the tears escaped. Thick pools welled in her eyes, further distorting her vision. To worsen the situation, a dampness spread from where she had hit her head, blood trickling from the wound her fall had created.

Confused as she was, the glimmers of truth she knew were heart wrenching and jarring: Allen's involvement with the nefarious group, his motives, and his overall shift in demeanor. Allen had always been the goofy jock, but those amiable eyes, the same eyes she had once adored, cast their disparaging indictments upon her now. Meeting them, she saw a torn conviction in place of compassion, and her heart tore in two.

"*Why?*" she whispered, but he gave no answer. Allen's fingers spread as the same dizzying energy washed over his palm. He pressed it to her head, and calmness washed over her. The image of his trembling gaze danced in her mind, and just briefly, before the darkness consumed her, she saw his tears. As much as such a contradiction puzzled her, inviting her to resolve the paradox of emotions within herself and within his gaze, she fell into slumber.

There were several moments of silence as Allen carefully retracted his hand, and he bit his lips hard, stifling any noise that dared to bleed past them.

"Finally. We've had enough setbacks as is," Oliver's voice called from behind them. Allen didn't deign to glance over his shoulder, his gaze never leaving Kendra as the robed demons lifted her from the ground and carried her away.

"You should have found a way to get this done a lot quicker. Between Intico ordering us to not harm a hair on the Blackwell kid's hair, and the fact he guards her, you were the only one who could do this. Now—Harvest is next."

Allen remained quiet, his mind far away, along with his gaze. There was a shift in the air that roused him from his momentary rumination, and his hand darted up, catching Oliver's hand when he tried to grab his shoulder.

Finally, Allen peered over his shoulder, staring into the similar gray irises of his father, and he glared.

"Since when are you so impudent, boy? You would never have married her. For ... what? To birth us a damned demonium? An impure mockery of our heritage? Ridiculous. Your mother would turn in her grave," Oliver spat.

Allen turned around, shoving past the man without another word. For once, there had not been a hint of envy in him when he had stared at the man. While he was still bound by the pact with the somnium, his obligation to the covenant remained. But in that singular moment, that festering voice that had haunted him for his entire life, envious and seeking to supplant his own to see him make the decisions he never could, had spoken to him again.

Sieghart no more.

Several robed demons congregated within the mostly empty warehouse where they conducted most of their meetings, training, and other nefarious preparatory work. Standing at Alysium's attention, they waited for her instructions, having been summoned by her.

"Should things go well with this meeting, none of you will need to lift a finger. I certainly hope this will be the case ... but should such measures be necessary, which I trust you are all of sufficient intelligence to discern, you will aid me. Until it is necessary, you shall remain hidden and obscured. To assure this, since I am certain your arcane proficiency is ill-suited to the necessary camouflage, the Sieghart heir shall disconnect you, so you may remain hidden."

She gestured her head to Allen, who had remained silent at her side until then. Although he had little will to help the covenant, he had no choice. Turning his gaze to the demons, he saw their leers, a shared disappointment embroidered in their despondent, blackened eyes. They awaited him.

He'd see them burned and scorned if that was a choice he could make. Their creed, bound in blood, meant little to him, and the family he was to discard himself to lead were but ghosts within the chambers of his empathy. But his insubordination was palpable to a fate worse than a simple afterlife in the shadows. The somnium, whom he had been forced to make a pact with, hissed in his head whenever he thought of diverging from their interests. Such was the case with pacts—they were not broken without mutual consent. An eternity sequestered within nightmares awaited if he were to deviate.

"When I use the eye of Jugo on you, it will last for roughly six hours. I will utilize it in such a way that, if necessary, you can break from it with minimal effort. You'll be on your own. I can't obscure the somnium without destroying their corporeal form," Allen explained, his voice dry as he scrutinized the demons—his former family. In the next breath, his right eye was bathed in darkness. In the center, a sickly green hue carved vertically; from it, indigo rivers stretched across the abyss. With energy shooting from the eye, there was a flash of red around the demons. Their connection and presence had been obscured.

With a blink, Allen's eye returned to normal. He let out a long sigh, pursing his lips as he glanced at Alysium.

"Prepare yourselves. We leave shortly," Alysium commanded, and with a snap of her finger, the demons dispersed. Turning to Allen for a moment, she said nothing before she turned to walk away.

"Wait," Allen said.

Alysium stopped in her tracks.

"Yes?"

"When will ... they take her body?"

"Very shortly. The fiend who will claim her awaits the blessing of the somnium lord. A complete dither of her caliber shall prove advantageous in enacting Harvest."

"I—"

"Out with it. I haven't time for such meekness."

Allen took a shaky breath, glancing across the warehouse at the stairwell that led underneath it—where Kendra was held.

"I want to speak with her—one last time."

Alysium frowned, her face scrunching in disgust before she folded her arms above her chest.

"You—the heir to the Siegharts—harbor such an attachment to a ... *human*? Or whatever abomination she is considered now. The difference matters not. Such sympathies toward lesser beings are wasted. The first time, the demonium I am tasked with placating slew the hounds you sent after the policewoman. Your failure the second time with the abomination was unacceptable. That's why I sent those mutts the third time to ensure there were no further setbacks. Now ... more blood is on your hands as a result, no?" She shifted, her nails raking her arms as she glared. "Kill your attachment and be done with it—lest your bloodline fall to ruin."

"To Inferos with the Siegharts," Allen hissed, his gray eyes living up to the stormy sky they resembled. "I will do what must be done. I will kill all that remains of myself once I've spoken with her."

There was a boiling silence as Alysium scrutinized Allen, his words mirroring a sentiment that she, at one time, had harbored. The desire to kill the expectations that entailed her existence. But even deeper was the vestige of love—the forbidden kind that would see them exiled if pursued. Instead, she had run from *him* and sought solace in the arms of one whom the Alastairs had excised.

Abomination or not, such a shared fixation would forever weigh on their hearts.

"You have until the end of the night. I will clarify as much to the somnium. After that—Harvest begins."

Without another word, Alysium turned and walked away. The sound of her heels clicking echoed through the hollow warehouse. And much like its ephemeral existence, Allen's sympathy was the same. All that was left was to kill what was left of himself.

Alysium had known Zane as a rambunctious boy. He had been a young teen when she had trained him, honing his power into something serviceable to the Alastairs. His latent abilities were something she had admired, having witnessed his power grow from a dull spark to an uproarious blaze. In no small part due to herself, he had become something frightening to most demons that opposed him, and that was why they needed his power. *Why Eridionne needed his power,* she thought.

Alysium swept her silky obsidian hair over her shoulder. Her legs dangled from atop the building, her flowy, black dress whipping in the fall winds that kissed her. There was a subtle chill that permeated, making her wish she had worn leggings as well. She hadn't initially planned on such an inconspicuous location, and it was colder than she thought, but she had her reasons. As the chill settled into her moonlit skin, she was reminded of similar chilly nights when she had worked with Zane, specifically how he naturally warded off such cold with his naturally warm body temperature. He always joked that he'd go nude if not for social convention. It wasn't as strange an idea as it had sounded: Zane's kin within Inferos didn't wear clothes due to the clothing-unfriendly nature of their demonic forms. Such was the case with flames and cloth.

Her black eyes, blending with the night, shifted across the glimmering city below. As large a city as Chicago was, it felt small to her from the high vantage point. And no matter how many times she stared down at it, she found herself apathetic to what animated it. The humans' lives meant nothing to her, insignificant in the scheme of her loyalties and yearning for vengeance. She tightened her delicate fingers on the cloth of her dress, recalling her initial pleas to Darrel before he had forged the ambition she had come to rely on as a bastion. It was all she had and all she needed.

"Makes you think about how small we are, huh?" a voice called from behind Alysium.

Turning her head, Alysium saw Zane. Standing with a rueful smirk, he approached with an alien amicability that was foreign to her memory of him. He had grown significantly from when they last met, towering over her. The blaze, fire demons, were tall, but Zane was not quite as imposing as the primonium, the unevolved demons which were most common in Inferos. Alysium levitated from the rooftop floor, landing softly with only a subtle gust to make her dress ripple. Her dull expression turned into a more amenable one, a phantom of a smile tugging at her lips.

"We are not small," Alysium said.

"Only our presence," they both finished in unison.

There was a pause.

"You always enjoyed overlooking cities from high up," Zane remarked.

"As a young girl, I always wished to be a bird, so I might fly far away. Now ... I know where I belong."

Zane took a step toward her, shoving his hands into his parka's pockets. It was appropriate for the weather, but the article puzzled Alysium, wondering why he encumbered himself with it, given he didn't need layers to remain warm.

"Why do you wear that?" she asked.

Zane looked intrigued, cocking an eyebrow.

"Cause it's comfortable. Gotta really appreciate the craftsmanship," he said.

Alysium frowned but disregarded his comment. It was ultimately inconsequential, or at worst, favorable to her. Holding his gaze, she crossed her arms, her face exterminating any semblance of emotion.

"Do you know what happened when you left?" she began.

Zane snorted.

"No, but I bet you're gonna tell me."

"You should perhaps consider the context," she chastised.

"Right ... sorry," Zane muttered.

Alysium turned her back to him, her eyes downcast at the city again as she distilled her memories.

"The plan fell apart. And we retreated with our tails between our legs. And like guilty mutts, we were punished. Each of us ... personally"—she took a deep breath—"by none other than the Alastair heir. That ... repugnant Alastair *son of a bitch*," she hissed, her face twisting in her pained rumination.

"Zaldionne," Zane spoke listlessly.

"My punishment ..." Her stare became desolate, her nails digging into her arms, becoming sharp as she drew blood.

"Alysium ... don't," Zane pleaded softly.

Alysium relented, her grip easing as her eyes refilled with conviction.

"Zane ... salvation is upon us." She tore her grip from herself, her nails coated in blood as the wounds on her arm sizzled shut. She swung around to face him, her boot stomping into the brick of the rooftop.

Zane's eyes darted to the side, meek to her imposition in the revelation of her plight.

"The somnium, Harvest, it will set us free from the chains of the Alastair's oppression and allow the family to become what it is destined to be."

"Harvest?" Zane perked his head at the mention of the infamous term. The fact Alysium was more animated than she had ever been before only added to his growing concern about what the Covenant of Augury was brewing.

"Harvest," she repeated, "is upon us. Where all the souls garnered will allow the somnium to take their vessels. With their corporeal forms finalized, the Alastairs will have no choice but to bow before us. Your power would prove fruitful in rectifying what the Alastairs subjected you and I to." She stepped toward him, extending her hand. "Join Eridionne and I, and we may see justice. The Alastairs will have no choice but to bow before us!"

Zane's mouth was agape, glimpsing the fanaticism Alysium had adopted, realizing how grave her repression rendered her. The more she spoke, the more apparent it was she was not the same woman he had once known—the same woman who had fostered his abilities.

"This *Eridionne* who hatched this plan to sacrifice an entire city of people to nightmarish monsters is an ass-hat bastard," he declared, which earned a glare from Alysium.

"*Watch. Your. Tongue,*" she hissed. Then she snapped her fingers, a crackle of purple energy coursing through her as she awaited Zane's decision, her optimism thoroughly tested.

Zane's eyes narrowed on her hand, wary of the pact she sought with him. Pacts were a commitment of power and will that would sooner see the realms perish than break. The distress in her eyes, the direness they harbored, stirred an unholy mixture of guilt and disgust within him. Such a concoction fermenting inside him was her intention. That was why Alysium was sent this time. Nobody else held a semblance of a chance to sway him. Alysium, for all her faults, was a demon that he harbored a bond with, a bond he would see spared in spite of their opposing convictions.

The wind ferociously whipped around them, stirring the night with further ominous influence. They stared into one another's eyes with polarizing resolve and waning sentiments that sought to demolish said resolve.

"It is time, Zane. Will you join us, or will you reside with the prey?"

Bemused by the choice he was given, Zane fervently understood that refusal meant death. The polarity between his demon half and human half were made readily apparent once more, the duality of his allegiance, and the contradiction of his dreams were challenged once again.

However difficult the decision was for him, his answer came quickly.

"Team prey all the way. I think our fashion is much more bearable, and frankly ... I could give a shit about your vengeance if it means enthralling an entire city to those discount-Venom-looking things." Zane flashed a resolved smirk, cocking his eyebrow at her. "And ... this is the part where you kill me, right?"

"Obviously," she declared flatly, the wind dying as the world stood still.

With how quickly Alysium's decision came, with how quickly she had killed her hesitation, Zane buried his remorse. The deadening silence that ensued allowed the ambience of the city to cut through the tension, providing an anticlimactic chorus to the coming carnage. Zane turned his back to her, casting his gaze to the abyss of the night outstretched above them. Neither of them spoke. Zane could only remember the various times they sparred, and how, as he gradually improved, he had to hold back. However, he couldn't have been certain of where she stood now, if she, too, had held back during those sessions.

"Alysium—I don't want to kill you."

Of all the demons he had slain, of all those lives he had taken, Alysium was not one he'd have foreseen. His hands clenched at his sides, and he inhaled a breath of respite—the calm before the storm. He turned around once more, seeing she had taken her position far behind him. She was clever to establish such a distance.

"Five meters a second ... that is how quickly your flames can travel."

"Sweet of you to remember," Zane spoke flatly. He crouched, crossing his thumbs before clasping his fingers together, forming the terra-diablo sign. Energy pulsed from his hands as he focused, then he slammed his fingertips into the concrete beneath him, and sparks of crimson and orange flew with pulsing energy that vibrated the floor. Two walls of concrete rose in front of him, causing a cloud of dust to form when they were struck by bolts of purple energy.

Demonic alchemy was one of the many useful skills Zane had cultivated, allowing him to alter and manipulate matter so far as if he had a catalyst, that being his energy, and knowledge of the chemical components. In combination, he manipulated the molecules with demonic energy against their natural inclination.

Alysium knew of the skill and had seen him use it plenty when they fought with others or with each other. She lowered her hand, still abuzz with the hostile energy she had shot at Zane. Her irises narrowed, turning purple, the whites consumed by darkness as she manifested the traits of her sin. Her skin took on an ashen hue, and claws grew from her fingertips as curved black horns protruded from her head, arcing inward.

Zane's anticipation was nothing less than what she had expected, but she had hoped he would have hesitated. Then, she could have ended things quickly. But now, it was clear she had to take on her true form to finish the fight. Of course, her subordinates wouldn't have been quick enough to get a hit on him without her. Maybe if they had used bullets, but such demons harbored great shame in utilizing the technology of humans in combat, seeing it as beneath them. Zane, however, clearly lacked that sentiment. That was why It hadn't surprised Alysium when he reached behind and drew a gunblade.

Zane aimed and shot, and the bullet pierced a covenant demon in the knee. He had anticipated they weren't alone that entire time, and despite the several demons surrounding him being invisible, he could clearly distinguish their positions from their body heat, something he could subconsciously track.

The shot demon howled in pain, toppling over in shock, and his wound sizzled violently due to the anti-demon bullet Zane had loaded in his weapon. Anti-demon bullets would corrode the insides of demons with a special mix of rosemary and other chemical reactants. As such, the demon found his flesh and bone dissolving where the bullet had hit him. He wouldn't be getting up anytime soon, which was what Zane intended, wanting to keep one of them alive. He would have tried to incapacitate Alysium, obviously, but he knew her too well; she'd never talk.

Alysium, acutely aware of what Zane had intended, whispered an incantation that snuffed the life from the demon without so much as a breath from him upon its completion. Zane clicked his tongue, seeing they had prepared for such a thing. It was victory or death. The demons bombarded him with several bolts of energy, and he rolled forward to avoid them, jumping to his feet. When he stood, Alysium kicked him back, sending him skidding toward the edge of the building, where two of the covenant members grabbed his arms and held tight with glowing palms. When he realized what was about to happen, Alysium had already channeled energy into her palm, positioning it to blast him. The demons utilized suppressant spells, keeping him from conjuring his flames or channeling energy while in contact with him.

Zane hated what he had to do, but with swift recourse, he dropped his gunblade, slid his arms through the sleeves of his parka, and ducked. He was free for a moment, his eyes darting side to side before he blasted the two assailants with explosive fire. The intense heat rended flesh from bone and boiled their blood into a mulch atop their frames. They had no chance to scream as their heads and torsos were burned to a crisp.

Alysium's bolt of energy shot above Zane's head, instead, tearing through his parka harmlessly. Another bolt shot from her hand, but he conjured a wall of flame that dispelled the blast harmlessly. Now that he had a moment to breathe, he focused on analyzing his situation.

His eyes flickered as he homed in on the energies surrounding him. Standing straight, he glanced down with a frown, seeing his favorite parka had a hole blasted through it, rendering it useless. Even with its special fireproof nature, there was a limit to it. His eyes returned to the surrounding scene, where he saw three of the covenant members standing spaced out from Alysium, all cornering him to the edge of the building they stood on. Despite his own skill, he was clearly disadvantaged, primarily because of Alysium's formidability.

He took a deep breath, unleashing a loud grunt as his fire swarmed his form. Not only did it act as a deterrent to them getting close, but it also functioned as a basic shield to any attacks he wouldn't anticipate. It made him nearly impenetrable to low-level attacks like the ones the grunts had been using.

A dance of blazing orange and purple lit the night from atop the building, the demons engaging in a perilous fight to the death. Gunshots rang with echoes through the sky, bullets finding their targets. Soon, only Alysium and Zane remained. Sweat dripped down Alysium's face, the heat from Zane's flames invoking her fatigue.

As assassins of the Alastairs, they were acquainted with their means of attack, defense, and respective capabilities. While she had failed to kill him with the finesse of an assassin, he failed to, or refrained from, inflicting a decisive blow against her as well. A battle of attrition in the truest sense. Whirls and lashes of flame and dark magic collided.

And it was when Alysium had exhausted a significant pool of her magic that Zane held his palm out toward her. A massive wave of flames shot from it, closing in on her rapidly. Holding her hands out, a wall of purple energy formed in front of her, acting as a shield that diverted the flames safely around her. Retaining the flames, she was forced to expend her defenses for several seconds, quickly eating through her reserves. When the flames had finally ceased, she was on the brink of exhaustion and dropped to her knees.

Zane walked toward her slowly, his flames flickering into a dull light before extinguishing entirely. The sounds of his boots crunching the battered concrete echoed as he closed in on her, despondency in his gaze. He had steeled his nerves. But when he prepared to incinerate her, just as he had the others, he froze. Something tugged inside him. An illogical nostalgia as he saw her harrowed face, her defeated eyes that were clenched. Not with fear, but anger. He had never defeated Alysium when they sparred, and this was the first. His victory, ironically, was cold, much to his despondency.

"I ... can take you prisoner—"

"Stop that ... damn humanity! I don't want your pity. I don't want your mercy. I refuse it!" she snapped. Her head rose and her eyes widened with an alien confusion within her. For all the brutality she saw Zane employ in their time together, it was now, when he forwent a demon's ruthlessness, that he exhibited the greatest power to her. She was not defeated by a *demon*. She was defeated by a *human*, and it sickened her.

Mercy. She was unfamiliar with it, yet despised it; it was as if a cat spared a mouse. Something unbecoming of the Alastairs—but intrinsic of Zane, as she now saw and abhorred.

"That isn't my humanity, Alysium," Zane protested. "I believe my demon side, too, is capable of mercy and compassion. *I*"—he gestured his hand atop his chest—"believe you're capable of mercy and redemption. There's nothing inherently human about it, and that's what you fail to understand. Demons ... don't have to forgo these sentiments."

"I said stop," she spat. She gazed upon his face one last time, and with a moment's respite, she made her peace with her death, but only her death. A *human* would not kill her. She would die by a demon. With a rueful gaze fixed on her body, she raised her hand to her stomach, her trembling fingers seeking comfort as they rested atop her navel. Steeling her nerves, she went still, her thoughts drifting to the future she had envisioned, one of justice and renewal. She dreaded *they* would not see it.

"Forgive me ..." she whispered and bit down hard with a mysterious crunch.

"No!" Zane called out, kneeling by her side, but it was too late. The poison had entered her body. Foam accumulated at the corner of her mouth, and she slumped to the floor, convulsing for several painful seconds before she went limp. *Dead.*

He didn't know what to think at that moment. In spite of her intentions to kill him, he found himself mourning her. When he served the Alastairs, he would have thought such a sentiment was irrevocably human of him, but he grew beyond the sins of his past. It was indicative of himself rather than any creed or circumstances of his birth, a power discovered irrespective of misfortune or proclivities. As he gazed upon her, the paradox of her visage was not lost on him. It was the most peaceful he had ever seen her. Regardless of her hatred of the Alastair, she was not spared their propensity toward wrath, and in death, that wrath was alleviated.

If only that wrath could have been resolved in life, Zane thought. Perhaps in another world, in other circumstances, she'd have been happy, but that was fruitless thinking on his part—thinking demons condemned.

Remorseful, Zane held his hand out toward Alysium, his expression tightening as he thought of the one grace he could still grant her. The returnal incantation, while useful in cleaning up demonic corpses remaining from a hunt, was more complex than it appeared. When used, it returned a being's body to where they had felt they belonged—a sentiment Ichor knew within the soul of all. Where that was for Alysium, Zane didn't know, but it was the least he could offer her.

"May you find peace in the shadows ... sanguine," Zane spoke, and Alysium's body dissipated into light. Her form shimmered, fading bit by bit until she was gone.

Zane closed his eyes, turning from the scene. A dreaded report came next, but he would not lament the approaching tedium. For now, he reflected on the measure of life—how fragile it all was.

Zane walked to the edge of the building, overlooking the city that glittered in the dark. The world would never know what transpired, despite the cumbersome guilt—despite the justifiable defense of his life, and maybe even the city, from what he could fathom. The path of fate, similar to string, twisted and bent. Threads of life were often cut to preserve the others, and no one would ever be the wiser.

For all Zane knew, he could have inadvertently doomed everybody rather than saving them. He hated such internal pontifications about the fragile threads—meaningless minutiae of what could have been. Consequential, but obscure, the paradox settled into a hollow sentiment a demon was supposed to admonish.

We are small.

Jessica despised politics, be it of man or demon. Sometimes, she could hardly tell the difference, which concerned her more than it annoyed her. Yet, there she was, using her authority to call forth the Alastair family's head to an emergency meeting. It wasn't easy to tug strings as tenuous and uncertain as those of demon nobility, but it was entirely too pertinent for her to refrain, which was why she personally sought to speak with the Alastair's head.

Between the reports she received from Eden, Zane, and the festering intrusions of the Sieghart family, she had expedited mitigation efforts. As she attended this meeting, she authorized a raid and apprehension of the Siegharts in Chicago. Bureaucracy was the death of civility, and as much as she had to defend many processes, she had her reasons for subverting typical regulations.

Still, a teleportation rift between America and France was extraordinarily difficult, even for a woman of Jessica's magical prowess. It had taken more than three hours, multiple times more than it would for any other native location within a thousand miles from the Hunters' HQ, but she finally arrived. The Château de Alastair. One of their many estates, but it was the one where she was granted an audience.

Sequestered in the east countryside of Paris, the château was nestled near mountains and vibrant, lush fields. Given their family's fortune in winemaking, typically for the most elite in society, they were easily the richest of the noble demon families. It was past dawn, and the sunrise shaded the landscape through the fog creeping from the land. As early and inconvenient to the Alastairs as it was, the importunity stressed by Jessica spurred such an abrupt meeting. It also helped that she persisted in leveraging their infamy against them. Jessica would be remiss if she didn't cynically remind them that several years ago rogue members of the Alastairs acted *against* the family's ordinance and almost sacrificed half of Athens, tarnishing the family's credibility.

Jessica tipped her hat down, masking the upper half of her vision from the bright sun that threatened to blind her from over the horizon. The thought of her being susceptible to a sunrise's glare despite teleporting halfway across the world subtly amused her, seeing as there were far more prescient things she had considered. Sun-blinding was not one of them.

Jessica marched along the cobblestoned walkway, the arches and stone of the chateau coming into clearer view as the architecture gradually obscured the sun. Tilting her hat back up, she squinted her eyes. The sight of the stone carvings of the family crest was embedded in the garden's paved center, which consisted of various elemental symbols compiled into one shield-shaped crest. A crest the family forged due to their high elemental affinity.

Jessica was greeted by two demonic butlers in black long-coated tuxes, dawning their unabashed demonic appearance with inhuman skin tones, black sclera eyes, and horns. Their true forms did little to intimidate her, however, and they could tell when she stared her convictions into their monstrous, slit red pupils. A bewitching smile flashed across her face, serving as a warning for their cooperation.

No words were exchanged, and they directed Jessica up the stairwell and hurried her into the manor. They marched through the impractical, hollow halls and led her past the various vintage art and statuettes that adorned the home—as gaudy a display as any, corroborating what Zane had recanted to her and Ethan when they recruited him. It would be a marvel if it were less gratuitous and under different circumstances.

Two snaps echoed as they entered an assembly room, causing the butlers to turn around and leave Jessica. Embroidered crimson leather sofas symmetrically adorned the room. Sitting in the northern portion of the room was a woman dressed in a robe with white fur framing her collar. The Alastair crest was embedded in a silk sash that ran across her bust, casting a dim glow in the sun-spotted room. Her slit purple irises were framed by black sclera, and she eyed Jessica dubiously. Jessica could guess several reasons why, seeing that the woman was none other than Eridianne Alastair, the matriarch of the Alastair family. And with less-than-short notice, amusement was the last thing either of them expected of one another.

"General Blackwell, to what do I owe the pleasure?" She spoke with a thick French accent, her voice deep and tinged with sardonic displeasure.

Jessica took her seat across from Eridianne, removing her hat. Her jade-green leer clashed with Eridianne's transcendent gaze, matching it in both depth and prominence.

Eridianne pushed a hand through her curly black hair and coursed a finger up her S-shaped, silvery horns, an idle habit of her impatience.

"Dire straits on our end, unfortunately. As well as the fact it pertains to the Alastairs. One of my hunters has just slain a demon, a certain Alastair woman who sought to overthrow the main family—you. She was apparently doing so through an alliance with another demon family and a group of somnium that have emerged. Not to mention, the kingpin of the somnium uttered your family name in reports I have received," Jessica said. Her pensive stare was met with an equally inquisitive expression from Eridianne.

"And who from my *tribu* do you speak of?" Eridianne inquired, referring to her family in French.

"I would presume you're familiar with an Alysium Alastair, correct?"

Eridianne cocked an eyebrow, shifting her gaze up as she searched her thoughts.

"Vaguely ... an assassin of my son's? Something of the sort. It wouldn't surprise me that she would seek vengeance. She abandoned her creed, perhaps chasing after my bastard son."

Jessica's head perked. *A bastard son?* It was unusual to expect such a thing as Eridianne to have a child out of wedlock. Yet, she had no known husband currently—following his demise in the Athens incident.

"Tell me about this ... bastard child of yours."

Eridianne scoffed.

"And what if I refuse? It is of no concern to you."

"Might I remind you of where your family stands after the Athens incident?"

Eridianne furrowed her brows, rolling her eyes and cursing in French after several moments.

"How often must I repent for that incident on behalf of the disgraced? Fine. My bastard son is formerly known by the name Eridionne. I believe he's some kind of police from the last report I received from my agents."

Jessica frowned, confused by the implications. Then it clicked. A demon of tenuous origins, cast out and acting as a police officer. It had never been disclosed in prior conversations between the Hunters and the Alastairs, in part due to their begrudging history with Zane, whom Ethan had poached following the aforementioned Athens incident.

Jessica had a grave suspicion she now needed to confirm.

"And this bastard son ... what does he go by now?"

Eridianne frowned, her eyes locked on the ceiling as she racked her head for the name. If it had been more consequential to her, she'd have remembered it sooner.

"Darek ... Daren ... D-something ... Carver?" Eridianne muttered.

Jessica froze, her suspicions having been confirmed. It was clear to Jessica now what had been occurring. A disowned demon heir gone rogue, which had become a recurring incident in much of the demon world, but this time, it pertained directly to a genocide of humans. Jessica's fingers curled into tight fists, her eyes shutting as she lowered her head, aware of how little time they had to correct such a thing.

Jessica stood abruptly, causing Eridianne to give a perplexed stare.

"I appreciate the information. This is where our meeting shall end."

Eridianne sighed happily, appearing relieved at the end of their meeting. She didn't enjoy the excessive interrogations she had to endure following the Athens incident, this one included.

"If that is all, I have much to attend to. I trust that we will not be blamed for whatever is going on?"

"You will not, so far as no information further links your influence to the investigation. Keep your nose clean, and we'll have no problems." She placed her hat back on, preparing to leave the room. Of course, butlers were waiting right outside the door to escort her off the property.

"Au revoir," Eridianne spoke distastefully, curling her fingers to wave goodbye.

Jessica walked fast, driven by the dire revelation before her and the Hunters. There was far too much to sort out with the little time she suspected they had.

Once off the property, Jessica phoned into command, having her own report to deliver to Commander Evans at the Chicago base. She held her earpiece and waited until she had connected.

"General Blackwell," the operator said.

"I need to be connected to the Chicago units, stat!"

"Right away, ma'am."

Moments of silence filled the void as Jessica paced in front of the estate. Her breathing was labored as she waited, not used to the connection process taking as long as it was. There was a muteness, so she knew the operator attempted the transfer, but why the operator in Chicago didn't pick up yet was more than concerning.

"General Blackwell?" the operator from before spoke.

"Why didn't the transfer go through?" Jessica asked, her voice tense as she clenched her free hand.

"Ma'am ... the Chicago base is offline."

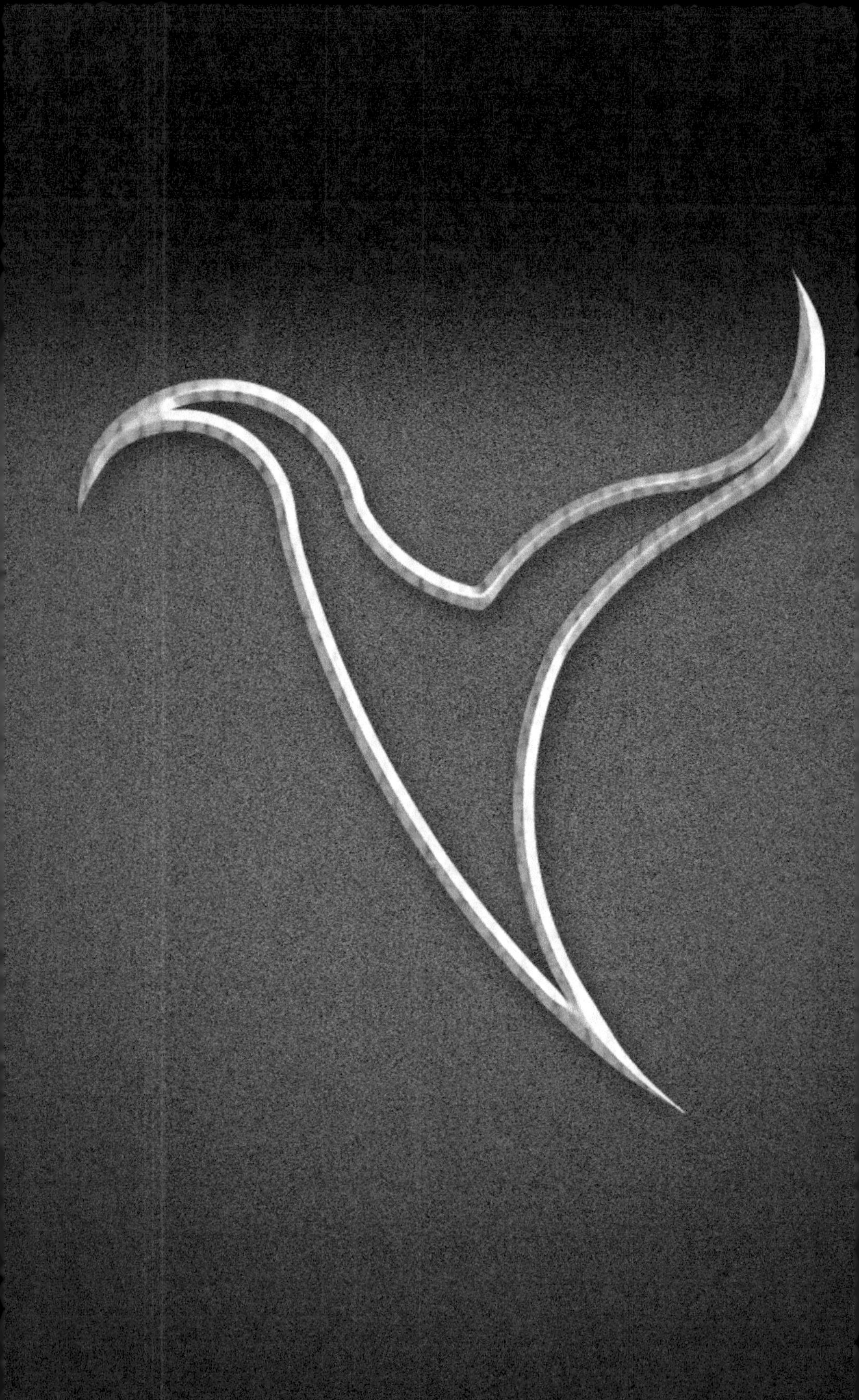

ELEVEN

BREACH OF HUMANITY

"This is on brief notice, but the raid will take place in approximately one hour. We've assembled your departments and will delegate your roles accordingly," Commander Evans said. The furrows of his brow intensified as he scanned the group of uniformed hunters that had crudely assembled in the engineering center's garage. Formal assemblies weren't an intended function in the base's original layout. As a result, the engineers and mechanics had to put their work on pause, much to their annoyance.

Among the crowd, Eden and Zane stood toward the front. Eden feigned composure in the face of their coming assignment, his guilt buried in his conviction. While he wanted to blame himself, he refrained; it was unproductive. Instead, he steeled his nerves for the coming operation.

Commander Evans interfaced with the hunter gauntlet on his wrist, tapping the holographic screen before the group's hunter gauntlets and bracers blinked. Several holographic projections of the Sieghart mansion shimmered in front of them.

"Ardent, Blackwell, Larson, and Schaefer, you will all be a part of the infiltration team. Grayson and Tracy, you'll be in charge of scouting. Carter and Jackson, you two will be in charge of hacking and maintaining comms. Reference the positions laid out on the maps sent to you. You will rendezvous and commence this mission. Afflict *no casualties*. Only non-lethal tools and force are authorized," Commander Evans said, glancing at Eden with skeptical scrutiny, but Eden showed no visible reaction.

Commander Evans turned his attention back to the hunters. "I don't want to hear about any accidents. Arm yourselves with appropriate equipment and incantations to finish this as quickly and *quietly* as possible. Upon determining Kendra Mallory's location, she is to be sought out, rescued, and returned to base. Do I make myself clear?"

"Yes, sir!" the hunters answered in unison, even Eden, begrudgingly.

"Dismissed!" Commander Evans yelled before exiting the garage with a stiff stride past his subordinates.

Eden knew it would be strange to utilize non-lethal options, given that for years he had only trained to kill. But, as a demigod, he was naturally better equipped to carry out the duty, seeing as his strength and barrier granted him generous leeway to get close to demons.

Hunters made their way to the armories to prepare for the raid, and Eden cut through the swarm, stopping when Zane obstructed his path.

"Geez, I just finished my own squabble, and I'm already in another one. I wanted to nap," Zane complained to Eden, warranting Eden to show apathy.

"Have you tried an energy drink?" Eden suggested dismissively.

"I've had like three today already. I don't need flame jitters or a heart attack, whichever comes first."

Eden shrugged and rolled his eyes, placing his hands on his hips as he tore his gaze from Zane. Hearing steps approach him, he turned to see Yuki stop in front of him, her iridescent eyes showing concern.

"What led to this?" she asked Eden meekly.

"Long story," Eden muttered. In spite of his underlying guilt and their mission, Eden summarized the events to Yuki. He had a soft spot for Yuki, a sentiment shrouded in darkness that transcended his reclusion. His cold demeanor melted with the consideration of their past strife, and he couldn't help but conjure a warmth he showed very few when speaking with her.

"Mm ..." Yuki hummed, nodding her head. She paused for a few moments, her finger on her bottom lip as she thought. "I think ... you did the right thing at the wrong time. Does that make sense?"

"I don't think so ... but don't try to placate me. It's still my fault."

"I'm not trying to cheer you up." She sighed. "I'm assuring you that your heart was in the right place. It was a situation you couldn't have predicted to be the case. Who'd have known the Siegharts were after her all this time?"

"I was negligent," Eden affirmed.

"You chose *now* to start making sense?" Zane asked sarcastically.

"Zane ..." Yuki groaned, eyeing him warily.

"You're right, you're right," he said, backing away with his palms up before walking off.

Yuki turned back to Eden, giving him a firm nod as she held a fist up to him.

"We got this. We'll get her back," she said. She adjusted the sheathed photon saber on her hip, a weapon consisting of two stacked blades attached to a rubberized hilt with a bulky, reflective pommel at the top. Attached to the hilt was a switch for deploying the built-in stun gun.

Eden cracked a smile at her words, briefly tapping her fist with his own.

"Agreed."

Night stretched across Chicago. The hum of the transport truck was filled with tense silence. Subtle grooves in the road caused the hunters to jostle in their seats, with the encompassing darkness cascading over their faces. Parallel on either side of the cabin, the hunters were seated, inspecting their weapons or contemplating in silence. Eden's arms were folded beneath his chest, creasing his coat. His gloved hands were clenched into tight fists, ready for liberal use throughout the raid. His taut expression spelled his intentions plainly, which invoked the other hunters to worry if there would be deaths. Commander Evans's earlier insinuation became plausible in their minds.

A van trailed behind the truck, packed with various technologies and a satellite on top. Inside the van, Andrew and another engineer sat, both already operating equipment from their seats. Andrew's fingers typed away on a tablet that synchronized with the neighborhood's power grid. With precision, he programmed the various electric junctions that were found, along with an overview of the electrical layout of the neighborhood. He placed his finger to his earpiece, tapping the button.

"This is Carter. We've mapped 70 percent of the local grid. ETA ten minutes until we're ready to go dark," Andrew said over the radio.

"Copy," several voices chirped over the radio broadcast.

The vehicles came to a stop at the outskirts of the neighborhood, where the hunters would walk to the Sieghart mansion. They exited the back of the truck, wielding their weapons and equipment. All were in uniform, except for Eden and Zane. Eden dressed in the same black coat and tactical clothing as he usually did, whereas Zane ditched his casual wear for cargo pants tucked into boots and a tactical vest atop a gray long-sleeved compression shirt. Zane was picky about what to wear because of his flames, and for several reasons, he refused to wear the standard hunter suit. Legitimate, albeit vain, reasons.

"Insenseilis," the group muttered, a faint blue shimmer coming over their forms. With a nod to one another, they marched toward the mansion. Within the darkness, the homes of the neighborhood shimmered with lights coming from inside. No doubt the residents and servants of the Sieghart mansion were unaware of the approaching hunters, and the element of surprise was on the hunters' side.

"Three—two—one, going dark," Andrew said. With his announcement, the mansion's lights, along with the neighboring homes and street posts, shut off. "Open sesame." The gate rose, and the hunters made their way down the driveway and toward the porch.

It was silent. Then it wasn't. The breach had commenced. Pops and thunderous marching rang throughout the mansion. Smoke spread from their grenades, and the house staff soon found themselves incapacitated by the hunters' nets, cuffs, and other means of subdual. They pinned the staff to the ground, binding them with energy suppressant incantations upon their defeat. It had happened too fast for the demons and normal human staff to react with precision, hurling the home into chaos.

Eden had swiftly dealt with the servants in his way, gunning for one energy in particular: Oliver Sieghart's. He was the prominent target of the raid, as expressed by Zane's reports. A dangerous foe that required his specialty in close quarters to subdue without casualties, less the Sieghart patriarch's eye of Jugo thwart their efforts entirely.

Eden had navigated the tight corners to find Oliver's study, where he detected Oliver's energy. Bursting through the solid door, he quickly scanned the room for his target. Upon spotting him, Oliver's right eye was trained on him with a twinkling green light glowing from its depth. For a brief moment, with a flash of red, Eden's energy had weakened. Having anticipated this, however, Eden persisted in his trajectory and leaped across the room before slamming his fist into Oliver's temple.

Oliver yelped, his eye becoming dull and dark. He crumpled to the floor with a harsh crack, and Eden's fingers clenched through tufts of his hair as he slammed the man's face into the floor. The wooden boards beneath him snapped and splintered.

"Don't move, or I start breaking bones," Eden declared. Thunderous energy resonated from within Oliver, a guttural growl sounding from the pit of his chest.

"Don't tell me what—"

Eden yanked Oliver's arm behind his back with ease and, resolutely, snapped it into an unnatural angle, causing Oliver to yell out in pain as he writhed beneath Eden.

"Don't fuck with me. Talk. Where's Kendra!"

Oliver's tongue was stone, refusing to speak despite Eden's tightening grip twisting his snapped arm further. Even then, Oliver merely continued to grumble obscenities and pant beneath him. Eden grabbed Oliver's other arm, preparing to snap it next until he heard footsteps behind him.

"I'll take it from here with the interrogation. Hold him still," Zane said, entering the room. "Your lackeys are all subdued, by the way. So don't expect any backup, Ollie."

"*You*," Oliver spoke between sharp puffs of air through his clenched teeth.

"*Me*," Zane agreed snarkily, strolling over to Oliver and crouching in front of him.

Eden yanked Oliver's hair to force his gaze up to Zane.

"We were supposed to be allies!" Oliver howled.

"I told you we're only allies if you allow us to be. You've done a shit job of that. So, how about I cut you some slack and say that I don't know you're a lying rat-faced bastard? That leaves us with the glaring connections between Alysium, this *Eridionne*, the somnium, and you—the Covenant of Augury, I presume?" Zane glared. "Then add into the mix Kendra Mallory's last known address being here ... you should start talking."

Oliver glared daggers at Zane, challenging his gaze at first. While Zane exhibited nonchalance, even on the bad days, he held firm with his harsh leer, wishing to express his distaste. Within seconds, Oliver relented, battered and crushed by the weight of the covenant's failure.

"Kendra ... I know she's friends with my son, but I don't know what you're talking about with the girl be—"

Eden's grip tightened suddenly, and he growled.

"Cut the bullshit," Eden warned.

"Ow, ow!" Oliver cried. Zane furrowed his brow, holding a hand up to Eden to tell him to ease up again.

"How about this ..." Zane started. He held his index finger up, a flame slowly flickering to life on it as he ominously waved it in front of Oliver's right eye. "You tell us where she's being held. Eden will go and check. He tells me you lied ... I burn your eye of Jugo out." A trick of assassins, Zane reared his *demon* side to Oliver in that instance. Both he and Oliver were aware that without the eye of Jugo, Oliver's claim as the family's patriarch would be challenged, leaving only his son as the legitimate head.

The candescent flame flickered in front of Oliver's face, casting a hard shadow and reflecting in his eyes. Within that flame, he saw something beyond misery and pain, but a shame he'd be forced to wear in disgrace even in his captivity. He'd have preferred death over that, and they would not grant him such lenience. That much, he was certain.

"Oh, and say something stupid like ... *I don't know...* and I'll burn it out right now." Zane offered a sardonic smirk, his glare sharpening. "*Tick-tock,*" he said melodically, waving his finger, earning an amused huff from Eden.

Oliver swallowed hard, cracking with haste once Zane levied his threat. Should his eye have been burned out, it could regenerate, but they were all aware of that. Demonic regeneration had a limit predicated on the severity of injury and the available supply of Ichor flowing through their body. Should the amount become too low, or the injury be too great, the injury would become permanent. In this case, Oliver's claim as the patriarch and heir of the Siegharts would be sundered.

"Warehouse on Blackhawk and Sedgwick ... she's beneath it. Access the lower level from unit number twelve. There's a basement beneath the manager's office," Oliver grunted out.

Eden looked at Zane, and they nodded at one another.

"Go, I'll take it from here," Zane said.

Eden relinquished his grip and let Oliver's arm fall limp. He decided to take a shortcut, bursting out the window instead of taking the stairs. He would go to the warehouse immediately and without backup behind him. Time was of the essence, and he could get there much faster than the rest of his comrades. With this in mind, he informed them of the location over the comms as he shot through the city.

Zane held his hand out toward Oliver, and orange energy flashed in his palm.

"Religo!" he spoke. Oliver's arms suddenly snapped behind his back, wrists bound in rings of orange energy. Given his broken arm, Oliver groaned in pain from the sudden restriction. Tossing and turning, he spat curses and writhed on the ground. Zane glanced at his palm, admiring his handy work since he hardly used basic magic.

"So ... Oliver, or should I say ... Aldo?"

Oliver briefly stopped his pained grunts, his eyes wide with disbelief as he stared at Zane.

"Where did you get that name?" Oliver hissed.

"I do my homework, my good pal. The Sieghart name is of Germanic influence, if my history of the noble umbra demon houses is correct. Oliver is hardly a name I'd associate with that. So, I did some digging." Zane crouched next to Oliver. "Several years ago, you changed your name to Oliver, a derivative of Olivier—a French name. Originally, I chalked it up to you trying to be less presumptuous doing business in America, but between that knock-off *Chateau De Fleur* and your new alias, it's obvious to me you're just chasing the coattails of the Alastairs," Zane alleged. A smirk carved his face as their eyes held. "Leviathan would harbor a pride toward you that even Lucifer would envy."

Oliver growled and continued to thrash, deeply unamused with the allegations Zane assailed him with. Zane stood, cracking his neck as he glanced out the broken windows, pondering idly. After several moments of Oliver's pained grunts and his wandering thoughts, a pang rang in his stomach, and it audibly grumbled.

Zane snickered, turning his attention back to Oliver.

"While I have you … any good taco spots around here? Asking for a friend," Zane said, earning him an unamused glare in response.

The halls beneath the warehouse possessed a dark, dreary tone. It had once been a storage center, now repurposed as a make-shift prison for those the Covenant of Augury had taken—be they dead or alive. Allen had seen far more dead than alive when he had visited.

There were no other prisoners at that moment but Kendra, the recent batch of corpses—fed to the hellhounds. Some of the storage cages served as a holding kennel for said hounds, who obediently waited for their next meal. Occasionally, Intico would even show up to extract the souls festering within the hounds, adding their power to its own. Harvest would take a massive well of energy to commence and maintain, a necessity for the hoard of somnium to sustain their forms for a substantial period.

A rancid scent permeated the cell on the far end, where they had once kept the bodies. Within the neighboring cell, what remained of the police officer's equipment was lazily stored in old crates. Such guile had crafted this playhouse of depravity that Allen detested. Even being there made him want to vomit.

There had been whispers of an ulterior motive to the somnium, and while it was plainly obvious to Allen that they were not to be trusted, his father thought differently. Briefly reflecting on one of his relatives, who in their failure during the hit on Archer, was offered as a vessel to a somnium. Such failure was never tolerated, further driving his trepidation to have this final conversation.

With such nefarious aspirations as to help Darrel overthrow the Alastairs, Allen saw the true purpose of their unlikely alliance. Oliver cared little for a different Alastair regime—only that they fell in their prominence. He always sought for their family, the Siegharts, to reign above the other families—a reverence with no rival. Skirting the Kohen Treaty, he sought to evade the scrutiny of the Hunters, claim power, then do away with contemptuous measures of peace between humans and demons. To that end, he swallowed his pride and played the nefarious game of alliances, even if it meant working with a disowned Alastair, to one day see their bloodline envy his own. He saw Darrel not as an ally or an equal, but as a *damned demonium*. As he saw it, the Alastair family would no longer be the chip on his shoulder. Under Darrel's leadership, they would soon live within the shadows of envy he always spoke ill of.

Allen's footsteps echoed in the sequestered storage halls, and the closer he drew to Kendra's cell, the more that voice in his head pecked.

They want vessels. They want us.

The infernal voice in Allen's head reminded him of this again and again. Oliver made his blood boil in his veins. When the man had compelled him by magic to make that pact—to take the somnium's hand—he hadn't slept soundly since. Slowly, his rebelliousness had been whittled away, and what was left was a desolate boy. Kendra could never forgive him, nor did he think he deserved such sympathy, even if Ichor herself ordained it.

With such a hopeless reality settling in, he condemned his remaining self-pity to Inferos, and at last, he arrived at her cell.

"You're not human anymore. Stop pretending you still are."

This irrevocable truth haunted Kendra, but repeating Eden's words granted her a hollow acceptance of her reality. It was all she could do as she dangled helplessly in her cell. The footsteps came to a stop in front of the door opposite her, but it obscured Kendra from seeing who was on the other side. There was no rebellion left in her, and her curiosity was encumbered by fear. Faintly, the husky scent bled through the door, and her eyes narrowed, glued to the floor with a rousing anger inside of her.

The door unlocked and opened with a creak, and Kendra's eyes tightly shut, shielding herself from the beams of light that rushed through the crack and illuminated parts of the cell. Allen stood there, quiet and pensive. There was trepidation in his ensnared breath, but shoving his hesitation aside, he clenched his fists and stared directly at Kendra, meeting her gaze when she slowly looked up at him.

"I can't imagine that it means much, but I really didn't want things to end up the way they did," Allen said.

With a hollow gaze, Kendra stared at her *friend*, ruptured emotions behind her glassy eyes.

Allen took hesitant steps into the cell as additional light seeped in from behind him, enabling Kendra to see his face, but she didn't want to look at him. Nobody in her position would. She especially blamed herself for having trusted him, for having turned to him against her better judgment.

She couldn't have known, and by no account, including Allen's, was she to blame. A victim's dilemma, as was unfortunately common.

"You don't have to believe me. Shit, I wouldn't ... but I only ever intended for it to be you. Kendall wasn't supposed to—"

"Kenny ... you're telling me ... you were," she croaked. Her head throbbed wildly, disorienting her for a moment.

"Responsible," Allen confirmed. Pacing in front of Kendra, he cast his eyes to the ground to avoid her harsh gaze, her scrutable silence more damning than ever. He couldn't coherently piece the story together in his head. He had rehearsed this moment plenty, but reckonings never accommodated.

"Katherine was too good a detective for her own good. We—they needed to get her off the case without arousing further suspicion. But then ... the somnium thought she was best kept alive for Harvest, and your death was deemed necessary to spare her to that end. That's why I had no choice." He took a shaky breath. "It was only supposed to be you ... I didn't know Kenny would ..." His hands balled into tight fists, and he slammed one onto the adjacent wall, but his building distress would be eclipsed.

The air squeezed Kendra's lungs, a burning sensation crawling from her stomach to her chest. Her head throbbed, but she endured its debilitation with her harsh ire, evolving because of and toward Allen—the *demon* responsible for Kendall's death.

"You had no right!" she howled, choking sobs leaving her trembling lips. Regret or not, it mattered little to her. *It was supposed to be me,* she thought. "You heartless, spineless son of a bitch! You should have killed me yourself! She would still—she was supposed to ..." Her voice cracked, uncontrollable sobs escaping her lips before she bawled.

Allen flinched, his lips pursing as he formed a grimace.

"I didn't want to hurt either of you," Allen said meekly, biting his bottom lip hard as tears gathered at the corner of his eyes.

He never had a choice.

Allen thought back to the many memories that he shared with Kendra. Regardless of what she thought at that moment, they were real. He had enjoyed his friendship with her and Kendall and was all the more jaded when he was forced to end it, serving them up as kindling to the flames of ambition. "But then you changed into something else, and I had to finish what I started."

"My sister!" Kendra spat, thrashing and kicking again. Rope tore into her, scoring her skin and turning it a blistering red. She inhaled a burning breath, attempting to exhale the flames she became accustomed to. Too unsteady earlier, she hadn't noticed her bindings were filled with a strange energy that tingled on her skin, a power suppressant enchantment she was unaware of.

"I'll fucking kill you!" Kendra shouted. And she continued professing her hatred and scorn in an increasingly cracking voice.

"Now, they want both of your bodies. The somnium." Allen reached up and wiped the tears from his eyes. Brushing his cheek, he faintly remembered the tenderness he and Kendra had once shared. "I begged ... but they wouldn't relent. I thought if it was just your mom, I could spare you at least. But I"—the words caught in his throat as he held back more of his tears—"I never wanted any of this!" He broke into sobs as a memory with Kendra resurfaced.

It had been New Year's Day, and they watched the holographic firework show in the city. A brilliant display of technology combined with the flashy explosions of fireworks—a sort of compromise for environmental purposes. As they had watched the fireworks, he had been in his head—the somnium's hiss and the festering guilt of his future involvement hadn't been lost on him then either. And without prompt, he had felt Kendra lean into him, for warmth, she had claimed. He had been jostled from his ruminations, and when he had least expected it, Kendra had kissed his cheek.

That memory was shredded by the corrosive screams coming from Kendra, and so too was the memory of her smile. Joining the altar upon which these things burned was his name and what was left of him.

Allen Sieghart—no more.

A barrage of footsteps echoed through the hallways of the underground facility, booming with urgency. He snapped his head to look behind him just in time to see the shadow barging into the room. It was entirely too quick for Allen to react, and he found himself launched into the wall from a swipe to his face. His cheek swelled with pain as he hit the wall with a sickening crack. A boot landed on Allen's temple, pinning his head against the wall and thrusting his world into a dizzying array of colors.

Kendra had strained her voice raw from yelling, becoming breathless by the time Allen was attacked. Though her struggling had ceased, she quietly stared at the silhouette that had appeared to save her. Unmistakable crimson eyes glimmered in the dark, staring down at Allen with contempt. *Eden.* While her anger still festered, she remembered his words once more, and her eyes lowered. She assumed he was angry with her more than anything.

Eden's gaze shifted to Kendra, his expression softening when he saw her intact. He then scrutinized the ropes binding her—third-rate magic-suppressant bindings, something he was familiar with. Removing his foot from Allen's head, he approached her swiftly, stopping shy of her before he fumbled with the knot holding her wrists in place. After a moment of failing to untie it, his arms glowed red, and he tore the rope from her wrists.

Now free, Kendra crumpled to the floor, catching herself with a searing pain shooting through her blistering, raw wrists. Blood came rushing back into her fingers and caused them to tingle. It was slow, but her wounds continued healing; the gash on her head and her raw wrists emitted smoke, the cells regenerating.

There was but a moment of silence before darkness consumed Kendra's eyes, and a blazing hue radiated from the center of those abysses—an incomparable wrath from Inferos itself. Her humanity aflame, her visceral gaze found Allen writhing on the ground. Without hesitation, she lurched forward, claws scraping against the floor. Mounting Allen, her hands wrapped around his throat and squeezed hard, her claws digging into his skin.

Eden watched with a blank stare. He had pondered interfering, but his objective only kept *him* from killing. It said nothing of Kendra, as she was not a hunter. As far as he was concerned, Allen was scum who deserved death. However, there was something that tugged within him as he watched Kendra squeeze the life out of the boy. He couldn't place it exactly, but something appeared amiss within her—a conflict.

Kendra's fingers clenched tighter, digging into Allen's neck with her newly conjured demonic strength. It would only be a matter of seconds before Allen would succumb.

"Are you sure?" Eden asked. His tone was flat, devoid of any deeper sentiments or regard for Allen's life, which was literally in Kendra's hands. He vaguely recognized Allen from school, his English class, which further explained how he could have lured Kendra, how he could have deceived her and evaded even his scrutiny. Being a Sieghart with the eye of Jugo, it was no surprise he had made himself inscrutable, escaping Eden's ability to detect the supernatural.

Kendra, however entrenched in rage she was, at least heard Eden's question. It simmered in her head for a few moments, and she clenched Allen's throat harder.

"He deserves to *die*. He's the reason Kendall is dead!"

Eden couldn't blame her. He'd do the same in her position. With her answer, he shut his eyes, turning his back to her as her strangulation escalated. The sounds of Allen gasping and Kendra grunting were all he focused on now.

"I won't stop you. Do what you feel is best."

Kendra's fingers tightened their hold on Allen, flames surfacing atop her palms. That same wrathful fire spilled from the corners of her mouth with each puff of air that she exhaled, her grip straining against the contours of his neck. Tighter and tighter. Allen writhed beneath her. His glassy gray eyes opened, glued to Kendra's demonic visage. As she stared down at him, memories of Kendall flashed through her head: her smile, her laugh, them playing together. *All gone because of him.*

Allen wheezed out a weak gasp, his limbs going limp as he stared up at Kendra. There was a resignation within his fluttering gaze that further incited Kendra's fury. His mind went blank, but he shut his eyes, surrendering. The color fled from his face, and her burning hands seared their shape into his neck like a branding iron as she strangled him.

There was a rush of blood to Kendra's head. The sensations bombard-ed her: the scent of burning flesh, the sight of his oxygen-starved face, and the tension of his neck as she wrung the life from him. But then, uninvited memories coursed through her mind.

There was the time they went to the museum together, and he made terrible jokes about the art for the entire trip. He took her to what was now her favorite ice cream parlor in Chicago, and he had bought her a cherry vanilla swirl. And she had taken him shopping in the fashion district, where they had tried on various outfits together and even wound up buying some things. Then there was the time they went to the jazz festival and secretly shared a beer together; neither of them enjoyed the taste. It had been the most rebellious thing she'd done, and she doubted her mother would have been amused. Finally, there was the kiss on the cheek she had conjured up all of her courage to give him at midnight on New Year's Day. Originally, she had intended to claim his lips, but she had lost her nerve to turn him to face her.

Tears spilled down Kendra's face, her eyes widened in mortification as the reality came crashing down on her. Whether he deserved it or not, she couldn't bring herself to cross that barrier and kill Allen. She released him, letting him breathe a deep breath at last. Kendra stared at her trembling hands. Her conviction prior to that moment was gone, diffused into the sentimental memories. The flames on her palms ceased, smoldering. Her vision blurred with the tears that pooled in her eyes, distorting her waning vision.

She stood on unsteady legs, still staring down at her demonic claws as searing heat permeated her skin. *A monster.*

With that damning sentiment rehashed in her head once more, her emotions became too much for her to handle. Her tears spilled down her face, and heavy wails breached her lips.

Kendra's decision to spare Allen surprised Eden. He saw no redemp-tion nor reprieve from the sins he had committed. Allen had irrepara-bly taken something from her, a theme he saw as all too common from demons. *They take until there is nothing left*, he thought. The toll should have been Allen's life, but Kendra chose differently. Her cries alone resonated with him, inviting in emotions he had long since buried within himself—a remembrance of repression.

The weight of the unforgiving world had repeatedly crashed down on Kendra, and she had been through entirely too much. No doubt, the vengeance she desired burned hot inside her—it was only natural she'd see it quenched. Sparing Allen seemed irrational to Eden, and he knew she thought the same. But it was human of her, and all too well did humans succumb to their emotions, however irrational.

Eden turned to Kendra, considering her plight and how he had wrongfully contributed to it. He concluded that he was wrong about her. It was irrefutable, in fact. Bawling before him, she was—without a doubt in his mind—a human.

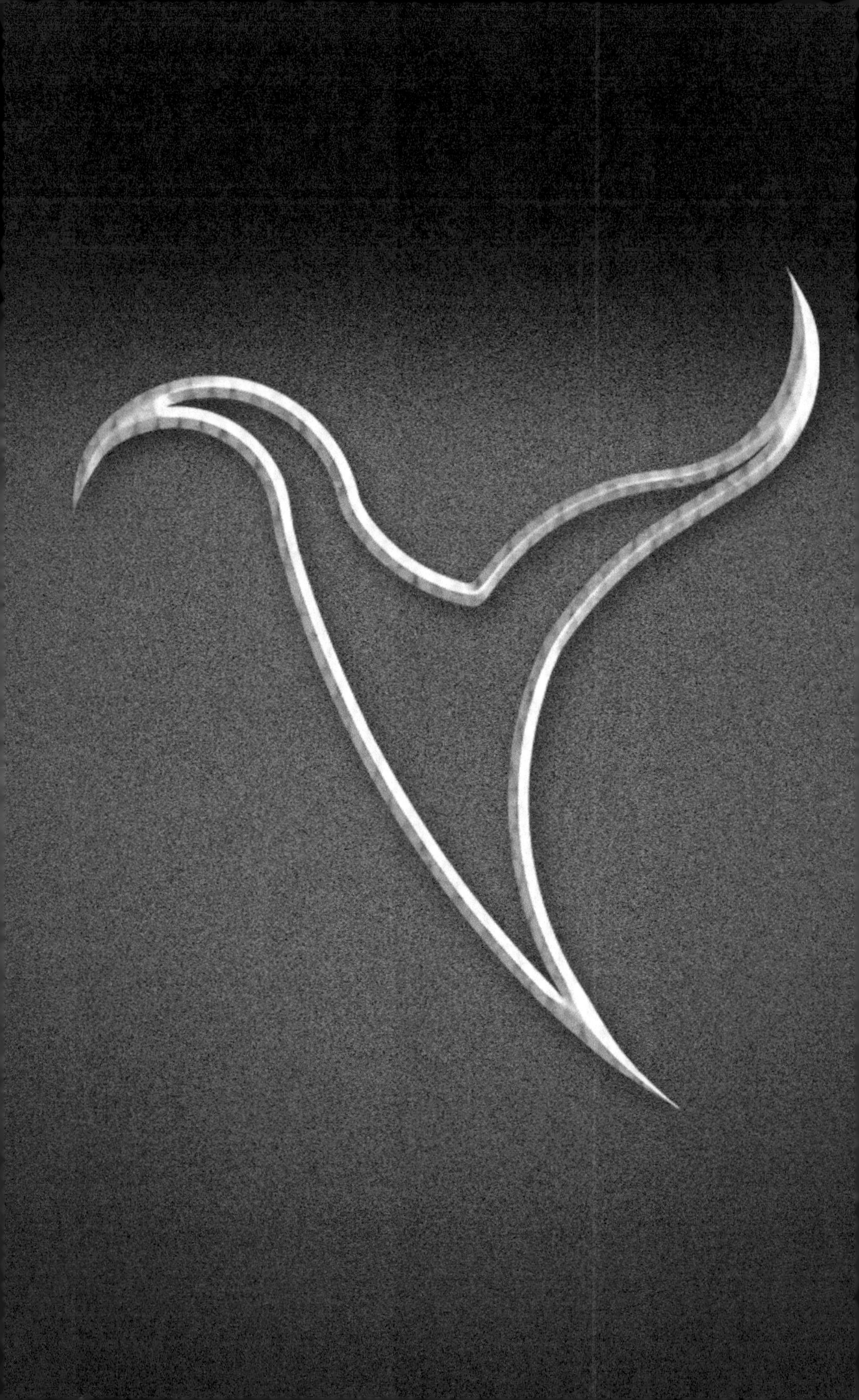

TWELVE

EVIL DESCENDING

Ominous winds stirred high above Chicago, rustling Darrel's coat as he stared down at the city. His gaze was hollow, devoid of enthusiasm or his usual fervor. Everything had fallen apart, and as far as he was concerned, all was lost. The sun set behind the city, and, similar to the light of hope he harbored, darkness descended upon the city. As the sun departed with its light, Alysium's untimely departure rendered his heart as dark as the city would become.

A single tear escaped his left eye, and he clenched his fists tightly, the air around him cracking with his wrathful power that manifested through his coalescing grief. He thought to relinquish any hope that remained and take the plunge from atop Willis Tower. With his death, the Covenant of Augury would be no more.

"Your humanity is showing, Carver," Intico's voice spoke, echoing around Darrel.

"You could never understand, *fiend*," Darrel spat, not bothering to look at Intico.

There was a harrowing silence following his statement, and his feet trembled as he wrestled with impulsive, intrusive thoughts. As grizzly as everything felt within his mind, there was a whisper of dissent from within. An undying desire gnawed at his anguish and supplanted it with the wrath coursing through his veins—a wrath he scorned the Alastairs for harboring. As descendants of Satan, the Cardinal Sin Ordinance of Wrath, they, too, possessed the eternal sin that animated their notorious power.

"*We* understand much. I envy the humans. Ignorant, yet privileged to harbor such sentiments with the life *Mother* gave them—the same life she deprived from us without an accursed dependency on you humans," Intico said, manifesting from the shadows as it walked toward Darrel. For once, it refrained from wearing the infamous unfeeling grin of the somnium. For once, Intico's expression suggested ruefulness.

"We thrive from the glimmers of sin humanity possesses, and grow attached through an intimate fear, becoming something that invokes an irrevocable integration of sin. Why we exist, I know not, but we will have what was shamefully kept from us ... what was *stolen* from us. You and I, Carver." Intico held its hand up to the sky, an insidious energy swarming it as the vestiges of all the lives that were stolen during the Covenant of Augury's scheming surged. The faint screams of souls forlorn and torn away from their corporeal forms echoed. Robbed of their agency, they would become kindling for the blaze of the covenant's goals—an ambition Intico sought to remind Darrel of.

Darrel turned, his eyes sharpening with a glare as he heard all of his malfeasance coalesce in Intico's form. The officers he offered up as sacrifice and the citizens he saw *disappear* to fuel disarray. He cared not for the anguished screams of their souls. The lives he sought to avenge by cleansing Mortale of his despicable bloodline no longer mattered. No such remedy existed any longer, nor dreams of renewing his bloodline. He had desired such with Alysium. The dream of their desired family would forever haunt him, but that dream's death gave birth to a festering wrath that even Satan could envy if he had still lived.

Alysium's body rested on their bed, having manifested within their home prior to his journey to the top of the tall tower. A somnium had notified him of what had transpired—the battle with Zane and how she committed suicide upon her defeat rather than become a prisoner and accept mercy. To the very end, he knew she had sought to not impede his ambitions—but she had failed to realize that she was integral to that ambition. Without her—without *them*—it was all hollow.

Darrel shut his eyes tightly, hoping to wake up from the nightmare that taunted him. His hand still remembered the softness of Alysium's belly when she had shared with him that the Alastairs, by their union, would be reborn. She was dead now. Both of them were.

Feeling Darrel's internal lamentation, seeing his anguish turn into a resolve beyond fear, allowed Intico to manifest a smile that stretched beyond its face. It carried with it the power building around Intico's form, rapidly expanding until it shed its glimmering white appearance in favor of an insidious miasma that ascended into the sky.

Emerging from the shadows behind Intico, several somnium formed. The miasma that loomed over them continued to expand, swallowing the darkening sky and painting it black.

"Carver, it is time," Intico said.

Instead of plunging himself from atop the building, Darrel relinquished something far more important. He submerged his humanity deep within the depths of his blossoming wrath, his untethered sin that no longer sought to justify the evil he had committed, but to bask in it and allow himself to begin anew. He could unleash his scorned, terrible potential. Signifying this renewal, his skin became as ash, and his curved horns emerged from his once slick black hair, now frenzied with his thundering energy. His purple aura whipped around him, bolts of energy cascading across his body as he approached Intico, holding his hand out.

"You made a deal with the Devil, and now ... he arrives," Darrel said, his voice dark and distorted with chaos. Something far more atrocious spoke from within him. The absence of anything he deemed human within himself left along with his original desire to overthrow the Alastairs. There was no desire left to tie him to the family. Indubitably, he missed Alysium, even her insistence to call him by his original name he had long since abandoned. If it meant seeing her again, he would have reclaimed that name, his mantle and claim as heir, in spite of his loathing of them. Along with her, however, all vestiges of that name and its significance perished. Now, all that was left was to destroy the Alastairs. He cared for nothing else after that.

Intico's smile returned to its form.

"Attaboy," Intico cooed and reached out, grasping Darrel's hand. With their joined palms, ruptures of scarlet light bled across the black sky as if it were torn fabric that oozed with fear and wrath alike. The quietude was stormed with the hiss of the somnium, and the city was married to the culmination of their unholy pact.

Harvest.

Their hands separated after several seconds. Darrel walked past Intico and the somnium—loyal soldiers ready to lay siege and claim what they were deprived of.

"If you're vanquished, Harvest will be lost for good this time," Darrel spoke, eyes fixed on the platform plastered in the center of the rooftop.

"Not a snowball's chance in hell," Intico spoke, chuckling darkly as it fixed its gaze on the city below—excitedly anticipating the ripe vessels. It knew that merging with them completely would take several hours once they began, but they didn't have several hours. Incomplete as it may be, once they joined with their chosen vessels, they would need to assist in dispatching any remaining obstacles. With how hastily they had enacted Harvest, there was not enough energy to accelerate the process sufficiently to their original plan. As such, they had to have additional fail-safes in place.

"Magenta," Intico spoke.

A somnium slightly taller than the rest, dawning a pinkish hue within the ghastly whites of its eyes, approached Intico.

"My lord?" Magenta responded.

"Watch over Carver and ensure the hunters do not reach the top of this tower. The energy didn't fully nullify the signals they utilize, and if by some small miracle they make it here ... that would be most disadvantageous. Do what you need to and claim your vessel when it is time."

Magenta narrowed its eyes, glancing at Darrel before chuckling.

"Of course, my lord," it spoke, slowly melding into the shadows cast beneath the miasma permeating around them.

Intico turned to face two other somnium, beckoning them forth.

"Scarlet, your dedication has not gone unrecognized since your bout with my vessel-to-be. Without your efforts, your own desired vessel would not be. As is the case for you, Lapis. You are both indispensable. As promised—your vessels await. You will be among the first to realize what it means to *be*." Intico turned to Scarlet, grinning darkly. "As for you, Scarlet, Burgundy shall assist you with your acquisition. Once you have claimed your vessel, you both will assist in my assault on the Hunters' base in the city. The powers of an umbra and homuntium dithered will be ... advantageous."

"Yes, my lord," Scarlet and Lapis replied in unison. The two somnium snickered, the shadows latching at their feet as they and several other somnium were swallowed by shadows, disappearing.

Intico stepped forward, the remaining somnium behind it following as a vivid shadow formed, shrouding them slowly. The somnium's dark chuckles echoed in the night, evolving into audacious laughter that ruptured the relative peace the city had mistakenly thought it knew. With leers that consumed the city, their vision became shrouded in darkness.

Now certain of its awaiting dominion, its promised *vessel*, Intico gripped its top hat and spoke.

"*My brethren, let Harvest begin!*"

A convoy of armored vehicles was transporting Kendra and Eden back to the Chicago base. Kendra held herself snuggly within the confines of an SUV that was positioned in the center of the convoy—safety reasons had been cited. Eyes still glazed, she kept her head down, evading the light that spilled through the window. She processed Allen's treachery and chastised herself for the fate of her sister, the unsettling revelation chipping away at her. Unable to reconcile those emotions, she plunged them deep into the pits of oblivion. She knew no greater evil than the evil Allen had subjected her to, and despite her rescue, everlasting darkness filled the hole in her heart.

Eden contemplated silently next to Kendra, his eyes closed and his arms crossed. The windows glinted with lights from the street, flashing across their faces throughout the ride. A low hum filled the silence as they drove through the streets. At night, traffic usually died down, and they quickly approached the base.

The night was eerily quiet, which Eden only gave a passing thought to. Mindless entertainment increased the number of citizens who were out and, subsequently, traffic. It was odd that things were so tranquil. Their mission was over, and they made a breakthrough in the case pertaining to the Covenant of Augury. With as large a head as Oliver's severed from the covenant's ambitions, Eden could only imagine the somnium following suit next. It was only a matter of time until Intico would resurface to make its claim or fade into obscurity when its fleeting energy supply was exhausted. With no corporeal foot soldiers at their behest, they would have to rely on scrounging up the nightmares of the citizens artificially, which would hardly prove sufficient to create the army the covenant had sought.

But then there was the matter of the potential moles in the police department. Eden suspected that Darrel was somehow involved in the matters plaguing the city, with as asinine a decision as revoking their access to pertinent crime scenes and information from their dwindling department. The Hunters planned to investigate that matter as well, but that night, they relished their success and Kendra's rescue. Oliver and his clan were in their custody, and their wealth of information was ripe for the picking.

However unpreferable the Hunters' continued custody of her was, Kendra was physically fine. Her head wound had healed, yet the dried blood remained stained on her face and cheek. Caked in grime from her captivity and bleeding, saying she felt gross would be an understatement. She picked at the thighs of her joggers, content with pulling her clothing from sticking to her body in the absence of a shower. However, her jacket had been utterly crusty and saturated with blood. While she and Eden had waited for the convoy, she decided to dispose of it in a trashcan.

Several trucks had arrived to collect the demons inside the warehouse. She still couldn't believe Eden had managed to incapacitate all of them when he had infiltrated. There weren't as many of them as she'd have expected, but the logistics of nefarious demon organizations weren't something she could accurately speculate on. And in that moment, she cared little to try.

When her human visage had returned, the wisps of chaotic energy receded back into her depths. Her claws and fangs receded into their human states, and she blinked, her blazing red eyes returning to their royal-blue hue once more.

"You okay?" Eden asked, peering over at her, having broken his own contemplation. He could detect the subtle shift in her energy as if it was obvious.

Kendra closed her eyes as she breathed a deep sigh, shaking her head.

"I see ..." Eden spoke quietly and returned to looking out the window. They both sat in silence from then on.

Whenever thrust into situations relegated to normalcy, Eden's awkward mannerisms showed. He was much more accustomed to the ways of the supernatural and the pressures they came with. The nuances of emotions, expression, and other matters of human interaction were jarring to him.

It seemed long ago, despite being less than a month, but Eden remembered seeing Kendra prior to her plights, and how charismatic and happy she had been. Seeing her thrust into this darkness, seeing her joy ripped away from her piece-by-piece, was something he was all too familiar with. The spark of hope in her eyes had dulled, barely present. While he was far from a ray of sunshine himself, the more he saw her eyes lose their luster, the more he wished he could have been more focused that day he found her mauled.

As much as Kendra blamed herself for her situation, Eden blamed himself too. If only they could be so perfect, unlike humans, they could have avoided all of life's perils. But unfortunately, they were both afflicted with their imperfections. As such, they would suffer through the human tribulations that lay before them.

The convoy came to a stop. Riddled with various vehicles that rested in the middle of the road, the usually bustling Downtown Chicago lay barren of pedestrians. After waiting for several minutes, the drivers of the convoy became impatient. Liberal use of their horns did nothing to spur traffic to resume. There was no movement at all.

Eden perked his head, his eyes warily tracing the streets outside the windows and windshields. It was too quiet. The driver in the SUV with him and Kendra glanced down at his hunter gauntlet, pensive for a moment before he reluctantly raised his hand to his ear, tapping his earpiece.

"This is Menendez. What's the holdup?" the hunter asked.

"Traffic's stalled for some reason," a voice chirped back over the comms.

The hunter pursed his lips, not buying the explanation given to him.

"It's been this way for several minutes. What's the deal ahead?" the hunter continued.

"Just ... piles of cars."

Eden scanned the environment skeptically, focusing on the surrounding energies. It was as strange as their driver thought it to be. No activity at all. He detected human life forces, but there was something *off*. Despite his acute sensing abilities, he was unfamiliar with such an odd composition to what he initially assumed was distortion.

One of the convoy vehicles creaked violently, and something heavy tore at the roof. Glittering, pointed white fingers plunged through the ceiling of the vehicle, startling the hunters inside. Another set of sharp digits plunged inside, wrenching the metallic frame open, and something peered inside, a warped screech emitting from an outstretched jaw. Inhuman, the thing's ghostly eye sockets had no specific line of sight to track. It was humanoid with rippling skin surging with white and black particles—a clamorous, speckled energy that subtly pulsed.

The surrounding omens reacted as if the air itself had become fabric that was tearing at the seams, revealing an enigmatic red glow underneath. It offered an insidious grin when it had found the hunters, and the group yelled out, fumbling to draw their weapons. It lunged inside and swiftly pinned a hunter down, its fingers piercing into his flesh as it lurched its head back. A sick crackling clicked as its jaw opened impossibly wide, and it prepared to bite into the hunter beneath.

Yuki, as quick as she was, drew her photon saber. Lunging forward, she impaled the creature through its mouth and engaged the stun gun. It let out a warped yell as it tensed up and lurched back, unpinning the hunter beneath it.

A hunter threw the back of the truck open, and another hefted the creature, tossing it out with a loud grunt. He drew his pistol and, without hesitation, blasted half of the magazine into the creature. Upon impact, the anti-demon bullets hissed, smoke leaving the bleeding wounds; it resembled what they saw with demons and their wounds, prompting theories about the nature of the creatures.

The air shifted, growing strangely cold. During the initial chaos, several of the *things* had descended from the rooftops, plummeting onto the vehicles with heavy thuds. The creatures put their metal-tearing affinity to use with the rest of the vehicles, their fingers plunging into the cabins and wrenching them open. The hunters rushed from the truck that was initially attacked, their eyes locked on the creatures.

The glittering fiends prowled in the streets, some abandoning their infiltration of the vehicles upon spotting *prey* out in the open. Echoing, distorted groans projected from them, and their eye sockets were wide as their heads turned toward the exposed group.

Gunfire rang from the convoy van, driving the creature to withdraw its arm from the hole it had created in the roof. The sound did not deter the rest of the creatures, who quickly advanced on the exposed group.

There wasn't a lot of time for the hunters to reflect on what they were dealing with. They drew their pistols, took aim, and opened fire on any of the demons in sight. Bullets zipped through the air, piercing into their flesh—or at least that was what they assumed it to be. Some fell to the ground, limp, whereas some had a sense and dodged out of the line of fire, jumping to the roofs of the surrounding convoy and civilian cars, sprinting along them with a rigid lurch.

The last one lunged at the group, emitting an ear-piercing shriek, but its face met Eden's boot. Seeing their wild tactics and vicious potential,

Eden called Avenger to his palm, and with three swift slashes, he cleaved the remaining demons that charged his comrades.

Avenger was coated in blood, but the blood seeped into the metal of the blade after a few moments, disappearing. Eden sheathed it and inspected the bodies of the fiendish assailants in pensive perplexity, deeply confused by their arrival.

While Kendra had desired nothing more than to ruminate in silence until the world ended, the multiple gunshots along with the yells from the hunters had torn her from her despondency. With the perturbing scent of blood filling the air, maintaining her idleness became unpalatable. Ignoring Eden's order to stay in the SUV, she exited, eyeing the scene warily. Eden appeared annoyed by this, but she ignored him. Though the corpses weren't moving anymore, the odd composition of their animated skin peeled, dissipating into white energy. The scent, albeit tinged with a faint pungency, was all too familiar. *Almost human,* in fact. The horrifying realization dawned on her when she saw what was beneath the dissolving energy—human flesh.

The rest of the hunters exited the vehicles in the aftermath. They gathered at the scene, peering at the corpses of the demons that had attacked them. Laying before them, the creatures, despite being demonic in nature, were alien to them. Even Zane, who had experience with all manners of demons, was clueless. Seeing what was beneath the strange energy that dissipated appalled all of them.

"They're ... human," Kendra murmured. The faces, containing horrified expressions, had shown a glimpse of the dark truth of their reality. These were humans who had been subjected to the dark ambitions of the somnium. Humans who were victims of *Harvest.*

The energy that left them ceased to disappear, and a haze left from their open mouths, gathering a short distance away from the hunters. The haze coalesced into tall, lanky humanoid forms, forming into several somnium. Having evacuated from the bodies they had inhabited, they glared at the hunters, their gazes rife with what one could only presume was ire. Understanding their disadvantage against the armed group of hunters, they fled behind the nearby building, and the hunters decided to not pursue.

It was apparent to Eden and Kendra what was going on. After all, Eden had experienced Intico's attempt at taking his body, and Kendra had witnessed it. The moment Kendra saw another of the somnium, she knew what it had meant. Somnium demons had possessed each of the humans—no—they had merged with them. What they had become was the dithered, a name none of the hunters were privy to yet. They surmised by appearances alone that the merging hadn't completed, seeing as the somnium had emerged from the human corpses.

Eden had briefly been a victim of the same process when he fought Intico. The memories of what he had experienced—what *they* had experienced—caused him to tense in disgust. He was positive that the humans had suffered until the very end, submerged in a ceaseless nightmare of the somnium's twisted machinations.

Zane crossed his arms, his eyes shifting up from the scene before he looked to the sky and froze. There, sitting astride layers of gray clouds, were the same distortions that the demons of unknown specificity brought with them. Undulating tears in the fabric of Ichor itself stretched and distorted, becoming something unrecognizable. The atmosphere itself had become underlined by a hiss. Some hunters reflexively checked their earpieces in disbelief over the noise, it being their first time encountering the precursor of a somnium's presence. Upon confirming it was not faulty technology, a hunter turned to Zane.

"What the hell is this, Captain Larson?" he asked.

Zane pointed at the sky, his expression marred with worry. More disturbing than anything, he was silent, offering no clever quips to alleviate the mounting tensions.

The hunters fixed their gazes on the sky. Mouths agape, they watched the utter malformation of the atmosphere above them flex and descend.

"Is that ... the source of the hissing?" Yuki asked, her eyes narrowing.

Eden marched past one of the dead bodies, tapping the pad of his hunter bracer to interface and switch his earpiece to the long-distance command channel.

"Blackwell to command, do you copy?" Eden asked, holding his earpiece as he waited for a response. But he only got interference. Shaking his head, he looked back at the group. "Nothing."

A few other hunters tried the same on their earpieces, but it was to no avail.

Andrew folded his arms, snapping his finger.

"The van may be able to get a better signal. Let me tune it," Andrew said, rushing over to the stationary van. Climbing inside, he tuned the complex console of knobs and dials. A minute later, he tried to dial into command himself.

"Carter to command, do you copy?" Despite his efforts, there was still no answer, nor a signal, according to the console. Disconcerted, Andrew dreaded imagining what their lack of a signal entailed.

"N-no dice!" Andrew called out and climbed out of the van.

Yuki paced as she racked her head for answers or potential solutions.

"Maybe if we get back to base, we'll be able to reach them?" she suggested.

Zane shook his head, sighing as he glanced south of their location.

"I don't think our problem is a lack of good signal ... there's interference from this strange distortion. And I can feel it south of here. Somewhere tall, but I don't know Chicago well enough to pinpoint where that could be," Zane said.

"I think Z ... I mean, Captain Larson is right. Besides, we had contact with command without a problem just minutes ago," Andrew said.

Eden had lived in Chicago for the past two years, but he hardly had memorized the city for a variety of reasons. Despite his various hunts, something had always occupied his mind, detracting from his memorization of the city's layout and landmarks. However, he turned to Kendra, meeting her gaze and finding determination in her expression.

Kendra processed Zane's statement for a few moments. She was very familiar with Chicago, and given they were somewhere near the Gold Coast, she parsed the qualities Zane had mentioned. She knew exactly where it had to be.

"Willis Tower," Kendra said. The hunters' attention landed on her. "Tallest building in Chicago ... Willis Tower. It's south of here!" There was skepticism in the hunters' eyes, but Andrew showed more faith in his own scrutiny, socking his fist into his palm.

"It makes sense! If they established that as some sort of ground zero for whatever this is, then it stands to reason that if we can set up a signal booster at the top, we can bypass the interference and restore comms with command!" Andrew said, his eyes wide and glimmering with renewed hope.

Staring pensively in the direction of the tower, Zane thought about the logistics of getting their other engineer, Bryce Jackson, there.

"Alright, I'll get Sergeant Jackson to Willis Tower," Zane said.

"Negative, Captain," Bryce spoke up. He stepped forward from within the crowd, sucking in air harshly through gritted teeth as he limped into Zane's view. Confused at first, Zane cocked an eyebrow with an expectant stare, but then he spotted it. Present a few inches up his left leg were three distinct vertical slashes through his suit. Zane cringed at the sight, knowing if not for the suit, the damage would have been gravely severe. "One of those things got me pretty good. An expedition through the city with more of them probably lurking? I can't ... I'm sorry."

Reflecting for a moment, Zane knew the circumstances were less than optimal.

"Shit, don't worry about it. Sergeant Tracy, get Jackson back to the base in one piece. When you get there, spur the rest of the hunters into full mobilization. We're beginning citywide evacuation procedures. Groups of no less than three are to sweep the city and facilitate evacuation procedures at the designated evacuation sites in our database. Copy?"

A youthful man, Mark Tracy, stepped forward, holstering his pistol. He placed a hand on Jackson's shoulder, nodding at Zane.

"Copy," Mark said. But he hesitated. Taking a moment to reflect, he and Jackson exchanged looks before he returned his attention to Zane. "Ah, and what about running into any more of those demons? They're ... still human, right?"

Zane's eyes averted to the ground for a moment, scrutinizing the stretched maw of one corpse. Even to the very end, the human appeared to have been screaming. Agonizing was too soft a word to describe their fate.

"Avoid killing them only if you can ... but do what you need to do to protect yourselves and civilians," Zane said. Tense silence surrounded them for several moments.

"Right. Leave Jackson to me," Mark said and walked off with Bryce leaning against him.

"Wait, if Jackson is out of commission ... who does that leave to restore the comms?" Andrew asked, his large blue eyes flicking between the group with concern.

Zane eyed Andrew, cocking his brow.

"You, of course," Zane said.

Andrew didn't register the statement immediately, blinking with a blank stare for a moment before his expression caught up to the situation.

"Wha—me!" he questioned, pointing to himself incredulously.

Smirking, Zane stepped toward Andrew and placed his hands on Andrew's shoulders.

"Yup. Escorted by yours truly!" Zane said, snickering. "Second field mission on the same day as your first, eh? We'll make a hunter of you yet."

"I was only supposed to be auxiliary support ..." Andrew whined. He had only ever served as a junior engineer at the primary base, and recently, the Chicago base. This had been his first mission as a field operator, but still, Commander Evans had insisted he *get his feet wet*. Losing the nerve to argue further, he slumped his shoulders in defeat.

Zane averted his attention to the rest of the hunters, crossing his arms.

"I'll get Private Carter to Willis Tower and we'll get comms back up and running. Blackwell, you're in charge of the rest in my absence," Zane spoke, flashing a rueful smirk. "What's your move?"

Eden glanced at Kendra and the rest of the group, his pensive stare beckoning questions from the group.

"Wilson and Daniels, stay behind to guard the convoy. Won't be good if the somnium free the umbra demons. The rest of you and Kendra—come with me. We're heading to the Chicago Police HQ to devise an evacuation plan. We have to utilize their radio infrastructure to broadcast to the citizens. After that, I'll make my way to the base to ensure we're mobilized before I rendezvous with Zane and Andrew at Willis Tower," Eden said, turning on his heel. "Now—on me!"

"Roger!" the group repeated. Diverging off into two groups, Zane and Andrew ran south, and Eden's group traveled north. The convoy guards stayed behind to ensure their demon prisoners remained prisoners.

Kendra jogged to catch up with the group, who were far faster than she had anticipated. She could understand Eden's speed. Then, in her memory, she recalled one of the conversations she had with Andrew, wherein he explained that the hunters' suits helped augment their physical capabilities. Andrew, by far, had been the most helpful in explaining these things, given how specific and eager he could be. Shaking the thought from her head, she refocused on the present situation, still wildly confused about the *plan*.

Kendra joined Eden's side, perplexed by how calm he was. The situation appeared insurmountable, instilling a mortal fear in her akin to when she first saw Intico.

"Eden, is this that *Harvest* thing that somnium spoke about?" Kendra called.

"I don't know," Eden called over the wind, and Kendra groaned, annoyed by her persisting ignorance.

Kendra couldn't fault the hunters before her for not knowing. The circumstances were far from normal, even by their purported standards. As they ran, the status of the citizens became apparent. Bodies littered the streets, rested in cars, and piled in the stores. At first, Kendra assumed they were dead, but she could see them breathing visibly, and energy still emitted from them.

"They're only asleep," Kendra said.

"The work of the somnium, no doubt," Eden alleged. His ire spilled from his breath when he mentioned them, the bitter memory surfacing from his last confrontation with Intico. And in that memory lay the answer they sought. Wrenching words from memories he had thought he suppressed, the statement Intico last spoke surfaced: *I will have your body soon enough—come Harvest.*

Eden carefully pieced together the various details he was aware of throughout the investigation into the Covenant of Augury that spanned several months. They had terrorized the police and collected bodies, sowed insomnia throughout the population, and used hellhounds to collect souls for a singular purpose—Harvest. The fact everybody slept left them vulnerable, primed for merging. It was why Intico had used a sleep-inducing miasma to exhaust him. If it were a simple matter of killing, Intico would have done so.

It had been less than twelve hours since Archer's death, and the Siegharts were in custody. But as nonsensical as it seemed, Harvest had commenced. The specifics of the phenomenon were unknown to Eden, but he had assumed such an orchestrated ritual would have warranted greater diligence in its execution. He speculated it had to be premature, but more than anything, he knew what the throes of desperation could spur even the most cunning demons to resort to.

Eden focused ahead, seeing several crashed cars along with flashing police lights cast from behind a building. It was almost overwhelming how much they needed to do, but their current directive took precedence. That was reaffirmed when they heard gunfire coming from near the police vehicles they spotted. Eden held his fist up, and he and the group came to a stop. More gunfire echoed through the desolate block, causing a good deal of concern to creep into Eden. He could detect demonic energy signatures from where the gunfire rang, accompanied by screams.

The group was only a few blocks away from the headquarters. Searching the energy signatures where the gunfire sounded from, Eden hadn't detected the peculiar signature of the dithered. He intended to ensure they and the somnium would remain far away from the surviving citizens. Standard firearms wouldn't prove effective against the dithered or the somnium, given their magical nature and regeneration capabilities—something their anti-demon rounds counteracted. Eden could only guess that the police had been the ones shooting, and with the somnium as the only candidates as targets, Eden assumed they were in mortal danger.

"Ardent, Grayson, you two deal with the demons. When they're eliminated, rendezvous with us at the headquarters," Eden said, glancing at Emily and the other hunter he ordered, Joseph.

Kendra perked her head up, glancing at the group of hunters. A younger man with bronze skin and short, curly brown hair stepped forward next to Emily. He had well-defined muscles becoming of a hunter, more toned than Vicente had been. His last name, Ardent, was peculiar to her, being quite uncommon. It was the name of her former boss, James Ardent, but he didn't resemble James. However, there were explanations that could explain that away.

"Roger," the pair of hunters replied. Joseph shifted his attention to Emily, and she nodded at him. Raising their rifles, they diverged from the group and sprinted around the corner where the gunfire rang out.

Eden waved for the rest of the hunters and Kendra to follow him again, and they continued their trek through the city. Upon reaching the street of the Chicago Police HQ, the once mighty indictment of crime had become a final hold-out against the somnium and dithered. Various vehicles had created a blockade on either corner of the street, flashing lights and gunshots ringing from the perimeters. Officers were barking at each other over the indiscernible noise. One of the most prominent orders came from a megaphone an officer was using to direct a line of citizens that stretched beyond the perimeter made by the police.

"Everybody, approach the station in an orderly fashion," the officer called over the megaphone.

The group approached a barricade that separated the desolate streets from the encumbered block connected to the headquarters building. Multiple officers in riot gear stood as an impediment to their mission. Eden ordered the group to hold their hands up as they approached, and upon noticing them, the officers stood attentively, their rifles held stiffly. Trepidation seeped from their pores, as was evident in their shifty demeanor. An officer held his hand up to signal them to stop, but upon taking notice of the group's attire and weapons, the police aimed their guns.

"Who are you guys? Keep your hands where we can see them!" an officer yelled in a shaky voice. Their paranoia was palpable. "W-what's with the weapons? Identify yourselves, now!"

Neither Kendra nor Eden blamed the officers. By every regard, the situation inspired fear and confusion alike, and the elusive nature of the group was no longer obscured. The officers were connected, and the obscuring incantation did not affect those who were connected. The situation, albeit tense, was something they had to navigate carefully.

With their training, the hunters could conjure a barrier capable of protecting them from the police bullets. However, if it came to a firefight, there would be little hope of completing their mission to utilize the police's infrastructure to mitigate the harm to the citizens. As impulsive as he could be, Eden understood that much, and he nodded at the officer.

"I'm Private Blackwell of Organization X. I'll provide my identification badge to you via band. Open a tunnel for me to send it," Eden said. The officers' stares were intense, weapons still aimed at the group they found to be entirely too suspicious. However, Eden's punctual statement provided a sliver of ease, and after exchanging some stares, an officer lowered his weapon, raised his wrist, and tapped across the pad of a device he wore.

"Organization X? Tunnel's open," he said.

Eden interfaced with his hunter brace, the holographic screen emerging. With a few consecutive taps along the screen, the officer's own screen flashed, and he watched the officer review the ID badge. Unfortunately, the officers' hesitation became apparent to Eden as their eyes shifted between Eden and the badge multiple times.

"We're under strict orders from our acting chief to not deal with Organization X," one spoke.

Now, it was Eden's turn to show ire, and he glared at the officers.

"Do you realize what's going on here? This is *our* jurisdiction," Eden growled and gestured his thumb to himself with a tight, quivering fist. "Deputy chief of police or not, Darrel Carver has no place hindering our mandated duty. We need to speak with the highest commander available *now*."

"You heard me. You're not civilians evacuating and have no authority or jurisdiction. We *can't* let you inside the evacuation zone."

Kendra's hands had been slack, but gradually tightened into pulsing fists. *They can't be serious. Why were they ordered not to cooperate with the Hunters?* she thought. The state of the city hardly called for arbitrary proceduralism, especially when faced with forces beyond human comprehension. Still, she knew there had to be a resolution—and preferably one that didn't involve gunshots between either party. Then an idea struck her. She wasn't a member of either group, but she had connections to the police, and plenty of experience speaking to them.

"If I might," Kendra stepped forward, hands raised, "I'm Kendra Mallory. My mother is Detective Katherine Mallory with the Chicago PD. These guys have an urgent message for the highest-ranking officer available from the department ... but I get that you can't let them through. My mother told me all about the chain of command and all that crap. So, can I go through? I'm just a civilian who was saved by them." The officers exchanged glances, one of them lowering his weapon as he eyed Kendra. He took a deep breath.

"You're Mallory's daughter?" Kendra nodded, her hands still held in the air.

"My mother has dedicated over two decades to the department. The least you can do is grant the request of her scared civilian daughter," she said succinctly.

The officers continued exchanging glances. The officer who had spoken relaxed his stance, pulling his radio piece on his shirt close and calling his captain over the radio.

Kendra sighed in relief at the progress. As uncertain as her chances of successfully getting through were, she assumed she had deescalated the situation considerably. She took several steps back to stand next to Eden, who gazed pensively at her for several moments before speaking.

"What are you doing?" he asked.

Pursing her lips, Kendra replied,

"Saving my city."

"Then ... if you get through, we need to talk to them about cooperating in the evacuations. If demons are attacking the shelters, they won't stand a chance against them."

Kendra nodded, exhaling unsteadily.

"Roger," she said, mimicking their punctual speech.

Several minutes passed—minutes Eden knew were wasted. Finally, a tall man, the police captain, approached the barricade, eyeing the group warily before his eyes found Kendra.

"Mallory's daughter?" the captain asked.

"Yeah. I need to speak to the highest-ranking officer in charge at this station on behalf of—uh—Organization X. It's urgent." Kendra swallowed hard with pleading eyes, silently praying that the captain would let her through.

"We're not supposed to work with Organization X by the command of the DPC," he said.

"I'm not a part of Organization X. Think of me as ... a witting citizen petitioning on behalf of their interest." He stared silently for a few moments, a puzzled expression on his face. Then he snorted.

"Fine. But no guarantees he'll talk to you. He's running around like a chicken with its head cut off. I'll do you the solid out of respect for your mom."

Kendra's eyes lit up as she nodded enthusiastically. She had done it, and relief washed through the group, collectively letting out their sighs of relief. Eden patted Kendra's back, and she nodded to the group before following the captain through the barricade.

The tumult in the surrounding streets was a grizzly sight. Several citizens lined up with sunken faces that were plagued with dark eyes. They nodded off while standing, some even collapsing outright. Several more were already collapsed at their feet, supported shabbily by relatives or friends who could hardly hold themselves up. Patchy darkness allowed the red tint of the distorting waves to color the street ominously, further propagating the dread among the citizens. Kendra steeled her nerves, feeling she was the *lucky* one in comparison. She at least had a grasp of what was happening. For them—astonishing confusion and supernatural whiplash. She intimately understood that herself.

Kendra and the police captain entered the lobby, carefully pressing through the narrow tunnel within the crowd. Worming their way through, they navigated to the stairwell, which was mostly unoccupied by the citizens.

As she scanned the scene, Kendra's fingers reflexively curled inward. She had visited that very building plenty of times with her mother, but this time was different. The entire city was on the line, resting on her shoulders with only the chance of mitigating the damage the demons could commit. Chicago was a large city. It stood to reason that even the few dozen hunters present at their Chicago base couldn't handle the gargantuan task of defending it—let alone the meager group waiting for her outside. In truth, she had little faith in her own capabilities, let alone theirs, but not once had a lack of faith ever stopped her from trying. It was something Kendall used to commend her for.

The silence between Kendra and the police captain was interrupted.

"She alright?"

Kendra looked up at him, tilting her head in confusion.

"Detective Mallory. She took a leave of absence weeks ago. She alright?"

Kendra pursed her lips, her eyes suddenly downcast. Her mother hadn't been alright. The slow descent into grief was hardly what one would consider *alright*. Trauma dumping on behalf of her mother was not on her itinerary that day.

"She's hanging in there. A lot is going on, as I'm sure you know."

"Yeah. I can't say that it's easy on you guys."

They stopped speaking.

Once on the second floor, they brushed past the bustling officers and personnel. Squawking conversations about the state of the city filled the room, and from what she had gathered, their wider communication infrastructure was down and attempts at contacting other relevant authorities were unsuccessful.

"Ma'am, I know it may sound like your father, but do not open the door. I repeat. Do *not* open the door for *anyone* you think is on the other side," a woman said from within the dispatch center, barely audible among the uproar of ringing from the phones.

Kendra stirred from her focus, recalling something her mother had said that was reminiscent of the conversations she overheard. The idea of familiar voices calling from behind a door. While haunting on its face, it suggested there was a parameter the somnium operated within, a boundary she wondered about. Surely, the somnium were capable of easily breaching a door. The reason for their tactics escaped her.

Having navigated through the hectic scene, the captain waved her over to a door with a plaque that read *Commander Thompson*. The captain knocked, and a buzz rang before he opened it. He gestured Kendra inside and followed after her. The office was clean and well-kept. They stood before a front-facing desk with folders neatly stacked along the surface. Behind the desk sat a stout, light-skinned man with salt-and-pepper hair and a scruffy beard. Dark circles sagged below his teal-colored eyes as he leered at the two with a puzzled expression.

"Why are you bringing a citizen to me at a time like *this?*" Commander Thompson asked the captain with a puzzled expression.

The captain furrowed his brow, nodding his head at Kendra to urge her to speak.

Kendra swallowed hard, digging her fingers into her palms. A ball got stuck in her throat as the pressure crept up on her. As articulate as she could be, the mounting pressure added a gravity that was absent moments prior. Summoning the courage to speak, she stepped forward.

"I'm Kendra Mallory, daughter of Detective Katherine Mallory." She took an unsteady breath. "I'm petitioning on behalf of Organization X. The state of emergency that is going on is far outside the police's understanding or capabilities to curtail without them."

The man nodded along with her statements, a frown forming once she had mentioned the Hunters' alias. A heavy sigh left his lips as he pinched the bridge of his nose. With a shake of his head, he returned his tired gaze to Kendra and stood.

"Listen, I understand how things look, but I can more than assure you we have this under control," he spoke condescendingly.

Kendra's thumbs dug into her palms, her focus strained to ensure that her claws wouldn't manifest. So easily was she dismissed with as ill-inspiring a line as the commander had delivered. There were plenty of criticisms she had heard about police as an institution, but experiencing this at such a critical juncture was the most palpable vindication of some arguments she had endured.

An uproar of screams echoed through the building, snatching the three's attention. A familiar essence in the air roused Kendra, prompting her to tense as she turned to the door. Insidious energy emanated through the department, accompanied by a dreaded *hiss*. Kendra cursed the timing of one of the somnium arriving, knowing that none of the humans, armed or not, would be able to deter it.

"What the hell is going on?" Commander Thompson snapped.

Kendra bolted out of the office, the two officers in tow as they sought answers over their radios. She hadn't registered why she sought the somnium; the idea that she was mostly powerless still plagued her. A hybrid with untrained power, more equipped than most humans, but she felt she couldn't defeat a demon. Still, she understood that she could, at the very least, serve to distract it, not to mention she could regenerate if harmed.

They came to a stop in the lobby outside the dispatch center when a reverberating cackle bombarded them from all directions. The sensation was ubiquitously disturbing to everybody, Kendra and the officers included. They looked around, panic marring their faces as sweat descended their brows. Then they saw it. Lumbering up the escalator, a lanky somnium slowly appeared.

How the somnium had gotten inside escaped them, but there it was. Aside from how nefarious and evil their actions suggested they were, their sapience was abundantly clear. Kendra knew it had to have a reason to be inside. The law enforcement personnel around them scrambled, leaving their desks upon seeing the fiend approach. It occurred to Kendra that they could perceive the demons pervading the city now, suggesting that Harvest had connected all the humans.

Swallowing hard, Kendra tensed as their gazes met. Those ghastly white sockets widened with its impossible grin expanding beyond the borders of its face. It had found her. Its arms swayed loosely at its sides as it took long strides toward them. Deceptive in its lumbering approach, it was faster than it appeared, each step taken with the purpose of compounding their fear.

The officers didn't hesitate, drawing their pistols and firing at it. The bullets pierced its thin body multiple times, leaving behind holes that oozed luminescent, glittering white sludge. It didn't slow down in the slightest, its cackle becoming syncopated and more audacious. Before their eyes, the bullets fell from its form, and the holes sealed quickly.

"How the fuck? Ineffective!" the captain called out.

The somnium snickered, dusting its shoulder as if to mock the officers' attempts at damaging it. Its eyes narrowed as it settled its attention on Kendra squarely.

"There you are, my precious vessel. Kendra Mallory, oh how I've longed to bask in that chaotic spark of scarlet light within your soul ..." it hissed, its mouth opening as a noxious haze oozed from between its teeth.

Kendra's breath halted in her chest. It knew her name. It was there for her. Her heart pulsed rapidly, her mind swelling with panic as she thought of what to do. Normal bullets didn't appear to have any effect on it, making her wonder what chance she stood with her claws and flames. However imposing it was, she knew she was the only one that stood a ghost of a chance at combating it in this instance. She had no idea what could kill the thing, but she had to fight however she could. There was no time to hesitate as it neared, and she took a deep breath before swallowing her trepidation.

Kendra yelled, rushing toward the somnium with her right arm drawn back. The officers didn't have time to reload when she charged it. Familiar anger coursed through her. Her blood boiled and became hot as an all-too-familiar itch coursed through her fingertips, causing them to turn black and sharpen to long points. Before her, the somnium lowered its stance, its eyes narrowing as she neared it.

"Kid, get away from that thing!" Commander Thompson called after her.

Coming into striking distance, Kendra swung at the demon, but it caught her wrist with ease, snickering as it hoisted her into the air. She dangled from the ground as it raised her high. Panic jolted through her as she thrashed at the demon, ferociously kicking her feet into its surprisingly sturdy frame. Smoke spewed from the corners of her mouth, her teeth tightly clenching as she struggled in the somnium's grasp.

Seeing those long, sharp teeth in front of her—so close—caused her to choke up. Her wrist tensed in its cold grasp, a display of how woefully outmatched she was against it. She was no hunter whose nerves steeled in the face of danger, nor was she nearly as brave as she had feigned in her charge.

There was a moment of silence as she stared into its fathomless eyes. She gleaned an eternity of torment within their depths—a remorseless voracity that consumed all before it to achieve its ends. *Helpless again,* she thought, remembering seeing Vicente dying before her eyes. *Helpless again,* echoed once more, and she deigned to think back to Kendall being helplessly torn apart as they were pinned to the ground. Those burning eyes that haunted her nightmares surfaced within her own as she conjured a rebellion against such sentiments that tore through her veins. Should she have relented to their despair once more, she feared a purgatory of torment awaited.

She had her flames. No longer suppressed, she could hear their cries within the depths of her soul, screaming at her for liberation from their cage. They had always come in response to an intensity of her emotions, and while she had sparse success in the past, she had never been as in tune with them as she was now. Her emotions, while marred by a chilling fear, were enough. Fearful fury would ignite her retaliation.

Fury culminated on Kendra's lips, heat crawling up her throat. As steam spilled through her clenched teeth, they became a burst of flames that jetted from her opening mouth, consuming the demon's form in a fiery hue. A hit at point-blank range, it proved immediately effective. The somnium's fingers went slack, releasing her wrist from its grip as it hissed loudly, convulsing in the fire that danced along its shadowy visage.

Kendra landed in front of the somnium, watching it stumble and jitter as her flames washed over its inky silhouette. It had been scorched severely, its body seeping with ooze as its skin undulated, attempting to reform as it had with the bullets. If she had learned anything from watching Eden fight Intico, she didn't assume that it was defeated. Not knowing any technical weakness of the thing, she could only venture that the location she presumed its heart to be was a good place to target. She arched her arm back, her fingers pressing tightly together and going rigid. She had seen what her claws were capable of by accident plenty of times. They easily shredded what they raked, and they could pierce through durable material. She didn't know what the demon was made of, but she bet its rippling, carapace-like flesh couldn't be harder than metal.

Kendra jabbed her hand through the demon's chest, and her entire body shivered as if she had plunged her arm into snow, the sludge coating it. The somnium exhaled a pained hiss, sounding similar to a deflating ball, before slumping forward limply. Heart throbbing wildly, she focused, trying to conjure flames on her hand and arm as she had done with Eden. Her hand sparked, and her temperature rose rapidly. Flames burst from her pores, spilling from the cavity left in the somnium's chest. The light drained from the fiend's eyes and ceased its noise, prompting Kendra to tear her arm from its chest. At last, it toppled over next to her—dead.

Heavy breaths escaped Kendra's lips in steamy puffs of air. She had killed a demon. The prospect terrified her, as was evident in her astonished gaze glued to the residual sludge that dissipated from her hand. Through the intense aftermath, she forgot about the spectating officers, consumed by the moral confliction she wrestled with.

The pair of officers had watched the entire encounter, dumbfounded. The captain swallowed hard, lowering his pistol as he glanced at Commander Thompson, who was still slack-jawed and stunned into silence.

"Commander?" the captain called, but no response came from the man.

Kendra finally caught her breath after several seconds, her demonic visage receding as she calmed herself. While difficult, she finally returned to her human appearance. Her ferocious gaze found Commander Thompson and the police captain, adrenaline still coursing through her.

The police officers' gazes showed fearful trepidation, locked onto Kendra, then glancing at the dead somnium. In such tumultuous uncertainty, the police captain, as the only one animated of the two, unsteadily aimed his gun at Kendra.

"You're not human ... are you with them?" the police captain alleged.

Kendra glared. For several seconds, such a question astounded her. In her admonishment of their palpable irrationality, she pointed to the dead somnium at her feet.

"Does it look like I'm with them?" Kendra spoke, cutting the tense silence.

"It said your name. You could be trying to get us to let our guards down. What's your game?"

"My game is to save our asses!" Kendra yelled, pointing at the exit that was downstairs. "And in case you haven't noticed, your bullets do jack shit to them! What *guard* would I need to tear down? Your bullets wouldn't do shit to me!" Kendra took a deep breath. "Look around. Do you think you can handle this without Organization X? Without me? *No, you don't* have it under control!" she yelled, her words dripping with venom.

As ridiculous as it was on its face, she remembered the paralyzing nature of perceiving demons for the first time. An intrinsic panic followed, and the more one dwelled on the thought of such creatures, the more prone to phantom despair they were. She recalled such unbecoming words of despair leaving her own lips after her tarot reading with Kendall.

After several seconds, Commander Thompson pursed his lips, reaching out and pushing the police captain's gun down, much to his subordinate's bewilderment.

"Okay, okay. Yeah. We have no clue what the fuck we're dealing with here," Commander Thompson conceded. He paced for a moment, cupping his mouth with a rigid, trembling hand. "I'm gonna speak with those Organization X guys. We need their help."

Finally, Kendra thought. She stood straight, turning on her heel as she approached the stairwell.

"Let's go then," she called to them.

The captain and commander exchanged weary glances before they followed her, warily creeping past the somnium's body as if it would jump up again. The crowd in the lobby had all huddled in one corner of the room, all wearing panic-stricken faces. They had undoubtedly seen the somnium demon. Kendra, the captain, and Commander Thompson pushed through the crowd and exited the building.

Outside, the barren streets were littered with viscera and the bodies of several officers, former dithered, and somnium. However, the attrition persisted. Gunfire rang out as the hunters and officers desperately struggled against the somnium and several dithered that attacked. Close to the HQ building's entrance, one such dithered shot a streak of purple energy through a police officer who had fired at it, splattering blood across the streets and nearby civilians. Unlike the other somnium, this one had the shape of horns atop its head, and it smiled chaotically as the officers fruitlessly shot at it.

Suddenly, a loud pop rang out, and a bullet collided with the dithered's head, blowing it open with steam coming from what remained. From across the street, Emily perched atop a police van at one of the barricades, her rifle smoking from the shot she had taken.

A loud yell snatched the attention of nearby police officers as a somnium held down an officer with its talon-like feet, while holding another up by their vest. The somnium turned its attention as it heard someone approaching rapidly. Behind it, Yuki charged, her photon saber pointed toward it as she closed in. As it prepared to counter her, a flash of bright light flickered from the pommel of her saber, and the creature stumbled, releasing the officers from its hold. With a slash across its legs, Yuki swept it from its imposing stance, kicked it to a prone position, then jammed the saber through its chest. Letting out a hiss, the creature looked up to see Yuki's pistol pointed at its face. She fired a single round, blasting a hole through its head before she withdrew her sword and holstered her gun.

The battle ended shortly after, and throughout the street, several officers lay dead, surrounded by their comrades that shouted over their radios for medical attention. However, it was far too late. Deep lacerations carved their bodies, all of which had hemorrhaged blood. The officers who had been blasted by the magic-wielding dithered had died immediately, few having any salvageable remains.

Looking around at the scene, Kendra and the high-ranking officers came to a stark realization. The demon that had slipped inside was the result of an overwhelming show of force. There had been entirely too many of them for the meager group to eliminate without casualties. It was a painful end that saddened Kendra to witness, prompting her to hold back tears as she clenched her fists. Nearby, she saw several hunters lingering, checking the corpses with skeptical gazes and drawn weapons. Finally spotting Eden, she and the high-ranking officers jogged over to him as he ripped Avenger from a corpse before sheathing it.

With the chaos temporarily settled, the hunters held their palms out, chanting silently. Each time they muttered *sanguine,* white light encapsulated the somnium's shadowy forms before their corpse dissipated. Eden did the same to the corpse he stood before, then he looked at Kendra as she and the officers approached. He sighed in relief upon seeing her and exchanged glances with the captain and commander.

"Jesus Christ ..." the captain muttered, his eyes wide as he registered the grim scene around them.

"We couldn't save all of them, I'm sorry," Eden informed tepidly, giving a remorseful scowl as he glanced behind him.

Commander Thompson ground his teeth, his weary eyes dilating.

"You're ... the Organization X guy ... right?" Commander Thompson asked.

Eden nodded.

"I am."

"I'm Commander Thompson," he greeted. "Listen. I'm technically not supposed to be working with you guys, but our acting chief, Carver, isn't anywhere to be found. Can't reach him at all. Seeing as I'm the next to assume control over the department, I'm ready to cooperate with your organization. I just want to protect everybody from whatever the fuck these things are."

Eden was silent for a few moments, searching Commander Thompson's eyes for conviction. Fear. But with it came cooperation. He was glad Kendra had convinced the man, since he had been ready to incapacitate and coercing them into assisting.

"As do I. What I need from you is the location of each evacuation shelter so I can send our members there, along with an order to your officers present at each shelter to cooperate with us. We're the only ones equipped to kill these things," Eden explained.

Kendra didn't hear the rest of what they discussed, still fixed on the memory of the fight. The visceral gravity of utilizing her powers to kill something had been paradoxically exhilarating and haunting. The subtle friction on her hand as it had pierced through the somnium, the icy prickling of its matter coursing down her arm, and the crackles and pops of boiling it alive with her flames replayed in her head. She fixated on the hand that had done it, uncontrollable tremors plaguing it.

"Kendra," Eden said. She blinked a few times. Eden, Commander Thompson, and the captain were staring at her.

She hadn't realized she had zoned out.

"Yeah?" Kendra answered, snapping to attention as she clenched her hand repeatedly.

"Kendra, you're going to be staying here," Eden said. Kendra's mouth went slack, her eyes narrowing before shaking her head.

"What? No! I have to—I mean, I should be helping!"

Eden's gaze softened.

"You *are* going to be helping. You and Joseph are staying here. The officers told me how you put that demon down ... and if any more of the somnium come, they'll need both of you." He grabbed her shoulder. "I'm counting on you, Kendra."

Kendra sucked her lips in and averted her eyes to the ground yet again. Eden didn't seem the type to trust easily. She couldn't think of a reason he would trust her after all the trouble she'd caused him, but it was exactly what she had wanted. This was her home, and despite the turmoil festering in her mind—the lingering trauma that weighed on her—her goal was to defend it. Suppressing a smile, she nodded at Eden.

"Roger."

Their attention was drawn to a subtle noise that echoed in the distance. A droning whir that resonated from above neared them. Eden withdrew his hand from Kendra's shoulder, turning toward the sound. He didn't sense demonic energy from whatever it was, inspiring confusion beneath his concern.

"What now?" he muttered. The sky above flickered with small green lights attached to objects obscured within the red-tinted darkness.

Once it was on top of them, a subtle pulse of a human energy signature resonated through Eden, and he squinted, wondering if it was who he was thinking.

"Looks like you beat me here!" a deep, gruff voice called from above.

Upon hearing the voice, Kendra's eyes widened as she saw the hovering objects descending, with someone dangling beneath it. She would have recognized that voice anywhere; it belonged to her former boss.

"James?" she called out, confusion riddling her as she saw his silhouette come into view. A line connected to James's wrist attached him to a large, hovering drone with four propellers. Given how large its silhouette was, it was clearly something military in both grade and design, especially if it could carry James through the sky. However, the group could hardly see it.

"Fancy seeing you here too, kid, but I suppose that ain't a surprise," James said, landing beside Kendra with the drone still hovering, but he disconnected the line from his wrist. He was dressed in jeans and a black soft-shell jacket with eagle patches on both arms. A hefty military-grade shotgun was slung across his back, and several rounds of ammo shells lined his abdomen. He glanced at Eden, gesturing his head toward Kendra. "She's tough as nails. I wasn't worried 'bout her."

"I knew if anyone'd be alright, it was you, but what the hell are you doing here, James?" Eden asked.

"Same as you slackers. I'm tryna help," James scoffed, gesturing his hand above as several other drones hovered, and crates dangled from them. The drones descended around them, set the crates down, and disconnected from them.

"Wait," Kendra began, approaching James. "You know Eden—the Hunters?" Kendra frowned, glancing between James and Eden while crossing her arms.

James gave an amused smirk, cocking an eyebrow.

"*Special. Client,*" he echoed, causing Kendra to slump her arms in defeat and mutter to herself.

"You brought supplies?" Eden asked James, eyeing the crates warily before he approached one. Kicking the top off, he saw inside there were several stacks of anti-demon ammunition, some of which were already in magazines.

"More crates are already being delivered by my drones all over the city to the evacuation sites. I was on my way here to speak with Commander Thompson and advise 'em to equip these rounds so they can actually kill those tall fuckers." James looked at Commander Thompson, raising a brow. "Whether their aim is good or not is on them, but might as well make the bullets count."

Commander Thompson crossed his arms, glancing between James and the ammo crate.

"Always knew you were a kook, James, but what the fuck?" Commander Thompson said, sighing as he approached the crate and grabbed a magazine for it, eyeing it as if it were dubious. He glanced at Eden. "James with Organization X, too?"

Eden sighed and nodded.

James eyed Eden before rolling his eyes and gesturing to the hunters who were gathering behind Eden.

"Go give them the orders they need. I'll make sure Thompson gets the message out to work with us and use the rounds. I'll be staying to watch over this site since it's the biggest. Allot your hunters as you need to," James said, nodding at Commander Thompson and approaching him to discuss.

Eden nodded and turned on his heel, facing the hunters. He whistled to get their attention. Providing them with the coordinates to several evacuation sites, he gave punchy commands as to where everybody would go. The hunters nodded, pulling up the coordinates on their hunter gauntlets before dashing off.

For all his awkward mannerisms when they interacted, Kendra saw none of that present as he commanded the hunters. He was in his natural element. Her hopelessness slipped away the more things had developed.

Once all the hunters had dispersed, Eden turned to face Kendra, nodding at her.

"I'm going to go check on the base. Once I'm done there, I'll check on Zane and Andrew before meeting you here again," he said. Then, jumping high into the air, he used his maneuver bracers and zipped off into the night.

From behind her, she heard footsteps and turned to see Joseph approaching her. She had thought back to her earlier curiosity, given his shared last name with James.

"You and me, huh?" Kendra greeted and glanced at James, who was still talking with Commander Thompson.

"Mhm. You, me, and my old man. He told me you used to work for him ... I don't envy that. He used to bitch at me when I didn't hold a flashlight at the correct angle. Can't imagine his attitude toward someone who he actually paid," Joseph said, smirking as he adjusted the strap holding his rifle to his back.

"He can be a bit of an ass ... yeah. He's not the worst, though. Paid me alright and worked with my school schedule. Didn't even seem upset when I had to quit after ... you know."

Joseph flexed his brows, grunting with a hint of surprise as he turned away from Kendra.

"Well ... I'm gonna talk with him before taking up my station. Give a holler if you need anything," he said before walking toward James, leaving Kendra to her thoughts for now.

Kendra pressed her hands to her shoulders. She felt she should have been colder since she only wore her tank top. Snuffing the thought, she released her breath and relaxed. The sense of hope building inside of her finally registered as she pondered the developments. She had done her part to convince the police to cooperate, and now, they could utilize the small opportunity that arose. Furthermore, Eden trusted her enough to help. Meager numbers or not, the Hunters were their best chance at survival, but her faith resided with Eden especially.

Tenacious as he was strong, Eden was a wall the demons would need to break through. But there was one demon Kendra knew who could. Intico had defeated him in their last confrontation, and she wasn't certain he'd be able to handle the fiend on his own. Transcendent with a voracity for Eden's body, it would stop at nothing. Without a doubt, the two were destined to meet again.

When he left, he had to know that a reunion with Intico was inevitable, but he persisted. Unbeknownst to Kendra, she had come to admire that unyielding stoicism. She turned, looking at the sky where she had last seen him. Even when he knew he couldn't win, he had dragged himself back to his feet in order to protect her. With him facing overwhelming odds, the adversity gave birth to an irrevocable imperative that echoed in Kendra's mind.

Eden must prevail.

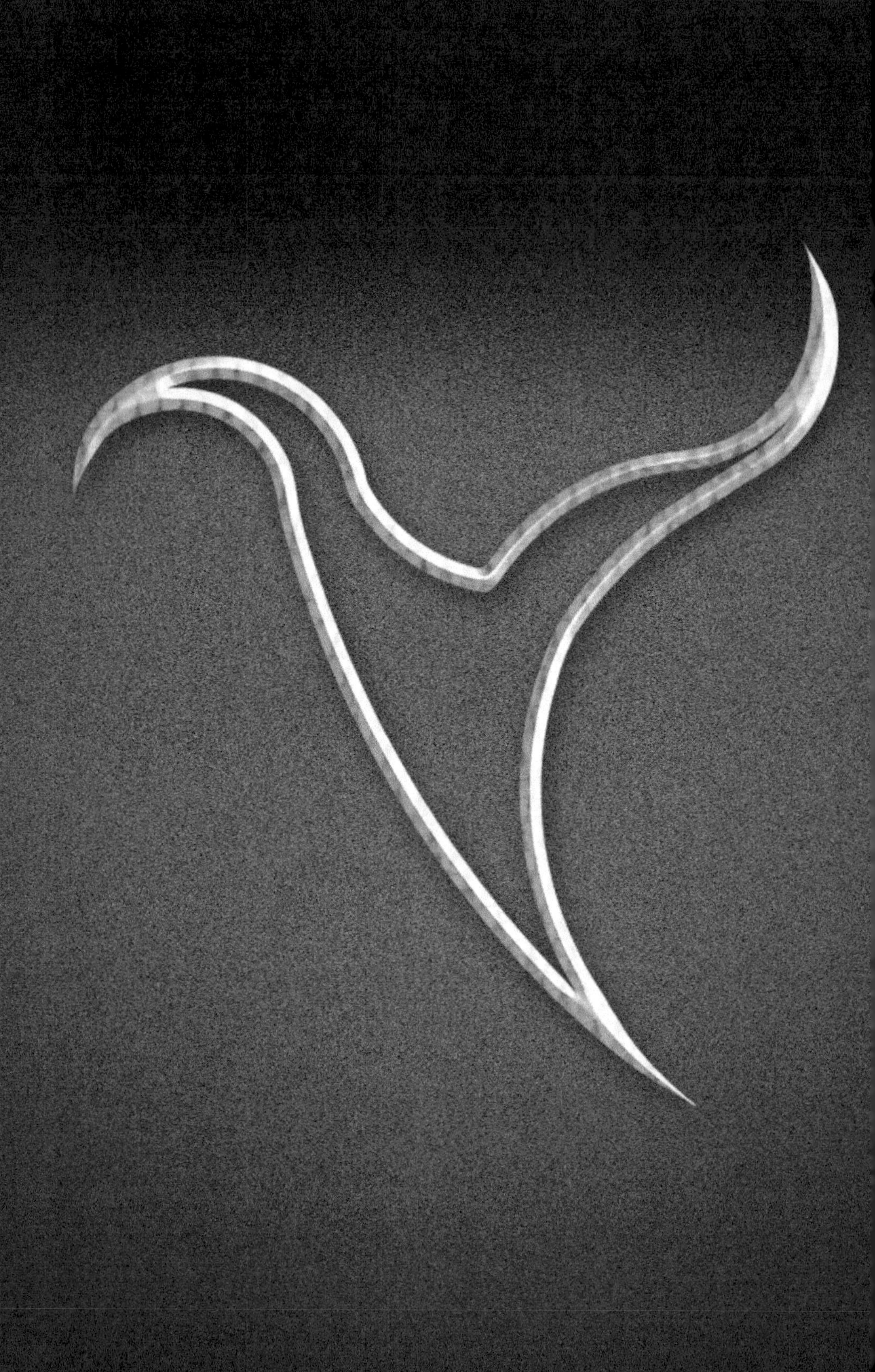

Thirteen

Ghastly Reunion

The energies composing Harvest were entirely *wrong*. The warping of space and light was disparate from Ichor's once serene displays. Eden had been accustomed to Ichor his entire life, and until that day, he had never witnessed such a perversion of its sanctity. Dashing through the desolate streets, he had plenty of time to ponder it. Within the eerie silence, the architecture of the city was far more appreciable to him—albeit under less than preferable circumstances.

Irrespective of his sensibilities, he was fixated on figuring out how to bring an end to Harvest. The hunters from the raid convoy were dispatched to the various evacuation sites that the police sent out to the citizens' smart bands, assuming they were awake to heed it. He was on his way to the Chicago Hunters base to rendezvous with the rest of those who were stationed there, who, to his knowledge, weren't aware of Harvest. Furthermore, there was the state of their communications that was pressing, further feeding his assumption of their ignorance. Their communications in the field were compromised, but he wondered if the communications infrastructure on base was operational. Upon not receiving an update from the raid team, they undoubtedly would have contacted HQ or vice versa.

Eden speculated on the nature of the ritual pervading the city. He and the hunters on the team hadn't been affected by it—yet—but there was a pattern, a range of functions Harvest appeared to operate within.

With that, it stood to reason that not all citizens were affected equally or as effectively. Many slept in the streets, yet many were also still awake in the evacuation zones for reasons unknown to him. Nonetheless, the somnium still posed a ghastly threat to the survivors, as was apparent by their direct attack with the dithered on the evacuation zone.

A faint voice cried nearby, and Eden came to a stop at the corner where the sound had projected from. The voice he had heard was that of a young girl—a child. Of all the potential victims, he knew he had to save a child. The girl's voice cried repeatedly, the banging of a door echoing from its location. Rushing down the street, he approached the archway where the sound came from, expecting to see a somnium since he detected its energy. A gate leading into an apartment complex was pried open unnaturally, and he rushed through, approaching the child's voice.

"Mommy, please! Let me in, please, Mommy! I'm scared! The scary tall thing is around the corner!" the girl's voice shrieked, wailing and crying as she persisted.

Panic swelled in Eden's chest, and he flashed with a burning red aura as he dashed through the hallway, turning the corner. He saw it. Standing at the door where the child's voice had come from, was a somnium. Nobody else was near, but the demon hunched in front of the door, its large hands curled and repeatedly banging on the door.

Eden was furious, his wrathful ire burning in realization of the cruel ruse of the somnium. It could have easily smashed through the door and sought its *vessel* inside, but what it did was far more insidious. Like how cats toyed with their prey when caught, the predatory demon stirred guilt and doubt as a primer to its attack, a *seasoning* of fear to ensure its prospective vessel would be more palatable.

The somnium turned its gaze onto Eden, but it hadn't the time to react before Eden had sliced its head off along with its arms.

"Sanguine," he muttered, staring down at the crumpled corpse as Ichor returned its essence to her veins. Whoever had been inside the apartment unit would be safe now, but there was hardly a moment's respite.

Gunfire rang out in the night, the boom echoing loudly in the neighborhood. Given the reverberation, Eden could tell it wasn't police gunfire.

He closed his eyes, focusing on the nearby energies for a moment. Hissing resonated against a much softer, frantic energy signature, one that was marred by the vestiges of malice, the perturbing signature of a human sought by demons. Cursing to himself, Eden sheathed Avenger and dashed out of the apartment unit.

The desolate march past apartment units, abandoned cars strewn throughout the streets, and several sleeping citizens suggested how dire Harvest was. A once bustling metropolis turned into a ghost town out of a horror film—complete with eerie creatures lurking in its corners in search of the humans. A weak waft of the miasma even patrolled the blocks, seeping into any building one could take refuge in. There was truly no respite for those who had no means of defending themselves, even if they *thought* they could.

On the adjacent block, a man aimed a shotgun at a somnium, the demonic entity standing in place a few feet from him. It had been advancing toward him until a moment ago—before the man had fired his gun. Peppered wounds marked the somnium's form, its black skin shifting and closing around the small holes that were blasted into it. Taking no risk, the man cocked the gun and shot the demon three more times in succession. Each time, the demon had merely stared with a beguiling grin. The gun had run out of shells, and the demon hadn't even flinched.

The somnium's long arm reached out and grabbed the man by his neck. Letting out a yell, he thrashed against the demon, but it was to no avail. In his struggle, he dropped his gun, and when hope seemed lost, a flicker of red streaked through the dark. In the next moment, the somnium's arm was severed, freeing the man from its clutches, sending him tumbling to the ground. In the dark, Eden's crimson leer scrutinized his *prey*, supplanting the nightmarish white glimmer from its eyes with his own, filled with a far more powerful fury. It took notice of its assailant, but it didn't get a chance to retreat, as much as it tried. Eden closed the distance and sliced the demon's head off.

"Sanguine!" Eden declared. With the incantation, every trace of the somnium disappeared. Eden's breath was labored as he stood before the man, having pushed himself harder to rescue the man on time. The man was petrified. He had nearly been merged with, and much to the benefit of his mental sanctity, he was ignorant of the fate that almost befell him. Dark circles carved his eye sockets, a clear sign his resistance had been pressured to near breaking.

"The fuck was that thing!" the man said.

Eden cocked his eyebrow, sheathing Avenger as he shook his head.

"Find your way to the nearest evacuation center. There's one a mile south of—"

"Like I'd trust those goddamned tyrant-ran centers. I'll fight these damn things off myself! Things just need a good slug instead of birdshot."

Eden grabbed the man by his collar, yanking him close. Of all the matters of his limited time, arguing with a headstrong civilian reminiscent of a cynical, conspiracy-driven uncle was not on his itinerary. Eden's demeanor shifted; usually aloof or damning, he glared, annoyed by the man.

"Ditch that thing and go! Your bullets won't do a damn thing to them!"

The wind blew harshly around them, accompanied by a hiss, which could only mean one thing: more somnium. Carried by the shadows, they manifested into their imposing, terrifying forms within the dark, positioned at the corners of the street alongside abandoned vehicles. Eden released the man with a shove, drawing Avenger once again as he eyed the demons warily. Whereas they initially approached, the demons paused, their pensive, ghastly eyes narrowing and fixing on Eden suddenly. Something was amiss, and Eden doubted it was the somnium's tenacity for the civilian's body.

"Go. *Now,*" Eden demanded, his eyes flicking to the man's gun before he approached it. He stomped on it hard, breaking the frame and neutralizing the weapon—just in case the man got *brave* again after his command.

The man stared wide-eyed at the three demons that appeared in the dark, realizing that their attention was not focused on him. He briefly stared at his smashed gun, realizing that if Eden could break it with a stomp, then he would be remiss to defy his order. Taking not a moment longer, he nodded and ran off into the city.

The night, however odd, had not perplexed Eden nearly as much as that interaction with the man. He sighed, clearing it from his mind. He couldn't allow himself to be distracted by fighting against several somnium at once. They certainly would make him regret it if he did. Once the man was out of sight, he initiated his assault, leaping from his position toward one of the somnium.

The demons showed no hesitation, but truly, Eden found no qualms about their bravery. More than all, he hated when demons ran away from him; chases were tedious, and as he had learned, often a means to other nefarious ends. As acute a hunter as he was, an unintuitive fact involved understanding a tactical retreat and what it could entail. His brief ignorance of such a concept several weeks prior still haunted him and would forever remain carved into Kendra's life.

The somnium, possessing only their natural means of defense, poised their sharp fingers. Eden had learned that attacking their fingers often just deflected his blows—provided he swung more precisely than he did with power. That was why when it moved its hand to block his attack, Avenger flared red, filling with energy as he applied heavy force into the slash. Its fingers were hard, but with sheer might and Avenger's infrangibility, they were sliced through. With a loud crack, the fingers flew off, and a stream of glittering white energy hemorrhaged from the carved stumps with two fingers dangling from it. The somnium recoiled, and Eden followed by swiftly removing its head with a well-aimed slash.

Then there were two, but suddenly, he was vulnerable. He was open and outnumbered, and the somnium seized the opportunity to rush either side of him, closing in from the vestiges of the shadows they could travel through. His armored coat would prevent any fatal wounds, along with his other natural defenses, but he couldn't afford to be slowed down by any injuries. He wouldn't have been able to follow and react to their attacks from that distance with such little time, but something changed within his vision. Their movements appeared sedated, slower than they truly were.

The moment stretched in Eden's mind—precious time he had needed. He crouched low as the somnium's fingers swiped at him, soaring harmlessly above his head. Dodging successfully, he was unscathed, and the demons were almost frozen in that outstretched moment. He jumped, slashing both the somnium's heads off in one swipe.

"Sanguine," Eden muttered, and the three somnium corpses dispersed into nothing.

Eden hadn't recalled his senses being as acute as they had been the moment prior. He maintained that he adapted best within the crucible of battle, and such an opportune evolution he welcomed with verve. Sheathing Avenger, he turned his attention back toward the direction of the base, his next destination. With no further time to absorb his newfound ability, his tumultuous journey persisted.

A warehouse positioned on the south side of Chicago served as one of the many Hunters bases throughout the world. Mostly isolated from other buildings, it provided an optimal location for their operations since the inception of their investigation into the Covenant of Augury. Red bricks compiled the building in a two-story structure with assorted black windows lining the street-side view of the warehouse. It was one-sided glass, as permitted for confidentiality. Out back was a shipping yard, given that it was a repurposed warehouse before establishing their operations. The vehicles that weren't a part of the now-deserted raid convoy remained stationed in the lot. Lining the proximity of the building were hunters armed with rifles, vigilantly fixated on the eerily silent city.

After several more minutes, Eden came into view of the base. With heavy breaths, he slowed to a stop. While his inhuman capabilities were a marvel to even a high-level athlete, his limitations were tested on his journey back to the base.

A hunter who stood guard outside the main entrance spotted Eden, calling for the attention of the others as he approached. Eden slowed to a crawl, glancing around to see no apparent signs of distress. The fact they were surprised to see him hardly suggested any pertinent information.

"Tracy and Jackson ... did they make it here?"

The hunter paused and shook his head.

"We haven't received word from anybody. You're the first we've seen from the raid team since everything went radio-silent," the hunter explained, his brow furrowed as he glanced around, confusion painting his face. "Where are the others?"

"Damn it," Eden hissed. The two hunters would have made it to the base, provided their journey back wasn't perilous. Their absence suggested it was. Despite their willingness to lay down their lives, as their duty entailed, Eden considered himself intrinsically responsible for not petitioning for them to be accompanied by an additional hunter. However, because of their insufficient numbers, he hadn't entertained the idea initially. There was no time to lament, however, as the rest of the hunters needed to be mobilized against the looming threat to them and the city. He steeled his nerves and turned to the hunter.

"Listen, the city is overrun with the somnium and other creatures—humans they've merged with. We need to mobilize immediately. Where's Commander Evans?" he asked.

"Commander Evans is inside, trying to get a hold of HQ. I'll radio him that you're here with a report." Eden nodded in confirmation and marched through to the base. He scanned his hunter bracer at the keypad beside the door and entered. The familiar halls were as bright as usual, and one could easily find themselves lured into a false sense of security. He knew of such hunters who would.

Despite not having been assaulted, the hunters present were on high alert in the advent of Harvest. Units usually inside the facility were either stationed outside or patrolling the perimeter. Non-combat teams worked on reestablishing the communication infrastructure, to no avail. Pending further updates, defense contingencies were established in the wake of the demons lurking the city.

Eden scoured the base until he found Commander Evans in an office. He was tucked into a desk, analyzing a holographic screen projecting a profile on the somnium, a file in the demon compendium. And with various undertones of unease, he precariously glanced up to eye Eden entering the office. Eyes bloodshot with dark circles beneath, his image was starkly different from hours prior. Bolting from his seat, he stood, slamming his palms on the desk.

"Private—what the *hell* happened out there?" he demanded.

Eden crossed his arms.

"The somnium began their plot—Harvest," Eden said. He glanced around the office briefly, noting its claustrophobic walls and its fortified position in the base. Commander Evans hardly acknowledged his own demeanor—shaky and more timid in tone—but Eden doubted he was oblivious to the creeping darkness that festered in the air. Seeing the typically abrasive man's uncharacteristic, erratic behavior, Eden arrived at an allegation. *The commander is hiding.*

"Explain, damn it!" Commander Evans demanded.

"They're merging with the citizens. Zane and Andrew are on their way to deal with the interference."

"And what have I told you about name etiquette? Use last names when on—"

"You're seriously getting on me about that now? Listen, the city is bound to collapse soon if we can't mobilize our forces to the evacuation zones. The base to hell. The police aren't trained to fight demons. *We* are." Eden clenched his hand into a white-knuckled fist and slammed it to his chest. "We need to protect the citizens. Larson and Carter are already handling bypassing the interference. They'll get a hold of HQ for reinforcements."

Commander Evans tried to interject, but Eden persisted.

"I've already established a contingency operation with the Chicago Police Department and James Ardent. They're going to cooperate with us, and now it's time we hold to our end of the bargain. We need to send the hunters to the various evacuation sites. The raid team's convoy isn't enough to cover all the sites."

Commander Evans gritted his teeth, a palpable irritation with Eden bubbling inside him. He and Eden had never gotten along with one another. The envious commander always saw Eden's alleged prestige and preferential regard as a product of nepotism. Jessica typically defended him and made amendments to the penalties he incurred, fostering a festering disrespect in Commander Evans.

"You don't have the authority to make that decision, Blackwell. In fact, the *fact* that you went out of your way to pretend to is an infraction in and of itself. We hold our ground here until reinforcements arrive. I'm not risking any of our hunters. *Am. I. Clear?*"

Their gazes clashed with shared contempt. Even in crisis, Commander Evans held fewer sympathies toward the greater plight, especially when that plight related to Eden, even negligibly. The two bickered for several seconds before an ominous torrent of energy surged from outside the base, snatching their attention.

They both felt it—a permeating chill. Like a foul odor, the presence of the somnium invaded the surrounding area in a heavy wave of distortion, and the incessant hissing assailed their ears. It was louder than usual, and the energy, familiar in the recesses of Eden's mind, belonged to Intico.

Commander Evans zipped around the desk and shoved past Eden, dashing through the halls. This prompted Eden to take off after him. Bolting outside, the two came into the clearing of the nearby buildings looming in front of the scarlet-hued moon. The hunters had grouped up, standing before the buildings—heads upturned.

Eden's gaze fixed on the building that garnered the perturbed hunters' attention. A group of several tall silhouettes lined the rooftop, scrutinizing the hunters with their crescent, hollow eyes. In the center, a more imposing figure stood. The wind howled, and its cape whipped wildly in the wind's protest. Black wisps emitted from their forms, peeling and dissipating into nothing as their beings solidified. The somnium, and in the center, the somnium lord itself—*Intico.*

Eden reflexively lowered his hand to Avenger's hilt, taking a combat stance. There was only one reason that Intico and the somnium had arrived there. They wanted their bodies. Intico wanted *his* body.

"Blackwell. I sincerely am glad to see you are doing well. I doubted my brethren or the dithered would provide you with too much trouble," Intico spoke, its voice echoing through the night as if projected into the hunters' ears.

Commander Evans flinched, not having directly experienced the phenomenon of somnium speech before, but Eden only stared with hardened resolve.

"Ah. My manners ... you don't know what a dithered is, do you? It is what *we*—you and I—will become soon"—its smile stretched across its face—"but not just *a* dithered. *The* dithered!" The somnium cackled, filling the night with their shared voracity.

Eden's gaze narrowed, crimson eyes flickering with power. The streetlights had since blown out, leaving a darker battlefield in its wake. They would be at a disadvantage, especially with the hunters having to aim their guns. Eden took tentative steps forward, contrasting with the paralysis of his comrades.

Despite seeing Intico again, despite the dark memories rampaging through Eden's head, he was calm. He had conquered any semblance of fear that resided within him. It had been inevitable they would fight again, and he wouldn't have deigned to consider retreating.

"You're remiss to think I'd let you," Eden called out.

Their last battle replayed in his memory. One-sided as it had been toward the end, he had reflected on where he went wrong in it. Rash and without regard for his opponent's capabilities, he had been reckless, and that was not a mistake he intended to make again. Intico was a formidable adversary, cunning, quick, and resilient. There was no room for error. He would have to be far more careful. Compared to their last confrontation, he had evolved in both ability and sentiment. As hunters, it was their duty to face foes deemed greater than them, and as remarkable as Eden was, he abided by that same principle.

Eden shifted his gaze briefly to Commander Evans, who was frozen in place and trembling. The man who was supposed to be *his* superior wasn't equipped with a gun, vindicating Eden's earlier hypothesis. Fear was all too familiar a trait to Eden—one he scarcely ever acknowledged, but he wouldn't tolerate Commander Evans's fear in the most critical of moments.

"Commander, go turn on the backup lights." Eden shifted his gaze to Intico. "I'll deal with their leader." With Commander Evans still an astonished statue, Eden assumed giving commands—much to the contrary of Commander Evans's earlier contention. "Hunters! Show discipline with your fire and stay paired up! They can command shadows, so be prepared to avoid them. Now, we fight!"

Commander Evans, finally breaking from his fearful stupor, seized the opportunity and ran inside—an opportunity entirely too cherished by Eden's account. Within seconds, the base lit up. The demons had descended the surrounding buildings quickly, closing in on the hunters with a show of their speed and tenacity, and the battle commenced.

As bullets and yelling echoed, Intico remained static atop the building, its glimmering grin carving the night. Stretching further, that malevolent smile challenged the glare of the lustrous moon looming behind it. The somnium lord beckoned Eden, bowing in taunt as it removed its hat and held it out toward him.

"Come, Blackwell. *Dance with the Devil.*"

With its invitation, Eden aimed and fired his maneuver gauntlets, yanking him into the air and propelling him toward Intico. The wind whistled ferociously as he gained momentum, and he drew Avenger from his hilt. With a raucous clash, Eden and Intico's reunion was announced.

A thunderous clang erupted across the block; blade met shade as Intico's hat became a staff that challenged Avenger's threat. Intico slid back on the rooftop from the force before its talons dug into the concrete beneath, anchoring it in place. Eden landed in front of the transcendent entity, pressing with palpable might in their initial clash. The air became electric on the surrounding beings' skin, vibrating with an intensity most of them had never experienced.

Eden attempted to anticipate Intico's next move, its cryptic demeanor suggesting little in that outstretched moment. A nefarious being of fear would never make itself predictable, but therein lay the secret: fear in the unknown. Eden knew that much before they had clashed.

The somnium thrived on all manners of fear, and as its purveyors, such a proclivity was judiciously weaponized against their desired vessels. If Eden could maintain his nerve, he could mitigate the disadvantage already imposed on him. And much like the somnium's indubitable union with fear, he represented unyielding bravery, even if it led him astray. But there were no frays in the tapestry of his composure—no doubts in his plunge into the unknown.

Intico, unflinching, braced itself, its talons crunching the cement beneath. Eden's eyes flickered, the moment slowing once again. In the corner of his vision, shadows moved in close with glimmers of light. Somnium sought to intrude in the duel, but he wasn't daft enough to have believed that Intico would be *fair*; it wasn't in their initial fight, nor would it be in their rematch.

Eden was the first to make the next move. He sent a swift kick into Intico, repelling it from him. The subtle hiss from the somnium closed in, their presence surrounding him. He became a cyclone of burning crimson, his aura flailing in his spinning counterattack. The somnium had been too close to avoid his blows, and a flurry of slashes tore them asunder, scattering the vestiges of their being to the wailing wind.

The battle persisted as hunters' screams resonated in the night along with gunfire, but Eden hadn't time to safeguard them; he trusted they would watch over each other. Even if he had tried, he knew Intico wouldn't let his misdirected attention go unpunished, and that *punishment* would render his efforts obsolete at best.

Eden stomped his foot as he came to a stop, positioning Avenger away from himself as he faced Intico again. He lunged, but upon slashing its form, it dissipated—another illusion.

"Excellent—you've grown," Intico's voice echoed around Eden, distorted by the pressure their presence manifested. The streak of shadows it was sequestered within zipped around Eden repeatedly. Eden closed his eyes, focusing on the resonance of the surrounding energy. *Left, right, above, below.* The fluency with which Intico commanded and moved within the shadows was greater than any other he had faced. One mistake within the umbrage was all that it would take for their duel to end. He would not make such a mistake, and he conjured masterful patience in the mute moments, waiting until that familiar energy announced itself.

When the raucous hissing halted in that single moment, Eden's eyes shot open, and he spun around, slashing at Intico. Avenger's edge met Intico's staff, particles of tangible darkness shooting around them. With

Intico's initial tactic thwarted, their deadly dance was resurrected. The air shook with each clash, each blow rumbling deep in Eden's bones and arresting his breath. Akin to fireflies streaking and bouncing off each other, synchronized attacks turned the once stagnant air into an exuberant whirlwind of their respective fury—fury Intico would see joined into one being. But neither relented.

A thick, tar-like miasma projected from Intico's mouth, surrounding the rooftop in the dangerous sleep-inducing substance. Eden leaped from atop the building, plummeting toward the ground to escape it. Shifting terrains, Intico followed, grabbing Eden's leg in a tight grip. A heavy thud shook the ground as Intico landed. In the next breath, Intico's hand was severed by a swipe of Avenger, and Eden rebounded from the ground to his feet. They paused, and Intico chuckled darkly, showing the stump sprout darkness anew, its hand regenerating with resounding speed by demon standards.

The attrition persisted, and the hunters soon defeated their assailants. A few were injured, but alive and stable. They had prevailed only by tactical preparation and working alongside one another with foreknowledge of the somnium's proclivities. Now free to spectate, they struggled to follow Intico's and Eden's movements, especially in the encompassing shadows that Intico employed. This was not a battle they could perceive, regardless of their connection and training in utilizing Ichor. The magnitude transcended their capabilities. With it, there was an implicit consideration that fermented inside of them: none of them could challenge a foe such as Intico should Eden fail.

But their battle neared its end. Intico found itself consistently pushed back and unable to land any definitive blows. The somnium leader couldn't risk depleting further energy in the prolonged altercation further. Its reserves were tied to maintaining Harvest. Should it run dry before finding a capable vessel, Harvest would be over, and the somnium would have been denied their liberation from their bereft existence.

Intico not only had to weaken Eden and commence merging with him, but during the merging, there was a period of vulnerability it couldn't risk with its brethren slain. Should the hunters find the sense to shoot, it wouldn't be able to merge. It would be a while before its reinforcements would arrive, as well. Only one option remained: Intico needed to defeat both Eden and the hunters in the same breath—a literal imperative.

Intico jumped back, its staff dissipating into mist as white particles coursed around its form. The air became ice, and the wind, against all that was natural, stood still. Energy expanded around Intico, and it hovered, head twitching. The coalescing energy swarming gathered at its mouth while a low growl rumbled in Eden's and the hunters' ears. It became more audacious and prominent the higher it hovered in the air, and the lights were crushed, plunging the base into darkness once more.

Several hunters, subjected to the intense pressure of the distortion coming from Intico's power, crumpled to the ground. The architect of fear that Intico was, through its power, the night prevailed once more, and the city beneath the somnium lord was swallowed in darkness. Dread washed through the hunters, their continued existence predicated on forces beyond their control.

Eden raised his head, glaring at Intico. A massive reserve of power was being summoned forth, a move he knew was not only taxing but also immeasurably dangerous—perhaps insurmountable. Malevolent and particularly destructive, the hiss of the somnium's desperation became a screech. The particles built into an orb, growing larger and increasingly imposing with an uneven, undulating surface. Specks of black invaded the white volume, and a haze of miasma swirled within the orb—a bomb. If it were to be launched at them, if the destructive force didn't kill them, the miasma would render them wishing it had.

"Blackwell, dodge if you must. But know that if you do ... they will die ..."

Only one possibility remained. *It had to be deflected.*

There was one way: a technique shown to Eden by his mother that could repel even massive attacks, physical or magical. Intico's growing orb of malevolence qualified as such. He never fully mastered it last they trained together, as it was an advanced technique requiring masterful and inhumanly precise control over one's energy. He had no choice but to execute it, or he dreaded what would become of his comrades who couldn't escape.

Eden sheathed Avenger, widening his stance as he drew his body forward. Energy gathered into his palms and flowed into Avenger's hilt. It crackled with red electricity, causing the ground to quake and splinter. Coalescing his energy and conviction into a resolution, he crafted a defense not only for himself but for his comrades. An array of flickering light proceeded with a howl from Intico, imploding around Eden as the bomb descended rapidly. Eden inhaled deeply. He saw the possibility all too clearly. The sphere would crash into the group and sunder them, bathing the city in miasma. The remaining hope—strangled. *That wouldn't happen,* he resolved. The bomb drew close, and his mother's voice resonated in his mind.

Remember, you must visualize what you are seeking to repel from you. You must imagine your own energy not as a show of power, but as an argument that convinces the attack's own force to push it back. Your own energy is not the force deflecting it, but the conduit through which the attack will resonate and reverse its path. As long as your own energy is comparable to or greater than your opponent's, you'll be able to guard yourself and others against any danger coming your way.

With a rupturing shriek in its herald, the bomb arrived.

The hunters shut their eyes tightly, accepting certain oblivion. But Eden drew Avenger in a clean arc, the edge glowing red with a wall of adjacent energy. It connected with the orb, a boom clapping over the field with raucous applause in the ensuing struggle. Deserting his propensity for exhibiting might, he conjured finesse. His energy sought to deliberate with Intico's bomb.

Eden's body dug into the ground from the pressure pushing in on him, igniting his calves and squeezing the breath from his lungs. Gravity sought to consume him, and he briefly feared the world would give at any moment if his legs didn't first.

But it didn't. Kendra's pained howls echoed in Eden's head, haunting him far more than Intico ever could have. He hadn't called upon every ounce of his strength simply to defend, but to avenge her anguish, to see all who wailed within Intico's stolen power liberated. With a guttural roar, his arm followed through in its swing, and Avenger deflected the bomb back in a show of Eden's resolve refuting Intico's. *They would not fall.*

The bomb of energy and miasma flew into the sky, back at Intico. The somnium dropped from the air, narrowly avoiding its own attack, eyes wide in bewilderment. Such an outcome hadn't been a possibility, a show of its own hubris—no—*infernal divergence.*

Eden saw the opening created, and despite his relative fatigue, he took it. He leaped toward Intico, frozen in equal parts mortification and pensiveness, and he swung Avenger at the bemused demon. Intico came to in the moment of attack, raising its hands to block the strike. A loud snap rang as its defenses were breached. Its severed hands fell aimlessly with trails of glittering essence, then Avenger met its neck.

Intico reeled back, avoiding the ending blow with only a gash on its neck. The somnium lord's energy reserves were lowered significantly. With the energy it took to regenerate from a *fatal* attack, it knew that if its head had been decapitated, it would hardly present a challenge to Eden any longer after regenerating. Even now, the stumps sizzled with white energy, the inky tendrils that sought to reform its hands a mere crawl of their former performance.

Eden landed, cracking the ground. His determined gaze was still fixed on Intico, intent on seeing it destroyed for good. Just when he was ready to lunge again, he saw that the once unchanging grin on Intico's face had become a sneer. This, perhaps, had been more disturbing to Eden than the intentionally haunted smile the somnium wore.

Its hat reformed on its head as it leered down at Eden, the pressure in the air alleviating as the heavy distortion over the area receded.

"You have round two, Blackwell ... but you haven't won the war, as the humans say. You may not yield to me ... but you will before the *vessel* of your failure. Anticipate the advent of our union," Intico growled, its voice echoing throughout the city. With a failure in its cunning plan, Intico sought to achieve an indefinite existence through less direct means. In their brief merge, Intico had glimpsed the underlying sentiments within Eden—his fears and drives alike. And while Intico could conjure fear through direct means of its magical dominion, it now realized it needed to conjure a fear invoked not by carnal self-preservation, but *guilt.* It was through this ephemeral guilt it would become everlasting.

Intico hadn't neglected its vigilance of its subordinates throughout the battle, despite its focus on its duel with Eden. Two notable dithered hadn't arrived, as one of Intico's subordinates had informed. Scarlet and the umbra dithered had been slain, which left one notable vessel unoccupied.

Staring into Eden's eyes with renewed confidence, the guile of its last resort formulated. Erupting with dark laughter, Intico retreated into the umbrage of shadows that carried it away from the base.

While Eden was prepared to give chase, he scolded himself for briefly considering it. Such was the unwise habit he sought to break. Even if he had, there was a surge of energies that closed in on their location.

They had won the battle, but inevitably, the threat had only been repelled, not vanquished. Intico was still on the prowl, and as much as he wanted to stop it, the approaching danger persisted—almost as if by design. A hiss permeated the air and inhuman screeches echoed from the nearby blocks—*the dithered.*

The hunters shakily stood to their feet, gathering themselves with renewed resolve—a cultivated faith in Eden. As much as Eden didn't wish to harm the dithered, there was no guarantee he could harmlessly incapacitate all of them. Certainly, his comrades didn't have the same luxury to do so. Intico had fled, but it was not vanquished. Its ambitions were unfulfilled, a herald of their next reunion. Eden, without a doubt, was its desired vessel, but he failed to discern its words in his anticipation of the approaching enemies.

The vessel of your failure.

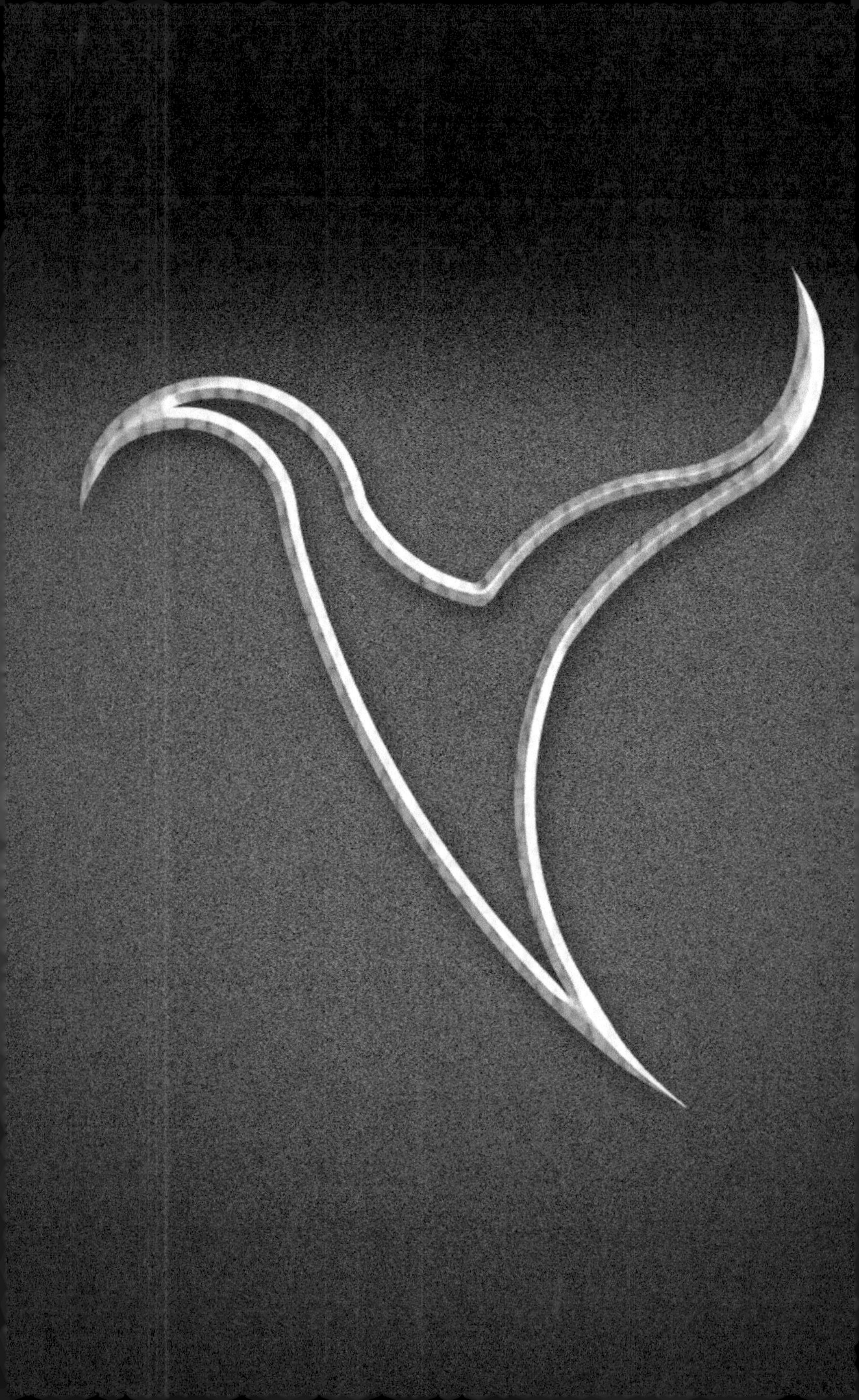

FOURTEEN

IMPREGNABLE INFERNO

The advent of Harvest allowed the somnium to maintain their beings throughout the city for as long as the ritual held. In their quest to claim vessels, this was critical, especially considering the less-than-optimal results of the ritual. There was an urgency in their continued persistence—even when they had merged with their chosen target. Three such somnium, left to the seclusion of their prowl, patrolled the slumbering streets of Chicago, inspecting the sleeping humans with voracious scrutiny. Coming across a group of young men and women sprawled on the cold streets, they crouched, inspecting them with delicate holds so as not to damage *their* prospective vessels.

"This one is too short," the first somnium sneered, holding a sleeping man in its grasp before tossing him back to the ground.

"This one is too tall," another somnium scoffed, holding a woman in its spindly fingers, inspecting her momentarily with an expression resembling disappointment. The irony was not lost on the first somnium, who gave the second a perplexed stare.

The third somnium's quietude suggested optimism, along with its grinning face—assuming its grin wasn't worn dubiously, as they typically were by its kin.

"This one is *just* right," the third somnium snickered, inspecting a woman with ebony skin. It was captivated by her shimmering dress that glittered similarly to the demon's incandescent eyes. Such a form blended with its gaze, a fixation forming as it gently pushed her into the ground, carefully prying her jaw open as its form jittered, its corporeal integrity dissipating in preparation.

The first somnium grunted, shaking its head at the second.

"Too tall? *You're* much taller, Sepia. Taller is better for adjustment," the first somnium hissed.

"Do you believe I enjoy being this lumbering, Maroon? Use your empty head for once! That's why we call you Maroon the moron"—it looked to the third somnium—"right, Violet?"

The somnium known as Violet turned to Sepia and Maroon, its eyes narrowing as it sneered.

"Will you both shut up? Merging is a sacred rite of passage from our pitiful existence. Refrain from your bickering. Even if you must merge with a suboptimal vessel, you can seek another later once the remaining pests have been dealt with. You have plenty of time before the merge becomes permanent!"

A spree of bullets whistled through the air, interrupting and riddling the somnium. The glittering white essence inside of them painted the sidewalk, and their forms twitched, critically damaged by the bullets that were fired.

Zane held his gunblade out in its focus-fire state, the state in which it was only used as a gun with the blade portion still folded in. The carved grooves along the weapon subtly glowed with heat waves emitting from them, the traces of flames fading. The barrel smoked still, embers scattering to the wind before he hit a switch on the side of the weapon, releasing the revolver drum. Seeking to remain ahead, he removed bullets from the straps along his vest, reloaded, and holstered the weapon.

"Oh, that's just precious. They're naming each other!" Zane snickered, reaching up and scratching his cheek as he overlooked the desolate downtown district of Chicago. He wasn't overly familiar with the place, but in spite of that, he found it haunting to see the massive collection of unconscious humans, many of whom appeared to have been out enjoying the nightlife prior to Harvest. Several of the streetlights and neon signs had shorted or busted open—from a buildup of pressure, Zane surmised.

Unlike Zane's more lackadaisical demeanor, Andrew had been far more skittish and anxious; his blue irises, usually ripe with curiosity or unparalleled concentration, were narrowed and rapidly shifting their focus. With a palpable overstimulation perturbing him, he hardly felt at ease, even with Zane handling the demons they came across.

"What about it? Is this really the time to be noting irrelevant data on these things?" Andrew asked incredulously between his breaths. The boy had been carrying a heavy metallic briefcase of electronic components, heaving from having lugged it for what he assumed was several miles.

Zane dusted his hands and nodded his head.

"This isn't my first rodeo with demonic plots consuming a city, funnily enough. This one is less ... grizzly, believe it or not. At least the humans are alive. For better or worse, I can't say, but I'm sure most'll recover," Zane said and yawned. Cursing his indolence, he wished he had gotten a nap in before things had escalated, noting the lethargy creeping in on him.

Andrew eyed Zane warily, baffled that his comrade could be as casual as he was, even when considering the circumstances Zane had witnessed, or had been a part of. Zane never elaborated to him. Of all the various afflictions to plague the Hunters, he thought Zane's cavalier attitude was particularly vexing. And to his learned sleuthing, many others held similar views of the half-demon man.

Zane snapped his fingers.

"Oh, right," he chirped, turning to the dead somnium and holding his palm out. "Sanguine." The somnium's corpses dissipated into light, leaving the slumbering humans that were beneath them clean of their presence. "Come on, tower's about a mile thataway. We're almost there."

Andrew's eyes were slightly glazed, a phantom fatigue fermenting in his mind, coaxing him to idleness. *Tired.* Andrew's endurance wasn't as developed as the other hunters, not having committed to the full course of the Hunters' physical conditioning yet. Accustomed to more sedentary tasks or ones that involved mostly using his hands, such physical strain was alien to him—and he wanted to remain a stranger to it for as long as he could. He found himself struggling to keep pace with the somnium's miasma methodically working its way through his system. As it stood, several miles of hiking through a demon-infested city while carrying a heavy briefcase was not part of his usual itinerary.

Is it natural to feel my heart this much? Andrew thought as he wheezed. Their trek through the once vibrant city was as ominous as it was excruciating on his strained legs. In such times, he seriously reconsidered his long-term viability in such a career, but even with his labored, miasma-filled lungs indicting his conviction, his obligation to the Hunters remained sturdy.

Zane spun around, jogging backward as he met Andrew's gaze.

"I can tell you're worried," Zane said over the wind. He had been stealing glances at Andrew. Contrary to his appearance of nonchalance, he was dutiful, and his desire to defend Andrew far superseded his easy-going nature. Andrew didn't specialize in combat, albeit he had received *some* basic training, and Zane was abundantly aware of the risks he undertook alongside him.

"H-huh? No. I ..." Andrew stammered between breaths.

"Remember, we're *both* hunters ... and I won't let *anything* happen to my lil bro." Zane beamed at Andrew before spinning back around.

Andrew stared forward at Zane, barely registering his words with his heart throbbing in his ears. But Zane's smile ensured him everything would be alright. Just as it had been before. He was a hunter now, that much was true. In spite of his low constitution and peculiar mannerisms, they had recruited him for his aptitude, which he had displayed, leading to benevolent developments that saved several lives. Not a day went by without thinking of how his life—or lack thereof—would have been, if he had remained a sickly child who was a ward of the state. The fact he was alive was a product of Zane advocating on his behalf. Given the advanced technology and funding the Hunters possessed, he was cured of his illness and granted a purpose. Subsequently, he was inclined to live up to in his fostered altruism. They needed him, both the Hunters and the citizens of Chicago.

Resolve reestablished, he increased his pace. With both hands, he held the suitcase away from his legs to avoid kneeing it, as he had already done several times during their trek.

Zane glanced at Andrew, a smirk pulling at his lips.

"Woah, second wind?" Zane asked.

"Something ... like that," Andrew spoke between breaths.

"I was never good at pep talks, so I'll pat myself on the back for that."

The two hunters eventually made it to Willis Tower, encountering a strange absence of enemies for the rest of their trip. Andrew's wheezing had taken on a life of its own. Sweat saturated his face and caused his skin-tight uniform to become stuffy. As protective and useful as it could be, it served as a heat trap during prolonged physical activity. Many got around that through their barriers, which they alleged helped regulate their temperature. Andrew was not nearly as precise with his energy control yet, and even with his suit's capabilities of augmenting him, he considered himself terribly ordinary.

Zane hated wearing the standard suit, and he didn't need to—as per his condition when he originally became a hunter. When on tactical missions, he opted to wear black cargo pants, a long-sleeved shirt, and an armored vest with ammo and his gear in various pouches and slots.

The megalithic tower before them was incalculably large up close. Glass panels lined the entire building, glossy with light spilling from inside of it. It contrasted largely with the surrounding buildings, especially in one detail that Zane and Andrew immediately noticed. The sky above the tower rippled with distortions and dimensional tearing more significantly than anywhere else. The clouds were ghastly and black, swirling visibly around the head of the tower, with red ripples surging through the sky and dispersing over the city. Even the miasma was stronger there, creating a thick fog.

Andrew's mouth was agape as he watched the hideous distortions. The most apparent thing was the fact that the ubiquitous frequency plaguing Ichor was most prominent there. It spurred a sick anxiety to well in his chest. Such were the perverted distortions when humans were introduced to it. Given Zane's lineage, while it disturbed him, it wasn't as intrinsically repulsive. However, what it insinuated certainly disgusted him.

"How do we even get up there?" Andrew asked, not having thought that far ahead.

Zane stroked his chin, squinting his eyes as he shifted his gaze between it and the ground. His creativity stirred, imagining a plethora of possibilities. It would be easy for him to get himself to the top using a propulsion of flames. However, that prospect bored him, and it only applied to him. In his following consideration, demon alchemy was the next thought that surfaced.

"Good question," Zane muttered to himself. He was lost in thought for a few moments, but a nearby disturbance snatched his attention right away. Clicks and gargles of distorted voices echoed from around the corners and above, obscured within the miasma. From all directions, several dithered appeared.

Andrew squeaked in terror, watching with wide eyes as the various dithered lurched and closed in around them. Unlike their somnium counterparts, they were not as imposing and suggested the inverse color scheme of the somnium. The undulating, glittering white skin cloaked their human visage, but their faces contorted with a shallow quality dissimilar to their original forms—like their mouths and eyes were projections atop the face rather than intrinsic to it. To further signify their threat, their fingers were sharp and pointed with claws, which Andrew had seen tear open the steel frames of their trucks and vans. One swipe, if unfettered by their protective barriers, would be enough to eviscerate them. With such an uncanny, unnatural quality to both the somnium and dithered, Andrew didn't know which was more terrifying.

The distortions only grew as the dithered neared them, causing Andrew to search for an escape. He placed the briefcase down and thought of how best to survive the situation. What was more frightening to him was the speed at which the dithered ran toward them, and the sheer numbers they harbored. Andrew believed Zane to be powerful, but that many dithered would prove more than a challenge for him to disperse safely, let alone while protecting a less-capable young hunter at the same time.

But Zane was a trickster of sorts. His nonchalance was not to be mistaken for incompetence, as was commonly the case, much to his enemies' detriment. Zane's eyes flickered brightly as fire coursed down his arms. The air flickered to life around the two hunters, sparking and filling with bright red embers. Orange-hued flames streaked across the ground, erupting into a burning shield that repelled the dithered from closing in on them.

With the scorched air, Andrew covered his face, nearly stumbling from the fire's radius himself.

Zane's eyes danced between the various creatures that advanced toward him. Their movements weren't as predictable as the somnium's, sloppy and uncoordinated, as he'd expect of demons inhabiting an unfamiliar body they'd yet to adjust to. The demons had transitioned from tall, lumbering forms to the more stubby and limited ranges of the human forms they inhabited. It would be far odder if they weren't hindered throughout their adjustment.

Zane sighed to himself, pained at the prospect of dealing with the dithered. He was more than capable of safely incapacitating them. However, there was an air of uncertainty given their sheer numbers and the handicap of protecting Andrew simultaneously. It was far sounder a strategy to bite the bullet and kill them, much to his chagrin.

Without dwelling on the odds, Zane got to work. Flames of less-than-lethal magnitudes scorched the demons at his command. They flickered in brief flashes, forming waves of embers rather than the orange and yellow walls that he had repelled their initial advance with. His magic was especially amenable to their continued existence; it was hot enough to repel them and halt their movements, but even this had its limitations. Zane formed a terra-diablo sign before he placed his hands on the ground and thrust his energy into the pavement. The pavement rippled with energy, distorting the cement around the stumbling creatures' feet and bolting them into place.

But he couldn't contain all of them. More closed in, brazenly rushing through the flames with shimmering energy surrounding their forms, protecting them. Zane groaned to see they had learned to create a basic barrier, something that would make this more troublesome. Without dwelling, he rushed to Andrew's side and kicked a dithered that jumped at him. Zane flashed a reassuring smirk at Andrew and went back to fighting off the demons with his flames and occasional melees.

However, this was not a winning battle as far as Andrew saw it. This was a prolonging of the inevitable: them being overrun. Another pessimistic conclusion resurfaced. *Useless,* Andrew thought. His skill with a gun was awful, as the instructor had put it politely in the few times Andrew had used one. His limited range of non-lethal self-defense options didn't seem useful either—two sound grenades that were experimental and effectively needed to be tuned for their target to be of any use. The somnium were not a target he had tuned them for, but despite his trepidation, he sought to utilize the time Zane had bought.

Andrew grabbed one of the sound grenades from his belt, a device consisting of numerous speakers and an amp that was filled with energy from a crystal containing a reserve of Ichor. He synchronized it with his hunter gauntlet before dialing to the tuning channel. The various sounds emitted around them were analyzed, the frequencies being scanned and adjusted. He hypothesized if he tuned it to the inverse frequency of their hiss, it would prove an effective counter.

The tuner had established the prominent frequency of the demon-infested humans, and Andrew adjusted it to the inverse and uploaded that data to his grenade. He bit his lip hard and pulled the detonation trigger on the grenade. Three ticks and it would emit that selected frequency. He tossed it high into the air, aiming to have it detonate above the dithered assaulting Zane.

Zane became overwhelmed the more he tried to maintain a non-lethal front against the somnium. Sweat dripped down his face as the creatures broke through his waves of shallow flames and swiped at him with their claws. In their unrelenting savagery, they shredded his vest in a matter of moments. Much to his dismay, he pondered the necessity of utilizing lethal force to blow the demons back. With his obvious repulsion at the thought of doing so, he imagined they were taking advantage of his hesitation. But much to his coming reprieve, an opportunity approached.

Descending, the sound grenade went off above the group of dithered's heads, blaring a continuous shriek of the frequency that they reacted adversely to, but neither Zane nor Andrew were affected. Zane blinked in confusion, only seconds away from burning the creatures before seeing them seize up. The dithered dropped to their knees, convulsing and jittering with distorted yells and clicks, the frequency from the grenade bombarding them to great effect.

Zane didn't question the opportunity that presented itself and immediately pressed his palms to the ground again. The cement distorted beneath the dithered's feet and bound them to the ground.

Andrew panted, still out of breath from their journey to Willis Tower, but he had an optimistic smile that presented itself as a result of his successful *experiment*. Zane looked down at him and grinned while snickering.

"Nice work, lil bro," Zane said, walking toward him with his hand held up. Andrew reached up, jumped, and high-fived Zane with a matching grin more emblematic of himself than the fear he had shown a minute prior. He still couldn't believe the grenade had worked. Astounded by his accidental prescience, he made a mental note to finalize the design and submit it as an official prototype when the crisis was over.

With the grenade having worn off, the dithered stared with frustration, yanking their legs to no avail. Then they tried clawing at the ground, thrashing repeatedly with even less success. Once it was apparent they were stuck, they let out a resentful roar. A black mist spewed from their mouths and coated the area in darkness momentarily. In a few, short moments, the somnium that were inhabiting the dithered had manifested in their original forms.

"Cursed hunters, you will *not* be ascending that tower," one of them hissed.

Andrew doubled back, stepping behind Zane.

"Wait, they can separate? That's cheating!" Andrew complained.

"Well ... at least the humans are free," Zane muttered, grabbing his gunblade and flicking it out. There were six somnium, which, as he calculated, was the exact number of bullets his gunblade held.

Given the relative proficiency the somnium had exhibited in their dithered form, what Zane had not accounted for was their magic proficiency. When he fired the first bullet, it appeared to hit the somnium, but its hazy form jittered, dissipating into nothing. An illusion.

A tendril of shadows latched onto Zane's ankle, lifting him up and flinging him into a nearby building, separating him from Andrew.

The somnium exchanged glances, nodding as half of them went after Zane, while the others marched over to Andrew, leering with ominous intent cloaked behind their hollow eyes.

Back on his feet, Zane groaned. Tendrils of shadow lurched at him, and he reflexively combusted, causing the solid magic to recoil at his sudden flourish.

"Okay, cheap shot with the umbra kinesis," Zane complained aloud, cracking his neck. It was easily presumed he had been caught off guard even in that moment, a mistake he usually capitalized on with his deceptive demeanor. As an assassin of several years, he was taught to be unassuming, but he took it to an extreme that only he could pull off. The somnium were remiss of such a quality, one emerging behind him and preparing to run him through with its spindly digits, but Zane caught its wrist and weaved to the side. With a swipe of a flaming arm, he sent the thing into the wall in a concentrated burst of flames, incinerating it.

The remaining two somnium, seeing this, halted in their advance as Zane turned his auburn gaze onto them. Zane smirked sardonically, stumbling forward to emphasize the danger of his deceptiveness, raising his gunblade and aiming it at them. He refrained from immediately firing, however, pensive as he stared them down for a moment.

"Uh ... what's your names, by the way?" Zane asked, quizzically raising an eyebrow.

The somnium exchanged glances with one another.

"I ... am Ebony."

"And I am Ivory."

Zane smiled, his eyes going wide as he laughed. He suddenly thought back to conversations he had with a hunter comrade of his, Drake, whose aloof demeanor only ever cracked in the face of revelations as comical as the one before Zane now.

"Oh, I get it now! What a *colorful* naming scheme you guys have. Oh man, Drake isn't going to believe me when I tell him this!" Zane stifled his laughter, clearing his throat.

"Those names are too cool for such ordinary somnium. I'm afraid I only have *one gun* for the two of you, but don't worry, I play the piano, and I've got plenty of keys ..." A realization struck Zane, and he glanced down at his tattered vest. He frowned when he saw the plethora of his ammo supply missing—likely scattered somewhere around the humans he saved. Sighing, he forwent telegraphing his retaliation and fired his gunblade twice, blasting the somnium apart before holding his palm out and grumbling the returnal incantation.

Zane stumbled out of the building's lobby with a sour expression. He had a phantom hunch he'd need all the energy he could muster coming up, which he had hoped to preserve it by using bullets.

"Tall orders ... short supply," Zane said to himself, clicking his tongue. He then walked past the dissipating somnium as he returned his attention to the others that were after Andrew.

The somnium walked with a slow, awkward gait toward the young hunter, watching him cower in amusement.

"Aren't you a little short to be a hunter?" one taunted, prompting the boy to retreat backward slowly, glancing around for an escape.

His wide eyes searched frantically, but everywhere he turned, the somnium emerged from the shadows, greeting him with an ominous grin.

"Would any of you even want a vessel this pathetic?" one asked.

"Not me," another replied dismissively.

"Me neither," the other said.

Andrew panicked as he considered what to do. He knew that calibrating his final grenade would take too long, and given the unpredictable stride of the somnium, he knew even grabbing the device would evoke urgency in them. Now familiar with its raucous potential, they watched his every move, snarling when their eyes found the device.

"Zane!" Andrew called out.

The remaining somnium crept closer to Andrew, taking their time for unapparent reasons. Feast or famine, they choose to indulge in gluttony, the fear Andrew exhibited enticing their patience and signifying their confidence. But their vision of the fearful young man was suddenly obscured, a wall of concrete emerging from the ground before they turned around.

In a flash of fury, an inferno closed in on them, bathing them in deadly flames they had yet to witness.

Crouching several meters from them, Zane's left hand was pressed to the ground, his right hand held out with smoke and embers emitting from his palms. By the time the flames crashed into the somnium, nothing was left for him to clean up with the returnal incantation.

"These things really get on my nerves …" Zane muttered, slowly standing as he yawned. "Alright, Andrew, we're good!" he called out to his young comrade, lazily marching toward Willis Tower. He took that moment of respite to reload his gunblade again, knowing he didn't have many bullets left.

"Geez, took you long enough!" Andrew whined, stepping from behind the concrete and dancing across the hot asphalt left in the wake of Zane's attack. Even with the insulated boots of his uniform, the heat surged through them. Jogging over to his suitcase, he reached down and snatched it up.

Joining each other's side, they looked up at the colossal building they'd somehow have to reach the top of. Pensively examining the building and its lobby, which they could still access, there was a lingering doubt about the elevators being functional. Even if they were, the integrity of them still being safely accessible was doubtful.

In the consuming silence, Zane mumbled to himself before glancing at Andrew.

"Y'know, part of me knows we could just go to the highest floor inside and just take a maintenance access to the rooftop … but that'll take way too long," Zane began. "That said—how about we fly up to the top?"

Andrew blinked in confusion.

"Fly to the top? Uh … how?"

Zane snickered and formed the terra-diablo sign before placing his hands on the ground. Concrete shifted around their feet and elevated them to create a platform that disconnected from the ground after a few moments.

"Uh, Zane?" Andrew squeaked, swallowing hard as he glanced between the platform and Zane, concern painted on his face.

"Andrew, how familiar are you with rocket science?"

"Not very," Andrew squeaked.

"Me neither, but gasses, of which there is an abundance in the air, are a thing I can manipulate with my demon alchemy … you following?"

Andrew gasped, his eyes dilating as he snapped his head around.

"Hey, hey. Just hold on tight to me … it'll be over before you know it. Promise. The city needs us, remember?"

Andrew's gaze shifted from the top of the tower to the platform, then back to the tower again. There was not a glimmer of resolve for him to conjure this time. Resigning himself, he shut his eyes tightly and clung to Zane.

Zane leaned down, careful not to weaken Andrew's hold.

Zane's energy pulsed through his palms, and the platform propelled into the air with a quick thrust from the cement beneath it. The launch allowed him to focus on the air beneath the platform, and he joined his fingertips together and crossed his thumbs, forming the ventus-diablo sign. Hydrogen primarily being present, the gas underwent a controlled ignition, causing the platform to hover. The level of focus he needed to maintain this was tremendous, but he was enthused to oblige.

Zane soon found his rhythm, and the platform shifted upward. Crawling at first, then gradually accelerating. Andrew's stomach dropped, his ears plugging as he kept yammering quietly about the fate of the city being in their hands. The platform rocketed high into the air, subtly wobbling as it brought the two hunters toward the top of the tower in seconds. Zane, exhilarated. Andrew, terrified.

The entire process was less than smooth, but Zane was aware of that as the platform subtly rocked. Andrew squeaked and prayed to whatever deity would listen, convinced this was his end with each jitter of the platform. When they approached the top, their acceleration slowed, and Zane tilted the platform. They hovered toward the rooftop gradually before landing. He wasn't dumb enough to drop the cement platform back to the ground from that height. It could easily kill the sleeping humans below.

Andrew almost fell over if not for clutching to Zane, who stood sturdily despite the forces he had commanded.

"Ladies and gentlemen, we have landed," Zane chirped, admiring his handiwork for a moment as he stepped from the platform, breaking from Andrew's grip.

Andrew collapsed to his knees, queasiness assailing him due to their turbulent journey to the top of the tower. Crawling off the platform, he thought he'd puke for a moment, but he pulled through without losing his dinner.

"Never ... again," Andrew said between his dry heaves, and Zane patted his back. As he inspected the rooftop, it became apparent how cramped it was compared to the city below. Zane had expected something grander for the second-tallest tower in the country, but they could at least walk around without the fear of falling off.

The sky ominously undulated and split with sickly, red energy indicative of the somnium—a source of the hissing that droned. In their exalted scrutiny, Zane had almost not heard it coming—a blast barreling toward him and Andrew. Zane held his hand out, a blast of explosive flames jetting from his palm, negating the blast.

A figure stepped forward from within the smoke, and it slowly cleared to reveal a devilish silhouette. Coming into view, a man stood, wearing a black outfit with a long coat that swayed in the wind. His harsh, blackened eyes fixed on Zane and Andrew, his ashen complexion shimmering with glimmering purple energy from the blast he had conjured.

"Carver ... it was you after all, huh?" Zane said in a flat tone. Despite the demonic visage he now dawned, he could recognize the familiar face.

Darrel was silent, pensively staring at them with an ominous presence about him. Before, when he and Zane had first crossed paths, he had *suppressed* his underlying hostility. Now, no such thing was necessary.

Darrel was unamused by their sudden arrival. In fact, he was outright furious, as was evident in his glare. *Of all ... my Alysium's murderer?* Darrel thought, his eyes flickering with energy as the indigo light sparked in his palm. The only solace he took was the fact he could have revenge.

"You took ... the only thing I had left in this world!" Darrel shouted as his energy coalesced into a humming orb that pulsed ominously.

Zane had suspected that Darrel collaborated with the Siegharts and somnium, perhaps as a willing thrall, but he was surprised to find out that he was also a demon. Demons were not allowed to serve in positions of authority in human society, which meant that Darrel had slipped under the Hunters' radar—somehow.

It made sense to Zane how and why the police had been targeted. They had a rat among them—one who sought to do away with their chief to seize power for himself. Even so, he would have sensed if Darrel was a demon, but given the collaboration with the Siegharts, he had an idea of how Darrel went unnoticed.

"Andrew, tuck yourself behind one of those antennas," Zane said. Andrew had been caught staring longer than he intended to, snapped out of his stupor by Zane's command. Stumbling to his feet, he grabbed the briefcase from the platform and ran. A streak of energy shot out at Andrew, but Zane unleashed another veil of flames to block it. When the smoke cleared, he returned the glare.

With Andrew out of the way, Zane's nerves settled a bit, confident enough to hold his own against Darrel.

"Why?" Zane asked as the smoke dissipated, the warm rush of wind still howling around them from the collision. Darrel stared with a despondent gaze, another swirl of energy manifesting in his palm.

"You have no right to ask that question, *murderer*," Darrel hissed, his teeth gritting hard as his glare intensified. "No. Things like you defy what they are until the last second. A monster—a tool once used by the Alastairs that now feigns regret. For what! Hunters? Humanity? Fiends like you ... like *us*, need not apply for sympathy and forgiveness. Not when the world has taken—"

"Woah, woah, woah. I didn't ask for your villain manifesto. I asked a simple question. Why? What's your angle? Keep it brief and punchy." Zane sighed, running his fingers through his hair. He hated listening to irrelevant diatribes about other's gripes with the world. At least Zane assumed it to be irrelevant. He didn't have the patience for cliché monologues after a long day and an increasingly longer night.

Darrel furrowed his brows and snorted.

"How's this for a reason? You killed my Alysium, and the Alastairs must be deposed, only now, after I kill you!"

"Much better," Zane said with a satisfied nod. "Now, mind telling me—"

More ferociously than before, the energy from Darrel's hand bolted at Zane with a loud screech. Zane knew his flames wouldn't be enough to counter this attack, so he leaned out of its path, dodging it. Zane reached behind his back, unholstered his gun blade, and aimed it in its focus-fire configuration at Darrel before firing two shots.

A shield of purple energy rose in front of Darrel and the bullets collided against it, hovered in midair, then dropped. Unrelenting, Zane switched the gunblade to its blade configuration before rushing toward Darrel.

The air shrieked as the blade collided with the energy shield and hovered harmlessly before Darrel's form. Except Darrel appeared to struggle, gritting his teeth and growling as his legs buckled from the force. Zane, as lanky as he was, was stronger than he let on. Sure, he wasn't as physically forceful as a brooding demigod, but he was still a demonium.

Zane's flaming aura rippled and coursed through the grooves and decorative valleys along the blade's surface. Darrel chanted in Latin, but Zane knew better than to let his opponent prepare a potentially game-changing spell. His flames bathed them in ferocious light. Heat swarmed, and Darrel's ward shattered, pushing him back into one of the roof's antennas.

Darrel panted heavily, reaching for his hip and grabbing his pistol, but he recoiled from the hot metal. While Zane had assumed he had brought his gun, it was mostly an accident that he had made it too hot for Darrel to handle.

In their continued attrition, Zane noticed a subtle change. Darrel's left eye became consumed by a harsher darkness. A red slit pupil and purple glowing veins manifested atop it—an eye Zane knew well.

Of all the things Zane could have predicted, this was not one of them. Darrel being an Alastair begged many questions. Harkening back to his final conversation with Alysium, he recalled her mentioning *Eridionne*, a name he knew was emblematic of the Alastair's naming schemes. He had heard whispers of a half-demon bastard child of Eridianne, and now, he personally confirmed that rumor. Seeing that eye, Zane knew he had to end things quickly.

The eye of Semita, *the leer of wrath,* was a dangerous ability to contend against, namely because of its infamous killing potential. And at that range, a single blast from the vengeful demonium would greatly damage Zane.

Darrel raised his hand, purple energy swarming in his palm before he thrust his hand forward to hit Zane. Knowing he couldn't afford to take that hit, Zane leaped back, aborting his own attack against Darrel, but Darrel launched it at him instead, now that there was distance.

Whereas before, Zane could afford to take a hit or two, with the eye of Semita activated, that was no longer an option. The eye negated any defenses of whomever it was cast on, no matter the power difference. Zane had spent half of his life under the umbrage of the Alastairs and had witnessed the gruesome ends many had met under the watch of such a grizzly eye. He still recalled the visceral scenes of Zaldionne blasting holes through those who assumed they could deflect his blasts when he had it active.

Zane sidestepped the bolt, his skin tingling from the proximity of the energy. Regardless of how the odds were now stacked against him, he understood how the eye worked. It relied upon sight. If it were a battle without sight, Zane could negate the eye's advantage.

Temperature detection, Zane thought. If he couldn't use his eyes, he would have to rely on his demonic awareness of the subtle temperature shifts around him, a perk of being half fire demon. It would be easy enough to track Darrel as long as things around them became hot, preferably inhospitably so. But first, Zane had to erase Darrel's line of sight.

Zane crouched and connected his palms to the floor. Energy surged through his skin and trailed throughout the ground around them as cement cracked and splintered. As it crumbled, flames erupted from the crevices. The concrete, pressurized, exploded into clouds of dust embroidered in a tapestry of fire. All around the two, the air was cloaked in a ghastly cloud of dust and embers

And, as Zane had intended, Darrel couldn't see. The glow in Darrel's eye ceased, and he searched. He could sense Zane's energy, sure, but seeing him was a whole separate ordeal, one he had been relying on.

"You hide, coward!" Darrel hissed, hurling a spiral of his energy into the wall of flames before him, where he sensed Zane. But it hit nothing.

A hefty hand found Darrel's shoulder, spinning him around before a fist covered in burning flames slammed into Darrel's jaw, searing his flesh. When it connected, an explosion of flames erupted, amplifying the force of the punch and sending Darrel tumbling across the roof. It was a hefty strike, sufficient to end the battle. Darrel was dazed, and his focus waned, his energy dwindling from the effort it took to regenerate from the incurred damage.

"You ever consider that my flames can feel just like my energy signature as long as I keep a little quiet?" Zane sighed and walked toward a disoriented Darrel until he stood over him. "You're a far stretch from Zaldionne. Any Alastair worth their salt wouldn't have fallen for that ... but I suppose you're not a *true* Alastair, right?" Zane scoffed, pressing Darrel into the ground with his boot pressing against his chest. "Geez, can you guys ever have some lifelong goals that don't involve subjugating humanity or something?" Zane sighed, flicking his gunblade to its hybrid form before aiming it at Darrel.

Zane had no further words for the man. He had exhausted his mercy with Alysium, and he knew Darrel's type all too well. There was no convincing such a man of the errors of his ambitions, not when there had already been so much death. Just as he clicked the trigger, cold, spindly fingers yanked his hand up, causing the bullet to fire harmlessly into the air. Zane looked up, seeing large white eyes staring down at him—a somnium demon. Before he could react, the creature lifted him and tossed him across the rooftop. He tumbled but caught himself by jamming his blade into the floor before he could slide off the edge.

Darrel gasped, regaining his composure and senses in those few lucid moments. His face was badly burned from Zane's attack, blackened with charred skin and dripping blood from the swollen cheek. When he lifted his head, he saw Magenta, the trusted right hand Intico had appointed to stand guard with him. He never understood why the somnium suddenly adopted names. He couldn't tell most of them apart, but Magenta had a familiar twinkle in its eyes, a semblance of the power Intico had gifted to it that distinguished it minutely.

Magenta's white eyes stared harshly at Darrel, a click echoing from it as it hoisted Darrel to his feet. Its pensive gaze bounced between Zane and Darrel. It deduced Zane had plenty of fight left, whereas Darrel had little to none based on his condition. Realizing this, Magenta cocked an eye and hissed.

"We wouldn't win this battle … we should retreat," Magenta spoke.

Darrel squinted and glared at Magenta, shaking his head with vigorous refusal.

"And leave all of our work to be destroyed by this clown? No, we will not yield," Darrel spat between his labored breaths, his face simmering as his demon blood worked to heal the damage.

Magenta was impressed and amused by the resolve it saw in Darrel, and a grin formed on its face—a grin befitting the somnium.

"Then you know what we must do, Carver," Magenta began. "The merge will be instant, and we cannot separate if you willingly become my vessel. The *you* that exists will cease to be—practically dead," Magenta explained, conveniently leaving out the other ghastly ramifications of their union.

Darrel's face twisted into a sickly grin, his trembling hand raising up to Magenta, his eyes flickering with the eye of Semita glimmering through the pervading darkness.

"I died when she did. As long as that hunter pays … that's all that is left for me."

With Darrel's final sentiment, Magenta took his hand. A veil of darkness enshrouded the two, obscuring them from Zane's vision in an inky blot of darkness imposing itself onto the infinite night.

Zane quickly switched his gunblade to its focus-fire configuration and shot at the two several times, running the drum dry. When he reached into his vest to reload, he was annoyed to find he had only one bullet left. Reluctantly, he clutched it and locked it into his drum before returning his skeptical gaze to the shroud of darkness. Feeling a coalescing of energies within the cocoon of shadows, he knew whatever would emerge, be it a dithered or some other perversion of life, wouldn't be good.

A chaotic cackle sounded from within said cocoon. The shadows melted into the floor, leaving a distorted, shadowy figure of glittering, purple-tinted energy with ghastly white eyes that were fixed on Zane. The lingering sentiment of Darrel's ire was plastered within its gaze, replacing the usual void in the dithered's eyes. Fixed firmly within its left eye, he saw the eye of Semita, its leer scorning any defense he could conjure once again.

It was in pressing times that Zane alleviated tense situations with humor, but nothing surfaced from his disturbed mind in this one—perhaps the grizzliest of developments. Within moments, the *thing*, Magenta, had closed the distance between them. The reinforced fabric of Zane's armored vest was torn from him, leaving his torso nearly bare before the fiend. In retaliation, Zane bathed the area in a spectacle of flames bursting from his palm.

Zane's labored breath filled the ensuing silence, smoke flooding the area surrounding him. The air was damp and rigid around him. Insidious eyes gouged Zane's from within the veil of smoke, and in a blink, Magenta greeted him up close. Suddenly, his skin stung in several areas, barraged by movements he couldn't follow. Slash after slash, its claws sundered his flesh.

Another burst of flames shrouded the immediate area, and Zane jumped back but found himself eerily close to the edge. He had thought that bit of distance would give him time to recuperate and mount an offense, but Magenta was cackling from within the haze left behind by Zane's flames. As it cleared, its palm was outstretched, and a surge of spiraling energy had formed atop it. The chaotic purple energy bubbled and crackled with power Darrel hadn't shown prior.

Time stood still and Zane stared with wide eyes. That attack was far beyond the scope of what he had expected, even with the two of them merged. The air shrieked around the dithered, and the energy shot from its palm and crashed into Zane quicker than he could react.

Zane became weightless—far removed from his prior poise. The ground had vanished from beneath his feet, having been torn from atop it and sent barreling through the air. The rampaging pain from the blast was the least of his concerns—at least when compared to the earth that he was hurdling toward. Death was imminent.

"Zane!" Andrew called out. He watched with wide eyes, fingers clenching the briefcase as he saw his comrade, his friend, hurdle toward his oblivion. He had been far too terrified and encumbered by the pressure from their clashing energy to reestablish their communications amid the chaos. It was perhaps a mistake he'd reckon with, or maybe a fruitless opportunity he hadn't taken. Either way, as he saw it, there was no further recourse.

That ghastly stare found Andrew next, and white consumed his vision. Sweat dripped from Andrew's brow as stuttered whimpers bled from his trembling lips. In its fear-inducing gaze, Andrew was paralyzed. The energy it conjured swallowed his agency, consuming it with an illusory display of his doom, an echoing of his fears manifested within the white abysses that gazed back at him.

But, as fate had deemed, Zane found himself still able to use his hands. His ears rang as the wind bombarded them, and the tower above narrowed in his vision. In that extended moment, neither helplessness nor despair ensnared Zane. Sparks of white consumed the center of his eyes, a burning flame enrapturing his semblance of humanity with a promise. Rather than supplanting it, it made a pact within his heart.

Andrew, even then, was his utmost concern. He had promised the boy no harm would come to him, and he intended to keep that promise even in the face of his demise by gravity. His convictions coalesced, and he sheathed his gunblade before his fingers reached for a vial on his belt, scooping it into his palm. The vial was embedded into an auto-injector, one that would eject the crimson serum inside of it into him upon jabbing.

"I'll burn brighter ..." Zane swore. His voice was lost in the wind, but the determination behind it would see the sky lit anew.

Channeling his demonic power and manifesting the form of his kind was a gamble, a heavy physiological burden on him. Although a risk, his promise was something he would never see turn to ash. Sucking in a harsh breath, he injected the serum into his thigh, and his eyes became black, a bright flame burning where his auburn irises once were.

Magenta slowly approached Andrew, a low clicking resembling a cackle resonating from it. Despite it being more efficient to blast Andrew—a quick, effortless task—the fear the somnium within it fed upon inspired its slow, methodical approach to introducing Andrew to oblivion. Andrew was of no threat to spur urgency.

Andrew, petrified, saw something worse than death as it approached. He could see it in its eyes. It gnawed away at his soul. A quick demise was a mercy it would deny him, but there was a flame burning yet.

"Carver!" Zane's voice erupted through the dense air. Flames surrounded him as he came to a landing atop the building, having conjured a powerful jet to ascend once more. His irises danced wildly within his eyes, a growing spark atop a canvas of black, a borrowed wrath sequestered in his blood.

Magenta stopped its advance toward Andrew, returning its attention to a stubborn threat that sought to challenge it again. Puzzled, it resurrected its prior objective of killing the hunter that had spurred its genesis.

A guttural growl left Zane's widening mouth, evolving into an uproarious yell. His skin darkened as if it were caked in soot. His hair became a torch, enshrined with curvy, grooved horns that stretched from his skull, serving as a flourishing effigy within the flames ignited around them. Valleys marred his skin, erupting with a flickering inferno that spilled from deep within his being. Standing before Magenta was the image of a blaze, Zane's secret, arcane form.

Andrew, now free from the paralysis that had coursed through him, bore witness to the display in awe. He was overjoyed to see Zane alive, but at the same time, he was stunned by the appearance of his rumored demon form. He had known Zane for years now and had been aware of its existence but had never seen it. Seeing it now harkened back to a comment Zane once made to him.

You'll know I'm in a pickle if you ever see it.

Orange and yellow, Zane's flames swarmed his limbs and body, forming a vortex. *Hotter. Stronger.* Zane's thoughts repeated such a promise, seeking to manifest the sinful power he had sequestered to remain true to his desperate vow. No ordinary fire would be enough for the creature before him. Those same flames burned more ferociously, the area becoming enraptured by a brilliant light. Eventually, their color was lost, and an infernal white energy coursed through the wicked flames.

The heat Zane emitted reached the dithered, the pressure following it caused it to flinch and squint. It fell silent, unsure of what stood before it now. Despite this brewing hesitation, it took its stance, claws outstretched with crackling purple energy bubbling from its palm.

"Carver is gone. Now ... you face Magenta."

When the dithered took a step toward Zane in preparation to dash, white flames blasted where it would have been.

"Die," Zane uttered, his voice distorted by wrath and chaos, barely contained within the gusts of his overflowing power. A series of flames whipped through the air and toward the dithered, prompting it to lurch out of its way several times. The heat was ferocious despite not having suffered a direct blow, hot air rushing past Magenta and dissipating when it reached Andrew. Even then, it was enough to make the boy recoil and shield himself.

Left. Right. Blast after blast, the dithered could hardly conjure an attack. While it dodged, energy formed in its palm, swirling and crackling before it launched a ferocious wave at Zane. The blazing demonium swung his arm and a wave of white fire jetted from the ground, advancing toward the dithered.

The energy was consumed in the flames, met by a greater power. And that was what Zane had plotted: creating a greater power that would serve as a shield in the absence of his barrier. In his demon state, his heart pounded with tenacity, blood coursing through his body with a burning heat that heightened his senses. He was more attuned and capable of reacting to the sporadic, quick foe before him—but at a cost. The amount of energy the form consumed took a massive toll on him. Even with his specially crafted serum to spur his body's ability to maintain such power, he had less than a minute while utilizing the white flames that manifested within him.

Magenta persisted stubbornly, coalescing a dangerous fusion of shadow and sin into a powerful beam, which it launched to meet the burning wave that Zane had conjured. It had assumed that if it could hold off, Zane would burn through his energy supply, having documented the notable strain such power incurred on its foe.

"*Burn out, stupid cinder,*" Magenta spoke in its distorted voice.

Zane sucked in a sharp breath and lowered his position. Heat surged and receded into flames that swarmed around his form, struggling to maintain such a taxing maneuver. Within the throes of their colliding energies, a small object caught his eye, a blinking, round device that approached Magenta. A sound grenade.

The device went off, a piercing shriek causing Magenta to shiver and convulse momentarily. In its obstruction, its own attack wavered. Zane's energy pierced through its defenses, narrowing with the hunter's focus and colliding with its eye of Semita, burning it out.

Andrew hadn't intended to involve himself in the fight, but even if it was minuscule, he had to make himself useful. He had to help his friend, and his faith was unwavering in Zane's capitalizing on the opportunity. Without a doubt in his mind, he knew Zane would protect him as many times as it took.

The damage inflicted was short-lived, however, as its regenerative capabilities almost instantly restored the eye. Following the sound grenade ceasing its debilitating noise, it turned to face Andrew, scowling as its eye of Semita flared brightly. It sprinted at the boy, fury flaring in its visage that swallowed the world in front of Andrew.

The promise Zane made, albeit echoing through his mind amid the chaos of his rage, remained central—a flame burning brighter than even his own. Shooting from Zane's horns, a streak of fire shot past Magenta, stopping just in front of its path toward Andrew. In a rapid combination, Zane utilized his demon alchemy to its fullest potential. He formed the ventus-diablo sign, and the flames swirled into a sphere, beneath it, a bubble swelling with hydrogen. He clenched his right hand shut, and the bubble popped, mixing with the fiery shell to create a directed explosion of searing flames that repelled Magenta away from Andrew. Seamlessly, he then formed the terra-diablo sign and slammed his left palm into the ground, causing a thick concrete shield to form around Andrew.

Trembling, Magenta rose slowly as its body hastily repaired itself, and its left eye flared once more with dismaying wrath upon meeting Zane's glare.

Its regeneration was troublesome, but Zane had one means left to hinder the abomination long enough to finish it off. He grasped the burning handle of his gunblade, pulling it from its holster. Raising it, he fired, and a searing bullet pierced its eye of Semita. Blasting through its skull, the bullet became a shooting star over the city, burning into nothing.

With the troublesome eye's regeneration hindered by the anti-demon bullet, Zane seized his opportunity and charged. He wrenched Magenta into his searing grasp, and the dithered writhed and clawed at Zane's arms, the sharp digits digging through his hardened skin and sinking into his flesh. However, the pain did little to overturn its impending sentence.

"By the way ... Magenta is a terrible name for a final boss," Zane said, his voice darkening as his grip blazed, the remainder of his energy gathering in his palms. In those last moments, his scrutiny maintained a sentiment to counter the impregnable wrath that had remained in Magenta—Darrel. Such wrath was damned before Zane, a measure of his own vows. Be it human or demon, he cared not. His answer was obvious.

"*Burn.*"

White embers flickered before Magenta's eyes, and its glittering form disappeared within the fiendish light that overtook them. An inferno of white consumed as energies collided in a violent breach, and two beings at once were turned to ash.

Magenta and Darrel were no more.

The rooftop was scorched black around Zane, who stood shakily with his blazing eyes fading—his flames doing the same. The light left him as his form shifted. His human visage returned, his horns and hardened skin melding back into his fatigued body. His clothes were almost entirely scorched off, but he was thankful he had maintained enough control to not accidentally burn away his pants. Being completely naked after an intense battle was not on his itinerary.

"Done," Zane muttered, his gaze turning to Andrew.

Andrew had his eyes tightly shut with his hands held in front of his face to shield himself from the dissipating heat. Slowly lowering his hand, the young hunter peaked an eye open when silence returned, and stepping from behind the concrete shield, he saw Zane. Battered and beat, he had been triumphant.

"Your turn, Andrew," Zane said loopily and slumped onto his back, breathing heftily with glazed eyes and a goofy grin.

It astonished Andrew how cavalier an attitude Zane maintained after the fierce battle, but that was the Zane he knew—it would be far more bizarre if he wasn't. Andrew would have tended to him, but there was the mission that he could now complete without interference. Before, even if he had attempted to establish their communications, their merged foe would have interrupted him. Now that he was free from distractions and outside forces, he could restore communications with the Hunters' HQ.

Zane stared into the sky, seeing the perverted red and black heavens staring back at him. Faintly, he still heard the infernal hiss of the somnium, even with his ears ringing. Magenta was gone, but *something* else remained on the prowl. Two halves of a whole, Harvest persisted.

Zane's grin faded, and the memory of the somnium lord he had met paraded in his mind. He tried lifting his arms, but they refused his commands, an indeterminable exhaustion washing over him, which he had staved off for longer than he had desired.

"Damn ... guess the rest is up to you, Eden. Don't fuck this up," Zane murmured before going limp, falling asleep despite the uncomfortable surface of the tower's roof.

Andrew carefully circled the borders of the base for the antennas. Even as the sky above was sickly, he was positive if he connected to the antennas of the tower, he could break through Harvest's threshold, bypassing the interference. He hoped that it would work, given all that Zane had done to get them there and give him that opportunity.

Andrew found a ladder attached to the base of an antenna. He swallowed hard, gripping the handle of his briefcase tightly with his right hand before slowly ascending the ladder. Upon reaching the top, he hoisted himself onto the narrow ledge where the antenna was firmly planted.

"Alright ... we got this." He popped the case open and sorted cables that he would need to attach to the antenna. Upon clamping three cables into place, he typed into the interface, logging in and waiting for the signal to establish. Seconds of eternity passed before the screen indicated a successful connection.

Andrew's eyes lit up as he cheered happily with a fist pump.

"Yeah!" he called out. He connected his hunter gauntlet to the console before touching his earpiece.

"This is Carter to base. Do you copy?" he spoke with a tremble in his voice. Moments later, the earpiece chirped.

"Carter? Yeah! We read you loud and clear!"

Kendra found Joseph to be both capable and agreeable. His firm command and focused aggression ensured no trepidation impeded the difficult situation they were all charged with. Despite his declaration of differing from her former boss, she saw that same confident competence burning inside of him.

The perimeters of the evacuation zone had been tested by the dithered. With the anti-demon bullets provided by James, the police held the perimeter, despite being unnerved by the somnium emerging from the humans' corpses. They hated gunning them down, but they had no luxury to spare the dithered as Zane or Eden could.

Many more citizens had arrived at the block of the headquarters building, sequestering themselves inside the surrounding perimeter. It was cramped, but with the transportation systems nonfunctional, there wasn't the option of optimizing the available space at the respective evacuation centers.

Kendra wormed her way through the crowd to reach the eastern barricade, where she found Joseph. The hunter lowered his rifle, a jaded expression on his face.

"You holding up?" Joseph asked, shifting his gaze to Kendra upon sensing her energy. Despite what his demeanor had suggested, he was remarkably in tune with energies and his surroundings.

"As much as I can," Kendra replied. "I find it strange that more of those things haven't shown up. Chicago is huge. There should be way more, right?"

"Well ... given how abrupt this all is and the timing of the raid, I'd wager they were running on a skeleton crew," Joseph surmised.

As Kendra and Joseph continued to discuss the circumstances, the streets surrounding the perimeter became eerily still. No further flooding of survivors, nor the demons and dithered. The two hadn't caught onto the suspicious change, however. Reprieve was a welcome change.

The sunken eyes of the officers and citizens alike became more pronounced, the faint miasma working its way through them. Humans, who had no innate resistance to the miasma, weren't able to resist Harvest's presence for long and soon succumbed to its slumbering effects. In droves, the crowd became eerily quiet and slumped to the ground.

"Is it just me, or is the miasma stronger?" Kendra asked, roused by the visible shift in its density. And the further she focused, the more her nose twitched, picking up a faint pungency drifting in front of the HQ building. *Somnium.* She was all too familiar with the scent they exuded by now, and the intensity of the miasma practically announced them.

First, the air shuddered, and the earth subtly quaked. A heavy breathing encompassed the block, its location indeterminate. Then came the *hiss.*

Kendra tensed, recognizing the particularly strong frequency that approached.

In response to the rush of stimuli, Joseph readied his rifle, scanning the area with a skeptical glare.

"Dad!" he called out, staring at the western perimeter to see if he was there. The sole standing figure left in the crowd, he spotted his father, who had his shotgun raised, carefully retreating over the several sleeping bodies toward their position.

"I'm here, boy! Keep your guard up! This one's different!"

Dark fog swarmed the three, a demonic growl clawing at their ears. *Intico.*

James was the first to be snatched into the recesses, a silhouette appearing within the surrounding veil and grabbing his shotgun before swatting him into a nearby police car. With a yelp, James tumbled to the ground. The alarm of the vehicle went off as Intico crushed the weapon in its grasp before dropping it.

Joseph fired his gun, and several bullets zipped through the air, appearing to collide with Intico's form, but its silhouette melded into the fog, disappearing entirely.

"An illusion? Shit ... Kendra, stand back!" Joseph said, his gun still raised as he searched for where the somnium lord would emerge. Kendra, overcoming her momentary paralysis, took to Joseph's back, carefully searching with him.

Kendra's first thought upon seeing Intico was that it had defeated Eden, but that thought was quickly discarded. If it was present in its somnium appearance, it made no sense that it would be after them as it was now. There were many questions that begged answers, but the answers were sought less the closer Intico neared her.

"James!" Kendra called, her ears carefully pinpointing where James was present, able to detect his faint, labored breathing. *Alive, but injured.*

Feeling the presence manifesting beside him, Joseph shifted his aim and fired several times. However, something tugged the muzzle of his gun, shifting it away as ghastly white eyes peered through the fog, glaring at both of them. With a crunch, the muzzle of Joseph's rifle was bent and scrunched, and the somnium lord snatched Joseph by the neck.

Joseph was pried from the ground. The transcendent demon before him easily shrugged off his thrashing, even proving impervious to the dagger he had drawn from his hips and attempted to jab into its hard flesh.

There were several moments in which Kendra was frozen, once again assailed by the familiar, icy grip Intico's presence evoked. Seeing Joseph flailing tenaciously in its clutches, her mind screamed at her to act.

Move! she scolded herself internally. She wanted to help, but something more primal told her to run. Every fiber of her being was locked in conflict, and the heavy, foul air shrieked insidiously as it peered into her. Within its gaze, she saw it. A damnation various entities were condemned to. Within the cold abyss of its very existence, there was endless fear—infinite suffering.

Suddenly, shadows traveled down its tattered, white sleeves, wrapping around Joseph before it tossed the hunter to the side, his body bound within its magic.

"Kendra, get out of here!" Joseph yelled, struggling in the shadowy binds to no avail.

Move! Kendra begged herself repeatedly. Then it snatched her from the ground, raising her to meet it face-to-face. It had purpose in its search for her—it *knew* her.

Kendra yelped and writhed in its grasp. Remembering how she escaped the previous somnium's grip, she focused on her form until flames conjured around her. Scorching hot, she became a torch, but Intico was unscathed by such power, presenting a far more formidable constitution her petty resistance couldn't deter.

It squeezed her tight, snuffing the air from her throat while leaning her back.

Before her dwindling vision, absent was its grin. Those eyes glaring into her blanketed her world in darkness, leaving only the wretched light from its eyes to color her as if it spilled from behind curtains. Within their depths, she glimpsed a fate akin to eternal damnation.

Intico watched the flames dwindle to nothing. Its fingers coaxed her jaw open as she gasped for air. Closer and closer, it drew toward her. It alleviated the pressure around her throat, allowing her to breathe again. And with Kendra's mouth open, it clenched her jaw, holding it in place as it closed its hand, drawing it back.

A means to an end, and that end drew near. A proposition. A darkness. A new creed to be born, irrespective of the blood of life it was denied. *Infernal* sentiments damned to a far more malicious existence; it saw before it the means of liberation. Eden's body was within reach through weaponizing the sentiment it recalled within him: a vow that would not break before he would. As its form shuddered and shed its corporeal anchors, Intico spoke.

"*Inhale.*"

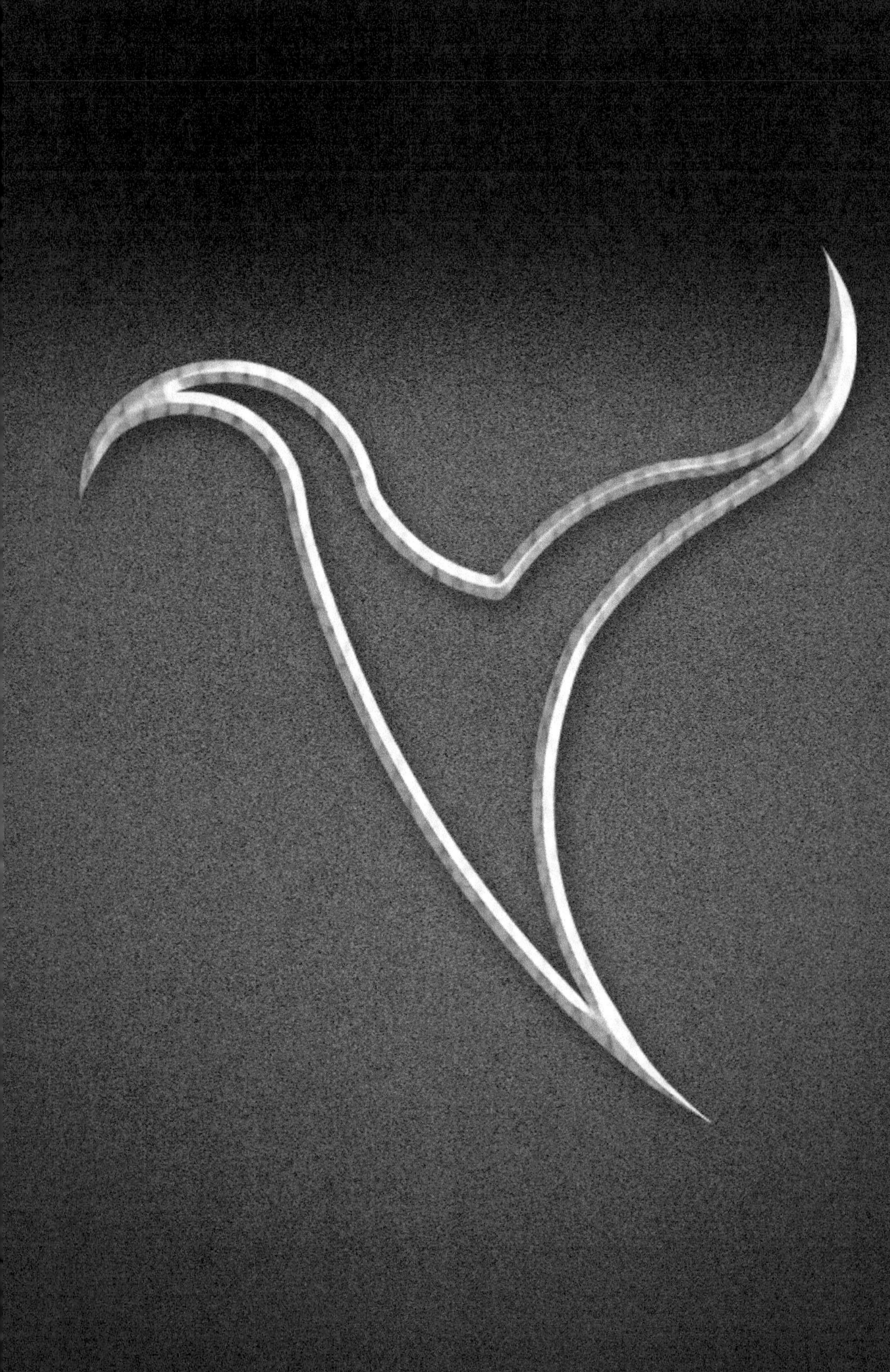

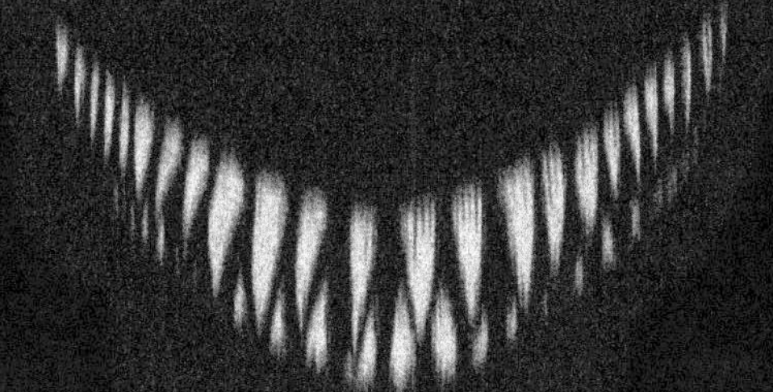

FIFTEEN

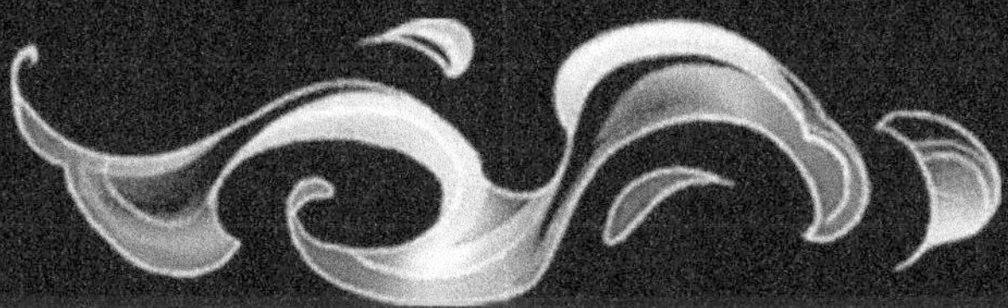

NEVERMORE WE FEAR

The somnium and dithered alike, cruel and tenacious, spared no means in their voracity for vessels. Within two hours, the city was thrust into disarray, despite the hunters' meager resistance and James's contingency plan. The air, quivering with shimmering pockets of red tears in reality, became a blasphemous display of the natural order. The omens, usually a balanced array of blue and red, were lost in the rotten scarlet waves.

The somnium surrounding the Chicago base had been vanquished. With the hunters' immediate threat dispelled, a slim majority of their remaining forces were commanded to patrol the city, defend citizens, and facilitate evacuations. Albeit insufficient, Commander Evans deemed the mitigation necessary—after some not-so-serene convincing from Eden.

But even if he successfully voided the spell cast over the city, Eden knew casualties were inevitable. Regardless of the hasty execution of Harvest, he and the hunters present were all that stood against the ambitions of the remaining purveyors of the Covenant of Augury. The glimmer of optimism that he possessed resided in Andrew and Zane. To ensure they had seen their mission through, he was on his way to rendezvous with them at Willis Tower.

He had nothing but time to soak in the horrors of the city, and his approach to the tower birthed a clawing tension that grabbed at his nerves. However sturdy his resistances were, his exhaustion steadily grew. It was inevitable that his mind returned to Kendra, his sympathy palpable. He could recall the traumas of captivity, compounded by the irrevocable sting of her festering traumas. Therapy would be the minimum of her requisites—if they made it out of Harvest alive.

Had he been further absorbed in thought, he would have been surprised by the incoming energy signature, followed by a searing strike that homed in from above. He halted in his tracks and jumped back right as the source crashed into the ground, a wave of fire scattering from the site of impact. Smoke clouded his vision, obscuring the scene before him, but as it cleared, a humanoid entity stood straight, eyes glimmering white with black-and-white speckled skin—a dithered. And with its scorching temperature, this one, too, was a trickier variety. Some of the somnium had been so fortunate in their melding, hastily exerting their former magical prowess—a command of the shadows and illusions.

While such trickery was not surprising from the dithered, there was a perturbing insinuation of the abilities exhibited by the one before him. Fire was not a typical display of the somnium—let alone the dithered. Abnormal among the abnormal, its energy signature was far more rambunctious. Rather than a subtle vibration and a hiss, it was a sweltering wave instilled with a faint shriek.

As the dithered swayed from side to side, Eden's scrutiny held. Such a puzzling creature granted him no respite to ponder, lunging at him. Claws dug into the ground, leaving scorch marks and a trail of flames as it took to all fours, further differing from the lurching gate the dithered were infamous for. As soon as it reached him, he jumped back, narrowly dodging the claw that swiped at him, leaving a streak of flames in its arc.

The fervor of his caution stirred Eden's hesitation, and his hand instinctively reached for Avenger's hilt. As he prepared to draw it, a familiar flicker of heat brushed over him. He exhaled breathlessly, his fingers quivering as he relaxed his stance. The swaying dithered before him exercised a ghastly smile as it crawled toward him, standing with a devilish look in its eyes.

"You ... failed ... me," it spoke in a feminine tone distorted by chaotic ripples of insidious energy, echoing with perturbed inflections.

Petrified, Eden gawked as the dithered drew closer. There was a struggle within its tortured energy signature, as if something inside was crying out. Opening its mouth once more, it projected a cackle imposed atop a cry, forming a wicked marriage encapsulating agony.

"Kendra ..." Eden whispered. There was no doubt in his mind that the dithered that stood before him was her. *How?* he thought. He doubted that Kendra, Joseph, and James would have been overcome by the somnium or dithered, but he could hardly parse through the limited explanations.

The dithered were elusive, and that mystery enshrouded the grim realization he contended with. There was no way to undo the process. The somnium, prior to the completion of the merge, could voluntarily abscond from their unwilling host. Such a thing was highly improbable, and the few displays of that phenomenon entailed something he sought to avoid. *The vessel's death.* As unscrupulous as the somnium had proven to be, Eden hadn't deemed its haunting taunt a lie. He had failed. Kendra's fate, sundered once again.

An aurora of flames burst forth from Kendra, and their intense, surging heat tested even Eden's barrier. Her stolen form coalesced with an intense energy she had not displayed prior. With such a powerful, secure merging, the underlying thought of Kendra's suffering would plague Eden. When Intico had briefly merged with him, there was an encroaching fear, a manifestation of repressed memories and machinations sooner scorned to oblivion. He knew whatever nightmares Kendra experienced, the agony they brought had to mirror the might on display.

When Kendra rushed him again, Eden barely had time to respond. He retreated back in time to be met with a wave of heat that ushered his evasion, causing his boots to screech against the pavement as he was repelled.

Kendra's claws tensed as she eyed Eden, a wrathful aura surging as she conjured flames in a swirling vortex. She screeched with a powerful, booming roar that quaked the street they stood on. Concrete cracked beneath their feet, cars shifted, lamp posts vibrated, and glass shattered.

Eden held an arm in front of him, shielding himself through the surge of power Kendra exuded. His trepidation overrode any further imperatives, be it necessary or not. He would not kill her. He couldn't.

Running on borrowed time, he dodged as many times as he needed to. He called out to Kendra several times, but without so much as a response, she rampaged through the streets, seeking to catch him. His attempts at hiding proved futile as well, as the somnium within her had judiciously used her keen sense of smell to track him easily. A pursuit of him through the city created a playground of uncertainty, of which his navigation was soon smothered. Vehicles scorched, buildings maimed, and any obstacle he hid behind was scorned by a burning voracity.

That borrowed time had to come due, eventually. A business center where Eden had taken refuge behind a brick wall designated for dumpsters. Erasing his breath, he nestled himself against the wall. He had broken sight from Kendra and carefully focused on the location of her energy signature. He had strained himself to maneuver through the city, weaving and dashing from various vantage points. Now, he was far enough away—or so it had seemed. But with the somnium, what things seemed to be was a gamble—one of which he had lost.

Embers flickered before Eden's eyes, a wavering ripple of heat tickling him. In a single instance, reality warped, and Kendra manifested before his eyes. She clutched his shoulders, claws digging through his jacket and into his skin. Eden pushed against her, but her grip didn't relent, and her searing temperature tested his resilience. The two wrestled momentarily, and Kendra tore him from the wall, pushing him across the lot until he was pinned to a stone building.

With no way to break from her hold, Eden strained to keep her from getting closer. She snapped at the air with her sharp, elongated fangs, and her claws melted through his jacket and raked his shoulders.

Tightly shutting his eyes, Eden cried out. His arms bent but never yielded to the mounting pressure, challenging not only them, but the vestige of his promise too. No matter the pain that assailed him, he remembered his vow, and Kendra, who had suffered enough, would not meet her end as long as he breathed. Conjuring his dwindling strength, Eden peeked an eye open, enduring the blaze that challenged it.

"Kendra ... you have to fight back!" Eden said, struggling to get his words out through the pulses of pain ravaging him. "You're stronger than it!"

Kendra's hollow eyes bore into him, narrowing in their scope as her claws clenched tighter, dragging another pained yell from him. Fire raged around them, barraging Eden's barrier and threatening to incinerate him should he lower his guard. However, something changed in her obscured expression. Her eyes flickered, a sliver of scarlet peaking for brief moments, and her fanged mouth opened.

"I'm ... not human anymore," she spoke in a distorted voice.

Kendra's tone, while diminished in its former agony, was damning. Her echoing a tactless sentiment he had once condemned her with reminded Eden of his deep-seated hatred of demons, a hatred he had carelessly turned on her. But he didn't hate her, nor what she had become. Above all, she was a reminder to him of what he most abhorred: irrevocable darkness. And the darkness he saw her contending against was the same darkness that he still fled from himself. The pain he sought to protect her from reflected his silent plea to escape from such sin within himself. Such liberation, while distant, reverberated from a brewing truth he yearned to embrace, despite how little he understood his own desires.

"I was wrong," Eden whispered. "Even if your body may no longer be that of a human, your heart and soul always will be."

His struggle had waned, however. His muscles became overwhelmed, unable to maintain their resistance and his barrier concurrently. Then the wall at Eden's back cracked, and he found himself met with the force that had overcome him.

Kendra bit into his neck, and Eden stifled his cries. While not the first bite he had ever incurred, it was the most painful, both physically and mentally. The reminder of his failure burned him far more than her power itself could. His legs buckled, and he slowly slid down the wall with Kendra's fangs firmly embedded into his neck.

Eden's neck pulsed, tensing with the fangs that had buried themselves there. It thankfully had missed puncturing anything vital, or perhaps it hadn't intended to inflict any fatal damage. Eden wasn't certain, nor did he try to decipher its intentions.

The flames grew more intense, and the tight clamp of her jaws remained firm. A surge of his strength held, and he reached up, grasping the back of her head and squeezing hard. Taking a deep breath, he prepared his final, true proclamation.

"No matter what you are ... you'll always be Kendra!" His resistance, albeit fading, was stubborn, and held to the cinders of hope he maintained. And it was joined by another. Deep within the depths of fear that strengthened the somnium within Kendra, there was a phantom hope that also had not abandoned her—a candle she had desperately needed within the encroaching darkness.

Gnashing and gnawing. Flesh was torn from bone, accompanying blood-curdling screams of agony. Kendra's perception was asunder, drowned in a sea of agony, fear, and guilt. Even though her own flesh had met the same assailment, its pain had since numbed when incessantly reminded of Kendall's agony. She condemned her sight to darkness, desperate to avoid watching the infinite cycle of Kendall being torn apart in front of her, a damnable memory she had been forced to endure with fresh, nefarious twists added to it.

"Please, Ken!" a pained voice cried across from her, drowned in the snap and snarls that droned on. "I don't want to die!"

Then the voice ceased, once again consumed by the ravenous demons that were conjured in the insidious immersion of the perpetual nightmare. Kendra's mind frayed, unraveling into a delusional fervor of voices barraging her from all directions. Screams, cries, of which many voices existed within it. Shivering, she was torn into repeatedly by the hounds that pinned her. The scars she had ruminated on and traced many times since the actual attack were reopened, sunken into with fangs and claws anew. The sweltering heat and pungent scent of the fiends permeated, invading her senses and denying her the oblivion she sought. Death would not come, nor would the violence diminish. Bound in ceaseless suffering, the hounds remained, and Eden never surfaced to save her.

An endless nightmare. The most haunting of her memories, inspiring the most visceral of fears—personally curated by Intico. The fiends knew no boundaries, or more accurately, forwent every one of them. There was no fear she had not been shown. No excruciating memory she wasn't forced to relive. Eventually, it settled on this one to torment her without relent.

An unknown force pried Kendra's eyes open, and she saw the burning bristles of fur from the hellhounds that tore into her body. Unfortunately, it hadn't consumed her entire vision. Past it, she saw rosy flesh, torn and shredded, being consumed by more of the demons. The sound of snapping bones and pained grunts assailed her once again, resurrecting the tears she had condemned.

In an alien thought, Kendra wondered why it hadn't been her instead. She should have been the one torn to shreds and consumed. *Envy.* The cardinal sin was given a vessel within her. Such envy was something she had never sought or found within herself before. Its emergence was boggling, but such darkness was granted a semblance of revelation in a voice that whispered among the sea of agonized yells. *They know not what they have. Such blessed beings render such a sacred gift forlorn.*

A thought not her own pulsed within the darkness of her being—one of the few discernible sensations she could still retain. *Pitiful.* That was all Kendra could deem such a thought. But soon, it too was asunder within the sea of thoughts—noise no longer to be perceived coherently. With that indiscernible despair assailing her, she resigned herself back to her personal hell.

Time after time, there was no resolution to the memory; there was no savior; there was no ... *hope.*

"I'm not human anymore," her own voice echoed, causing the world to vibrate. Darkness enshrouded Kendra's vision, oblivion teasing her once again—close but never arriving. *She's dead because of you,* rung through her head. *Bitter envy.* A cacophony of insidiousness envy and fear mingled into a noose that pilfered the breath from her.

However, in the ocean of declarations assaulting her, she heard *her.* A voice not from above, but from within, called out to her. She dared to peek her eye open once again, still seeing the horrid sight before her. *Who,* she thought. There was a faint voice that was drowned beneath a pool.

The world writhed and distorted, darkness stretching over her vision as red ripples tore across the scenery. As if she had been sleeping, she slowly remembered it: Intico, the demons that had sought her out, the betrayal. All of her emotions correlated to it came rushing back at once, drawing a grasp that reverberated in the ensuing void.

"It's natural to feel that way," a familiar voice echoed. Likened to a dream, she saw an impossible respite within the encapsulating darkness. No longer strangled within the suffocating sin she had been invaded by, Kendra blinked, a strange void of white surrounding her.

Kendra stood still, her gaze shifting around the infinite nothing. In this instance, she felt nothing. Her pain was muted, and there was the illusion of serenity in its absence. The accursed memories were distant within her immersion in the space.

Kendra attempted to call out, but her words never left her lips, her voice absent, as was her ability to move. *Hello?* she thought, blinking in confusion as she searched. Manifesting within the space, a crowd of blue twinkling sprites drifted around her, humming indiscernibly. The more she watched them, the more she could hear from them. Cries, screams, praying to whoever would listen; they were human voices calling out in fright and desperation.

A burning heat suddenly assailed her form, a sensation she became a stranger to following her mutation into a homuntium. The right side of her body became encased in a surge of red, her muscles tensing as malice invaded her thoughts.

Not human. Not human, the thoughts repeated, reverberating from far away in the void. Her fingers tensed, and her jaw tightened. Right to left, her demonic appearance marred her human features, and the words she vociferously despised assaulted her with their *truth.* The reprieve she sought had known its end, and she shut her eyes tightly, arresting her resistance once more.

"You are Kendra," *her* voice called. A soul emitting a familiar aura drifted near Kendra.

Daring to open her eyes again, Kendra saw the soul, whose ethereal shimmer exalted her.

"*You* are Kendra," the voice repeated. Blinking in confusion, Kendra realized who it was that spoke: Kendall. She immediately assumed it was another trick—a delusion meant to captivate her before plunging her into hell once again. "You're too cynical sometimes, Ken. Seriously, I didn't think I'd get the chance to be your guardian angel, or whatever I am," Kendall continued, giggling momentarily.

Guard me from what? This is ... the end, Kendra resolved, her eyes narrowing as they averted from the formless soul in front of her.

"Ken! Since when are you this murky? You're far from beat. You and I know it ... we can feel it—literally. We're a part of this thing right now, and we can feel what it feels. It probably doesn't know it, but you aren't broken. Why else would this Indigo-what's-its-name creep keep showing you that awful stuff over and over again? Be you human, demon, or the dastardly Fox of Ashwood High, you're still Kendra. And Eden knows it too. He hasn't given up on you—see for yourself."

The void shuddered, and within its leering expanse, two crescent white eyes opened. Intico's eyes. But rather than staring into her, they served as a window of sorts, a faint image flickering in the haze. She saw Eden's face, twisted in distress. Then she saw the crook of his neck and his hair.

A metallic flavor nestled on her tongue, and something warm invaded her throat. It was blood. Eden's blood. As if she had been parched, her throat became moist, and something deep inside of her was roused—a hunger she was familiar with but had staved off with the concoction the Hunters had provided her.

But when that primal call beckoned, she stood still. She had ignored the urge to seek out more of what had ignited the hunger within her again. A denial of what she abhorred. In such liberation, she remembered Eden. *Don't give in*, echoed in her head. She couldn't remember when, but she knew he had spoken those words to her. Then, she heard him call to her from reality.

"You'll always be Kendra!"

Will I? she thought. She remembered her abstinence from what she thought herself to be. When she bit Eden, her hunger for blood had fervently raged—an unending fever. *Gluttony.* Her hands had been tightly wrapped around Alan's throat, repressed from choking the life from him. *Wrath.* And now, there was the phantom sin creeping into her from Intico, a choice she had yet to overcome. In the absence of fear, this was all that was left. *Envy.*

"I was supposed to die ... but it was you instead. All that I can imagine lies ahead is more suffering. What's next? Intico leaves me and takes Eden's body. No matter how I imagine this ... it's over," Kendra levied, her voice returning to her at last. But within it, there was trepidation that tugged at either side of her. Human—demon. It didn't matter what she was.

There was a serene silence for several moments before the dark was illuminated before her eyes, the shimmering soul from before reappearing in front of her.

"Remember what I told you?" Kendall began, waiting for several seconds before the blue light swallowed Kendra, suspending her from the surrounding darkness and enrapturing her in the sentiment Kendall sought to impart. "It's never too late to change your story! Now stop doubting me and show them what Kendra the Kamikaze is made of!"

In that desperately needed revelation her cheeky younger sister had echoed to her, she found herself able to see where she stood at last. The frozen state of her being was thawed at last with such a childish reminder. Human—demon. In truth, she didn't know where to place herself, but that didn't matter. The ultimate sentiment was birthed from the crucible of her being and renewed hope.

I'm not defined by what I am—but by who I am—and what I do now. And right now—I'm still Kendra.

Resolved, her fists clenched, and her body emitted a scarlet glow. When the infinite darkness crept in around the glimmer of Kendall's soul, Kendra's aura flared, and the darkness retreated from her overwhelming scarlet blaze.

By her power—by her will—Kendra would see more than *her* story change.

Kendra's fangs retracted from Eden's neck. Strained and rigid, her claws withdrew, the tips caked in blood. She convulsed as her gnawing growls were distorted by the energy stirring within her body. The prominent flames that once cloaked her faded, and the glittering light and darkness coating her skill peeled.

Eden opened his eyes, watching Kendra writhe and clutch her head. The voice that spilled from her gaping mouth suggested a wrestling of forces, one voice screaming at another. A riot visibly raged within her, spilling out with her cries of rebellion.

"Get ... out!" Kendra roared. The air quivered from the vocal projection, and she tore at the essence cloaking her, peeling away the perversion to reveal her skin. Repeatedly, she clawed her way back to consciousness, expelling the darkness that sought to become one with her. Sundered in uneven chunks, she exposed her flesh from beneath the glittering skin bit by bit, separating the inky tendrils stubbornly clinging to her. Soon, black miasma spilled from her lips, embers igniting throughout, and with one final yell, she succeeded.

The air became shrouded in the miasma, which coalesced and gathered in a mass of darkness above Kendra and Eden. Kendra's claws tore into the concrete beneath her, carving the ground to brace herself as she expelled the miasma. Once it had evacuated from her entirely, she gasped a deep breath, the cold air rushing into her lungs. All at once, her senses reconnected to the surrounding world, no longer inundated by the sinister entity. Such a rush, intense and enthralling, made her dizzy. Promptly, she collapsed, falling into Eden's waiting arms.

In an event Eden thought to be impossible, Kendra had reversed the merging process. That fact was as astounding as her resilience, but also, it was a testament to something far more insightful—something he had yet to understand himself.

Fear. The creeping weed of sin—a darkness with which the somnium needed to incite for merging—was vanquished within Kendra. Without such fear, without such an anchor to human vulnerability, somnium could not remain within a whole being. Without a void to fill, beings of fear could not fathom what enshrined the person; they could not join with such unfathomable beings.

Eden and Kendra's labored breaths filled the ensuing silence.

Kendra's trembling hands pressed into Eden's shoulders, and she dragged her head up to face him. The wounds he was covered in, wounds she had inflicted, were immediately apparent. On her tongue, the taste of his blood still lingered. She had seen the moment she had harmed him—when Intico had harmed him.

The looming darkness pulsed with insidious red distortions. Now free of its vessel, it surged with a sinister hiss, and tendrils stretched out from the fog toward the ground. The once-still air howled with a shriek, prompting Eden and Kendra to flinch in unison as it formed a tall silhouette. Several feet away from them, Intico methodically melded from the miasma above. With its hollow eyes gaping from within the shadows, it found them. Intico chuckled darkly.

"You show such resilience. Both of you. But ... Harvest isn't over. Not until I have claimed what is mine," Intico spoke, glaring at Eden. The wind became still once more, but paradoxically, Intico's cape still danced behind it. Flashing a wicked grin at the two, it approached slowly. The fermenting hesitation it had fastidiously designed within Eden had run its course, and the result was a boy who could no longer mount the resistance that had troubled it for too long. By Intico's yearning—by its patience and guile—no divergence from Eden would further deny its desires.

Eden slowly raised his arms, pain shooting through his shoulders from the motion. Gritting his teeth, he grasped Kendra's arms, carefully shuffled her off him, and stood to his feet. He swayed at first but found his balance quickly. His and Intico's gazes met, and their conflicting ambitions once again clashed. The insurmountable pressure returned, but despite its cumbersome presence, Eden knew he had but this one remaining chance to hold true to the vow that had been tested and compromised one too many times. As long as he could draw breath, there was only one outcome he could accept. With such a conviction, he withdrew Avenger from its sheath.

As Kendra watched Intico, her blood ran cold, the chilling memory of its presence within her evoking a ghost within her. The true test of her desire brewed, the ultimate memory of Kendall's words bubbling as she met those gaping eyes once again. With shallow breaths, she braved Intico's transcendent approach.

"I told you that next time would be different. It's time for me to hold true to my word," Eden assured Kendra, positioning Avenger in front of himself.

"Finally, we are in agreement, Blackwell," Intico said.

Thus, their dance was resurrected. A battle a fatigued and injured Eden could not contend with for long. Through their attrition, Eden displayed the resilience Intico had come to adore, reminding it of its underlying desire to make such a constitution its own.

The air cackled with their collisions, assailing the surrounding environment with ferocious blasts from their respective attacks. The impetus of pain within Eden manifested within his slowed movements, flinching and relenting. His strength's ceiling had descended significantly, whereas Intico, with little regard left for the stability of Harvest, conjured all of its remaining power for their final battle. A power Kendra had briefly been acquainted with in all of its repugnance. The imprisoned souls, the product of the covenant's ruse, resided within Intico and fueled its formidable prowess.

Though Eden had valiantly staved off Intico for a short while, he had met his match quickly. Grabbing Eden once more, Intico hurled him into a building. The shattered glass loudly echoed throughout the desolate block, and Eden tumbled hard into the lobby of the building until he hit the counter. With the assaults on his fresh shoulder wounds, he sucked in air harshly, grunting loudly as he gathered himself and shakily stood once more.

Before he could cobble a reaction, a tendril of shadow from outside snatched Eden by the neck, yanking him from the building and into Intico's grasp.

Eyeing Eden warily, the somnium lord appeared to frown before tossing Eden into another building's stone walls.

"Fear ... more fear," Intico muttered, glancing away from Eden momentarily, briefly leering at Kendra. Seeing her remain on the ground, it turned its attention back to Eden and waltzed over to him. "I am all for bread and circuses, Blackwell, but I grow weary of this quandary. Cease your resistance."

"No," Eden muttered, clenching the pavement as he peered up at Intico, his crimson glare remaining resolute despite the pain coursing through him.

"You will submit. We will be one." Intico spoke with reverberating audacity as it drew near him. The dark of night became more prominent, a quaking perturbing the air as Intico's eyes grew and its mouth stretched wide. *"I will break you!"* it screeched, reality shuddering with its deafening energy.

Kendra's fingers dug into the ground beneath her. Beyond witnessing Eden's desperate defense, she noticed the Ichor surrounding them. The omens were scarce—signifying the life that was snuffed from the city.

Though faint, howls were carried by the wind, only detectable by her sensitive ears. The pain of the city's denizens resonated through her head, mirroring the pained cries she had heard when joined with Intico. So many were subject to the fate she had experienced firsthand—a cruelty beyond permissibility.

She shut her eyes tightly, unable to ignore the howls any longer. The vestiges of their cries and suffering illuminated a reality she couldn't allow to manifest. Should Intico have its way, the ambition it sought would know no bounds for humanity's will. A cruel thesis—a story she could change.

Kendra stood to her feet, burning eyes opening once more. No longer bound by fear, she accepted the urgency it birthed; it kindled her renewed agency. Fear, and all that it entailed, would no longer serve as shackles.

An inferno swelled within Kendra's chest as she sucked in a deep breath. The darkness encapsulating her soul, present within her eyes, ignited with a scorching blaze, ripe with embers that spilled from her. Her feverish skin emitted intense heat, and her fists unclenched, her claws extending. Through her sharpened teeth, a ferocious aura burst forth from her.

"Intico!" Kendra called out.

The chill of the night was challenged by the sweltering heat that came from Kendra, and Intico turned its attention back to her, looking over its shoulder.

Hotter, Kendra thought. She needed to conjure a flame capable of challenging Intico. Her heart drummed in her chest, blood racing through her veins and energizing her limbs. A streak of red crossed her vision before the surge of flames bursting from her took on a scarlet hue, incinerating the surrounding air. What she had coalesced was a spark that could burn the fate Intico had crafted for them.

Once unconcerned, Intico stared with bewilderment, turning to face her as she rallied her strength and courage. While her power was of note, no such concern emanated from Intico at this critical juncture. The heat was no different to it than any she had conjured before, and such flames were of no threat to it.

However, the imposition Kendra had summoned from deep within was not lost upon Eden. The scarlet hued flames were infamous among the more knowledgeable in their world. Intico, while briefly merged with him, had not gleaned this knowledge to foresee the danger that it faced. *Chaos flames.* Familiar, conjuring a forlorn memory, Eden welcomed it within his astoundment, and the once dreary city, bathed in darkness and perversion, was introduced to the bright flicker of paradoxical hope—Kendra.

Eden dragged himself to a kneeling position. His vision was hazy but still capable of scrutinizing the power that challenged their foe. Chaos flames were possessed with an infernal instillment of wrath: a pure, revered power found sequestered within Inferos. No shield or barrier could withstand their wrath, similar to the eye of Semita. Only—this power was more elusive. Despite its deep roots in the depths of the cardinal sin of wrath, it had not been those exhibiting or embodying such a sin that inherited it. Eden had only known one such woman who inherited the power, and at least to him, she had been far from a purveyor of wrath.

Kendra lowered herself to the ground, building power in her legs. The flames surged to a concentration in her palms before streaking down to her fingertips, coating her claws. As inexperienced and rough as her control over even her original power was, her imagination guided its development, a rough culmination of both her practice and her instincts. Akin to directing the current of a river, her flames coursed across her skin, following where she concentrated.

With black claws streaking bright red, she lunged. With fear conquered, flames to scorn, she swiped.

Intico raised its arm, preparing to endure Kendra's flames as it had before. Furthermore, as if to suggest its certainty, its impossible grin stretched across its face once more as their gazes reunified. Reflected within the abysmal void, that same scarlet spark within Kendra flickered, and once again, Intico prepared to cast it back into the abyss of fear.

Kendra growled out with the same intensity that the fire in her hands burned. Her claws sundered the chitinous black skin. Once serving as an impenetrable barrier, the flesh was easily shredded by her burning power, and the flames stretched across the severed limb, burning it to nothing.

Kendra's eyes traced back to Intico, cautiously eyeing the once transcendent entity as it stared with wide eyes at the stump.

A strained expression marred Intico's face. Grunts emanated from it as the stump smoked, but no tendrils emerged to repair what was burned away. It wasn't regenerating, prompting Intico's smile to twist into a perplexed sneer.

Kendra's glaring radiance showed no signs of dying, invigorated and riotous. Her teeth bared, fangs grinding against each other as she inhaled the warm air. She lunged once more, levying the same attack as before. Meeting Intico's eyes, she saw no glimmer of the same disregard it had shown before. It was vulnerable.

The tension in Intico's fingers released a revolting crackle, and the wind swarmed around it. Cape flapping, Intico dissolved. Having narrowly avoided Kendra's attack, it became intangible, forming into a circular shadow on the ground. That shadow zipped around Kendra, bouncing from object to object to avoid being tracked by her keen senses.

Repeatedly, Kendra whipped her head around, her eyes following it for only the first few moments. Tricky and erratic, it shot from corner to corner, then burst into black mist, shrouding the area in its immutable presence. The familiar scent of miasma wafted around Kendra, and she held her breath. Suffocating silence.

Intico shifted around her, but she couldn't track it fluidly. Without the requisite training or attunement Eden possessed, such a move was especially effective on her. A precise attack would likely miss and leave her vulnerable to its counterassault. Though her flames burned formidably, Intico could still easily snuff their remaining hope if she was reckless.

Coming to a decision, Kendra realized that precision was impossible, and albeit untested, something more broad and encompassing was her only solution. *In my chest,* she thought. And the heat surged within her core. Burning hot, it crawled outward, and she lowered her head. The pressure building inside of her bubbled until she could no longer contain it. With a yell, she unleashed a swarm of chaos flames around her, consuming the darkness, miasma, and any shadows that had maintained physical form around her.

Despite the mist being expelled, the wind still howled around them. Something stirred beneath Kendra's feet, causing her to stumble back. Intico's spindly, clawed digits shot up from her shadow, narrowly missing her. Despite her shaky footing, she aimed to swipe at Intico's arm, but instead, a tendril latched to her shins, tripping her. She tumbled to the ground. But before she could take a deep breath to prepare another burst of flames, the crushing weight of Intico's talon-like feet dug against her chest. The impact and subsequent pressure siphoned any breath she had in her body, but she still flailed her arms beneath the tight binding of Intico's foot. Choking gasps carried profanity from her lips, her burning glare staring up at Intico.

"It's a shame you are no longer a suitable vessel ..." Intico hissed, its talons digging harder, cracking the concrete as it crushed Kendra slowly. With its penetrating leer, it drew its one remaining arm back, the sharp digits poised as it prepared to impale her. Even with her regeneration, the expected damage would be too much to heal from. "Au revoir," it hissed at her.

She would die.

With explosive force, Eden's boots smashed into Intico's head, prying it from atop Kendra and sending it skittering down the road. The presumption of Eden's fatigue had echoed through both him and Intico, but that presumption, too, was arbitrary in the burning tenacity reignited within Eden. Seeing Kendra's final stand, seeing not her desperation, but her conviction that overcame all that had challenged it, was something Eden had to answer in kind. Even if he would suffer the consequences of his overexertion after this, there was no reservation to forgo.

Kendra stared at the sky above her, gasping deeply as oxygen rushed back into her lungs. When she saw the once condemning crimson eyes meet her own, she didn't see vitriol or despondency, but a faith rekindled, and an indisputable recognition of her.

"Come on," Eden said, his breathing labored and erratic. His skin burned and red sparks coursed across his form, causing his strained muscles to convulse further—a pain he would persevere for more than his sake. Bearing the consequences of their shared ambition, he offered Kendra his hand.

Kendra promptly took it, and he hoisted her to her feet before turning to face Intico. Trepidation was gleaned from the fiend waiting in the distance, a reluctance to lunge at them. Recognizing its hesitation, Eden knew it, too, had come to the same realization. Alone, they would perish by the voracity before them. Together, they would become the sunrise to vanquish the insidious night.

"What's the plan?" Kendra asked, turning her attention back to Intico, her claws held at her side, ready to lunge despite the ache resonating in her chest.

"I'll take point. Stay on me as I make openings for you to get close. It can't regenerate from those flames. Burn it with them."

"Roger."

"Let's go."

Eden took the initiative to rush toward Intico, shifting the angle of Avenger. Kendra, close behind, branched off, taking a blitz approach akin to coordinating in a soccer match. Intico grabbed its hat and flicked its wrist, the article transforming into its shadowy staff. Twisting the weapon in its grasp, it deflected Eden's incoming assault before turning to Kendra, who, upon noticing its persisting attention on her, kept low on its armless side and slid behind it. Forced to keep an eye on Kendra especially, it leaped away from them to acquire distance. Eden, however, didn't relent for a second, immediately taking after it, Kendra in tow.

Albeit imprecise, their combined assault kept Intico on the defensive. If Eden lunged in, Kendra retreated back and waited until it was opportune to strike. If Kendra closed the distance, Eden retreated to give her space to attack without concern. Much to Intico's displeasure, it found itself encumbered by their efforts.

At various points, Intico sought to retreat to the umbrage of the shadows, to become impermeable and escape their assault. But Kendra had blasted flames from her mouth, causing the shadows to retreat, denying it refuge within them. If Intico tried to attack Kendra, Eden was there to repel it back. It dared not tear its focus from Kendra, however. With an odd harmony, neither of them allowed Intico to prosper in its sly tactics.

Intico conjured a dark power within its arm, a hazy energy shrouding its staff as it slammed it down at Eden. In those precious that stretched in his mind, Eden drew Avenger back, visualizing the attack that neared him. With Avenger glimmering red, he swatted the staff, parrying it much as he had the bomb Intico had threatened the hunters at the Chicago base with. The staff repelled back, and Intico was wide open for a few integral moments, of which Kendra charged in for. Her burning claws tore into Intico's face, shrouding the left side in her flames and leaving a gaping hole in its hollow head.

Intico recoiled back, white particles spilling from the open wound and scattering its glittering essence to the ground as the chaos flames burned it. Its imposing energy diminished immensely, a significant portion of its power depleting from the damage it had incurred.

Now, Eden thought. Rushing forward, he slashed at Intico.

A loud pop resonated throughout the city, the shockwave cracking the surrounding windows of the buildings and cars. A brief struggle occurred between Avenger and Intico's staff, but as Eden built up the power in his arms and legs, the shadowy staff gave way to the pressure. As it snapped in two, Avenger ripped past its resistance and collided with Intico's abdomen and tore into it.

Intico let out a hiss as more of its energy spilled out. Kendra's attack may have been permanent, but the damage Eden inflicted could still heal, provided the blow wasn't a fatal one it didn't have enough energy to regenerate from. Retreating back, energy dripped from its form, coating the ground in what appeared to be a random assortment.

The two lunged at Intico, spirits high in their rebellion against its will. Then a snap sounded in the dark. Tendrils of shadow constricted Kendra and Eden's ankles from either side, anchoring their feet to the ground. They both internally cursed, and Kendra sought to focus her flames to burn through them. However, before she could do so, Intico lashed its hand out, more tendrils of shadow whipping through the air and grappling their wrists. With a swift yank, they were pulled to the ground, the other end of the tendrils held by Intico.

Intico jammed its digits into the ground, pinning the other end of the tendrils as its feet anchored into the pavement. Its remaining eye and flickering mouth enlarged, wriggling black skin peeling back. A dark voice hummed around them as the surrounding omens rushed toward Intico. As if swallowing them, it sucked in an endless breath and a white, luminescent orb formed in front of its mouth. Growing larger with each passing moment, it coalesced into incredible power.

Eden knew what was coming, and no matter how he struggled, as long as Intico remained anchored to the ground, he couldn't escape the bindings. He was still too fatigued to gather enough strength to break free, but Kendra was more than capable of erasing the bindings shackling her.

Kendra could burn away the bindings. However, there was the question of Eden. The energy Intico gathered was tremendous, and its gravity weighed down on both of them. If Eden was incapacitated, she stood no chance by herself.

But Kendra saw the silver lining to the tumultuous predicament—an irrevocable advantage. Intico stood still, an opportunity that she wouldn't squander, but the matter of *how* she would do it remained.

"Get out of the way, Kendra!" Eden called to her.

Her mind went blank, her creativity flourishing as she imagined how she could channel her flames into something far-reaching, capable of incinerating the somnium lord seeking to subjugate them. Her memories flashed through her head, and she remembered the moments right before the words Kendall had reminded her of.

You're chock-full of inhibitions that you need to let out.

Kendra's wrists raised, and her claws dug into the ground, mirroring Intico's position. She braced herself as best as possible, arching her back and tensing her leg. With her breath itself capable of scorning, she knew what she would do.

"I've got this!" Kendra called out. She eyed Intico, seeing its flaying, corporeal form flickering with instability. The words Intico had spoken to her overlapped with Kendall's instructions.

Inhale.

Focusing the heat within her body, she called it to her chest, where it stirred and welled. Tension built, and a radiant glow emanated from her chest to the rest of her body, turning her skin a hellish, glittering red. The omens surged around her as well, as if responding to the need she conjured.

Chaos flames spilled from the corners of Kendra's mouth. But even then, she didn't release. It wasn't ready. It became almost too hot for her to hold the bursting flames within her, but she held her breath despite her body screaming for reprieve.

The incredible pressure created by the building energies caused Eden to flinch. With a comparable force pulsing from both of them, Eden anticipated the final clash approaching, of which he hadn't resigned himself to either of the two outcomes. His eyes returned to Intico, seeing the mass of energy now enlarged. *It's ready*, he thought. *She's ready.*

The familiar screech from Intico's energy reached Eden's ears, and he turned to Kendra.

"Now!"

Kendra's eyes focused once more on the void of white staring back at her, and within its recesses, she saw a faint glimmer of blue. *Kendall.*

The white was soon eclipsed by darkness, and Intico's bomb shredded the earth beneath.

Release!

Pure fury coursed through Kendra's veins, and every hair on her body stood as fire-kissed bristles. The infernal energy she had conjured in her throat merged with her breath and imagination. *Consume all before you,* she commanded the flames. *Change our story.* Her mouth opened as wide as possible, and the incredible tension in her body burst forth in a long, scorching wave.

The darkness was assailed by flurries of scarlet red, and the cold was condemned to oblivion. In an instant, the bomb of malice that promised to engulf all that stood before it, to launch them into the despair of a soul-shredding nightmare beyond permissibility, was consumed.

Time stood still for the somnium lord. A tenacity drove its persistence as it saw its ambitions consumed by wrath. *No.* By hope. Intico's fingers and talons tore from the ground, and it jumped, escaping the path of the flames.

Kendra had poured everything she had to offer into her retaliation against Intico, locked in place as she unleashed all the pressure from her body. There would be nothing left in her once the wave of chaos flames had left.

A vain effort.

But the sentiment that had challenged Intico's had not been lost. Eden was a patient hunter, cunning and opportunistic. The various energies that paraded had provided the perfect distraction and camouflage. He focused on every shift and change in his environment, and his bindings relented in the moment Intico fled from its approaching oblivion. He used the last of his strength to tear free from them and unleash one last attack against Intico.

Intico hadn't seen Eden rush at him. In a burst of speed that stretched beyond Eden's limits, he jumped in the air and kicked Intico back into the chaos flames waiting below. Quickly pivoting, he twisted his body and shot the anchor of his maneuver bracer into a nearby building, pulling himself out of the way. He crashed hard against the building and slid down with a hard landing.

When Intico slammed into the ground with a harsh crack, the flames swallowed it. Nothing akin to pain had perturbed the somnium lord in its final moments, but even so, its hiss permeated the entire city as it was engulfed. Melding into the roar of Kendra's chaos flames, it went silent within the blaze. Intico became nothing more than a silhouette within the scarlet light, dissipating throughout the power Kendra had conjured to defeat it. Numbness swallowed it in the overwhelming heat of the flames. In a whispered scream, its voice projected from around Kendra and Eden, melding into the roar of Kendra's chaos flames. Soon, nothing of it remained.

The ground and infrastructure that were scorched by the flames were black and crystalized, having been melted or atomized by the intense power. The flames, with no more energy to fuel them, faded as quickly as they had come, leaving only embers and smoke in their wake.

Kendra gasped, sucking in a deep breath of reprieve. She trembled, smoke emitting from her skin, still red from the heat it had been subjected to. A low rumble lingered in her ears as she slowly whipped her head around, searching for Intico as if it would reemerge, but it was nowhere to be found, and the shadows remained still. At long last, the nightmare was over.

Kendra's gaze landed on Eden with a dazed expression. Her vision wavered, and hardly anything had come back into focus. She stumbled to her feet. The remnants of her glasses fell from her face and shattered on the pavement below. They had melted and become brittle in the intense blaze she had conjured. Smoke pervaded her entire form, and the fabric of her clothes had frayed and darkened. Thankfully, they remained intact. Sapped beyond anything she'd experienced, even the most brutal of soccer practices, a brisk breeze brushed past her, carrying her disheveled braid with it. Free from the pressures, liberated from the assailing dangers, she became almost weightless.

The quietude of the city was surreal. For once in Kendra's entire life, the city was truly asleep. Her absorption of the moment was soon interrupted by what felt like tiny droplets of water kissing her skin. *Rain,* she thought. But when she peered at the sky, there was no rain or clouds. The sky that had been cloaked in darkness and malevolent energy became a dull blue. Hardly a view befitting her efforts.

The omens that had been sparse appeared in a twinkling resolution, flooding the once barren sky. She hadn't always experienced them as vividly as she did now, as if their absence had invoked a sensitivity to their return. Their scarcity, which Harvest had invoked, was no more.

Harvest was over. Both Eden and Kendra could hear the omens sing a sweet symphony, faintly resembling wind chimes, and the hiss that had lingered in the air had died along with Intico.

The omens fluttered around the entire city, glimmering and bathing it in their cyan glow. Citizens littering the streets gently stirred, the miasma that had spurred and sustained their slumber disappearing.

Kendra closed her eyes, basking in the fresh air and omens song, but a faint whisper called to her, rousing her from her thoughts. When she opened her eyes, they had become their normal royal blue again, her demonic features receding, and the familiar light, playful voice called again.

"Ken," a light voice whispered.

Kendra's eyes widened. *This voice ...* She whipped her head around, desperately searching for the source.

The omens gathered around Kendra, a pale-blue light enveloping her.

"Ken." No longer a whisper, the undeniable voice of Kendall called.

When Kendra glanced behind her, she was greeted by a dazzling light encompassing a glowing orb, the soul inside Intico she had convened with. Kendall's soul. When the omens cleared, the visage of her sister, translucent and immaterial, stood before her. It was exactly as she remembered her the most: with a radiant smile stretching ear to ear.

"Kenny ..." Kendra croaked, her voice hoarse. She hadn't realized her throat and mouth had been so dry until she spoke.

"What did I tell you about doubting me? Look at us," Kendall began, gesturing to the omens permeating the city. "We're free because of you."

Kendra's eyes welled with tears, a tightness building in her chest as she choked back sobs. She had relived that nightmare many times, seen Kendall torn and maimed more times than she could count. Now, she got to see her little sister whole, at peace once again.

Kendall frowned.

"Don't go crying on me now, Sis. I know ... I won't be here with you anymore, but we get to have this moment—this last goodbye. Let my final memory of you be something less dreary, k?"

"No, Kenny! I need you still. I want you to stay. Please," Kendra choked out.

However, Kendall maintained her serene smile, despite the sorrow present. Slowly, she faded before Kendra's eyes.

"I can't, Ken. I'm tired, and *Mother* is calling. Tell Mom and Dad I love them a million." She exhaled shakily, her form shimmering as it flashed in and out of existence. "Please ... one last smile from my brave big sister?"

As best as Kendra could, without hesitation, she grinned as wide as she could; the tears spilling down her cheek provided a paradoxical display. In return, Kendall mirrored the grin, but no such tears marred her ethereal visage.

Then she fell back, floating to the ground slowly as her specter flickered.

Kendra lunged and grasped at the apparition, and to her surprise, it was heavy, as if she was real. As the light faded, warmth manifested in her arms, and the soft body weighed her down. She dropped to her knees, her eyes resting on Kendall's form.

Hope blossomed in Kendra's chest, and she leaned down, pressing her ear to Kendall's chest. But there was no heartbeat. Such an impossibility perturbed Kendra, defying the logic she had known. Unblemished and clean, but lifeless. It was like Kendall was sleeping. The fact that her body was in her arms was unfathomable, but the questions never emerged in the face of her sweltering sorrow. Grief reignited anew.

She had known Kendall almost her entire life. When their mother first brought her home from the hospital, the foggy memory of peering down at her little sister remained. Kendall's first words had been Kendra's nickname—Ken—the reason why she preferred that name. The countless nights they slept together after getting scared from telling ghost stories. Playing together. And as she stared down at Kendall, she saw those memories burn away with a bittersweetness lingering in their final goodbye.

Kendra could no longer sustain her composure, and tears flowed heavily from her eyes down her warm cheeks. With no more Covenant of Augury, no more somnium, and no more Intico, she finally had a chance to *feel*.

Eden's eyes fluttered open. He had slipped away briefly and hadn't seen the apparition or heard the last conversation Kendra had with her sister. When the omens had finally dispersed from around Kendra, he saw her holding Kendall's body. He, too, had seen the fate that befell the unfortunate girl, but he understood the baffling phenomenon: a blessing from Ichor. *An invaluable token of her love.*

They had liberated the city from Harvest and, subsequently, the torment it wrought upon all of Ichor. Such blessings were granted to those who earned her adoration. As rare an occurrence as it was, he held no doubt that was the case. Kendra had endured such torment for long enough, and Eden deeply respected her resilience. Be it a human or demon quality, it was Kendra's.

They both deserved a much-needed rest now. For Eden, everything hurt, and he could barely keep his eyes open. Despite this, he fought to remain awake as emergent energies manifested throughout the city, many of which were familiar. The Hunters had finally arrived.

Eden slowly raised his wrist to his face, tapping the interface to bring up the holographic screen. He navigated to the panic button and pressed it. Promptly, he went limp, resting his face against the unwelcoming, rigid surface of the building. His typically crimson eyes had faded to jade green again, signifying his depletion. In the next moment, he was asleep.

In such a world filled with dastardly creatures, humanity found itself prey to the whims of nefarious forces—those who dwelled in darkness: the subjects of sin and its purveyors. Within the deepest recesses of their hearts, they were ignorant of how truly thin the veneer of peace truly was—how fragile their sentiments and *humanity* were. Be it humans or demons that threatened the sanctity of their lives, they couldn't comprehend the horrors that lurked. Despite this grim truth, the bleak odds they faced against the instruments of evil were not insurmountable.

For that night, it was not humanity that had prevailed, but the testaments of overcoming such darkness in spite of their aversion to it. This darkness would forever persist beyond the demons, and the seeds of sin could find their genesis within all who were touched by Ichor. Even when plunged into darkness, finding oneself was beyond obligatory, despite the absence of *humanity.*

Kendra had, and many more were to follow.

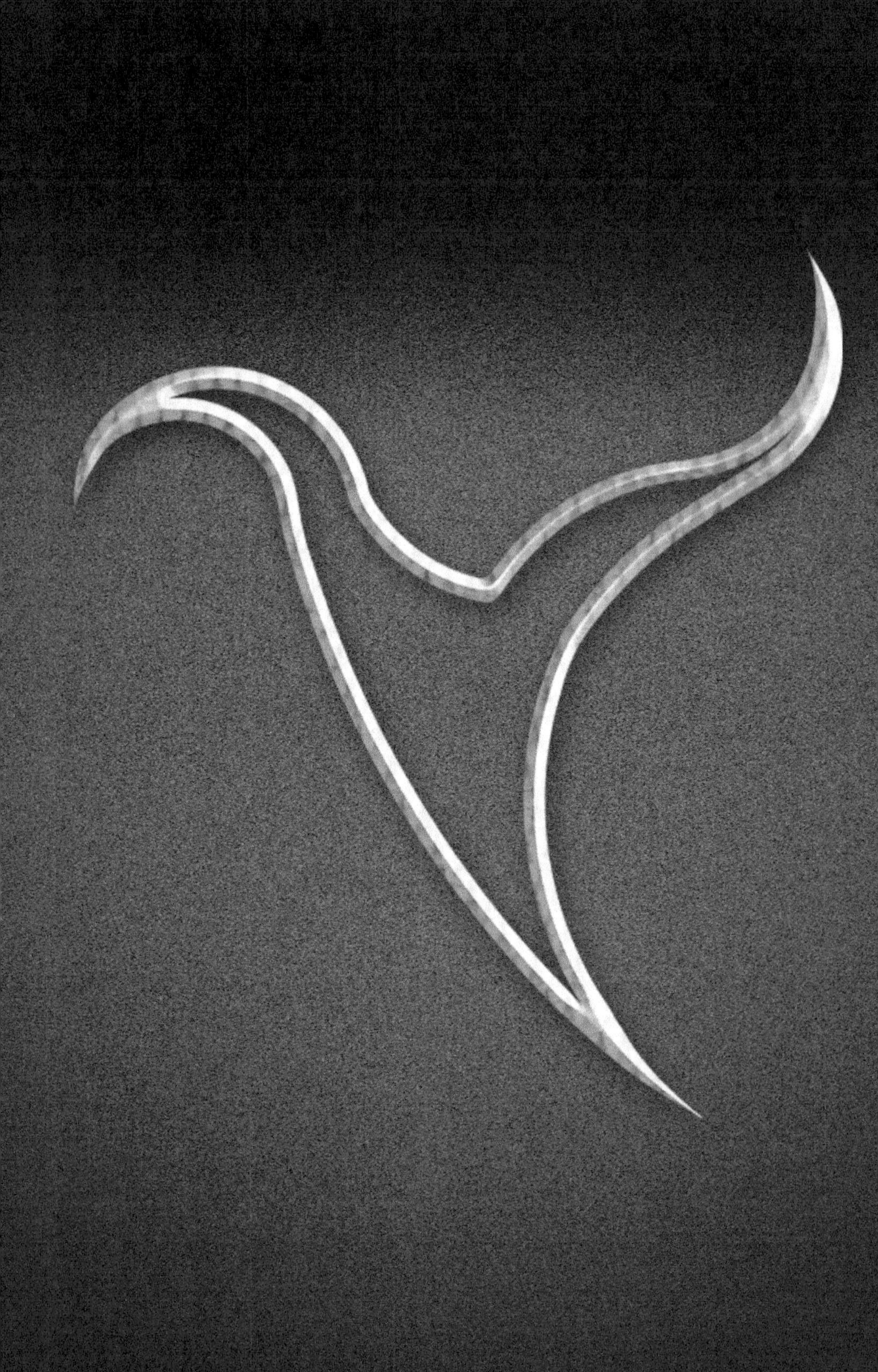

SIXTEEN

SERENITY IN GENESIS

The hum of helicopters permeated the city as several of the birds descended. The cityscape was sparsely lit, many of the lampposts and other sources of light compromised, save for the shimmering parade of omens. Given the uncertainty of their intel, they navigated the city carefully, and several hunters dispersed to the various evacuation sites and emergency signals from their comrades that had been stationed in the city.

Containment came first, and the borders of the city were locked down by the Hunters and National Guard alike. The entire city and the minor regions beyond it had been encompassed by Harvest's strange distortion. It had effectively blocked any signal to and from the outside world, which had further confounded and delayed the Hunters' arrival. With teleportation through Ichor hindered by the distortion, they were forced to utilize military infrastructure in Wisconsin to respond to Harvest—a process that had taken several hours after Jessica's discovery.

A helicopter descended on a desolate street that was littered with debris. The environment had seen battle, as evidenced by the cracked glass, scorched ground, and damaged buildings. Jessica pensively scanned the environment, tracking Eden and Kendra's faint energy signature. She leaped from the helicopter when she spotted them, her rapid fall suddenly disrupted by a burst of energy that flowed beneath her feet, cushioning her landing. Immediately, she rushed over and inspected the two carefully, seeing that only Kendra was conscious.

"Are you okay, Kendra?" Jessica inquired.

Carefully lifting her head, Kendra tensed a bit, holding Kendall's form close as she met Jessica's gaze. It was the first time she had seen the woman without a hat obscuring her features, and she couldn't help but further notice the strong resemblance she and Eden harbored. With a tepid nod, she gestured her head to Eden.

"He needs aid. I'll be okay …" Kendra whispered hoarsely, her voice no longer able to project.

Jessica eyed Kendra for a few moments, seeing the young girl in her arms—something that confused her until she remembered Eden's report from Kendra's attack. Shaking the thought from her head, she gave a rueful smile and rushed to Eden's side.

Seeing Eden's blood-saturated form covered in several wounds, she gasped, pulling him close and pressing her ear to his chest. Feeling his pulsing heart, she let out a shaky breath, holding him close to her as she stifled a sob. Fear had assailed her nerves since the revelation, and she had dreaded what she would find.

A heavy, emotional curtain opened within her, and she let out a soft sob as she embraced Eden tightly. Whispering her gratitude to the deities that would listen, she gently removed a light-blue crystal from her pocket. An easing aura flowed from it, washing over Eden's body and slowly alleviating his form of the worst of the injuries.

Shortly after, the helicopter landed in the empty stretch of nearby parking lot, and Ethan, along with several hunters, exited. They examined the scene vigilantly—seeking any additional threats that may have remained.

Confirming the safety of the environment, Ethan approached the scene where Kendra and Eden had defeated Intico, and a listless expression formed. He clenched his fists tightly, turning his attention to Kendra. He could tell she wasn't ready for an interview. As desperately as the Hunters would want explanations, he wasn't so crass as to pry into her earned respite, especially upon seeing Kendall's body in her arms. Briefly, an envious twinkle emerged in his eyes, and he turned to face Jessica and

Eden, approaching the two only after he scrubbed such irrelevant thoughts from his mind. There was too much work to do.

A sundry of conditions had assailed the citizens. Some were spared the worst and successfully evacuated or hid. Many had joined the sprawl of slumbering vessels subject to the somnium's selection. Of those that hadn't been merged with, they awoke sore and groggy, subject to examination later by the emergency workers that were dispatched alongside the arriving hunters. What was particularly pervasive were the traumas and confusion held among the population. This, too, would be addressed in the aftermath.

Spreading throughout the city, they gathered many of the citizens, or their corpses. Hospitals were soon flooded by the population, many reporting chronic fatigue, concussions, and other minor injuries.

The most adversely affected were the disentangled citizens the somnium had merged with. While many had been killed in defense by police and hunters, there were more who had been found in a catatonic state, still alive. Of their most ubiquitous symptoms, they broke into bouts of screaming and despaired babbling. Ultimately, these individuals were admitted to long-term care in psychiatric institutions, pending documentation and treatment.

Another part of the aftermath that remained to be solved was the widespread shock of an entire city having been connected to Ichor. Such a phenomenon, while containable in condensed occurrences, was a problem that warranted a strict lockdown of the city. For several days, the vast majority were methodically disconnected, condemning the cohesion of their memories to a fabrication of the truth, pending government statements on the event.

As for Kendra, she was eventually interviewed vigorously to acquire her knowledge of those involved from her perspective. Many of the umbra demons had taken their opportunity to escape at certain points, but some had been captured before the night had ended. Of the most notorious, at least, Oliver and Allen were in the Hunters' custody. In the ensuing interrogation, Oliver was less than cooperative, but Allen divulged much of the inner machinations of the scheme, at least that of which he was knowledgeable.

The ensuing containment and contingency operations required the Hunters, National Guard, and the semblance of law enforcement that still functioned. Darrel had left a tumultuous state of uncertainty within the Chicago Police Department. In the wake of his treachery, many were cross-examined to root out any potential sympathies and cohorts of his and the Covenant of Augury's scheme.

Pertaining to said investigation, in the following month, Eden and Zane elected to visit Julian Stroth on behalf of the Hunters. That afternoon, they sat across from the detective they had grown familiar with. Confined to Julian's office, they reviewed the various documents pertaining to the incident. As they spoke over the preliminary reports, it was not lost on either of the hunters how involved Julian had been in the investigation leading up to their own, and there were many questions left unanswered. With an unresolved curiosity held by the three, they discussed the details leading to their proposal.

"*Exsomnis*, huh? So that's what they're going with? Sounds like a corny cartoon villain's organization," Julian said as he scanned the document in front of him. The official narrative had deemed the group responsible as a terrorist organization that had been apprehended pending further investigation. The organization, Exsomnis, was a drafted scapegoat to stand in where the truth could not.

"What's funny is that I told them *almost* the same thing, and they went with it anyway," Zane spoke, smirking as he picked at his collar. Both he and Eden wore black suits, much to Zane's dismay. "Guess great minds do think alike. Right, detective?" Zane questioned, earning a nudge from Eden.

"Can't really say my mind is all that great. Right under my nose, that rat Darrel pilfered whatever integrity this department had and offered it right to the Devil. He was my friend for years, and you'd think I'd have known the guy ... but guess not. Still don't understand any of this shit," Julian complained. He rested his elbows on the desk, joined his hands together, and placed the lower half of his face behind them. "What *really* happened that day Darrel kicked you guys from the crime scene?"

"Well, just in my brief look at things, a rime, maybe, left us a gift to assist our investigation. If not for their interference, I'm guessing we wouldn't have even known, and Darrel would have been installed as the acting chief. I'm sure you can extrapolate what would have followed."

"The hell's a rime?"

"Ice demon," Eden answered, sighing as he drummed his fingers on the desk. "Pretty sure most, if not all, of them got wiped out centuries ago. Guess it wasn't all of them ..."

Julian shrugged, thinking about how farfetched the supernatural world's existence appeared—especially with technology everywhere.

"Isn't *Organization X* at all concerned about the truth of all of this coming out? Cameras exist everywhere in this city. Several must have picked some of these things up."

Eden shook his head.

"Regardless of what they called the group, it's not like you're going to find any tangible evidence anywhere to refute it. Normal recording devices can't pick up these things, otherwise, everybody would have known about demons several decades ago," Eden mentioned, tapping his finger on the desk as he idly glanced at Zane. "Anybody who could cohesively corroborate events has already been disconnected."

Julian gave a wry smile, shoving the papers to the side before adjusting his glasses. His visage showed discontent with the brewing allegation he was about to levy.

"Speaking of which—I'm next on the chopping block, huh?"

"If you were, we wouldn't be speaking," Zane answered, straightening his tie before clearing his throat. "In recognition of your assistance during the initial investigations, your meticulous documentation, and continued salience in the aftermath, we're offering you the opportunity to keep your memories intact—on the condition you join the organization. We could use a keen-eyed detective to help sort through the supernatural phenomena around the country." Their gazes met, and, mirroring Julian, Zane propped his elbows on the desk and rested his chin atop his clasped fingers.

"Where's the *but*?" Julian questioned, cocking his brow.

Zane snickered.

"You'll be under a permanent NDA, but other than that, you'll have plenty of resources and responsibilities as an investigator."

There was a pause, the two hunters locked in its hold as Julian pondered the offer given.

"I think I'm good right here, honestly. Don't know if I'm quite ready to leave Chicago. Lots left to tie up, and no firm foundation to commit. Can't imagine any of that is what you guys would want."

Zane sat up, shrugging his shoulders.

"Who said anything about leaving yet? It's hard finding people for this stuff, let alone capable people. Think of yourself as ... an informant until you're called on for your expertise. Only thing you'll have to do until then is study up on the curriculum and do what you do best. You won't even have to quit your job at the Chicago PD yet," Zane explained.

"Think of it ... as a link to your current life. Seeing as you won't be in a combat role, it's not necessary for you to live anywhere else or even maintain a training regimen. Just make yourself an expert we can rely upon. Only catch is you have to make a decision now, or you'll be disconnected," Eden further explained.

"All pressure," Zane quipped.

In the ensuing moments, Julian pursed his lips and thought in the following silence. He glanced at the portrait left on his desk, a picture of him and his colleagues together—including Darrel. Prior to his promotion, Julian had remembered the several conversations he had with Darrel. He always found the man brooding, but he was always punctual. Sometimes—he was even kind. Aware of such nefariousness, to know that they had all meant nothing to him was downright condemnable. The friends he lost to Darrel's plans—he wished to retain their memory with the truth.

"That sounds like a much better deal. Get a contract in front of me, and if the fine print is as you described, I'm in," Julian finally replied.

Zane nodded, and he and Eden stood from their seats.

"Smart man. Devils are in the details, especially in our line of work. Always best to read the contract, anyway. You ex-military by chance?" Zane questioned.

"My ex-girlfriend was a lawyer. It was … a glimmer of good that was left after that relationship."

"Amen to that," Zane sighed, flexing his brows before nodding at Eden.

"Quick question," Julian began, prompting the two hunters to return their attention to the fastidious detective. "This family of demons Darrel worked with … it's my understanding they were suspects of yours at first, but what prompted you guys to pull the trigger on a raid? Even our warrants aren't that quick to come."

Eden and Zane exchanged pensive glances, and Eden shrugged before gesturing his head toward Zane.

"Ah, well. They made the mistake of abducting a girl who we had already determined to be a target of the covenant. We caught her geo-pin at their mansion, and we had all the evidence we needed from that point on."

"Kat's daughter, right? Kendra?" Julian asked, earning a nod from Zane.

"As for the whole quick raid thing, our organization is aware of most of the demons that have integrated into human society. As dubious as it sounds and is, it's a measure our government takes to ensure that any supernatural conspiracies have a clearer paper trail to follow. Also, it ensures demons don't go trying to supplant human authority, as has been known to happen in several countries. Bit of an oversimplification, but you should get the gist. Given the imperative of managing demonic threats, the Hunters have extra leeway to deal with these things as efficiently as possible. Call it a … benefit of the job. Not exactly like we can take these matters to a normal court."

Julian sighed, sitting up and slapping his palms on his desk.

"The hell am I getting myself into?"

"Nothing harder than the hell you've already witnessed," Eden said, folding his arms. "Honestly ... if not for Kendra, things would have ended badly. We all owe her."

"That so? Someday, you'll have to tell that to Kat," Julian said. There was trepidation that followed; he frowned as he glanced at the picture on his desk one last time before he shut his eyes. "You guys don't seem the ... inattentive sort. You insinuated things like this have happened before, so why was the response so slow? This Harvest scheme lasted for several hours. Something more than a communications blackout had to have gone wrong ..." Julian pontificated, opening his eyes to stare at the two hunters.

Eden remained silent, averting his gaze while Zane scratched his chin, peering at the ceiling as he thought for several moments.

"I wonder about that ... but that's a story for another day. I'm still pretty exhausted from that last bout with Darrel. This is hungry work." Zane patted his stomach, his eyes lighting up with something he recalled. "Oh, speaking of which, can you point me to a good taco joint? I still haven't had a chance to really check one out since I got to this city." Zane grinned, pushing the seed of a hypothesis to the back of his mind.

Julian studied Zane with confusion before glancing at Eden, who flexed his brows in response.

"Two blocks from here. A place called Gonzalez's Taqueria. Can't go wrong with the birria, but they have pretty good vegan and keto options, too, if that's more your flavor."

Zane snapped, nodding his head.

"Thank you. I'll give them a visit. We allowed businesses to start operating again recently. Hopefully, they'll be open," Zane said.

"We'll be off now," Eden said.

With that, the two hunters left the office, returning to the SUV waiting for them out front. Zane undid the collar of his suit, sighing in relief as they approached the vehicle.

"Can't wait to get out of this thing. I hate wearing these suits. The material doesn't jibe with me," Zane said.

"Can't you get something more suitable tailored to you?"

"Not for work purposes. Some bullshit policy against the fabric I prefer."

Eden sighed, opening the back door of the car and stepping in.

Zane tapped the top of the car, garnering Donovan's attention.

"Hey, Don, go ahead without me. I'm gonna grab some tacos before heading back."

The older hunter glanced over his shoulder at Zane, furrowing his brow.

"For real this time?"

"Eden can vouch! I really gotta try out Gonzalez's Taqueria before I get sent back to HQ. Haven't had a single damn taco since I've been here. Can you believe it?"

"Considering I've practically been your taxi driver, I can. Still ... you're catching a different ride back home, kid."

Eden snickered at their interaction, shutting the car door before tucking himself into his seat and buckling in.

"Yeah, yeah. Gotta get my daily steps, anyway. Later, Don," Zane said, signaling goodbye before walking down the street merrily.

"Not gonna join him, Blackwell?" Donovan asked.

Eden shook his head.

"Got some things to do. I'll eat later," Eden replied, glancing out the tinted windows.

Faintly, the glass glimmered from the luminance of Eden's crimson eyes as he stared out at the city, watching the trickle of snow fall like frozen tears from the sky. He chose to ignore his hunger; he was too fixated on the coming conversation he sought to have with Kendra. Even in the aftermath, things were hardly opportune, but by Kendra's own admission, she wasn't sure it ever would be a *good* time to speak. Braving such tribulations was practically a requirement now, and while difficult decisions were plenty and ceaseless, above all, he knew he was the only one to proposition the possibility awaiting her.

A friend.

It was that same month, November, when Kendra and Aaron were called by the Western Chicago Psychiatric Institution. Katherine had been discovered alive among the various citizens who were collected by emergency personnel. Of course, both of them rushed there as fast as they could.

Entering the main lobby, Kendra saw several people with the all-too-familiar expressions of despair she'd grown jaded to. She saw it everywhere she went. *How many are here for the same reason?* she wondered. The drab room was beaten down by the familiar fluorescent lights medical buildings were known for—the kind that made it near impossible to tell what time it was outside. In their familiar glare, she was brought back to when she had awakened in the Hunters' medical facility, and she tensed with anxiety, dreading the revelations this memory would yield.

Aaron walked in behind Kendra, much less interested in anything other than seeing his wife. He took brisk steps toward the reception desk, Kendra in tow. The squeak of his boots on the vinyl floor alerted one receptionist, prompting her to peer up from the antiquated monitor she had intensely been staring into moments prior.

"I'm here for Katherine Mallory. I'm Aaron Mallory, her husband, and this is our daughter." He gestured his hand to Kendra, pursing his lips.

The receptionist's movements were sluggish, her gaze calculated and marred with fatigue. This, too, was but another symptom of the aftermath the preyed-upon city contended with. The father and daughter supposed that the staff hadn't rested since the offending night and accordingly offered their patience in kind.

The receptionist nodded and held a finger up before continuing to type on a physical keyboard for a few seconds. With a satisfied nod, she tapped the enter key hard and returned her attention to Aaron.

"Alright, sir," the receptionist began, scanning the screen. "Katherine … Mallory. Ah, yes. So, while visitations are in progress, you will both need to wait in the queue. You'll be accompanied by a psychiatrist to gauge any developments in the patients during interactions. Current wait is"—she glanced at the timer on her monitor—"about two hours."

Kendra stood behind Aaron as the receptionist spoke. Both of their shoulders slumped when they heard the reported wait time, their faces twisting in disappointment. Of course, they had no choice. They glanced at one another before nodding. While her father was certainly patient, as was necessary for his job, Kendra's supply was far more limited, especially given how the seconds dragged for her since her change.

The receptionist offered a wry smile. Her face scrunched up as she gave them a sympathetic nod. Her hand glided across the desk and reached into a filing cabinet before she pulled out a stapled stack of papers. Sliding the papers to him, she gestured to a bin of pens sitting on the opposite side of the desk.

"Fill out the paperwork, bring back your IDs, and then we'll go from there."

Aaron nodded and looked at Kendra, and she promptly removed her wallet from her pocket, fished out her ID, and gave it to him.

As Aaron sat in the lobby, Kendra approached a vending machine and used her smart band to purchase a can of water. She grabbed it from the slot, then went outside, escaping any prying eyes. She knew her father would be a while and opted to take her syn-blood dose for the afternoon. She at least tolerated the taste now.

Cracking the can open, she fished a packet from her coat, ripped it open, and dropped the tablet into the can. Once it had dissolved, she gulped it down and threw the empty can in a nearby recycling bin. She exhaled, her breath elevating visibly in the cold air. Sprinkles of snow fell from the sky, the first she had seen since last winter.

It was different. The snowflakes didn't bother her when they landed on her skin. She couldn't feel them, more precisely. The cold had bothered her less since her change, which she considered a more pleasant development. Still, she dressed as if the weather meant something, putting effort into her outfit for the first time in several weeks. She sported a long black puffer jacket that hugged her frame, a cyan scarf, which she had found to be hideous—a gift from Kendall, and beneath, she wore jeans and a pair of brown boots with beige fur at the top.

Kendra contemplated her mother, anxiety crawling up her throat the more she thought about what she'd see. She had heard nothing but tragedies across the news regarding the fate of several citizens who had been found following Harvest. With such dire expectations, she clenched her hands hard, digging her fingertips into her palms as she sought the absent silver lining. She had nothing but time to search, and for the duration of her wait, she desperately tried. However, sifting through the icy wasteland of her trauma-addled mind, she only found spools of ash.

Time froze along with the landscape, stretching endlessly before her as she ruminated in its cold embrace. She had lost her sister already, and she prayed to Ichor for yet another blessing. There had already been far too much tragedy, and her heart ached at the prospect of yet another loss. For two hours, these thoughts ruled over her as she carefully paced back and forth across the icy pavement. Eventually, she was jostled by a voice.

"Ken," Aaron called.

Kendra turned to his voice, seeing him peeking from the doorway. He ushered her over, and she promptly cleared her head and followed him back inside. From there, they navigated the halls of the building, following a nurse. If their nerves weren't already high, a middle-aged woman jogged past them, sobbing. A distant door was ajar and garbled screams echoed through the halls from it, followed by several medical personnel rushing in.

The nurse guiding them pursed his lips and hurriedly ushered them along through the halls. Eventually, they reached a room with a blue door, and they paused. Aaron was apprehensive, furrowing his brows as he took deep breaths, and Kendra retreated into her thoughts. They both watched the door with shared trepidation, fearful of the prognosis they would discern for themselves.

The door creaked open, and low groans permeated the room. A bed was parallel to the door on the opposite side of the room, and tucked firmly atop it, was Katherine. The room was bare, with hardly any equipment present besides a monitoring machine and an IV drip. The tube from the drip snaked beneath the blanket atop Katherine, presumably inserted into her arm. Standing beside her bed was the psychiatrist.

The nurse directed the two inside the room, closing the door behind them when they entered. Neither could see Katherine's face properly, but what was immediately apparent were her sunken eye sockets and thin, cracked lips. She appeared as if she hadn't slept in days.

As they approached, Kendra searched her mother's eyes. They were hazy and distant, completely divorced from the world in front of her. Kendra averted her eyes to the psychiatrist, who gave them a nod of recognition before clearing his throat.

"The good news is, she hasn't been adversely vocal since we've taken her in. Her vitals are stable, and her basic reflexes have been accounted for by the physicians. By most means, she is physically sound. However, we've had no such luck with her cognitive exhibition. The same as many other patients, she is catatonic and unresponsive to most visual and auditory stimuli," the physician spoke.

Aaron was silent, pensively staring at Katherine's face. Kendra hardly ever saw her father get emotional, but in this moment, she thought he might cry. He was optimistic, but not daft. She knew that he, too, could see that Katherine was gone. Lost in her head.

Kendra remembered vividly the experience of being merged with a somnium. What she saw—what she felt. The debilitating sensation of dissociating from all but one's fear—she couldn't have forgotten it if she tried. The fact she had reestablished her sanity from such a state was a mystery to her, perhaps tied to the fact she had ejected Intico herself. The specifics escaped her. Unfortunately, the others who had experienced being a dithered hadn't expelled the somnium by their own accord.

By a stroke of luck, her father had been called to go on a business trip the night before Harvest. Kendra had been grateful for this, assuming he, too, would have become a dithered if he had not. To become a dithered not only meant losing one's body to the somnium, it also meant losing the very concept of their self. The somnium didn't merely hijack their form in a demonic possession, an entirely separate phenomenon. They melded into the very being of their victims. Memories, body, and soul would be entangled with the somnium—entities of irrevocable fear whose minds could not be fathomed by the living. Even if separated, either by volition or force, the host's being would be sundered—lost in a sea of psychosis and despair.

"Mom?" Kendra spoke. Trepidation swallowed her. Despite suspecting that there would be no response, she called out anyway.

"Kat?" Aaron called. Although his tone was firm, his nerves were thin. He, too, received no response.

Grief had become an unwelcome acquaintance in their family for the past two months. A sense of jadedness was bound in Kendra's overstimulated mind. Only so much loss and misfortune could be processed before her emotions muted to such an extent that she could only process things logically. Eventually, she would. In weeks or months, it was inevitable. But for now, all she possessed was a familiar void that had replaced her heart.

"Dad ..." Kendra swallowed.

"I know. I won't keep you." Kendra saw the history flashing in her father's eyes. A familiar gaze once bathed in fondness, but now, there was a sorrowful desolation present. Katherine meant the universe to him, and with the stars that were in his eyes slowly disappearing, there was only a dark sky left in their absence.

She left the facility and made her way home. In the glum atmosphere pervading Chicago, she blended in too well—one more addition to the sea of solemn faces. The bus ride was silent and short, and she was once again alone as she treaded the snow-glazed ground.

Demons existed, along with various other entities she wouldn't have ever dreamed of. This was a reality she was no longer new to, but it still astounded her how little she had known of the world her entire life. There was a vastness within her to still explore, but she was unsure if she truly wanted to. The more she yearned for her old life, the further she found herself immersed in the surrounding beauty. The omens danced whimsically, reminding her that the nightmare was over. No infernal hiss, which had been present since she had become aware of the supernatural. With it gone, she found the newfound harmony to be a gentle reprieve in her silent stroll.

She froze in place, the flash of Kendall's face smiling at her in her ethereal brilliance. Her fingers curled tightly before she raised her hand to touch her cheek. Tepidly, her other hand reached to the opposite cheek, and she tugged on her face, forcing the same smile she had conjured for Kendall's departure. However hollow her enactment of the smile was, she wanted to emulate that serene smile that Kendall departed with, to grant her final request as her brave big sister.

In this mimicry, she found herself thinking back to what came next. The proposition Eden had broached with her days prior echoed in her mind, and while not as heavy as she had expected it to be, it was no less perturbing with the existing burdens plaguing her battered mind. Her hands fell to her sides, and her gaze dropped as she thought hard about what they had spoken on, but her resolution remained the same.

She would make her decision after graduation.

Summer was Kendra's favorite time of the year. The weather was mostly agreeable in Chicago around that time, and she enjoyed exercising in it. She recalled various trips she had gone on with either her family or her friends. In particular, Natalie's farm in Arkansas was a great visit. The strawberries they grew were a favorite of the locals, and she found herself prey to their delectable sweetness.

But this summer was far different. With the wounds of the year prior still freshly embedded in the city's memory, it was a time of transition. Life resumed, uncaring of the tribulations that ran through its fabric. No matter how many had tried to move on, the unnerving fear that violated the sanctity of the public conscience remained—be it in the despair of loss, or the lingering darkness that haunted them when they closed their eyes.

Kendra and Eden graduated from high school together that afternoon, the class of 2043. As monumental as Kendra had always imagined it to be, it felt unceremoniously hollow. There was a chasm where enthusiasm should have been. What awaited her was uncertain, no matter how long she had considered the options.

Eden, as he had reiterated innumerable times to her, always planned to dedicate himself to hunting. With school out of the way, he could entirely focus on his role with the Hunters. When he spoke about his ambitions, there was an underlying solemnness to it, as if it were daft to consider any other options.

Despite the months in which Kendra had spoken with him following Harvest, Eden was still embroiled in mystery. He didn't speak much beyond whatever subject was being discussed, and often enough, he resorted to silence and reclusion. His aloofness wasn't ubiquitous, however. He had his moments of insightful clamor and playful banter if she caught him on a good day. Kendra respected him, regardless.

As much as Kendra would have wished to attend any of the various after-parties or outings with friends and acquaintances of her class, she had another plan that evening, much to Natalie and Candace's sorrow. They were aware of her preoccupations.

Rosehill Cemetery was an architectural marvel, one best admired divorced from its connotations. Unfortunately, Kendra had no such luxury. She hadn't visited the grounds since Kendall's funeral, hardly able to summon the courage to visit, but it was imperative that she did.

The sun reflected a radiant golden hue against freshly trimmed grass that framed the road. The lawns stretched for miles, housing innumerable mausoleums and grave sites marching its expanse, and lush, viridescent trees cast soft shadows that kissed the landscape, bathing a sparse selection of headstones.

Cars lined the shoulder of the road. Plenty of parents and recent graduates were visiting graves. Kendra presumed that many had the same idea as her. The countless souls that had perished the year prior weighed heavily. As painful as it was, she tried to imagine how many others had been deprived of witnessing, or experiencing, the next chapter of their or their loved ones' lives. She knew she wasn't alone in that harrowing consideration, but it was alienating regardless.

Kendra walked along the grass, and it grew quieter the further she drew away from the others. The omens were denser in the cemetery for reasons unknown to her, but she ventured a guess why. As she treaded the path, a pleasant breeze caused her hair to flail in the wind—not that she minded it getting messy now that the graduation ceremony was over. Only one more thing remained.

An assortment of gravestones lined the grass, Kendra's eyes precariously scanning over the unfamiliar names. She could easily get lost searching for Kendall's gravestone, her memory of the uniform graveyard being quite hazy. However, she could smell the faint scent of forget-me-nots. Her father had delivered them to Kendall's gravestone the day prior. Even now, he waited in the car for her—per her request. She wanted to be alone.

Her flats dug into the grass as she came to an abrupt stop before the shimmering stone embedded in the ground. Kendall's grave. Her eyes darkened as she scowled down at it, her face contorting with the emotions she had feared would emerge. Buried, yet, pervasive in her mind. A joyous day was encumbered by an uncertainty she had to confront; she kept telling herself that, at least.

The lenses of Kendra's glasses became hazy, and she lowered her face as she trembled. It was too fervent a sorrow, and all too well did she know what was coming. She clamped her lips. And with a torrent of emotion erupting from within her, she let herself spill.

Tears cascaded down her cheeks, and she gave herself permission to remember Kendall again. The image of the two playing video games together several years ago. Kendra had almost snapped the controller when Kendall kept proving herself better. It was only natural she would be better, given Kendall had gamed far more than she had. She recalled how much Kendall had talked about wanting to one day design an astrology platformer game with the constellations embedded into the level design. The characters, which she had endlessly rambled about, would utilize magical tarot cards to defeat enemies—demons.

While Kendall proved more adept at video games and various dexterity-based feats, Kendra held the edge in their athletic performances—something she had never let Kendall forget. The many times they had raced on their bikes couldn't be counted, but Kendra knew she never lost. Kendall swore she wanted to play soccer too until Kendra had shown her up one too many times in middle school. Kendall managed to beat her in a foot race once and decided she'd join the track team, convinced it was her calling. Kendra hadn't faulted her for it. Kendall was a very fast girl. Faster than she had been.

If Kendall had never injured her legs on the trail, Kendra couldn't help but wonder if they would have escaped the hellhounds—just like she had the night she left from work.

The memories turned pearl white, and she blinked away her tears to focus on the letters engraved on the stone.

Kendall Mallory.

2026 - 2042

Beloved daughter and sister.

So desperately did Kendra wish they could be laughing and celebrating graduation together, but fate saw things differently. *It always did.*

The tears ran dry, and she composed herself with steady breaths. Despite being outside, she felt similar to when she was stuffed in that musty cell, breathing nothing but misery. She didn't surrender to such despair this time. Kendall's final goodbye, like her startling claps, pulled her back when her mind had sunk too far. In the confines of her mind, she resolved herself to make a decision. She had told Eden that the decision was not hers alone, but hers and Kendall's—at least the memory of her.

Boston University had extended her a full-ride scholarship for their forensics program. She had always admired her mother and the work she did. And while she didn't have much of a mind to thrust herself into the jaws of the rigid hierarchy of a police precinct, especially after her experience with them during Harvest, she was drawn to the bigger picture of their work.

She knew her mother would be proud of her, should her mind not have been sundered and secluded to a recess of unfathomable horrors. Not even the Hunters had a method of treating the former dithered. The underlying despair begged an unnerving prerogative brewing within the depths of her spirit. She had conjured that same urgency when she resolved herself to stand against Intico.

"That was her favorite color—right?" Eden's voice called out.

Kendra glanced down at the silk cyan ribbon that adorned her waistline, frilly and girly in the most obnoxious of fashions. She had remembered brainstorming a graduation outfit with Kendall last August. Kendall, more than aware of Kendra's aversion to overtly frilly things, had suggested a formal, sleeveless jumpsuit and a colored ribbon. Kendra would have gone with silver, her favorite color, but in this way, symbolically, Kendall had walked the stage with her.

"Yeah," Kendra answered in a hushed tone, her voice hoarse.

Eden stood behind her, still dressed in the simple black suit he had worn beneath his gown. Kendra had never seen him in formal attire, being used to his simplistic, colorless attire and leather jacket. Even with how colorless it was, there was a present reminder that he, too, had experienced the same world as her.

"Have you made your decision?"

Kendra stilled herself, ceasing her trembling as she studied the omens that pervaded her vision. Among the plethora of her thoughts was a truth she had discovered viscerally: demons are dangerous. In such a brief span of time, a relatively small group of them had brought Chicago to its knees, and that was one of the better outcomes.

Kendra thought of Vicente, with whom she had a brief, albeit reluctant, friendship with before his life was cruelly ripped away by the demons that had sought to capture her. Her former best friend, a boy whom she had harbored feelings for, was a demon who had seen her stripped of her humanity, had seen her offered to the somnium, had seen her sister's life torn away by hellhounds. She thought of her mother, who was now catatonic, lost in a sea of fear and disparate memories.

Kendra's eyes sharpened, a fresh clarity reflecting in her stark royal-blue irises. She turned around, her gaze no longer cast in shadow as she found Eden standing across from her. Meeting the stoic crimson gaze that revived her conviction, she sought to abide by those eyes she once scorned for their ire.

No matter what she was, she would focus on what she could be and what she would do now. Her story would forever change, but she sought to change it for the better. *In Kenny's memory.*

The once dejected girl standing before Eden was no longer the same girl that he had saved on that tragic evening. She was someone beyond strong. Without her, he was positive his body and mind would have been swallowed in an insidious eternity. As reclusive as he had always been, he developed a soft spot for her, a kinship established in the traumas the shadow of the world offered them. The festering darkness in her core was a reminder of that, and he could never diminish the strength it took to live with it. He knew what such darkness heralded, and the strength to overcome it was inscrutable even to him.

Kendra's answer was clear, even before she spoke it. The conviction that she manifested in her eyes condemned the tears that stained her face—the tears that could stain many others.

Kendra's eyes flashed a deep red, the strength within her quelling her sorrow and birthing ambition. Standing before her was a bastion against demons, a pillar she would stand beside to banish the darkness that pervaded them.

Inhale.

Release.

And she spoke her new testament.

"I'll become a hunter."

The weekend of departure had come. Kendra had spent all night packing her bags, which was surprisingly more difficult than any prior vacation she'd ever gone on, albeit this was far from a vacation. She wasn't sure when or if she'd see her room again and had to be conservative about what she decided to take. She doubted the dorms at the Hunters' HQ would prove to be accommodating to her full wardrobe. Still, she wanted a semblance of comfort and style for her days off, an anchor to her humanity, as she saw it.

She rolled the suitcase out of her room, resolutely shutting the door behind her. The home was empty as she stared down the staircase, and she paused to absorb the moment. She and her father had their goodbye dinner the night prior, and he had left for work when she awoke. Days before, she had a goodbye day out with her friend—one of the first she'd had in a long time, and one of the last for a long while, too. Thinking all of her goodbyes were out of the way, she considered herself ready.

Light bled through the windows, bathing the house in a soft glow. The banister cast columns of shadows that lined the hallway above it, and staring out the window, Kendra couldn't help but dread the trip ahead. She hoped the vehicle waiting for her outside had good AC. She enjoyed the heat, but she still hated stuffy air in a hot car. Furthermore, Eden had assured her the training would be tough, and despite how strong she already thought herself, she was certain he had factored in her strength when he made that claim.

Kendra's solace faded when she took one last glance down the hall and saw Kendall's door. She hadn't entered it since the morning of the attack—not having found the courage to do so. Becoming a hunter was a new genesis for her, but something still tethered her—something she had forgotten. A phantom compulsion overcame Kendra, and her fingers unraveled from the handle of her suitcase; it appeared she had one goodbye left after all.

With carefully placed steps, Kendra crept down the hallway. No such nefarious intent pervaded her mind, but great diligence had been placed into her approach to the door. It was shut, indicating that Kendall had to be asleep. She always kept the door shut when she slept.

Kendra extended her hand and carefully opened the door, the creaking of the neglected hinges filling the silence. She daftly expected a clap, reminiscing on the cheekiness Kendall had startled her with twice. But Kendall had no such foresight this morning; Kendra was prepared this time.

The dusty room was swallowed in darkness, the window and curtains still shut. On her dresser, a cyan hairbrush sat next to a pearl-white glasses case and an empty jar that once contained pumpkin-scented candle wax. She knew she had little time, but she thought, in her deviousness, she'd take something of her little sister's as a keepsake. Carefully, she opened the top right drawer, where she remembered Kendall stashed her tarot deck. There, within it, she saw the cards, and as she sifted through the deck, she found them. The three cards Kendall had drawn in their last reading session.

The tower.

Six of Swords.

Death.

Kendall would never even know they were missing.

Carefully, Kendra tucked the cards into her pocket and turned back to the messily made bed, as was characteristic of Kendall when she was in a rush. When not preparing for big occasions she was excited for, she always poorly managed her sleep schedule. Kendra guessed Kendall had been in a rush that morning for whatever reason—perhaps having overslept and nearly missed the track team's bus.

It had been the race.

Kendra had not thought Kendall to have lost that race, all things considered.

A paradoxical smirk marred Kendra's features as she dared to creep toward the bed.

Kendall was none the wiser.

Kendra stopped at the bedside, remaining dead silent, as if she were afraid to wake her precious little sister from her slumber.

And as Kendra stared down at the empty bed, there was not a doubt in her mind—exactly as Kendall had asked of her.

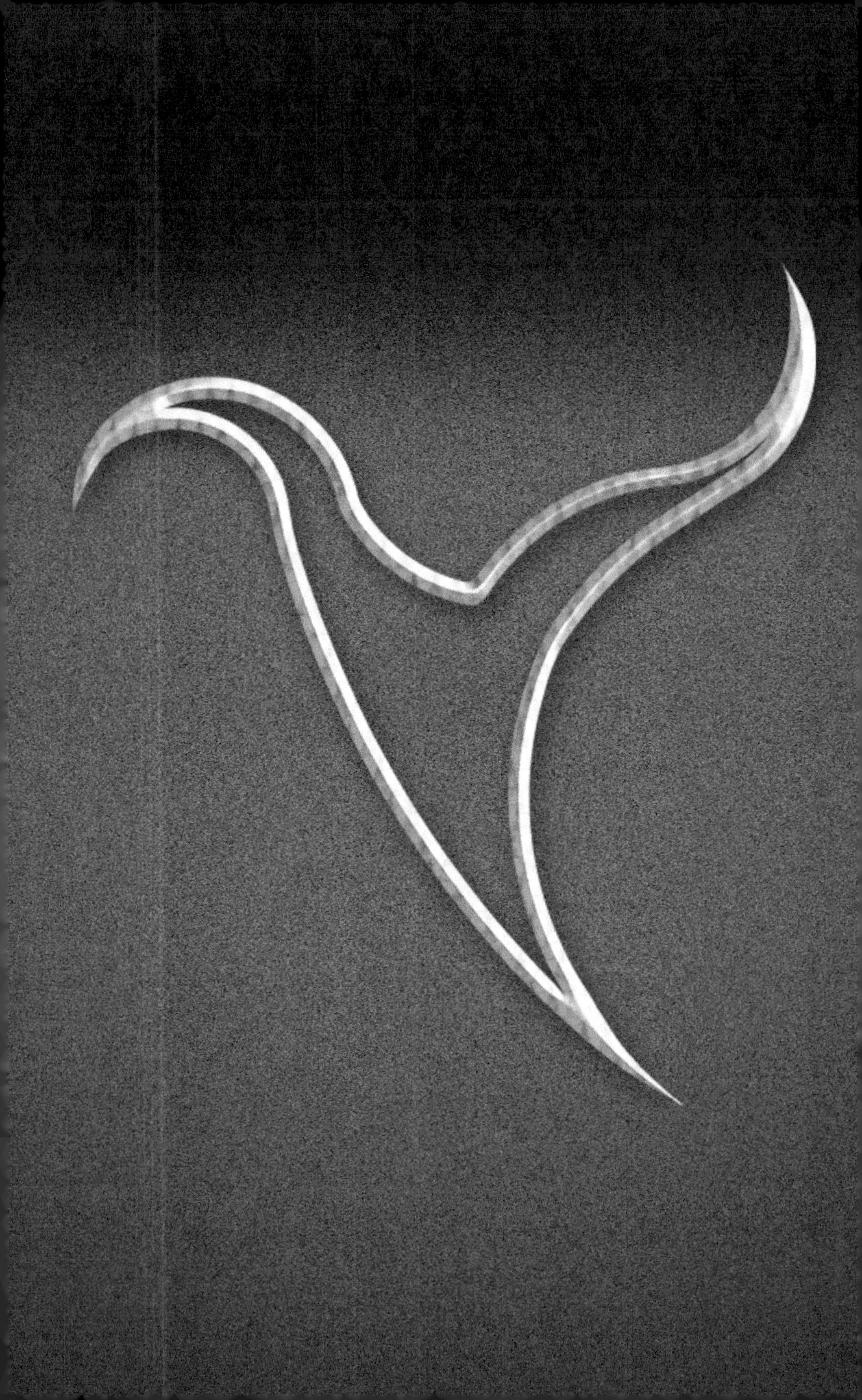

THE END

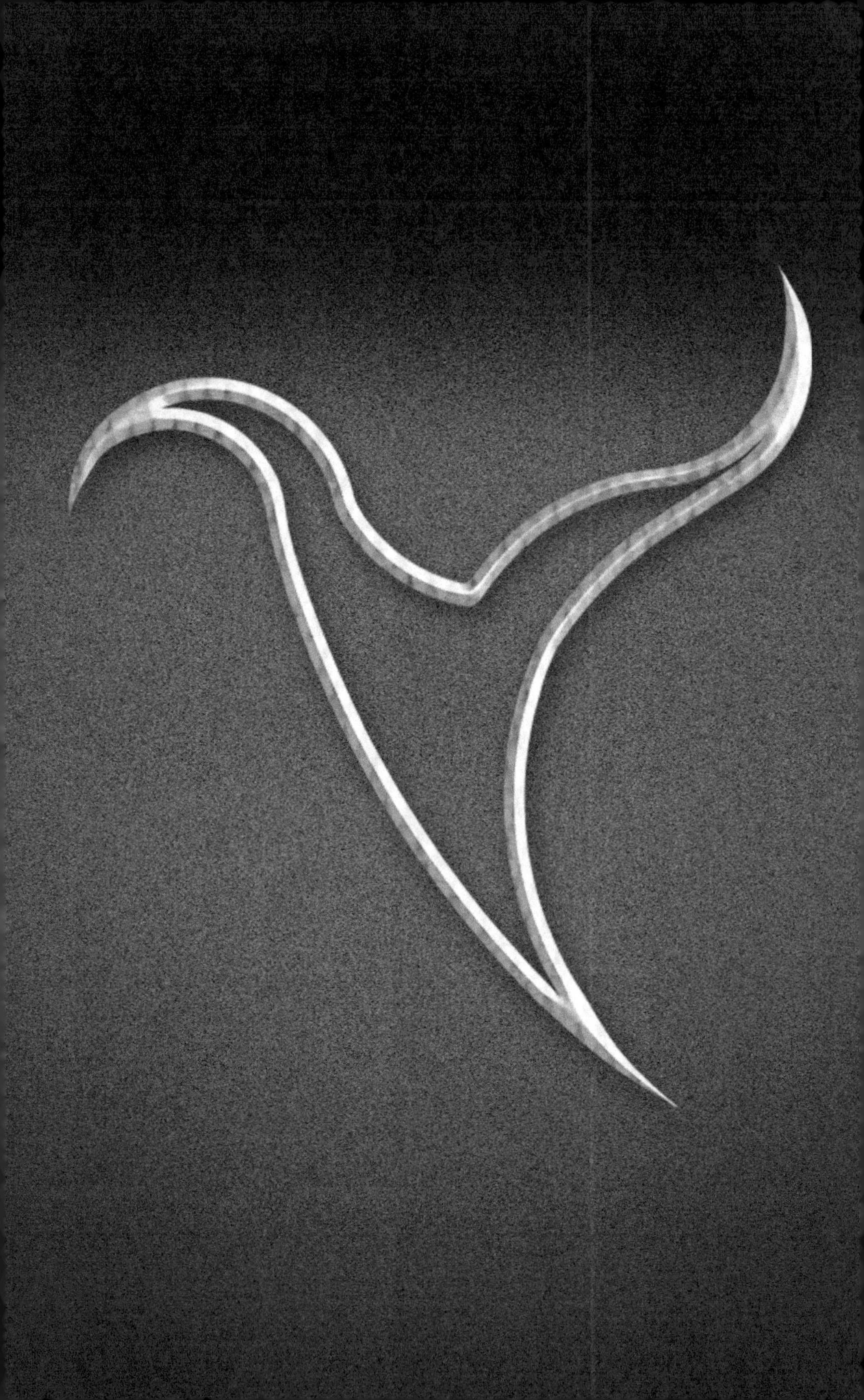

Thank you for reading!

Blood Creed will return

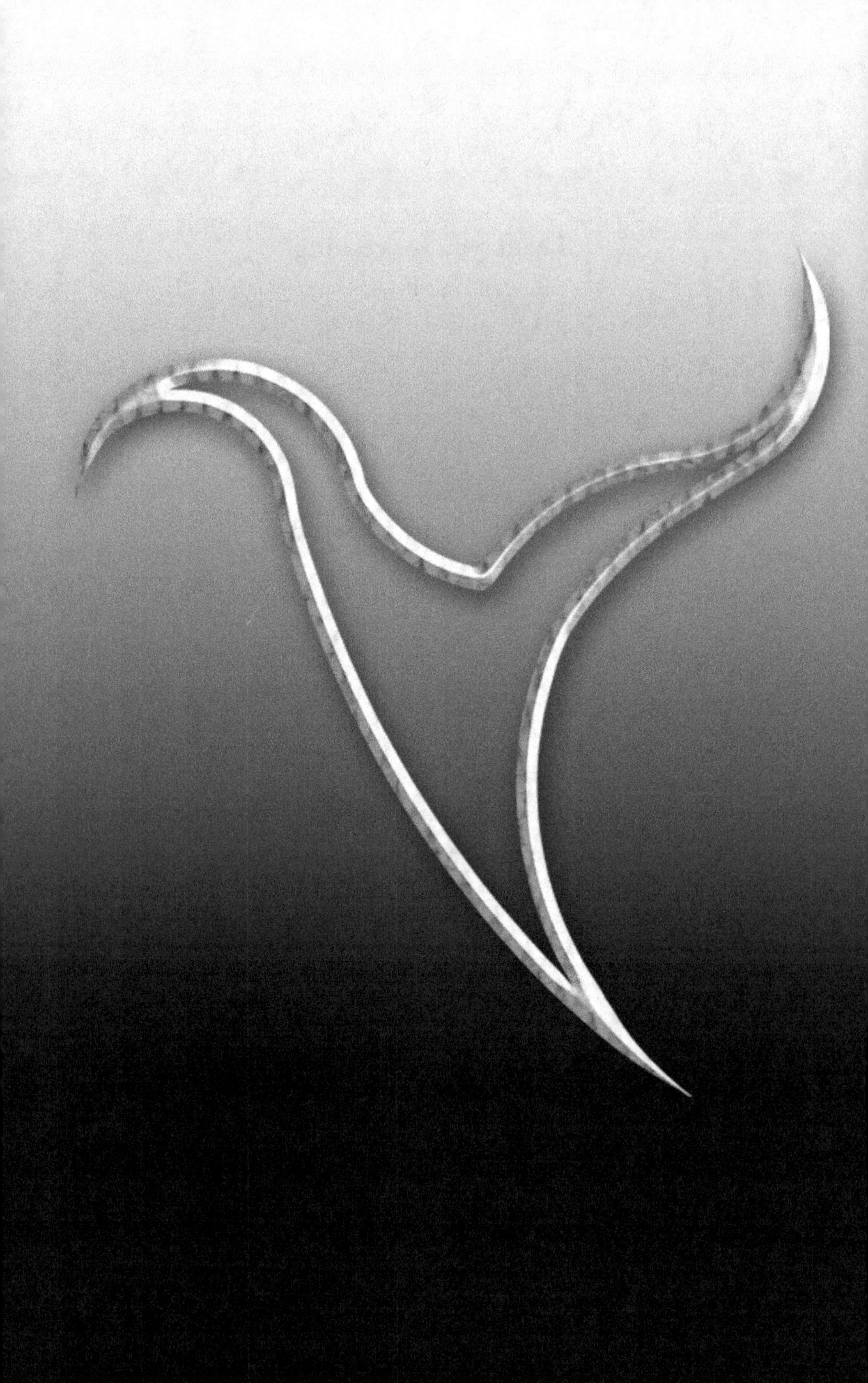

Many truths are obscured
from eyes forlorn, but
within the umbrage of such
tribulations, there are many

Revelations

Tributes

I commemorate my eternal appreciation of my friends and beta readers: Elijah, Savannah, Natasha, Philip, Devon, and Anna,

I thank my longest friend, Savannah, whom I call Savy. She has been instrumental in the development of these characters and world over the past decade, as it was when her and I first started talking online that Blood Creed's "Genesis" took place.

Elijah, especially, deserves a special place here, due to how he encouraged me to continue writing Genesis when I felt as if my writing wasn't good enough for myself, let alone anybody else. Because of his indomitable spirit, I forwent my doubts and persisted in the struggle of creativity to bring this book to you.

I thank my dear friend, Philip, who, atop providing me art, endeavors to endure my long rants about the lore of Blood Creed and has collaborated in forging ideas around it all for several years. Their monstrous creativity has helped bring about Blood Creed in more ways than I could condense here.

Lastly, I pay tribute to my artist, Anna. I first contacted Anna on her Etsy store in 2020 and commissioned her for art of Kendra. Her art painted the world of Blood Creed in a way I hadn't been able to imagine before, and while I originally hadn't been certain about writing this book, it was seeing these characters you have read about that invigorated me to bring their story to fruition.

In Loving Memory

This book serves as my testament to the memory of my late mother,
Shameka Phillips-Johnson.

Regardless of our strife, our love of books and poetry serve as the connecting threads of our indubitable bond.

If you would like to follow Eric or subscribe to his newsletter, scan the QR code below!

About the author

Eric Still is a dark fantasy and horror author based out of Los Angeles, California. Most wouldn't know it upon first meeting him, but Eric is autistic, and he is quite proud of the tribulations he has overcome. In fact, he has turned it into his super power, channeling his hyperfixation in order to craft his stories and efficiently utilize his creativity! Eric decided to become an author due to his  natural love for writing and poetry, and his deep desire to tell stories around lore he has created for over a decade. His love for all that is dark and macabre naturally spurred his desire to write within a genre that combined fantastical and horrifying machinations alike.

His hobbies include playing video games, reading (obviously), hiking, going to concert, attending goth venues (was it mentioned he's goth? Did his black cat make it obvious?), and spending time with his friends in general. He greatly enjoys meaningful conversations covering philosophy and can monologue for hours on a topic he's passionate and cares about!

He draws inspiration from several sources, from the dark world of Marvel's Blade to the Young Adult mythologies of Percy Jackson, video games like Skyrim, God of War, and Dead Space, and anime such as Re:Zero, Dragon Ball, and Full Metal Alchemist. He is certain that, if one is so discerning to catch them, they can glean several references throughout his books!